BOOK ONE

# The Sandrian Chronicles

# WRITTEN IN BLOOD

## Keith Montgomery

THE SANDRIAN CHRONICLES: WRITTEN IN BLOOD
©2016 Keith Montgomery
First Edition
Edited by Christina Hargis Smith
Proofread by: Maura Atkinson Butler
Cover art by Jeffrey Kosh Graphics
Published by Optimus Maximus Publishing, LLC

ISBN-10:1-944732-13-6
ISBN-13:978-1-944732-13-4

# Dedication

This book is dedicated to my wife and all those who dare to dream.

# Acknowledgments

Special thanks to my mother, who raised me the right way, The Critiques R Us Writer's group of Cleveland, Ohio, Christina Smith, Donea Boiner, Rod Collins, Earl Rohde, and anyone who ever took time out of their lives to offer me advice, opinions or encouragement. I'm the writer I've become because of all of you.

# Author's Note

One of my favorite books of all time is the Jungle Book by Rudyard Kipling. My favorite scene in the book was where Mowgli's wolf parents brought him to the council rock to be judged by the pack. Akela, the pack leader, lay upon his rock and called out "Look well, O wolves!" as one by one each cub was rolled out to be assessed. As authors and readers, we're a kind of pack onto ourselves. Authors roll out their stories, their books, their cubs to be judged by all. So many great authors have gone on before me. Now, it's my time. So, it is with great reverence that I present to you, my story, my book, my cub for your inspection and judgment. As a proud parent, I say onto you, Look well, O wolves!

# The Sandrian Chronicles
# WRITTEN IN BLOOD
by
## Keith Montgomery

# CHAPTER ONE

He leaped and sprinted, tearing through the brush as he tried to stay ahead of the…*Thing*. Its origin was unknown, but it had already killed his comrade and now it hungered for him.

They were both the best of hunters, yet neither of them had the slightest inkling that they were being stalked. They were tracking elk when it struck with terrifying and unnatural speed. It knocked him breathless to the ground then took down his companion. Marco's wail, as it sank it's fangs into his neck and ripped away a chunk of flesh, would haunt him for the rest of his days. The sight of spraying blood was forever burned into his memory.

He tucked and rolled onto his feet as the sickening sound of slurping reached his ears. He knew it was already too late as his cohort's body convulsed. Marco was dead. When the beast reared its head, the eyes sparkled like tiny jewels and were filled with an unholy malevolence. A horror was born of nightmares made into flesh.

Despite his head spinning, he bellowed in anguish, then launched himself at the murdering monster. It almost seemed amused as it backhanded him away like a bothersome gnat. Evaluating him, the creature pounced but he evaded it. The thing barely missed his throat with a swipe of its claws. Before it attacked again, he charged into the woods.

The wind whooshed by his ears, all he could hear was the snap of fallen branches beneath his feet and bah boom of his heartbeat as he ran for his life. Shoving past large shrubs and low hanging tree limbs, he struggled to keep his footing on the uneven ground. Suddenly, an angry roar came from behind him. His blood iced over. It was gaining on him. *Shit*!

As he cleared the trees, he spotted a stream, and summoned all the speed he could muster. There was heavy underbrush just on the opposite side; if he could just get there. Droplets splashed into his eyes when he hit the water's edge. Never breaking stride, he pumped his legs, fighting to maintain momentum the current was stealing. Reaching the bank he stumbled, reclaimed his balance, and then took off for the bushes directly ahead. Once inside the dense foliage, he ducked down and took a moment to catch his breath and hide from his pursuer.

Fragrant pine saturated the air. Moonlight shone down, trickling through the canopy, barely illuminating his hiding spot. His heart pounded in his chest. Sweat cascaded along his face. He prayed while he waited. Something warm oozed down his leg. He examined the limb, finding blood. *Damn*! Dread twisted his insides. The scent would lead it right to him.

Tending to the wound as best he could, he kept a look out, eyes frantically roaming around, searching. Minutes passed; there was no frustrated howl, no enraged roar. *Was it gone? Had it given up?* He damn well wasn't waiting to find out. He was a sitting duck if he stayed put. No choice, he had to risk it hearing him, it was time to get out of there... fast. Carefully, he moved further into the brush. Every rustle, every explosion of a stepped on twig seemed to resound like thunder. If only he could just snap his fingers and stifle everything.

Crack!

Another broken twig sang out. *Dammit, too much noise*! Stopping in place, he listened, body taut. Goosebumps swam up his arm. All was quiet, too still. Sweat beaded and ran down his back. There was still no sign of it.

It was baiting him. He wasn't stupid. It was somewhere nearby, watching. He had to keep moving and make an escape. Pushing warily through several dozen more yards of foliage, he made his attempt to get to the truck. It was his only hope. Glancing over his shoulder, he listened, it was now or never. *Go*! He ran like the devil was chasing him. For all he knew, it *was* the devil. At last, he reached the meadow where he and his partner began their hunt.

Once in the open, he concentrated. The familiar tingle of transformation washed over him. His muzzle receded. Ears shortened, whiskers withdrew from his face and his shiny coat retracted as he morphed into human form.

The change in his perception was instantaneous but his sense of urgency was no less acute. He had to go for help. That thing must be hunted down, destroyed. As for his friend, dear goddess, he regretted leaving him out there, but had no choice.

Even in the gentle, bluish white hue of moonlight, the beauty of the landscape was awe inspiring. There was little wonder why this enclave was so highly regarded. The wooded areas were unsoiled by human industrialization and the wide assortment of wild game was plentiful. The lakes remained so pristine you could practically see through to the bottom. But after tonight, there'd be only one reason to return to this place, to find, and kill that thing.

His spirit lifted. There it was, just ahead! The Toyota Four Runner sat where it was parked. He was nearly—. A prickly sensation danced across his skin. Jerking his head about, he braced himself, yet there was nothing, only the open field, the scent of wildflowers, rich pine, and moist earth. All seemed well, but the standing hairs on his arms told a different story.

It was here!

He broke into a mad dash. As he sprinted for safety, his vehicle grew closer. The faint odor of exhaust fumes hung in the air as he reached for the handle. Frantically, he tried yanking open the door, but he was viciously slammed into from the side. They fell to the ground and tumbled about as legs and arms wrapped around him. By his Lycan blood, its strength was unbelievable, as he thrashed and fought, but couldn't shake free.

Goddess Moon, its breath had the stench of a slaughter house, though that was the least of his worries. The creature seized his head, and with a turn, it exposed his jugular then drove its awful fangs into his neck. An unbelievable burning invaded him as blood filled his mouth. With a fast tug, he felt his throat give way.

Weakness overtook him. His limbs felt heavy like lead. His breathing became labored, and vision failed him. Darkness closed in as air abandoned his lungs. It'd won. The last thing he heard before his spirit fled him was the creature roaring into the starry night sky.

5

Blood, it was the wondrous spoils of another successful hunt. With a rush, her body came alive as she licked her fingers clean. Of all the creatures upon which she fed, Lycan was always her favorite dish. Nothing ever tasted so delicious, so delectable.

# CHAPTER TWO

He could smell it. Her blood was always distinctive. There was never any confusing it. And the scent drifting up to him was the fresh blood of mortals mingled with that of his quarry.

The low hanging clouds parted to reveal the lights of a Colonial style house below. Descending, he wrapped himself in shadows while the wind rushed by his ears, the sultry breeze whipping through his hair as his coat tails flapped wildly behind him. Closer examination of the property exposed an old tire swing that hung from one of two large maple trees which flanked the house, an S Class Mercedes was parked in the drive, outdoor furniture, a tricycle and assorted toys strewn about on the front lawn. He shook his head grimly as the scene swelled in his vision.

"By the Elder, mortal children dwell within. I must be swift!" he said to no one in particular, his voice, a rich, smooth baritone spiced with a hint of the West Indies.

At six feet eight inches tall, Adalius was broad shouldered and heavily muscled. A portrait of menace in black leather, he was an imposing physical specimen with long sideburns that ran to a well-groomed mustache and beard. His milk chocolate skin contrasted with a head of long, thick black hair that hung just below his shoulders, a gift from his great, great, grandfather, a powerful vampire with dominant genes.

His gaze drifted to the West Indian tribal emblem tattooed to his wrist. Once the brand of a hunted breed, it became a symbol of the strength and pride of his kind. He was Sandrian, a vampire with a heartbeat. Their species had more in common with humanity than any other immortal haunting the night. But, like all vampires, they couldn't survive without taking in blood nor withstand direct exposure to sunlight. Thanks to a sorcerer's cast magic, he was the exception to the rule. He was a Torlume, a day walker. A fact known only by his most trusted allies.

Malicious laughter greeted him as he set down on the driveway. Drawing his Glock 21's, he made his way toward the residence. He fumed. Only one thing could entertain a vampire so, and that was causing the suffering of another. They were enjoying themselves. His jaw hardened. That was about to change.

Concentrating on the house, he sensed no heartbeats coming from within. A heavy sigh escaped his lips. It was already too late to save those who called this place home. Bliss emanated ahead of him as he climbed the front steps. He knew came from feeding well.

Vermin. Most likely, the family was first subdued, and then bound. With children present, the intruders would force the parents to watch as, one by one, they eviscerated the young and dined on their innards. All females would be raped and drained, leaving the male of the house, by then utterly mad, for last.

Heaven curse him. He'd committed many of the same perversions time and again. At one time, he too had rained down death on mortals for sustenance. But just as often, it had been for his own enjoyment. Even now, a part of him longed for the rush, the thrill of pursuing, ripping open, and taking the blood of his terrified prey. Their terror was nearly as nourishing as their life fluid.

Skin tingling, his heartbeat surged. By force, he stilled his emotions. Deep within his being, the seductive caress of darkness called to him. Like a drug, its siren song, enticed him, trying lure him back to being the horror he'd once been. Back to being like his maker. So tainted was his soul by her evil, he might never be truly be cleansed of her or the blood on his hands.

*Enough!* He shook himself from his musings. There was indeed much to atone for but there would be opportunities to reflect on his regrets later. Tensing his body, he holstered his weapons and gathered himself, preparing to confront the vampires within and the demons from his past.

"I sense your delight. You shall pay a terrible price for the harm you have caused, as will your mistress," he said aloud to himself. Approaching the front door, he slipped free from his veil of shadows. Throwing out his hand before him, the door swiftly opened, slapping against the wall. He blurred through the entrance into the foyer. He paused. The room was in disarray. Furniture was over turned; lamps lay shattered on the floor. He continued on, his footfalls heavy as he followed his nose across the spacious living room, past an enormous, wall mounted television.

The scent of pot roast, vanilla cappuccino, and death greeted him as he approached the dining area. Upon entering, he was greeted by the gory scene of two vampires, a male and a female, and five dead mortals scattered about on the floor. The she-vampire busied herself, draining a small child while her counterpart chewed happily on intestines from a woman that lay before him. A dangerous growl rumbled from his chest. Sensing his presence the she-vampire looked up, hissing in anger and fear.

"Go find your own, Sandrian. This kill is ours!"

The male was on his feet and flashed toward him, grabbing his coat lapels. "Yeah, mother fucker, I think you should leave. *Now*."

His rage ignited. Driving his knee into the aggressor's groin, the vampire groaned and doubled over into Adalius' arms. In a skillful motion, he slipped a silver dagger from his trench, driving it up through the vampire's heart. The immortal crumbled to dust. Pressing her fists to the side of her head, the female screamed. He blurred. Catching her by the throat, he lifted the immortal, forcing her to the wall. Her feet dangled above the floor as he flashed his fangs.

"You bare her mark upon you. I want to know where she is."

The female clawed at his hand. "Let me go… cock sucker, you killed him!"

Accused of killing a thing already dead. Amusing. "His death occurred long before my blade found its mark. You waste my time, wench. Tell me where I can find her. I will not ask again." He applied greater pressure. The stubborn viper remained ever silent, ever defiant. It was impressive. Her toughness nearly gained his respect. Patience, however, was not an option. The answers he needed lay hidden within her. He knew how to get them. She was not going to like it.

"Very well, I will take what I need. "Her eyes widened as he psychically crashed through her mental barriers and into her mind. Carefully, he sifted through memories playing out like multiple cinemas until at last he saw *her* face. Anna, beautiful as always. Her words however, couldn't be made out. Apparently, this female paid little heed to her queen's plans. None of what he noted made any sense. He withdrew from her psyche. "Your maker will not be pleased to learn how little you value her plans."

Her head turned from side to side, eyes blinking as if waking from slumber. As she focused, her expression changed from fear to recognition, and then to contempt. Her face morphed into a sneer.

"Adalius. You were Anna's lover. Now you think you're going to kill her." She laughed bitterly. "Fool. She is forever and will rule this world long after you are dust and your kind are our fucking slaves. I don't care what you do to me. I'm not telling you shit. I belong to her. I will die for her."

"And die you shall but not befo—"

A dull thud took him by surprise. Her eyes collapsed in on themselves, her smile victorious as she crumbled in his hand. The rattle of his dagger on the hardwood floor drew his attention to his feet. She had reached into his coat, withdrew one of his daggers and plunged it into her own heart. Gazing down at the sooty remains, he scowled. Unfortunate, a possible lead lost, but it did not matter. He would find Anna no matter how long it took. The question was, where to look next?

Brushing his hands clean of the she vamp, he one by one examined the victims to ensure none would rise as one of her minions. Thankfully, the duo had been more interested in feeding than recruiting.

Drawn by the darkness of night, his eyes drifted to the bay window. Anna was out there somewhere. He forced himself to be still. Storming out in search of her would be ill advised. Leaving vampire slaughtered bodies lying about, risked them being discovered. Humanity would be forced to confront questions best left unasked. The survival of all in the supernatural realm hinged on man's belief that such things did not exist.

The Drayken had to be alerted. The bodies had to be removed and the murder scene cleansed. A viable cover story had to be made to explain the family's disappearance. Memories would have to be altered and records changed. But that is what the Drayken did. Taking out his cell phone, he hit the speed dial option. The line rang once, and then clicked.

"Identification number and password," the deep voice said, distorted by a voice changer.

"Identification number 961563. Password, Sandrian 216."

"Good evening, Master Adalius, how may we serve?"

"I have come across a vampire slaughter. I need a cleaner unit dispatched.

"Number of victims?"

"Five, including two mortal young."

"Triangulating your phone signal, stand by." Pause. "Your location is confirmed. Please hold." The line clicked.

He waited patiently, keeping watch on the drive, in case of unexpected visitors. Several minutes passed. The line clicked once more. "Your representative has been notified and will give you continued updates on this case file. A cleaner crew has been dispatched to your location. They should arrive within the hour. Remain there until that time. Touch nothing. Is there another matter I can assist you with Master Adalius?"

"Not at this time, thank you for your aid."

"The Drayken live to serve." Transaction concluded.

Blessed be the old ones for the Drayken. For thousands of years, the secret society had served vampires with their astonishing wealth and influence. Thankfully, a division existed to deal with slaughters and other messes left by rogue vampires.

After securing the home, he sat and meditated. Taking deep even breaths, he focused on soothing his anger. Control of emotions was a necessity. They only served to cloud his thoughts. *Have to think. Where would she go next?*

The closest major city was New Carrollton. That, paired with Anna's affinity for the fast life of a big city, suggested she might head there. With an analytical eye, he studied the ashes of the dead she-vamp.

Her loyalty to her queen was impressive. Such devotion made Anna even more dangerous.

His expression hardened. A few abject lessons would have to be doled out. Anna's underlings feared her more than they feared him. It was time they were taught the error of their ways. She may be the destroyer, but he was death.

# CHAPTER THREE

It was a sweltering summer night when Trey Thomas arrived in Cleveland, Ohio. The familiar smell of algae permeated the air of the lakefront city as he rode his Harley on the long winding road known as Martin Luther King Drive. The evening, devoid of even the slightest breeze, was heavy with haze and moisture, causing him to wipe his brow as he rode down the asphalt covered road way. *Damn, it was hot.*

A sheen of perspiration covered his exposed arms and it tickled as sweat rolled underneath his tank top and down his back. Headlights from oncoming cars were brighter than normal or just seemed that way to tired eyes protesting for long overdue sleep.

He blew out a breath and thought of ice cold beer as the heat from his engine joined forces with the air to surround him in a life sucking heat bubble which challenged him for every inhale he took. Familiar darkened scenery rolled by, a welcome sight as he gulped a deep lungful and smiled. He was home and his baby seemed to know it. The rumble from the bike between his legs seemed a little richer. His Harley was practically purring.

"I know, baby, feels good to be home don't it?" Lovingly, he patted the gas tank, feeling slightly rejuvenated. Damn shame this was a business trip. It'd been years since he'd come back. Most likely wouldn't be back now if his informant hadn't called and asked to meet up at the place of his birth, because he had intel. Something big was brewing in the supernatural world. Maybe this would shed some light on what the hell it was. The blood suckers in the last vampire nest he took down actually seemed relieved when they saw him break out his stake. It was starting to creep him out.

Passing the multitude of cultural gardens that lined both sides of Martin Luther King Drive, he rode by the Italian garden then the Greek and Latvian gardens, before he arrived at the ramp which led up to Wade Park Avenue.

As he approached Thurgood Marshall Recreation Center, he thought of his favorite snitch. He chuckled. Frankly, it was his *only* snitch. Why Kyle picked this particular location to meet wasn't clear, but what the hell, it was as good as any he supposed. Putting on his turn signal, he pulled into the rec center parking lot.

Boyishly handsome with a well-groomed beard and a creamy, coffee complexion, he was packing two hundred ten pounds of lean muscle on his six foot one inch frame. Straightening the bandana, on his head, he let out the kickstand and gave the area a quick once over. It was always a good idea to stay aware of your surroundings. Never knew when you might be walking into fang fest. Such was the life of a vamp slayer.

There were plenty of gnats buzzing' about, but the area was devoid of foot traffic and there were only a handful of cars passing by on the street. Satisfied that all was clear, he removed his walking cane from the luggage rack, grabbed the .40 cal out of his duffle bag and slid it into his jeans at the small of his back. Always be prepared.

Thankfully, there was an abundance of shadows. No sense in attracting any unwanted attention. It shouldn't be a problem though. This place wasn't much better lighted than he remembered as a child. Some things really never changed.

He checked his watch. "This better be good, Kyle, I pissed off a very sexy lady in Atlanta cause of this shit." Slipping his keys into his jeans pocket, he started off in search of his contact, torn between the need to know what Kyle had to report and the desire to jump back on his bike and ride off into the embrace and bedroom of leggy Monica.

Making his way down the sidewalk which ran the length of the rec center, his heart swelled in his chest. Despite the inconvenience, his mood was lightening. It was always good to come back to Cleveland, home, sweet home. Humming a happy tune, he reminisced about the days when he and his friends played football on the grass fields that surrounded Thurgood Marshall. It all came flooding back, memories of the good old summer yesterdays from his younger, wilder past.

Tammy Dalton. Damn, talk about a blast from the past. They were best friends back in the day, and one wild summer, passionate lovers. Trey hadn't thought about her in years. Funny how that stream of consciousness thing worked. Musings of childhood brought out a smile as he continued the stroll down memory lane. Things were so much simpler then, back before he discovered that it wasn't the darkness one should fear, but the things sometimes hiding in it.

Trey let loose a slow exhale, turning the mood somber as thoughts swung to Pops. He never stopped mourning the ole man's death. It seemed like a million years ago when they'd sit on the front porch on those hot summer nights when Pops *wasn't* away and listened to all the bullshit stories of hunting vampires and demons.

He never took that shit seriously. Just chalked it all up to a man trying to entertain and bond with his son. Pops was just spinning yarns and fantasies. Yeah, that's what he thought until that horrific day in Europe. It was supposed to be a quiet vacation with his wife and daughter. That day, everything changed. Forever. His eyes glazed over.

"Squash it, Trey, *now!*" he rebuked himself. It was time to reel it in. This little mental jaunt was heading back to that familiar place. Not tonight. Not the time. He missed Jennifer and Haley, his wife and little girl, but it was back to business. There'd be time to boo hoo into a pillow later.

Before he realized it, he came upon the baseball diamond where in the summer, they held league softball games. As kids they used to pile into the metal and wood bleachers and sit through game after game until the park lights would come on and illuminate the field and stands. He could almost smell the popcorn and hot dogs the vendors used to sell. Just the thought of those dogs simmering in that salty brine, the cooked just right onions, and that spicy brown mustard, made his empty belly grumble.

Inside the metal cage, surrounding the batter's box, stretching down the first and third base lines, he caught sight of a couple, necking. They picked a great spot. Nice and dark on the diamond, none of the park lights were on, so there was excellent cover.

A sly smile crossed his face as he thought of the times he and Tammy spent inside that batter's cage. There still weren't names for some of the things they did. A soft moan escaped the young woman's lips. He was about to turn and leave them in peace when he noticed the leather trench coat on Mister Lover Lover. *No way. It had to be a least eighty five degrees. Who would wear a coat like that in this heat but a fang.*

Trey decided that it was time to break up this little party. Reaching behind his back, he drew his .40, cocked the hammer, and stepped inside the batter's cage. The vamp had backed the girl against the metal fence as he fed, her moans becoming more pronounced as his hands slid underneath her skirt. The bastard was totally lost in his meal, otherwise he would've heard footsteps coming up behind him.

Trey gripped his pistol tightly. Interrupting a feeding vampire was a dangerous undertaking. As hazards went, it fell somewhere between jamming a metal fork into an electric socket and taking a header into a tree shredder. Definitely, a bad life decision, but fuck it, he was a slayer and short on time. He had to make it quick, didn't wanna to keep the dead man waiting. Kyle might get the happy feet and bounce. Just the thought of it ticked him off. If that limey bastard bolted before giving up the info he'd come so far to get, bad things would happen.

Carefully, he stepped into position. Lifting his cane high above his head, he swung with all his might, cracking the vampire on the back of his head. The bloodsucker stiffened and reached for the stricken area, the force of the blow dislodging him from the woman's neck.

"Owww, bloody hell! Can't a bloke have a bite to eat without some sod boppin him in the beanie!" The female stood motionless, still entranced, her vein leaking blood as the vampire twisted about and found himself staring down the barrel of a silver slug loaded gun. "Oh bugger, it's *you*." The vampire rubbed the back of his head.

"Evening, Kyle, baby, I thought we agreed you'd keep your fangs to yourself?" Trey lowered his weapon.

"We agreed that I wouldn't kill anyone. I still gotta eat same as you, ya bloody bastard. Owww, what ya hit me with anyway?"

"Silver tipped cane. May not kill a vamp but it's a damn fine attention grabber. Now let the girl go. You said you had info for me, so let's talk."

The vampire shook and rubbed his still stinging head. "Dammit, Thomas, your bloody timing sucks. No pun intended, mate."

He raised the cane again.

"Ok, ok." Kyle turned to the still immobile female. "Would have been grand, love. Now, if you please, be a good girl and hand over your driver's license."

Trey rolled his eyes.

Kyle shrugged his shoulders. "What? I'm just saving her for later." The female reached into her purse, withdrew her wallet, then her license and handed it to Kyle. "Thank you. Now, on your way. I need to talk with big daddy cane. Oh, and it's too hot tonight. You need to leave your bedroom window open." Kyle paused. "Blimey, we can't have you walking around looking like that now can we?" He leaned in and lapped up the blood trailing down her neck. Once he'd cleaned up the spill, he ran his tongue over the wounds, causing them to close and heal like magic. "Much better. Now off you go and no stopping till you reach home." The young woman walked away, still under his spell, leaving the two alone to chat. "And don't forget about the window," Kyle called out after her.

With that matter settled, Trey got right down to business. "Ok, spill. What's going on?"

Kyle watched the woman leave, then turned and fell into step with the slayer. "The grapevine's been abuzz with the chatter of darlin' Anna skipping her way back toward New Carrollton."

He turned to Kyle. "New Carrollton? Why would she go there?"

Kyle shrugged. "Kinda makes sense actually when ya think about it, mate. It was where she suffered her greatest setback. Who would think to look for her there?"

Ok, he had to admit, it did make sense. "Point taken. So what gives? Vamps I've run into lately have been jumpy. It has to be because of Anna. What's she up to now?"

"Personally, I think she's looking to settle in and set her plans for the future in motion."

"What are you talking about?"

"I'm talking about Anna. She's burnin' to shag the same ole and start a new age, with her and her merry band of knobheads sitting pretty in the catbird seat. With her in charge, it would be her kind on top of the food chain. Everything else would be kibble."

Trey stopped, mid stride. "She wants to start a revolution? That'd be suicide. Everything this side of perdition's flame would be gunning for her. Even she couldn't win that battle alone. She'd need allies, lots of them and who'd be willing to help her?"

Kyle shook his head ruefully. "Trust me, mate, there are plenty of psychos on every side of the fence who would gladly help her pull it off. Under the status quo, there are rules to be abided by. If Anna were the queen bee of this big blue hive, there would be only one rule; swear allegiance to her and the world is your bleedin' oyster."

Trey mulled over the implications of a world at the mercy of Anna. A chill shimmied down his spine. "This sounds like bullshit but you haven't steered me wrong yet."

"Bloody no, I haven't. You slayer blokes better do something about Anna before she does something about all of us."

"Trust me; if this checks out, Anna will be dust long before she ever lays the first brick in her kingdom. I *promise* you that."

Kyle slid out the driver's license from his trench coat pocket. "Smashing. Ok, I've done my part for king and country, now if you'll excuse me, I have a meal to finish."

Kyle started off but Trey caught him by the forearm. "If I find out you've snacked too hard on that girl…"

"Spare me the death threats, mate. I'm just gonna take a little and maybe have a little fun. Ciao for now." The vampire pulled out of his grasp and walked away.

"Kyle." Kyle stopped and turned. "Take care of that beanie." Trey smirked as his stoolie rubbed his head. Kyle flashed a mock smirk of his own and flipped him the bird. As he sailed off into the night sky, Trey watched him go then quickly made his way back to his bike. He needed to fuel up and pick up some sandwiches and bottled water for the trip. North Carolina was long drive from Ohio and from the sound of what he'd just heard, the clock was already ticking.

# CHAPTER FOUR

It was eleven thirty-five and the line of people waiting to get into Le Freak, New Carrollton's number one hotspot, continued to grow. The night club boasted a diverse clientele ranging from the young, up and coming Wall Street types to the hard hat and lunch pail set who paid daily homage to a time clock. Once through the double doors, though, it made no difference who you were or how you made a living, everybody was the same.

All who ventured into the stylish, contemporary, happening place came in search of something. Some came looking to escape the trials and tribulations of everyday living, some searching for a warm body or bodies to take home for a night of passionate fun, while others came for nothing more than to dance the night away.

As usual for a Friday, it was crammed with the dapper dressed and scantily clad. The lights were turned down low, bathing the room in a warm amber hue, as music weaved its magic over the crowd. Rich, soulful tunes alternated with hot dance tracks, while servers buzzed about like bees, totting drink filled trays, hustling for tips.

Among the crowd, there was one a little different from the party goers around her. Though entranced by the goings on, she hadn't come to dance or mingle. Her interests were more of a culinary variety. Anna sat at the bar casually sipping her wine, her grey eyes taking in the sight of the wealth of humanity who partied and drank about her. Tall and lean, her figure curving and regal with creamy, smooth, alabaster skin, auburn hair tastefully styled off her shoulders. There were enough bodies available to quench even her thirst, but she was no hurry. The night was still young; it wouldn't be long before her meal presented him or herself. In the meantime, she simply allowed the scene to envelope her.

Across the room to her right, a sexy brunette eyed a tall, muscular male standing near the dance floor, with drink in hand. She studied him, licking her lips. He was scrumptious. She made a mental note to herself, this one could be tonight's appetizer.

As he sipped his drink, he seemed to sense the eyes of the brunette upon him and turned. Sparks flew the instant their eyes met. He smiled. She smiled back, an invitation to approach her. He accepted.

The scenario played itself out, again and again, throughout the evening. Anna loved observing human courting rituals. She let out a whimsical sigh. So much had changed since she was mortal. Fashion in particular had evolved with the times, the new styles and fabrics, so exciting. They were refreshing, enticing, and sexy, more to her liking. For instance, the form fitting red dress she wore undoubtedly would attract dinner her way before long. It made *her* moist when she saw it in the store front window.

Three cheers for new fashion. Finally, liberation from the restrictive and mundane she'd always craved. Gone were those long waisted bodices and draped skirts she'd worn when she first arrived in this country, with her husband, in the 1680's. And good riddance to linen shifts, and those damned stays. How she hated those things, they were supposed to be a support garment but all they did was support her belief that males were intent on controlling women through the use of torture devices disguised as everyday attire.

Swaying in time with the music, she crossed her legs and lifted her glass of wine to her lips. Her high cut outfit exposed her shapely limbs as she perused the crowd. Males, on the hunt for new conquests, strolled by trying to engage her by winking. She, of course, winked back but nothing caught her fancy. She wasn't in the mood to settle tonight, but if all else failed, it would be a simple matter to overtake a mind and lead them to a quiet spot for a bite.

Without warning, every patron in the bar froze in their tracks. Even the music came to an abrupt halt. Anna looked about mystified, slowly setting her glass down on the bar top.

Magic. Someone had come to call on her.

Then Anna spotted her striding across the dance floor, the walk a smoldering glide of heat and sex. She slalomed smoothly through the sea of living statues, loathing shown in her eyes. She'd changed her hair and the clingy dress was seductive and somewhat out of character, but it was her. Sylvia. The night had just taken an unexpected downturn.

The new arrival sauntered up, took the seat next to her, leering with contempt. Anna's smile was mirthless as she studied her newly arrived adversary. Hate wasn't strong enough a word to describe how she felt about this creature.

It was Sylvia who alerted the Vampire High Council about her activities in New Carrollton twelve years ago and brokered the agreement between the Lycan and the Council to form the joint task force, leading to the destruction of her nest and all of her children. Sylvia vehemently denied any involvement, but Anna knew better. She could always see the look in the sorceress' eyes, mocking her, taunting her. Sylvia was responsible, without question, and she would see to it the cockroach got what she deserved. Retribution would come and when it did, inflicting unspeakable suffering would be only the beginning.

"Sylvia, so nice of you to have taken time off from your cud chewing to stop by." There was never any love lost between her and the sorceress.

"You always were such a bitch, Anna. You do know, of course, what they do to bitches. They put them to sleep."

She fired a hard glare. "Is that a threat, Sylvia?"

"You may take it any way you wish." The sorceress regarded her coldly.

*****

The hairs on Sylvia's neck bristled as she faced her hated nemesis. How could she ever have considered this *thing* a friend? They'd met long ago at the annual Mystic Coalition Ball, a black tie gala. Admission was strictly by invitation only. Despite numerous precautions against unwanted guests, Anna managed to finagle her way into gaining access. It was no small accomplishment. Wielders of magic had long since learned how to shield their minds against vampire influence. Even an

21

immortal, four hundred years her senior, would have been hard challenged to pull off what Anna managed to do. Impressive to say the least and it proved to be the first red flag that Anna was something more than simply vampire.

Sylvia had admired Anna for her resourcefulness and made it her business to introduce herself. Soon they were chatting like old friends and giggling like schoolgirls at the stuffy and arrogant Gyland, the elitist class of the Coalition, and their strict adherence to archaic rituals.

Looking back, it was obvious Anna wanted nothing of her friendship. It was all a ruse in an attempt to take possession of the Algeus, the forbidden book of dark magic. In her hands, the book would have made Anna all but invincible. Cleverly, Anna alluded to the book one evening during casual conversation and barely concealed her disappointment to discover only the most powerful among the Coalition were ever allowed near it. Sylvia was just a Myona, back then, an apprentice, far too inexperienced to gain access to the evil text but her friend and lover, Julius, was another story.

The vicious little whore wasted little time turning her attention to him, using her wiles and cunning to lure her beloved into bed. Julius may have been a womanizer, but thankfully, he was no fool. He quickly saw through Anna's veil of treachery and for the sake of all, banished the book to a nether dimension, ending her plans of possessing it forever. Enraged, Anna launched herself screaming into the night. He'd made a bitter and terrible enemy. Soon after, Julius was found dead in his abode. Anna's reprisal had been swift and lethal.

To her outrage, the Coalition's investigation was ruled closed, citing inconclusive evidence. It was ludicrous! Everyone knew who killed Julius, yet none had the courage to stand up and charge Anna with his murder. Even the Coalition feared Anna's growing might. They were cowards, one and all.

It fell to her, the only one who gave a damn, to avenge Julius. Time and again, she'd hunted and battled the vampire only to find herself barely holding her own. Anna simply was too powerful. Only her quick wit allowed her to survive many of the encounters. It forced on her a cold, hard truth. Until she completed her training, she would never possess to skill and power needed to kill the Destroyer.

So, she immersed herself in her studies, pushing her endurance, mastering one spell after another until she surpassed even her mentor's abilities. Anna's dominance over her was at an end.

"So, are we going to sit here, gawk at each other and trade insults, or did you actually want something, Sylvia?" Anna lifted her glass and took a sip.

Eyeing her enemy, Sylvia crossed her legs. "We're aware of what you're planning. The coalition is, even now, debating on what to do about it."

Anna arched an eyebrow. "I'm truly flattered that the great and powerful Mystic Coalition has taken such an interest in me, when I'm sure they have so many more important things on their busy agenda to concern themselves with."

Her lip curled with disdain. "Spare me, Anna. Anytime someone of your stature embarks on a plan to cause such monumental change in the status quo, it demands our undivided attention. Normally, we wouldn't interject ourselves into vampire affairs, but this isn't strictly about vampires, is it?"

It wasn't the kind of news the blood sucking bitch wanted to hear. The last thing she wanted was the Coalition to start sticking its nose into her plans. Anna tried to hide it, but Sylvia knew she'd struck a nerve.

"My, you truly must be unnerved. I've barely started my nest building and already I'm being monitored," Anna said, her lip twitching ever so slightly.

A direct hit.

Sylvia leaned in toward her. "Yes, we are concerned. But, understand *this*, Anna, I don't care what the coalition decides. I will not sit idly by and watch the world fall into your grubby, little hands."

Anna laughed out loud. "And what will you do to stop me? Run doe eyed and weeping to the Lycan and the High Council again? You're just a second rate sorceress with a few petty parlor tricks. You're no match for me, Sylvia."

She smiled. Time to show Anna a real trick, this one would kill her. "Is that what you think? You look pale, dear. Perhaps you could use some sun." Casually, she lifted her hand. Anna watched transfixed as tiny pinpoints of light appeared on Sylvia's skin and quickly expanded.

23

Soon, it was entirely illuminated with the glow of yellow sunlight. Anna stared wide eyed, hissing fearfully. Sylvia gazed at her extremity as if inspecting her nails.

"Beautiful, isn't it? I can control the intensity of the light; make it as dull or bright as I wish." She looked upon Anna's expression with keen satisfaction. "I've added a few new parlor tricks, but you can see that, can't you?"

Sylvia rose to her feet and eyed Anna bitterly, her skin returning to its natural hue. "This is your first and only warning. Stop what you're planning or I will. I *do* hope I've made myself clear, vampire....for *your* sake."

Anna's eyes sparkled with rage. "You day is coming, witch. New powers or not, I will kill you, Sylvia!"

She met the vampire's unflinching gaze with a withering glare of her own. "Oh, I so look forward to you trying." She turned and started away as the patrons and music reanimated as if nothing had occurred.

*****

Anna watched as Sylvia disappeared back into the partying throng. Angst flooded her mind. The sorceress had become a serious threat. Fortunately, the fool had tipped her hand. This new ability would've come as a very unwelcome surprise in battle. She would have to find a way to counter her magic then kill the sorceress, once and for all.

"Hi, is this seat taken?"

She turned and feasted her eyes on a fine-looking, well dressed hunk of American beefcake. Square jawed, clean cut, intense blue eyes, and a smile that would melt the polar ice caps, he was glorious.

"No, please sit down."

He took a seat next to her and smiled. "I'm John, pleased to meet you."

She put on her most seductive smile. The cat was about to seduce the canary. "Hi, John, I'm Anna, nice to meet you too." She shifted on the bar stool exposing more of her legs. Reaching out with her aura, she enveloped him, projecting sensual arousal and welcome. They shook hands. Anna licked her lips in approval. The prey had an amazing physique, stylish haircut, manicured nails and tailor made suit. Truly, he was a male who took good care of himself.

"Your hands feel like ice, Anna. Would you like my jacket?"

"Why, thank you, John but I'm fine, really."

John nodded, looking her over. "Well, Anna, you are one amazingly sexy lady."

She smiled, her eyes roaming over her new friend. "You're very good looking yourself, John. In fact, I was just thinking you look good enough to eat."

# CHAPTER FIVE

dalius landed in an open field, fading into view as his cell phone vibrated for attention. He drew his weapons, leveling them in opposite directions. He reached out with his mind, scanning the wooded area about him, finding no contacts within his telepathic reach and only the scent of foliage and wildlife were present in the air.

Certain that he was alone, he returned the guns to their holsters, withdrew the phone from his trench coat and took the call. "This is Adalius."

"Where are ye, Ada?" It was Duncan Sinclair, his Drayken representative and good friend of twenty years. The familiar brogue of the Scotsman was always a welcome sound to his ears. Sadly, the call was most likely meant to update him about the unfortunate family he'd failed to save.

"I am approximately thirty miles south of New Carrollton," he said, keeping a watchful eye on his surroundings.

"Are ye sure about this, laddie? It's a long way tae travel if ye guess wrong 'at she devil could be headed anywhere."

"As sure as I have ever been. It is the closest major city, and need I mention her previous connection to New Carrollton?"

"Aye, there is 'at. Just be mindful, lad, she could be leadin' ye intae a trap."

It always amused Adalius that Duncan referred to him as lad. Though he was turned at the age of twenty six and still had a youthful appearance, he was in fact over three hundred years old, and was at least two centuries Duncan's senior.

"I have given serious consideration to the possibility, I shall be careful. Have you a progress report on the case file of the murdered family?"

"Aye, I do. I was sad tae hear about th' wee ones. Damned bastards should hae been staked to the ground and left in the sun tae burn." Duncan paused, "Ada, dinnae blame yerself. If there was anythin' at t'all ye coulda dain tae save those puir folk, ye would've."

"I do not blame myself for their deaths. Adalius cringed. He hated lying.

"You cannae hide it from me, laddie, Ah can hear the guilt flowin' through the lines."

They'd been friends too long. He couldn't hide his feelings from Duncan. "You know me well, old friend."

"Loch the back of muh hand. You've much tae answer for, Ada, let th' devil witch answer for her oan sins."

Adalius acquiesced, "I will not presume to debate your wisdom."

"Now there's a wise mon." The matter settled, Duncan got back to business. "We checked into th' family's background. They've too many connections in high places tae simply vanish. So, we've arranged a vehicle accident. All th' autopsy reports have been prepared an' our fowk will see tae it aw th' investigators an' th' medical examiner are dazzled tae ensure consistency in their reports."

Thorough and efficient, that was Duncan and his Drayken brethren all over. "Thank you, my friend. Please see to it that floral arrangements are sent."

"Already taken care of." Duncan was the best. Every Drayken hoped that when they retired, their service would be rewarded with being made vampire. It wasn't a guarantee. Sometimes the only recompense was the gratitude of the clients. But no one doubted that when the time came for Duncan Sinclair to call it a career, with his renown for excellence and going above and beyond service, he would justifiably join the ranks of the immortals.

"Be advised, I've taken it upon myself tae see tae some arrangements. You are now th' proud oaner of a townhouse on th' outskirts of the city. You should be receiving the coordinates and address oan ye phone directly. Weapons includin' yer sword and additional ammo are already in route and should arrive within th' hour."

It was like Duncan could access his mind; often the Drayken anticipated his needs and acted before the request formed in his thoughts. "Impressive, you never cease to amaze, Drayken."

"An' am a fantabulous dancer too."

Adalius smiled. "I need not be reminded. As I recall, it was how you stole Samantha away from me."

"Ah did nae such a thin', Ah simply provided anither option and let the lass make er' choice."

He could hear the smile in the Scotsman's words. "Is that what you choose to call it?" he needled his friend.

"It's th' story I'm stickin' tae."

Adalius checked his timepiece. As much as he hated it, it was time to say goodbye to his friend. "As always, it was good to hear from you but I must be off. Wish me luck, Duncan. Anna must be located and destroyed, for all of our sakes"

"I'll do better than that, laddie, mah flight leaves in two hours. I'll contact ye th' minute Ah arrive in New Carrollton."

He blinked in surprise. "You are coming here? But what of your other clientele, surely…"

"I've already spoken with Drayken elders, they agree that th' destruction of Anna should take top priority. Mah other clients will be assigned a new Drayken representative until further notice."

Obviously, he wasn't alone in recognizing the threat Anna represented. "That is welcome news. Where are you now, my friend?"

"Sydney, Australia."

Australia. That would mean it would be many hours before Duncan arrived. "Indeed, what has occurred there that requires your personal attention?"

Duncan chuckled. "It's called a vacation. E'en we Drayken, need a wee bit an R an' R from time tae time."

He closed his eyes and sighed. He had intruded on his friend's hard earned time of relaxation. "Forgive me old friend, I did not desire to disturb your time of enjoyment."

"Nae, ye never need apologize tae me, Ada. You're my friend."

"And I shall ever be yours. Very well, I shall see you soon."

"Aye, that ye will."

The line clicked, ending the call. Adalius returned the phone to his coat. He was about to take to the sky when a familiar tingle danced up his spine. He drew his weapons. "I know you are there, show yourself and be recognized." The air before him shimmered. A form took shape, then substance.

Adalius scowled. "Gautier."

The vampire, tall and lean with ear length platinum blonde hair, smiled maliciously. "Hello again, Sandrian. I can't tell you how long it's taken me to track you down, but as I recall, I warned that I'd find you no matter where you went."

Gautier was an aristocrat in the immortal hierarchy with an acute hatred for him and contempt for Sandrians as a whole. His sentiments were far from uncommon. Bigotry and hatred against his kind had been ongoing since long before the pyramids were erected. Throughout the centuries, Sandrians were persecuted and pursued by other vampire kind. The carnage and bloodshed nearly resulted in their extinction.

The air about Adalius became agitated with the crackle of psychic energy. "Do you also recall, what I said would come to pass, should you ever come after me again?"

A smirk spread across Gautier's lips. "Actually, I do. You threatened to kill me."

"You will find, son of Dracul, that I am a male of my word." Adalius noted the handle of a sword protruding from behind the vampire's back.

Gautier moved toward him, his eyes sparked angrily. "You know, a threat from you would send shivers down the spine of the average immortal. But unlike those commoners, I have no fear of you. Quite the opposite, I feel indebted. Hunting you, Sandrian, has rejuvenated me, given me purpose. I'll so miss that after I've killed you."

Adalius exhaled an annoyed breath. *What was it with villains and their need to monologue?* "I have yet to be slain by words, Gautier. You wish me dead, then come try your hand."

"Yes, you're quite right. Let's cease this senseless banter and get on with the fun." Gautier blurred forward, striking him with a hard left

29

cross. Ever the opportunist, the southpaw pressed the attack, firing a swift punch to the midsection, driving precious air from the Sandrian's lungs. Adalius fired a counterpunch; Gautier caught it in his hand. The vampire beamed, backhanding Adalius away.

Infuriated, his own eyes blazed teal as Gautier charged. Skillfully, he deflected a left cross meant for his head and caught the vampire with a violent uppercut, lifting Gautier off his feet. Adalius went on the offensive, catching Gautier with a series of viscous chops. Gautier threw a desperate punch. It was expected. He batted away the punch and caught the vampire with a roundhouse kick, knocking Gautier backward.

Blood flowing from the cut on his lip, the Frenchman smirked, "Nicely done, Sandrian. Pity I'll have to find a new past time when you're gon-"

Adalius blurred forward, knocking Gautier's words back down his throat with a shot to the chops. The vampire hit the ground, his legs rising to the sky. Wiping away the blood from his split lip, Gautier sat up and glared.

Adalius winked. "I was under the impression you had come to fight."

Gautier snarled, "You...*dare*!"

Adalius' eyes narrowed. "Indeed I do, Draculson. Rise, I am becoming bored."

"I will rip out your spleen, Sandrian. You are dead!" the vampire roared.

He had him. Adalius had him and he knew it. Gautier was a sound fighter and more powerful than himself, but he was arrogant, and undisciplined. He would use those vices to destroy Gautier.

"So you have said. Yet I continue to stand unharmed. Something is obviously wrong. Perhaps you are not applying yourself."

Gautier, still unsteady, rose to his feet, blade in hand. "I intend to apply this sword to your throat, mongrel."

Adalius regarded the irate vampire, motioning for him to bring it on.

Gautier gathered himself. "I am going to carve you to pieces for stealing my Anna from me. For taking what's mine."

He held his ground preparing for Gautier's assault. "I cannot steal from you what was never yours. Anna made her choice, Gautier, she found in me, something perhaps lacking in you." Adalius' grin was wicked. A taunt. It worked.

Gautier, his eyes gleaming bright red, charged screaming at the top of his lungs. Adalius flinched. The rage radiating from the aristocrat was astounding. It slammed against his senses like a physical force.

Gautier swung the blade across his body in a downward arc. Adalius matched his speed, dodging the would be fatal blow. Gautier exploded in frustrated rage, wildly swinging the sword like a thing possessed.

Adalius ducked underneath, side stepped to the left, then tucked and rolled to the right. He somersaulted over and out of the way of Gautier's mad swipes. The attacker roared, aiming for the Sandrian's left flank, but Adalius leaped over the blade then snapped a roundhouse kick to the immortal's exposed face. The blow spun the Frenchman around. He staggered and fell. Adalius moved in.

Gautier rose to his knees. "No more, Adalius. I will leave you in peace. Please, have mercy!"

His brows dipped. The vampire was up to something. "You think me a fool, Gautier, whatever you seek to do, I will…"

Gautier scooped up a hand full of sandy earth, tossing the debris into his eyes. Blinded, Adalius staggered back. Gautier sprang to his feet, and wasting no time, he fired a punch, landing it flush on Adalius' chin. He blinked, trying to clear his head.

The aggressor swung his blade, slicing Adalius' shoulder. Gore flowed from the wound. Adalius countered with a hard right but it failed to slow the emboldened immortal. Gautier back handed Adalius, the sword handle gashing him above the eye. Blood seeped from the wound, into his eyes, partially obscuring his vision. Gautier seized the opportunity driving his broadsword into Adalius' abdomen.

He groaned. The silver in the sword seared his insides like a branding iron. Gautier's smile was cruel. With a grunt, he shoved the sword deeper, the tip breaking through his back. Swiftly, the nobleman withdrew the blade. Adalius, doubled over, going down on one knee.

Gautier's smile was vicious as he ran his finger through the life fluid that stained his blade. "Now *that* was satisfying. I have longed to feel the split of your flesh," he said licking the blood off his fingers. "I took care to avoid piercing your heart that, of course, would've been fatal. Still,

31

wounds from silver can be excruciating. But you know that first hand, don't you?"

Adalius pounded the ground. Through sheer force of will, he rose unsteadily to his feet.

"Yes, get up, Sandrian. You'll spoil my good time if you die so easily."

He steadied himself and assumed a defensive stance. The wounds were healing but not nearly fast enough.

"Much better, now don't be a buzz kill and die too swiftly. I want to savor this." Gautier lunged forward swinging his sword. The first stroke sliced across Adalius' bare chest. The second scored a deep wound across his thigh. Gautier admired his handiwork.

"You're slowing down, Sandrian. Are you tiring? And those nasty wounds, they don't seem to be closing as they should. You've not been feeding." Gautier clicked his tongue. "You've grown soft, Adalius. You've actually come to care for the well-being of mortals. Denying yourself a proper feeding because of some absurd sense of nobility. Bah, I will torture and maim many in remembrance of you. Whatever could Anna have seen in you?"

Adalius faced his foe, focusing on one task, killing Gautier.

"No snide remarks, Sandrian? You must be more injured than I realized. But worry not, you're suffering will soon be at an end. When I'm ready to end it."

Looking upon the Frenchman, he did the last thing Gautier expected. He laughed.

Gautier warily lowered his sword. "What are you laughing at, Sandrian dog?"

Adalius continued laughing.

Gautier was far from amused. "Answer me, what do you find so amusing?"

Ignoring his wounds, Adalius focused. His strength was slowly returning. He just needed to stall a little longer. "Is it not apparent? I am laughing at you. You're a buffoon, Gautier, a jester, a clown. Here you track your prey across the globe, have them primed for the kill, yet all you can presume to do is preen and prance about like a spoiled princess. Indeed, you are killing me. Not with your blade but with your endless caterwauling. The temptation to hurl myself upon your sword to spare my ears more of your drivel is overwhelming. Can you not still your tongue, if only for a moment?"

Gautier's expression flashed from bemusement to stark outrage. "Enough, Sandrian, I shall slice out that insolent tongue and eat it before your dying eyes." The vampire started forward.

*Yes, come closer Gautier. Closer. Closer....And now*! Adalius leaped into the air and delivered double axe kick as Gautier came into range. The first leg knocked the sword from his hand and sent it sailing straight into the air. The second caught the startled blue blood underneath the chin, snapping his head back, his body arching from the blow. The instant he touched down, Adalius dropped to one knee and fired a thrust punch to the immortal's mid-section, doubling him over. As Adalius rose, he slid his arms under Gautier's armpits, hooking his arms and pulled back as the sword came down, lancing through the vampire's back, impaling him entirely.

Gautier cried out. As a subtle sizzle reached his ears, Adalius drove his knee into his adversary's face, sending the immortal stumbling away. He went after Gautier, blocking out his own pain. There was no turning back. Only one would walk away from this confrontation. Gautier groaned, frantically reaching for the sword handle was well out of his grasp. He sensed the Frenchman's panic.

He was losing; Gautier would soon breathe his last. "It ends here, Gautier." Adalius caught up to his prey. Reaching for the sword handle, he yanked it free, bits of charred flesh clung to the blade. The tormented vampire roared, then turned. "I warned you not to pursue me, that next time we met, I would destroy you. That time has arrived. Farewell, Gautier, death has come for you!"

Adalius swung. The sword sliced through neck bone and cartilage, severing his head. The vampire's body crumbled to dust at his feet. His strength spent, Adalius sank to his knees. His wounds were still closing, albeit slowly. He needed rest and more importantly, blood. He had to feed and soon. Reaching for his phone, he hit the speed dial, as the remains of Gautier drift away in the breeze.

Gautier was every bit the menace he once was. By destroying him, Adalius had taken another step taken toward redemption. The line began to ring. Relief washed over him when he heard the familiar click.

"Aye, what is it, lad?"

"I have been attacked. It was Gautier."

Duncan growled, "Dammit, Ada, did ye kill him this time?"

"He is dead." His skin tingled as the healing continued.

"Aboot bloody time, Ah tauld ye tae th' kill the snobby bastard years ago."

Adalius took in a painful breath. "I am regretting that err in judgment…as we speak, old friend."

"Ye need tae feed, ah can hear it in yer voice."

"Your concern is appreciated, but you need not worry abo—"

Duncan's voice went up an octave. "Ye have tae feed, Ada. Ye cannae get around it, ye have tae have blood, mon!"

"And feed I shall, you have my word. Now, if you please, add a new coat to the list and have it shipped to the new dwelling."

"I'll tend tae it, now go and feed. If ye need anythin' else, contact me."

"I shall. Thank you, old friend."

"Just be safe, an' Godspeed, laddie." The line clicked and went dead. Adalius willed himself to his feet, taking a sample of air into his nostrils. Good, just what he needed. There were deer close by. Hardly his first choice, but he dared not take a human vein in his condition. If he went into blood lust, the result could be deadly.

He gave one last glance at the remains of his nemesis, bowing his head. "Rest well and be at peace, Gautier." Silently, he lifted off the ground and flew off in the direction of the deer and blood he so desperately needed.

# CHAPTER SIX

She had a death wish. That had to be it. Why else would she, a happily married wife and mother, be carrying on an illicit affair with a real live vampire or a real dead one, depending on how you looked at it. Checking her watch, Marie turned into the parking lot of the Cove Motor Inn and drove toward the rear, scanning the darkened area until she spotted a silhouette in the distance, among the trees.

"Oh thank goodness, she's still here." She was running really late but it couldn't be helped. She had responsibilities. Exhilaration washed over her, as she drove toward the figure while her outraged conscience pitched a bitch about the loving husband and father who had done nothing to deserve this blatant betrayal. As she approached, the individual turned in her direction.

Marie's heart sang as her headlight beams fell upon the waiting Trish, who smiled happily and waved. Hurriedly, she pulled over and parked her Volkswagen next to a walnut tree, switched off the engine, and put on the park brake. The reliable station wagon had once again delivered her safely to her destination.

Giddy from excitement, she couldn't wait to feel the embrace of her lover. When Trish suggested she wear something sexy for their rendezvous, Marie had nearly soaked through her panties. Trish was turning her into a total sex fiend. After their steamy encounter in the university stairwell the other night, she'd gone home still very much aroused, and literally attacked Logan, her husband, in the kitchen, as he was preparing dinner. The bedroom could wait. She couldn't.

They'd gone at it like a pair of horny teenagers, kissing, groping and pawing, trying to get to the good part before the parents came home.

Their lovemaking was rough, raw, and primitive. Tenderness was cast to the wind. She hadn't been in the mood for a gentle hand. After all the delicious things Trish had done to her, she wanted, she needed to be taken, conquered, possessed. She scratched and clawed like a cat in heat, their bodies tangled and joined, flesh against flesh, calling out curses and each other's names.

Neighbors beat on their door for quiet. But there was no stopping. Logan was deep inside her, driving her to the breaking point and beyond. His back arched, he pounded her, slapping against her, claiming what was his. And when he hooked her legs and jack hammered her like he knew she liked it, she dug her nails into his back and exploded in molten ecstasy. He wasn't far behind. Groaning like an animal, sweat pouring off him, he threw back his head.

The instant his body seized, his cry tore through the apartment. His seed filling her, she came again in incandescent climax. She couldn't tell who screamed the loudest. They'd collapsed, spent and panting, but far from done. Luckily for their son, Jason, he was spending the night at her sister's or it would've been pizza night.

Tonight however, she made sure dinner was prepared. After the family was fed, she told Logan she and her girlfriend were going to have a ladies' night out. The last thing she wanted was a multitude questions. Trish *was* her friend and they *were* going to be together. Technically it wasn't a lie.

With her long, brunette hair pinned up, gold blouse, and black pants on, she grabbed her purse and slipped on her flats. Not bad, just not the outfit she'd wear for Trish. Purse over her shoulder, she kissed her men good bye then headed out the door. Just in time to run right into the super's nosy wife. The busybody often prowled the hallways engaging residents, searching for juicy gossip or spreading it. The woman was TMZ on two legs. She had to admit though, the lady always had the good dirt.

The latest hot topic was the woman in 213. She'd been entertaining three men for the past week. They were all seen going in but nobody had come out. Often, moans and shouts could be heard through the door and down the corridor. Three men, wow. Guess shame wasn't a word in everyone's vocabulary. After leaving Geraldo to her gossip distribution, she'd gotten in the car and driven two blocks to a Wendy's to change, so damn hot and bothered, she could barely sit still on the car seat.

But, even if she had the guts, the instant she even thought of sexing three men, her mother would claw her way out of the grave and smack her into the next time zone. Still, just thinking about it... it had to be the blood. She'd been drinking Trish's blood. Something about it, gave her inner slut a get out of jail free card. Just a drop of it made her totally and wildly uninhibited. It was exciting and scary at the same time. Logan, of course, noticed her newly found, high octane sexual appetite. Sometimes he gave her the suspicious eye but she simply attributed it to her new exercise routine and the yoga classes she had been taking. She assured him in the sweetest of ways that there wasn't another man. And it was true, Trish wasn't a man.

It was extra a muggy evening. The heat wave made for stifling days and little relief at sunset. The wind blew through her hair as she sang along with the radio and thought of her hot date. A mischievous smile teased her lips. Her outfit was gonna knock Trish's socks off.

Stashed in the trunk, was a pair of ebony, lace top, thigh high nylons and her sexiest black 'fuck me' pumps, along with the black pleated mini skirt Logan had banned her from wearing outside the house. The matching silk blouse she purchased earlier that day complimented her outfit nicely. Just thinking about how her vamp lover would react, sent a tingle dancing down her spine.

When she walked in Wendy's to change, she drew a few sideward glances as she strolled into the restroom. But when she came out, outfit on, lipstick applied, hair flowing about her shoulders, every head in the place turned. Her skin tingled at the eyes roaming her body. Such a turn on! She practically strutted to the car.

She rolled to the restaurant driveway, and yielded to traffic. Casting her eyes to the dining area window, she spied a young man staring at her like a hungry lion. That was until his date caught him in the act, dumped her drink into his lap and stormed away. *Ha! Served him right.*

Marie opened the car door and slid a leg out as Trish approached. She lusted at the sight of the alluring vamp. *Damn, she looked hot in her red leather mini skirt and matching corset.* Her golden hair was loose and free, her eyebrows arched and her lips were lush with color of candy apple red lipstick. With her firm breasts, narrow waist, flared hips and long toned legs, the vampire was sex itself.

She exited the vehicle, her blouse open showing off her cleavage as Trish rushed into her arms. Backing her against the car door, Trish kissed her passionately. Their tongues swirled together. Intense excitement, coursed through Marie's veins as the sexy vamp yanked open her blouse, sending buttons flying. Trish's eyes sparkled like jewels, her gaze traveling from Marie's eyes to her shoulders, down to her breasts. Marie's nipples hardened under the fiery scrutiny.

Delicate hands slowly glided over the supple lines of Marie's waist and hips as the vampire leaned in. Marie took in her scent, spicy cinnamon and sweet. They coiled around each other, like angry serpents, their bodies surging and relaxing in a rhythmic dance.

"I'm going to devour you, utterly," Trish, in a husky voice, whispered into her ear.

Marie shivered. The sound of that voice, the feel of her body, the touch of her hands....*Oh. My. God*! "You better," she sighed.

A gentle exhale escaped Trish's lips as Marie's hands roamed down and over the vampire's tight round ass.

"I missed you," Trish purred like a happy kitten in her ear.

Marie bit her lower lip as Trish trailed tickling fingers up and down her spine. "I missed you too, Trish."

The vampire's eyes twinkled with mischief. "I see you decided not to wear a bra."

Marie beamed. "I wanted you to have easy access."

Trish smiled, her fangs extending. They looked like ivory daggers. The vampire moved in, her lips covering her own. Marie's respiration seized in her throat as Trish's probing hands worked underneath her skirt. A soft whimper escaped her lips. Marie parted her legs allowing access.

The blonde smiled, ducking her head. Marie trembled as Trish trailed her tongue down her neck. Marie's pulse quickened. Fisting the blonde's hair, Marie sighed as her lover worked her way down, toward her nipples.

Licking her lips, Marie hissed as slender fingers stroked her through the silky material of her panties. With a gasp, Marie threw back her head, as Trish's hand ducked underneath the lace, cupping her, stroking her.

Marie's legs quivered, her hips rolling with a mind of their own. She was good and wet, soaking as Trish worked her, sliding one, then two fingers inside, exploring, torturing her.

With supreme effort, she shoved Trish away. "No, not here," she said with what strength she could muster. Taking the vampire's hand, she led her to the room she'd rented earlier in the day. Marie trembled as she guided the key toward the lock. Trish took her hand, holding it steady as the key slid in.

They forced their way inside, closing the door behind them. Trish took Marie into her arms, kissing her hungrily. A heavy breath escaped the brunette's lips. Trish slid her hand under Marie's skirt, caressing her pussy. Shivers of delight raced over her body. She cried out as Trish latched hold to a nipple, slowly, deliciously drawing it past her lips, into her mouth.

Marie surrendered. Hooking her leg around Trish's waist, Marie softly whispered her lover's name as the vampire forced her against the door. Painting one nipple, then the other with her tongue, Trish suckled and teased, making love to her. A low growl rumbled in Trish's throat. Carefully, the vamp rolled the lace panties down over Marie's hips, allowing them to fall freely to the floor.

"Mmmm, you belong to me now," the blonde said in a husky voice.

It was true. She could never, would never, deny Trish anything. Whenever the vampire hungered, she would relent. If Trish asked her to commit murder, she'd gladly do so for another sensuous bite from her fangs and more of the unbelievable rapture of that amazing tongue.

She'd never felt interest or attraction to another woman before. Yet now, all she wanted, all she craved, all she needed, was Trish. She had taken her to heights not even her husband, who she loved with all her soul, had ever taken her and she wanted more, much more.

Trish kneeled down and smiled up at her. Marie knew what was coming next. *God, yes.* She widened her stance, pushing her hips forward in invitation. Trish indulged her. Marie's stomach muscles trembled, as Trish traced her tongue down her body leaving a searing trail in its wake.

Stopping to lave around her navel, Trish slowly delved inside. Marie's body seized. Hissing and groaning, Marie ran her hands over her aching nipples while Trish slid her free hand down between her own legs. With surprising strength, Trish hooked Marie's legs over her shoulders. The look in the blonde's eyes made her heart skip a beat, as Trish ducked her head. Marie writhed, her breath came in gasps. The soft warmth of that magic tongue, curled and swirled around her sensitive clit. Marie threw back her head, her body arching. Trish was gentle, suckling with exquisite tenderness. The vampire was tireless, relentless as she continued to torture her with unbearable pleasure.

"Oh *Gawd*!" The sweet sting of fangs. She hissed. Hips undulating, she came as the vampire fed from her, taking what she needed and giving so much more. Suckling and swallowing, Trish shuddered. A gentle tug of her clit sent her off on the wave of yet another orgasm. On and on, riding wave after delicious wave of pleasure, each climax stronger than the last, Trish satisfied her, completed her.

Just when she could stand no more, Trish released her. Marie panted as butterfly kisses and tender licks guided her into reentry. When she could do something close to focusing her eyes, she looked into her lover's face and smiled. Trish, blood trickling from the corner of her mouth, smiled back.

She ran a finger through Trish's hair. It didn't matter how much the blonde took from her. What Trish gave her was well worth it. The world started to spin, she felt disoriented and weak. Everything moved in slow motion. The carpet came up to meet her. She fell into Trish's arms that bore her up and carried her to the bed. Laying her gently down, Trish took her place next to her.

Tears streamed from Marie's eyes. Images of her spouse flooded her thoughts. *What was she doing? This was wrong on every level. The lies.* She hated herself for all the lies. But it was…so…damn…*good*! Trish wiped away the falling tears, gazing into her eyes.

"It is time to decide, my love. Are you prepared to accept the gift I offer you?"

She struggled to reign in the myriad of strong emotions. "Trish, I've thought about it, I really have but I…I just don't know."

Trish kissed her cheek. "I know you love me, I sense your thoughts and I feel what is in your heart."

"You can read my mind?"

"Yes. I can also control mortal minds and alter or erase short term memories. As I get older, I will gain the ability to effect long term memories as well."

"Have you been controlling me this whole time?" Her anger flared.

"No, my love, I swear, everything you have given, everything you have felt has been of your own free will. I have seduced, not controlled you."

She knew the truth when she heard it. Trish wasn't lying. But now with her desire sated and mind clear, other unanswered questions began to bloom. "Are there others like you?"

Trish nodded nervously. "Yes and so many other things you cannot begin to imagine."

Marie shuddered. All the things she once considered childish fears, stepped into the light of possibility. In her youth, she remembered being terrified of going anywhere near her mother's closet. An icy cold would grip her, as if something were watching, but her mother always said it was only her imagination, now she realized that something malevolent may very well have been hiding in that closet.

"What do you want from me, Trish?"

"I want you. I offer my love, my heart. What we have shared is but the beginning of what can be yours. My powers and abilities, they can be yours as well if you become my mate. Come with me, Marie. Join me in immortality."

It felt like being swept down a wild rapid, it was all happening too fast. Yes, a huge part of her wanted to leap at Trish's offer, but there were other things to consider.

"What of my husband and son, Trish? I don't know if I can just leave them. What if I refuse to accept? "Trepidation filled her.

Trish took her hand and kissed it tenderly. "I would simply wipe your mind. You would have no memory of our ever meeting."

*No.* Her heart broke. It was hard to breathe. *A life without Trish? Unbearable. Unthinkable.* She loved her husband but...

"I sense your conflict, Marie. I can offer so much more than your husband ever could. Come with me; remain forever young, vibrant and beautiful. Come with me and together we'll watch the rise and fall of kings. We'll feed upon the blood of royalty and make love in the

41

bedrooms of their palaces. We will take what we want, when we want, and no one will tell us we're wrong. And I will love and make love to you throughout time."

Her head was swimming. It was an offer seductive as Trish herself. Spending an eternity with Trish and being forever young...it was too much to resist. "Before I give you my answer, promise me something?"

"Anything, I would do anything for you."

"If I say yes, you must promise me, we will turn both Logan and Jason."

"I promise, my love. We will turn them both. Your husband will be my husband, your son will be my son. I swear to you on my own blood."

Marie took her hand, gazing into her eyes. "I love you deeply. I accept you and your offer. Remember your promise to me, I hold you to your word. Now take me and make me yours."

Trish smiled, tears welling up in her eyes. "I will honor you as well as your wishes, my love. Soon, we will all be a family."

Trish leaned in and kissed her. Enveloped by the seductive aura of the vampire, Marie sighed, spreading her legs wide as Trish settled between them. Her heart hammered inside her chest as the vampire's tongue, slipped between her lips, wrapping around hers in sensuous dance. Yielding to Trish and the power of her aura, Marie surrendered her body. Her blood. Her soul.

Trish moved down, covering her neck with loving kisses. Wrapping her arms around her lover, Marie arched into the vampire as Trish showered her with loving attention, her tongue once more working its magic.

She rolled her hips against the vampire as Trish's tongue brushed her neck. Her breath came out in pants as Trish purred. Fingers glided down over her flat belly, down between her legs, caressing, stroking, probing. Trish flicked her clit. Marie moaned, soft and long.

A nip of her neck. Marie clenched her teeth. Trish was gentle but she wanted...more. As if sensing her need, the vampire responded, her stroking becoming more vigorous. The blooming in her core began. Her muscles rippled. Her heart pounded. Trish stroked faster, leading her, driving her toward... *oh God, shit*!

The sharp strike of fangs. Fingers slipped inside. Marie's mouth stretched open. She came as Trish drained her. On and on, she rode the wave as the vampire clung to her neck. Clutching Trish's body, she held the vampire's head to her throat, wrapping her legs around Trish's waist. Marie clung to her lover, forsaking life as her strength failed her. Trish possessively sank her fangs deeper. An intense sensual pleasure seeped into her mind. Marie cried out. *Please don't stop!*

Thoughts not her own flooded her mind. Trish. The vampire's entire living and undead life spread out before her. At the same time, she knew the vampire saw into her life as well. They were joining, merging, their souls becoming intertwined. It was beautiful, and the most intimate thing she'd ever experienced. She felt Trish's pleasure on top of her own. She was totally vulnerable, exposed, and accepted.

Trish loved her for all she was. Marie embraced their union as the vampire fed. Trish shuddered as she came, her moans, so sexy, so delicious. Like Trish herself. They belonged to each other. Trish released her. A wet thickness hit her lips. Marie licked in the metallic tasting fluid.

"Yes, drink it down, my love. Take it all in."

She did as instructed, drinking down the trickle that became a steady flow. It was done, they were mated. They belonged to each other, bound forever more. There would never be secrets between them.

Marie groaned. Her insides ignited. Horrible burning consuming, her chest collapsed. Her breathing ragged, hands trembling, she reached for Trish. The blonde took her hand, stroking her hair.

"Shhhhhhh, you are dying, my love, but I'm here. Soon, you'll need never fear anyone or anything ever again."

Through their link she knew Trish smiled. Marie found comfort in the blonde's beautiful face as the void swallowed her away.

# CHAPTER SEVEN

The Fifth District police department was watchdog to some of the toughest neighborhoods in New Carrollton. Inside the old squad house, in the holding cell area known as the Cage, which housed arrested citizens waiting to be processed, a fight broke out between two prisoners from rival gangs. A gaggle of officers hustled to separate the combatants while several other suspects were brought struggling in through a back entrance. Shouts echoed off the walls as street walkers from the vice sweep of the previous night, stood in line and argued amongst themselves while their pimps, pointed bling adorned fingers and complained of police tactics and brutality.

Assorted individuals sat at tables filling out police reports, while others waited to post bail. Briefcase carrying lawyers and public defenders made their way back and forth across the great room, on their way to represent clients facing charges ranging from assault to burglary to attempted murder.

Detective Arnold Page shook his head as he and Theo Richardson made their way from the cafeteria toward an old stone staircase. Page, a silver-grey fox with thinning hair who wore blazers and ties, looked like he'd be more at home in a courtroom than a homicide unit. A twenty year veteran of the force, he'd managed to wiggle his way out of several promotions which would have resulted in him becoming a desk jockey. That'd be the day. He was a detective, a damn good one. His place was investigating crimes, not pushing pencils. Medium height and build, Arnie sported a large, somewhat bulbous nose broken at least twice. Badges of courage he'd earned on the mean streets of his youth, where he sometimes found himself on the opposite side of a police interrogation room table.

To the brass and the assholes of the precinct, he was Detective Page. The gumshoe with the mind of a steel trap, tenacious as wolverine when it came to pursuing justice for the victims of the crimes he investigated. To his friends, he was Arnie, just a good Joe.

As they passed the Cage area, the rumble continued. The gang members were locked together, tussling as officers tugged and pulled, trying to separate them.

"Who the hell put members of the Dragons and the Vice Lords in the same cell?" Arnie yelled out, as he shook his head. "Doesn't anyone pay attention to the shift briefings?"

He and his partner continued past the station desk, toward the staircase leading to the detective squad room, sidestepping more officers racing to the Cage. As they looked back, one of the brawlers was being dragged away to the overflow cells in the basement. Taking the stairs, they headed up toward their desks with lunches in hand.

"What idiot put them together in the same cell? They've been blowin' each other's brains out the past few weeks." Arnie fumed.

"Cut 'em some slack, Arnie, we're all a little off our games right now. "Theo Richardson, in his jersey and jeans, was good looking and athletically built with dark, wavy hair, a clean shaven face and a vicious right cross. Arnie took the younger man under his wing when Richardson made detective. Hard-nosed, loyal to a fault with stones the size of medicine balls, Richardson didn't bite his tongue, compromise his principles, nor pulled any punches when it came to speaking his mind. If he thought you were full of it, he'd make sure you knew it. The kid was his partner and best friend.

While his was his ability to analyze, Richardson relied more on instincts. The kid said he'd sometimes just get a feeling when he worked a case. Like an itch in his mind. When doing police work, there were times you went with your gut. Often he told Theo to trust those feelings whenever he got them, never ignore the little voice when it told him something wasn't adding up.

As they continued up the stairs, another group was making their way down. An attractive brunette, carrying a clipboard, passed them as they ascended the staircase.

"Hi, Arnie." The young woman smiled warmly.

"Hiya, Hazel, how are ya, sweets?"

She brightened noticeably when she saw Richardson. "Hey, Theo." Richardson gave her a

quick hello as he made his way upward. Arnie looked back over his shoulder and watched as Hazel dejectedly made her way down.

She was a ray of sunshine in heels, blouse, and knee length skirt. What a looker. Hazel had long auburn hair, gorgeous eyes, a killer figure, and toned calves that in his youth, would have had him slobbering like a hound. If he were twenty five years younger, he'd give her a run for her money. He nudged Richardson as they continued their climb. "You know, kid, for such a great detective, you can be pretty dense."

Richardson rolled his eyes. "What are you talking about?"

He rolled his eyes. Richardson wasn't *that* dense. "I'm talking about Hazel, doofus. She's crazy about you. Why don't you ask the girl out for Pete's sake? "

"She's nice Arnie, she really is, but I guess I'm still not ready."

Arnie grunted. "Kid, far be it for me to tell ya how to run ya life but…"

Theo stopped walking and turned. "Don't start with me, Arnie."

Arnie threw up his hands defensively. "I ain't not startin' nuthin', I'm just saying that it's been six years. You could at least allow yourself to have a little fun."

Richardson's eyebrows rose. "Look who's talking? When was the last time *you* had a night

out?"

Arnie sighed. "*That's* different. I was married to my wife for thirty five years when she passed. I'm done. You, you're young, bright and handsome. You still got ya whole life ahead of ya."

They reached the top of the staircase and headed into the break room. The heavenly aroma of java hung in the air as Richardson made a beeline for the coffee maker.

"Hmmmm, looks like a fresh pot to me." Richardson picked a mug from the stack next to the coffee maker then reached for the pot.

"It is. I made it ten minutes ago."

Richardson paused. "*You* made the coffee?"

"Yeah."

He set the pot back in its place. "Think I'll have some tea instead."

Arnie grunted. "You sayin' my coffee makin' skills aren't up to your standards?"

Richardson grabbed a tea bag from a tin container, dropped it into his coffee mug and reached for the pot of hot water. "I'm saying your coffee making sucks." Richardson filled his mug with hot water. Steam rose from the cup as another detective walked into the break room, reached for a mug and filled it with the fresh brew.

He patted Richardson on the back and nodded toward the other detective. "Now there's a man with discriminating tastes. He knows good coffee when he sees it."

"Hey, McGee, I wouldn't drink that if I was you," Richardson said as he headed toward the doorway of the break room.

"Yeah, why not? "McGee asked, concern making its way across his face.

"Arnie made it," Richardson replied then looked back and smiled as he exited. Arnie gave the thumbs up.

"Fuck!" McGee looked like he'd swallowed a turd. He motored to the sink and dumped his mug.

"Come on, McGee."

"No, Page, that sewage you make isn't fit for cleaning toilets. Now stay away from the coffee maker."

Arnie threw up his hands then followed his partner out. Making his way toward the squad room, he sidestepped a speeding clerk with an arm full of files bound for the captain's office. What they needed was a cop directing floor traffic, it wasn't the first time he'd been nearly run down by one of those guys. He had to pick up the pace but he finally caught up to Richardson.

"I'm sorry, Arnie, but I'd rather drink a gallon of lighter fluid than swallow a drop of your coffee. Coffee, Arnie, how do you screw up making coffee?"

47

"Bite me."

Richardson chuckled as they approached their desks which were pushed together and facing each other. "Not even with Bricker's mouth."

Bricker looked up from his desk. "Hey, you keep my mouth outta your mouth, Richardson."

"Arnie made coffee, have a cup?"

Bricker cringed. "I'd rather drink scalding acid."

Richardson gave him the 'I told you so' look.

Arnie's expression soured. "Fuck all a you."

Bricker grinned. "If you promise to stop making coffee, old man, I'll even wear a garter and nylons."

The two detectives took their seats, each placing his lunch before him. Once settled, Richardson picked up the conversation. "Speaking of garters and nylons, how did your date with Tonya go, Bricker?"

Bricker flashed the grin of the wicked. "Great. She's my kinda girl, hot, blonde, stupid, inexpensive, and *loves* to suck a dick."

Along with assorted groans, Richardson rolled his eyes and shook his head. "You are the absolute epitome of class, Bricker."

"And I'm a fuckin stud, too!"

A voice from a cubicle behind Bricker blurted out, "Macho, Macho Man!!"

"Hey, you losers are just pissed that I saw her first."

Captain Williams, tall, lean, and graying at the temples, made his way out of his office.

"Alright, that's enough. Let's cut the chatter and start giving the taxpayers their money's worth, shall we?"

"You mean you want us to actually work for our money? What a dick," Bricker joked.

The captain's nostrils flared as he fired a look at Bricker that would have cooked meat. "Not tonight, Bricker. I just got off the phone with the commissioner, who just got an earful from the mayor. We've had four dead bodies turn up in the McClain Park area in the last week. Everybody wants to know when we're gonna catch this murdering psych job. The heat is on to bring this bastard down, gentlemen."

Richardson turned about in his chair. "So, do they think we're just sitting around with our thumbs up our asses?"

The captain's expression softened. "Nobody doubts we're doing our best, Theo, but I was notified that if we don't nail this down, the mayor is threatening to call in the Feds."

This announcement was greeted by a series of groans and expletives, not to mention his stomach rolling over as the captain held up his hands.

"Look, I don't like it any more than the rest of you but it's an election year, so I don't think I need to tell you that nervous voters can make for a very nervous mayor, who's up for re-election. That's the hand we've been dealt, gents, so let's catch this lunatic before we have to deal with the suits from the government."

The captain returned to his office. As for the rest of them, it was back to the business of hunting down a maniac. Richardson turned and opened the Styrofoam container before him. Grabbing his corned beef sandwich, the kid took a bite. Placing his sandwich back in its container, Richardson wiped his hands and reached for the file that had become his new preoccupation.

Arnie rolled his eyes. Theo tended to take some cases too personal. He had to learn to separate his emotions from this job; he'd wind up in a loony bin.

"Kid, will you give that Pearce case a rest? Between that and the McClain Park investigation, you're gonna go bonkers."

"I promised Mister Pearce I wouldn't give up, Arnie."

Arnie set his own sandwich down, picked up a napkin, and wiped his mouth and hands. "Ok, he said his wife was having a ladies night out and never came home. In my experience, that so-called girlfriend was most likely some Joe she met in one of the classes he said she was taking at the university. The fact that her body hasn't turned up says to me she's likely alive, kickin', and doing the nasty with some new beau."

Richardson flinched, most likely from a visual of his own wife in another man's arms. "You saw his face, Arnie. He was adamant his wife would never leave him and their son behind."

"They never believe it until they see it with their own eyes."

Richardson laid the file on his desk. He had a point and the kid knew it. "I'll give ya that but..."

"This isn't about *his* wife so much as it's about *yours*. Admit it, kid."

Richardson paused, blew out a breath and rubbed his face in his hands. "Maybe so, but I know how he feels. If I can help him find his wife…"

Arnie held his hands up in front of him. "I get it. Just promise me you'll give yourself time to rest. We need your head clear, fresh, and in the game while we hunt this nut job."

Richardson nodded, continuing his lunch as he read.

He really felt for the kid. Richardson's wife vanished six years earlier in much the same way as Mrs. Pearce. He knew Theo would never give up looking. Maybe helping Logan Pearce find his wife is a way of coping. Maybe the kid needed to find her almost as much as he needed to find his own wife.

# CHAPTER EIGHT

The moon cast long shadows as music and muffled chatter from within the club drifted out and up into the starless night. In a darkened corner, behind an old filthy trash dumpster, Anna held John in her arms while drinking from his neck in long pulls. The alley smelled of urine, ripe garbage, spoiled meat, and old grease but it provided enough cover for her to feed without fear of discovery or interruption.

Alleyways were never her first choice, especially when they reeked like this one, but they usually afforded vampires in the mood for fast food the opportunity to dine in relative peace. Tonight's entrée was fresh dressed human male, pickled in bourbon. Though she preferred Lycan as a rule, tonight, she was more in the mood for the subdued flavor of human blood. To her delight, John was diabetic. He was practically a living, breathing stalk of cane sugar.

It was relief not to experience the bitter aftertaste caused by the medications mortals used to control the affliction. Either John had skipped taking his meds or he wasn't aware of his condition. Originally, the plan was to turn him, but once she tasted the candy flowing through his veins, she simply couldn't bring herself to stop.

Males. She hated to admit it, but hunting them was becoming a bore. They were all the same, whether human, vampire, Lycan or other. All tended to do their thinking with their dicks. Show a little leg, flash a little cleavage and badda boom, badda bing, dinner was served. Tonight was just another case in point. She'd slipped on her most risqué outfit and spiked heels, walked into that meat market of a nightclub, crossed her legs, and like clockwork, along came din din wagging his tail behind him.

It was bad taste to grumble about an easy meal but she was a huntress. She lived for the thrill of the chase as well as the spoils. You could lead a male to the bowels of Hell with the promise of sex. Where was the challenge in that? Her body surged from the new life flowing into her as John's heartbeat slowed to a crawl then went silent. Such a shame to lose out on making a new child, but at least he didn't go to waste. She chuckled to herself, wondering if he had a sibling and if said sibling had blood as sweet.

As John went limp in her arms, she bent down to scoop him up when she was startled by the clapping of a pair hands coming from the rear of the alley.

"Bravo querida. Bet he was good to the last drop." From his scent, Anna easily determined that the new arrival was vampire. Tall, deliciously wide at the shoulders, sporting dark shades, he was dressed in an Oakland Raiders jersey, black jeans, a chain necklace, and Timberland boots. He was one hundred percent hard ass, dripping testosterone, totally male, and she absolutely wanted every drop of him.

Pity she'd just eaten. This brown skinned immortal, at least half Latino, was solid as a brick wall, with a buzz cut that gave his appearance a hard edge. Generally, she preferred longer locks on her men, but the close cropped look suited him. It was far from the only thing she found to her liking.

As the vampire removed his shades, she saw the most gorgeous hazel eyes she'd ever seen on a male. He moved toward her, his gaze unwavering, gait wasting little movement. Her nipples puckered, and moisture pooled between her legs. Without a doubt, this vampire was the sexiest neck pricker she ever laid her eyes on. But that baby face wasn't fooling her. She'd seen his kind before. He was a rogue, a snake, and most likely a cheat, but she wanted this sexy beast inside her. And nothing was going to stop her from making it happen.

The gleam in his eyes and the growing bulge in his jeans, told her all she needed to know. He wanted her as much as she wanted him. He came to a stop a few feet away. Well out of arm's reach, but close enough to count the hairs of his debonair mustache, he feasted on her sleek figure. Desire singed the air between them.

Anna marveled. He wasn't the least bit afraid of her. No, he was anything but. *How interesting. How very refreshing.* Subtly, she breathed in the musky cologne of his skin and visualized all the scandalous things she ached to do to him. Noting the flare of his nostrils, the corners of her mouth curled upward. He could smell her arousal just as she could smell his.

"He was delicious, actually." Anna licked her lips as she surveyed the immortal with approval.

The rogue grinned, the tips of his fangs peeking from under his lips. "Glad you enjoyed. Now that you got your grub on, we need to talk."

Anna lowered John to the ground as she turned. "Really, talk about what exactly?" She braced herself. There was the rustle of feet on the rooftops above her and at the mouth of the alley behind her. They were all wrapped in shadows but she could feel them.

"Seems we have a mutual problem that I think we could help each other with."

She arched an eyebrow. "And who is *we*, sexy?"

"You, me, and my employer."

Anna stepped over John's lifeless body, sweeping a stray lock of hair from her eye. "Well, lover, I'm afraid I do not chit chat with errand boys. When your *employer* wants to converse with me, he'll have to do so in person. So, nice chatting with you, tootles. "She froze at the sound of the multitude of rifle bolts being pulled back.

"Uh, uh, querida, I didn't dismiss you. I think you need to listen."

Carefully, she did a mind sweep of the alley. They were all locked, loaded, and aiming their assault rifles in her direction. Her eyes blazed, fangs lengthening as her anger flared.

"I could kill you before your friends could begin to squeeze off a shot." The vampire shrugged casually. She sensed his emotions. He wasn't afraid to die. Good, they were all just a cat's whiskers from doing just that.

"Most likely I wouldn't survive the bum rush, but sweetness, not even *you* could tiptoe through all the silver that'd get sprayed your way should you decide to get froggish. So, shall we die together or would you care to hear me out?"

She assessed the situation. It wouldn't harm her to listen to what he had to say. If it turned out that his proposition was a waste of her time, then she would kill him and his little friends too. Retracting her fangs, she took in a calming deep breath then exhaled.

"Proceed."

"Thank you. I'm Padre. We, of course, know who you are already. As I was sayin', we have a mutual problem. I'm speakin' of those dried up, fangless, self-important mutha fuckas on the Council. They be in our biz and I know they be in yours. So, my employer was wonderin' if you'd be down for a merger."

Folding her arms across her chest, she eyed Padre suspiciously. She hadn't the slightest interested in joining forces with this vampire hoodlum and his master. On the other hand, it never hurt to have allies. "You want to team up, so to speak. Tell me, Padre, what exactly is your *biz*?"

Padre cleared his throat and smiled. "You can call us...entrepreneurs. There is a huge market out there and we are prepared to meet the demand for our product but those dry bones keep stickin' they limp fangs in the way."

Anna did a quick scan of Padre's mind. "You peddle narcotic laced blood?" She did the math. "Ahhh, you're drug dealers."

Padre grinned sheepishly and shrugged. "Potato, spud, sweetness. Point is, like you, we having expansion issues cause of them dried up fossils."

Mentally reaching out to the armed vampires, she sensed heightened anxiety. Even heavily armed, with their advantage in numbers, many weren't convinced they could stop her if it came down to a confrontation. They weren't all foolish enough to believe they could take her. "Well, Padre, we apparently both have grievances with the High Council, but aside from the great pleasure of seeing them all staked, what would be my motivation to partake in this business endeavor? Put simply, what's in it for me?"

Padre counted off on his fingers. "One, you get the old dirty bastards out your long and curlies. Two, you get to remake the vamp world in your *very* hot image."

*Interesting, but it seemed a bit too perfect. What was that saying when something seemed too good to be true?* "Assuming I agree to this little business arrangement, what's to prevent your employer from pulling the big double cross after the Council's been dispatched?"

"We in this strictly for the bank, querida, long as you keep your hands off our proceeds, we stay out your castle."

While she digested that, she caught Padre's eyes drifting down toward her legs. Subtly, she shifted her stance, exposing more thigh, giving him a better view. "You sound confident, Padre, but are you certain you're prepared to take a bite out of this very large cake?"

Padre flashed a toothy grin. "Oh yeah, we got the manpower and the hardware if you got the stones."

She had to admit being impressed with Padre's confidence. Moreover, she was impressed with him. He was wild, brash, and sexy as hell. He reminded her of Adalius, and how she still longed to have him at her side. "I'm intrigued. How long do I get to decide?"

"Take your time, querida, but don't take too long. Those mutha fuckas are dust whether you with us or not. We just thought maybe you'd want some of this action."

Anna studied Padre carefully. Did he truly believe it would be so simple? The High Council had faced many adversaries in its thousands of years of existence and crushed them all. Many lay dead, buried and forgotten. They were the lucky ones. The rest were held prisoner, in the catacombs below the Enforcer sanctuary. There, daily torture and cries of torment were the norm. The Council's wrath against their enemies was notoriously uncompromising. They never forgot, nor did they ever forgive.

"You do realize, of course, that by attacking the Council you would be facing Dracula as well?"

Padre's expression darkened, dangerous anger flaring in his eyes. "Fuck Drac too, we takin' every single one of them punk bitches down, you know what I'm sayin'?"

Anna nodded. "How am I to contact you with my decision?"

"Worry not, sweetness, I'll find you."

She raised an eyebrow. "Very well, I shall consider your proposal."

Padre beamed like a man who had closed a billion dollar deal. Muy bien, I'll get back to you in a few days; till then, sexy woman." Padre looked to his cohorts. "Vamonos!"

As they one by one retreated into the night, Anna quickly reached out with her senses to Padre. For an instant, all his thoughts and schemes were spread out before her like an open book. His mental shields, with unexpected strength, slammed shut. She flinched.

"Naughty, naughty, you didn't say Padre, may I. "The vampire winked and blew her a kiss as he slid on his shades, faded away and was gone.

She'd underestimated him. She wouldn't make that mistake again. Now alone in the alley, she fumed. They actually had the gall to threaten her. She could have easily destroyed them all. The only reason she didn't was because Padre was right, the Council had to be destroyed if her plans for the future were to be realized.

It was an intriguing proposition. If Padre and his master were as prepared as they believed, an alliance between them could lead to the elimination of the High Council, the Enforcers, and Dracula. She and her children would be left to step in and establish the new order.

Despite Padre's assurances, Anna knew the time would come when she'd have to deal with his employer. If she agreed to join them, she'd begin preparing for that day. It would start by gaining the trust and friendship of Padre. Through him, she'd crush his master and install Padre in his place, in exchange for his allegiance, of course.

In time, she was certain she could get him to do it. After all, power was an aphrodisiac and Padre looked like a vampire whose dick was always hard.

# CHAPTER NINE

Victor Sanchez was up, dressed, and ready to hit the streets for his morning run. He only started his routine three weeks ago but he already started to see results. He'd lost ten pounds and had more energy than he had in years.

All in all, he felt like a million bucks. Everything was coming up roses in his life, for a change. His boss had finally taken notice of his hard work and rewarded him with a promotion to head of the I.T. department. He was six months away from marrying his childhood sweetheart and his offer was accepted the day before on his first home.

Humming happily, he finished lacing up his sneakers. Sneaks pumped and tied, he grabbed the cordless phone by the bed, and called his fiancée. He hated waking her but she insisted that he called her before he went out to run. It was four thirty in the morning, the same time he ran every day. It really made him feel bad, interrupting her sleep, especially since she didn't have to get up herself until 6:00 a.m. but it was what she wanted, so he called.

As he sat on his bed, listening, the phone rang then at last she picked up. "Hey, baby, I'm up, dressed and about to head out....Listen at you, why don't I just call after I come back from running...Ok, mami, but..."Victor smiled. She wasn't going to budge. He was wasting his time and hers. "Ok, ok, I'll call you as soon as I get back...Baby, I'll be fine, I promise...I'll be careful...Ok, I love you too, bye."

He hung up the phone. Rising from the bed, he went to his dresser and grabbed the house key he kept on a chain, along with a few dollars, his cell phone, driver's license, and a small handgun. Stepping outside, he closed and locked the door behind him, then started his stretches in preparation for his run. When his warm up was complete, he speed walked from his stoop to the sidewalk, turned right, and began to jog.

It was sticky and humid. Just a preview of what the day had in store for the city. The meteorologist said there was a twenty-five percent chance of thunderstorms rolling through the area later that evening. *Yeah, right, that was what they reported two days ago and not so much as a drop fell from the sky.* He wasn't gonna take an umbrella. *Why bother?* It hadn't rained in so long that most of the lawns were turning brown. The heat wave had even less pity on grass than it did on people and animals. He laughed bitterly to himself. Seemed like the only one the weather hadn't slowed down was the creep committing all the murders in the McClain Park area.

That'd hit a little too close to home. He lived a short distance from the park. Now he found himself looking more over his shoulders and being more aware of the surroundings since the homicides started. He knew his love was on edge about him being so close to the scene of the crimes. Frankly, so was he. He couldn't wait to start packing so they could move into the house and away from all this.

Traffic was very light as Victor finished the first mile of his run. Funny, he never noticed how lovely the neighborhood was until he started jogging. He was sure gonna miss it here. As he passed the home of Mrs. Hudson, he shook his head. She had the most handsome yard in the neighborhood, at least she used to before the drought killed her colorful floral arrangements. Such a pity, she always kept that yard immaculate. She set the example for everyone to follow in maintaining a fabulous lawn and flower beds.

The last house on the block belonged to Mr. and Mrs. Porter. As he went by, the same blue Chevy was parked in the driveway as always. Who it belonged to, he had no idea. Mr. Porter worked nights and drove a black Ford. Victor sure hoped he'd be around to see the day when Mr. Porter came home a little early and discovered for himself who the Chevy belonged to and who his wife was entertaining.

There were a few less pedestrians and only a couple of other joggers out and about this morning. He'd given each a hello nod as he approached the next leg of his route on Payne Avenue. Working his eyes back and forth, he monitored his surroundings. He was close enough to the McClain Park that he began to get anxious. The revolver in his pocket provided some sense of comfort. He gave it a caress. Glad he had it with him. Hopefully, it'd never get used, but better to have something and not need it than to need something and not have it.

Victor's lungs were settling into a smooth rhythm. Up ahead, there was the silhouette of a shapely female, walking in his direction. Her hair seemed to flow about her like it had a mind of its own. *Weird*. There wasn't any breeze. As he drew closer, her assets became clearer. *Ay Caramba*! The blonde was the most beautiful woman he had ever seen. As he passed, they made eye contact. Nodding in greeting, he continued jogging. She returned the courtesy with a smile that made his heart skip a beat.

He continued down Payne Avenue toward the next turn which would lead him to the last leg of the run. Victor jogged, sweating like a hog, he had to hold his head down to keep the moisture from his eyes. Shaking his head, he wiped the perspiration from his face. He blinked. There was another woman coming toward him. Arms and legs pumping, he opened up his stride, building toward the big push to the finish. He nodded to the woman as he blew past her. She smiled.

*Huh?*

It couldn't be. That smile. *There's no way it could...could it?* He glanced over his shoulder. Gone. *Whoa, what the...* He stopped and turned, nothing, not another soul. "I would've...was I...What just..." Cocking his head like a confused puppy, he wiped his brow. He shook his head. Stress. Maybe Carmela was right, he needed to stop putting off that doctor visit. He'd make the appointment today.

The horizon took on a golden, wine hue. The time! *Santa Maria, he couldn't be late for his first day as supervi-* His stomach dropped into his feet as his body shot straight up. Arms like steel bands wrapped around him. Wind whistled by his ears, the ground shrank away. His heart hammered wildly, adrenaline pouring into his system. *Madre de Dios!* He struggled to yell for help but it was like something had stolen his voice.

Soft lips were pressed to his neck. With a sharp pinch, two needles pierced his skin. It should have hurt but instead, his mind flooded with pleasure. Legs wrapped around his waist, then the sensation of floating back to earth. He was helpless as they settled in the field of grass, those sweet, wonderful lips pressed to his throat.

Her body was cool, soft, and sensual like her moans. The pleasure intensified with each of her swallows. He was blacking out. He didn't care. She was killing him but he just didn't care. All that mattered were the two of them together. *Yes, empty his body, just please don't stop.*

The world faded away. The woman continued suckling at his neck. It was harder to breathe. His mind clouded over. His last thoughts were of his so very beautiful fiancée. Carmela was his best friend. It saddened Victor to know how much she'd miss him. His death would devastate her. The thought of her pain and loneliness ripped at his very soul. It was an agony he would take with him to the grave.

# CHAPTER TEN

It was only ten o'clock in the blessed morning and it was already eighty-five degrees. Arnie took stock of the crime scene, scowling as insects buzzed about his ears. All around the taped off area, crime scene investigators droned about collecting evidence. Birds sang from the branches of a nearby tree as before him, covered by a sheet; lay victim number five of the dead bodies that began turning up in the McClain Park area.

His expression soured as he reached into the inner pocket of his blazer, and pulled out a writing pad and pen. The BIC flew across the paper as he jotted down every detail he noted. The more he catalogued, the more his skin crawled.

The victim's name, according to the identification found on the body, was Victor Sanchez. He was found lying here by a little old lady who happened by while walking her pooch. The official cause of death ruling he'd leave to the medical examiner, but his best guess was the poor bastard bled out.

Strange that no significant amount of blood was found anywhere near the body or the crime scene; then there were the two peculiar puncture wounds on the victim's neck, just like the other four. Dammit to hell, there's no doubt about it, he'd seen this before.

Twelve years ago, Arnie transferred from vice to homicide just as bodies began showing up in the McClain Park area in much the same condition. The investigation went on for weeks. No leads, no suspects. Then, just as suddenly as it started, the murders ceased. Then of course, as if a series of vampire-like murders weren't spooky enough, all the victims' bodies were found in the morgue, not long after, with their chests cut open. Their hearts had been removed. Review of security tapes showed nothing and nobody saw a thing. The entire department worked that case for months, but every tip led to a dead end, so into the unsolved case files it went.

Arnie scowled. After all these years, could the rat bastard be back? The feeling in his gut said yes. This time, he'd get the perpetrator. Arnie would be damned before he'd let that maniac get away again. Running a hand through his thinning hair, he knelt down, lifted the sheet, and carefully re-examined the body. He wished the poor kid could tell him something, anything that would lead them to the sick fuck who murdered him.

"Arnie?"

He looked up as Richardson made his way toward the scene. "Meet victim number five." Arnie gestured toward the body as he rose to his feet.

"Same story as the others?" Richardson scowled, gazing at the body.

"Fraid so. Vic's name is Victor Sanchez. We found his ID on him, a few bucks, small revolver and his cell phone. We were all set to knock on doors to see if we could get someone to make a positive identification when his fiancée happened by unexpectedly." Arnie pointed toward a nearby ambulance where a woman lay on a gurney being attended to. She was being given oxygen as paramedics monitored her blood pressure while a female detective stood at the ready to conduct her interview.

"That's fucked up," Richardson said.

"Very. There wasn't sign of a struggle. He apparently wasn't robbed. The gun hadn't been fired. Like the others, there are two puncture wounds on his neck and the cause of death, just like the others, appears to be blood loss."

Richardson took stock of the crime scene as he removed his shades. "I don't suppose anyone's come forward to say they saw the whole thing and can ID the attacker?"

"Way too easy, and we can't have *that*, can we?"

Richardson ran his hand across his sweat covered brow, his eyes drifting to where Victor's body lay. "I wouldn't mind. It would sure cut down my spending on antacids."

"Ain't that the truth." Arnie continued to stare at the body. Richardson's gaze fixated on him. The kid knew him well.

"Alright, I know that tone and I know that look. What is it?"

Arnie squinted. The sun was beaming. "I was hoping I was wrong, but this isn't the first time I've seen this."

"You're talking about the murders that happened twelve years ago. I remember it. I was a senior in high school. But that was different. There wasn't any mention of the bodies being drained of blood in any of the news reports that I can recall."

Arnie nodded thoughtfully. "The commish and the mayor, at the time, decided not to feed that little tidbit to the media. Nobody wanted to give copycats ideas about trying their hand at blood suckin.'"

Richardson's brow dipped. "You don't think this is a copycat, do you?"

He paused. "No, kid, I don't."

"Arnie, you think it's him, the same guy?"

"My gut tells me, yes. It's the same exact M.O." Arnie sighed and shook his head. "We got to get him this time, Theo. We can't let this bastard slip through our fingers again."

"If it is the same guy, why would he come back and why now?"

Damn good questions. "If I knew that, it might go a long way to help us catch the sonuvabitch. They stepped back to allow the coroner's office to take the body away for autopsy. While Victor was being placed in a bag, they made their way toward the ambulance where the victim's stricken fiancée was receiving treatment.

Paramedics had begun loading her into the ambulance. The female detective who'd been interviewing her met them halfway. Damn shame she'd seen her fiancé like that. She was among the crowd that gathered when they saw the police taping off the area. Her scream, would haunt him until Victor's killer was brought to justice.

"She gonna be ok, Anita?" Arnie nodded toward the ambulance as it started to pull away.

Anita brushed her hair away from her face and hooked it behind her ear. "Her blood pressure is way too high. They're taking her to Metro General." She looked over the notes she made on a small writing pad. "The last time she spoke to the VIC was about 4:30 a.m. this morning, just before he went out for his morning run. He worked at Bennington Tech where he had just gotten a promotion and was preparing to start his new job today. As far as she knows, he had no enemies."

Arnie ran his hand through his hair once more. "Ok, we got five VICs, an I.T. guy, a bank teller, an admin assistant, a seamstress, and a security guard. All of them of different ethnicities and ages."

Richardson chimed in, "The only thing they seem to have in common, aside from being dead, is that they were all joggers who were out alone in this area."

"So our perp is maybe just an opportunist, so what do we do, do we put a curfew on the park area?" Anita asked.

Arnie sighed. "We could do that but the bastard might take his act on the road."

Richardson shook his head. "I think its academic, Arnie. People are already starting to give this area a wide berth. Soon as the press puts out word of another body found, folks are gonna start avoiding this area like the plague."

"Then we'll just have to supply our own runners. Anita, you're in great shape and I bet you'd look irresistible in those cute little running shorts.

Anita rolled her eyes.

News trucks arrived. Several people carrying cameras and microphones approached the crime scene. Richardson watched the ambulance drive away as the media members swarmed in their direction.

Anita clicked her tongue. "Here they come."

"At least that poor woman won't have to deal with this," Arnie sighed irritably.

Richardson slipped his shades back on. "Thank Heaven for small favors; she's already had a lousy enough day."

Arnie grunted in agreement. "If we don't run this lunatic down, she won't be the last having a day like this."

# CHAPTER ELEVEN

The blinding flash was quickly followed by a thunder clap that made the Earth tremble. Torrential rain danced wildly on the streets and sidewalks as residents, caught in the down pour, scrambled for cover. On the corner of Clancy Avenue and Watermill Road at Delany's Sports Bar and Grill, Trey strode in from the rain. Soaking wet, he removed his shades and shook the water from its lenses as another lightning flash lit up the district. As the thunder rolled off in the distance, he made his way toward the bar, water dripping from his head and the black bandanna. Stopping at one of the center stools, he unzipped his leather jacket and took a seat as the bartender moved toward him.

"Hi, welcome to Delany's. What can I get for you?"

"Beer, Genuine Draft, and a menu."

"Coming right up," The barkeep, whose name tag identified him as Scott, produced a beer glass from beneath the counter, filled it from the tap, and placed it in front of Trey on a coaster along with a napkin and a menu. "Take your time and let me know when you're ready to order." He smiled then moved off to wait on another customer.

Trey folded his glasses, placed them on the bar top, took a drink of his beer and looked over his surroundings. This place was nice. Sports memorabilia peppered the walls along with wall mounted, fifty inch, high definition boob tubes. Overhead cone shaped light fixtures provided just the right ambiance for a sports bar and were mated perfectly with the hickory wood floors and walls.

"Buy a lady a drink?" came from a woman seated two stools down, who flashed a sly smile.

"Sure, you know one?"

The strawberry blonde's expression darkened as she stood with a huff and started away. "Asshole."

"Moocher."

She slung her purse over her shoulder as she stalked off. "Fuck you."

"As if…"Trey watched her storm out the door, to the street and out of sight. A user if he ever saw one. He chuckled to himself. "In town less than an hour and already got a chick pissed at me, still got it."

His stomach rumbled as he opened the menu and began pouring over the selections. After coming to a dinner decision, he looked up to attract Scott's attention but, as if reading his mind, Scott was already on the move in his direction.

"Ready to order?"

Trey pointed to the bottom corner of his menu as the barkeep produced a pen and a small writing pad from the Delany's apron he wore. "It says here that if I can finish a dozen of the Four Alarm wings, the second dozen is free?"

"That's right, sir."

"Then I'll have an order of those and a side of cheesy fries."

The bartender nodded as he wrote down Trey's order. "Coming right up but I have to tell you, I been working here five years and I've seen plenty of tough guys come in and try, but nobody has *ever* finished a dozen of those things."

"Nobody, huh?"

"*No Ba Dee.*"

"Nobody until now, Scotty, let's do this."

"Alright! A man with guts, I'll put your order in, be right back."

While Scott moved off to the kitchen, he conducted a subtle visual sweep of the bar. Being a vampire hunter, all he needed was a glimpse to ferret out any blood sucker that might be hiding among the crowd. A quick scan confirmed no fangs present so he turned his attention to the three big screen televisions mounted high on the wall behind the bar. Stuart Scott was on the air and handling his business on the center screen so Trey made himself comfortable and enjoyed his beer while he waited for dinner to be served.

Sportscenter was going to the third commercial break as his meal arrived. The cheesy fries were piping hot and the wings still sizzling as the two plates of food were placed in front of him. The aroma of the hot peppers filled his nostrils, making his mouth water in anticipation.

"There you are, sir, can I get you anything else?" the bartender asked with a smile.

"Just some more napkins."

Scott reached underneath the counter, produced more napkins, and placed them next to the plate of wings.

"Thanks, Scotty."

"Sure, enjoy your meal and good luck. "He grinned then moved off to wait on another customer.

Trey plucked a few cheese covered fries off his plate, popped them into his mouth, then picked up the first of his wings and took a bite. He was pleasantly surprised. It had heat and plenty of it. Still, he'd expected….more. Just another pub that thinks their wings are…*Ohh shit!* His mouth and tongue burst into flames. Trey's eyes watered. Sweat poured from his scalp as if trying to escape the spreading inferno.

He coughed repeatedly. His nose running like a river, he took another swallow of beer trying to cool the burning napalm raging out of control on his palate. But the spicy heat only continued to build. Searing pain raged from the cut on his lip where the sauce had seeped in. It was awesome! In his youth, Trey often drank Habanera sauce straight from the bottle. Spicy, hot flavor was always his passion; one of them anyway. The other was Jennifer. It'd been five years since she and their daughter had been murdered by that blood thirsty psychopath, Anna.

Jennifer shared his passion for spicy food. She made Buffalo wings as fiery as their love making. When she died, her wing recipe died with her. He'd traveled from sea to shining sea but never found wings that could compare to hers, until now. These wings were crispy, boldly seasoned and bathed in a sauce that was '*in your face with a fuck you and yo mama too*' attitude. The spicy flavor slapped him in the taste buds and dared him to do something about it. He was in love.

He breathed in deeply through his mouth, slowly exhaling through his nose. Trey could almost feel the nose hairs being singed by the pepper that laced his breath as his system began to recover from the habanero induced shock wave.

Picking a napkin from the stack left by the bartender, he carefully wiped his mouth and cleared his throat, eyeing the remaining wings. The culinary courtship was over. It was time to get on with the serious eating.

"Everything ok, anything else I can get for you?" Scott had returned from cashing out another customer.

"Nah, everything is great."

"Alright, you kinda had me worried when I saw you coughing."

Trey licked the spicy sauce off his fingers. "No big deal, just the sauce introducing itself."

"Ok, if you need anything else just let me know." Scott moved off to wait on another patron who took a seat at the bar. As Scotty took care of business, Trey turned his attention to a baseball game, broadcasted on one of the other televisions, above the bar. Spearing another wing off his plate, he took a bite.

Damn. Boston was in the midst of a rally. Two men were on, two outs, tying run at the plate with a full count on the hitter. Trey frowned as he watched the pitcher go into his windup.

"Come on, baby, blow it by him. I got a hundred riding on this. "The batter sent a weak grounder right at the first baseman, who stepped on the base, ending the inning and the game. Cha ching!

It was amazing how much better his dinner tasted now that he was several hundred bucks richer. He'd have to catch up with that no good bookie after he took care of things in New Carrollton. After he finished the last of the wings and fries, he signaled Scott who immediately responded.

"You did it man, I'm impressed."

"There was never a doubt. I'll have my second order to go."

Scott smiled. "Done deal, I'll take care of that for you." He went off to place the order as Trey downed the last of his beer. Feeling content, he plucked another napkin from the stack and wiped his mouth and hands, basking in the glow of the best meal he'd had in quite some time.

"Is this seat taken?"

Trey's skin tingled from the silky feminine voice. "It will be when you sit down. "He prepared himself. If this was another moocher, he was gonna... *Oh my damn*. The tall brunette with legs that ran all the way up to her throat, smiled as she laid her purse on the bar and offered her hand.

"Hi, I'm Lisa."

"Trey Thomas.'" Trey accepted her hand.

"Nice to meet you, Trey."

"Likewise." A warm smile spread across his face. It'd been a long time since he'd been this happy to meet anyone. Lisa took her seat. Her smile was angelic with just a hint of mischief, twinkling in her eyes. "Never saw you in here before, this your first time here?"

"Actually, yes, I just got in town about an hour ago."

"Oh, visiting family or friends?"

"I'm here on business, I guess you could say." As he and Lisa chatted, Scott returned from the kitchen.

"Your order will be up in a few minutes, sir."

"Thanks, Scotty'"

Scott's eyes lit up as he acknowledged the new arrival. "Hey Lisa, you having the usual?"

Lisa checked her watch and nodded "Yes, please. Don't have time for much else."

"Coming right up. "As Scott went to the rear of the bar to retrieve a wine glass, Trey picked up the conversation with Lisa.

"So what do you do for a living here, Lisa?'

Lisa looked up at Scott's approach as he placed her drink on a coaster. "I run a hair salon and spa. Nothing too exotic, I'm afraid." As Lisa took a sip of her wine, the music coming from the center television interrupted their conversation to announce that it was six o'clock, time for the evening news. They turned their attention to the television as the announcer finished with 'This is Action Four News at six. 'The news program graphics faded and the camera panned in on an attractive news anchor.

*"Good evening New Carrollton. This is live at six Action Four News. Our top story, yet another body was found near the McClain Park area bringing the total to five in the past week. The victim, identified as twenty-five year old Victor Sanchez, was found this morning in a field on Payne Avenue. Police have decline to comment on speculation that the*

*recent homicides may be the work of the same serial killer who committed a similar rash of murders twelve years ago in the McClain Park area. Residents are urged to report any suspicious individuals to police immediately."*

Lisa shivered. "My sister and I were in middle school back then. My mother wouldn't let us out of her sight. Every day it was like a wagon train when classes let out. People left work in droves to pick up their kids, most businesses closed early, and it seemed like the whole city was under curfew. Then, just as suddenly as it started, the murders stopped. Weeks went by, and no bodies turned up, so eventually, everything kinda went back to normal."

Trey studied Lisa carefully. From the look on her face, other unwanted memories were beginning to surface. He hated to do it, but he had to ask. You just never knew what information might prove useful. *Couldn't push too hard though, if pressed too hard, she might clam up on him. He had to be smooth. Start with a simple question like...*

"So the killer was never caught?"

"No, but can I tell you something strange?"

Trey brightened. She was opening up on her own. "Sure."

"You promise not to laugh or think I'm crazy?"

He gave her his most solemn look. "Of course, I promise."

Lisa took a breath, her expression tight. "A friend of the family worked at the coroner's office back then. One day, I overheard her talking to mom. She said she saw the report on the coroner's desk. All the bodies stored in the morgue, from the McClain Park murders, were found with their chests cut open. Someone removed their hearts."

Definitely pertinent info, it sounded like a slayer dealt with the bodies in the morgue. If he could find out who, maybe his counterpart could fill in a few more details. Maybe this will bring him a little closer to finding Anna.

Lisa took a glance out the bar front window. "Look, it's stopped raining. I really hate to do this, Trey, but I gotta go."

"Alright, well it was nice meeting you, Lisa."

"You too, Trey, tell you what..."Lisa retrieved a pen from her purse then picked up a napkin from the bar, wrote out her name and number, then passed it to Trey. "If you have any free time while you're in town, give me a call."

Trey smiled, accepting the napkin. "Do you often hand out your phone number to men you meet in bars, especially with a serial killer on the loose?"

"I'm not into the habit, no." Lisa flashed her own pearly whites. "But you're ok, I can smell an asshole a mile away."

"Good thing I showered, huh?"

Her laugh was light and melodious. "Very good thing. Take care, Trey, call me." She rose from her seat with a wink, picked up her purse and made her way out of the bar. Trey turned to admire the sensual sway of her hips. As Lisa walked out, Scott, as if on cue, arrived with his wings, boxed and ready to go.

"You, my friend, are my idol. First, you polish off a dozen of the Four Alarm Wings, then you follow that up with getting Lisa's phone number."

"Come on, Scotty."

"I'm serious. There are guys in here who have tried for years to do what you just did in five minutes. She's very choosy about who she talks to, let alone give up her phone number. It must not suck being you."

"Trust me, Scotty, sometimes it really sucks being me." Trey thought of his life without his wife and child.

As if sensing his mood change, Scott retrieved another beer glass, filled it with Genuine Draft and placed it before him. With most of the other customers already gone; Scott stopped and chatted as Trey drank his beer. Full belly and feeling mellow, Trey raised his arms above his head and stretched. "That second beer hit the spot, Scotty."

Scott wiped down the bar top. "It was on the house. Anybody who could polish off those hot ass wings deserves a free beer."

"You think these wings are hot, my wife used to make wings that it'd grow hair on your toe nails."

"Holy shit, how did you eat it?"

Trey patted his flat belly. "Cast iron stomach, flame retardant tongue."

"You're a better man than me. So, ready for some dessert?"

"Nah, I'm done. I'll take the check now."

71

"Be right back."

Scott went to the register, rang up the order, then made his way over, handing him the check. He withdrew cash from his wallet, placed the money it into Scott's hands, and then returned it to his back pocket. "Keep the rest, Scotty. It's the best food and service I've had in a long time. The wings reminded me of home."

"Thanks a lot. Come again and say hello to the wife for me."

"No can do."

"Divorced?"

"She's dead. "Trey forced the welling emotions back into their cage.

"Oh… I'm sorry."

"You didn't know."

"How long has it be—"

"Five years." Trey picked up his boxed wings. "Keep the faith, Scotty and watch ya back out here."

Making his way out to the street to his Harley, he cranked it up and pulled out into traffic. Have to grab a room and check in with Maya. It'd be dark soon. Tired as he was, sleep wasn't in his immediate future.

# CHAPTER TWELVE

Jason Pearce ran like hell. He dashed through, around or leaped over puddles like his butt depended on it, and it did. Dad was gonna kill him. Be home before six his father said. It was now an hour past that. It wasn't his fault. He'd been playing basketball and didn't notice the storm clouds until it was too late. He had to ride it out underneath the school's overhang. The instant the rain stopped, he lit out for home.

The street corner was just ahead. The crosswalk light was changing but he wasn't slowing down. No way. If he didn't get home fast, Dad would ground him for life. It was still kinda cloudy. He was a little surprised to see so many people out and about so soon after the storm. But it wouldn't slow him down. He just imagined he was a running back breaking into the clear as he slalomed in and out, cutting right then left, spinning, stumbling as he charged toward the goal line.

The storefronts were a blur as he flashed and dashed across intersection after intersection. He knew them all by heart. There was Markie's DVD Exchange followed by Thompson's Flowers. That's where Dad said he bought roses for Mom for the very first time. How many times did Dad tell him the story?

He missed Mom. Tears welled in his eyes. She disappeared about a week ago, when she'd left for that girl's night out. Nobody's seen or heard from her since. Dad calls the police stations and hospitals everyday hoping for word but every day it's the same disappointment. She was just gone.

Antonio's Sub shop was next. His mouth watered as he smelled their fries. Nobody could beat their fries. At last, he came up on Mr. Wilcox' place, it was the general store where you could get all kinds of stuff, like juice, cereal, beer, and milk.

*Milk!*

He was supposed to pick up a gallon of milk on the way home. Jason slammed on the brakes. The sudden momentum shift nearly made him tumble to the ground. His Nikes squealed as he slid to a stop and turned, into the store.

Mr. Wilcox was seated behind the big glass candy counter as he sprinted to the coolers in the back. As Jason opened the sliding door, he heard Mr. Wilcox talking on the phone.

"I told ya, Toronto would blow that lead...Yeah, Cleveland won. That's another fifty bucks ya owe me, ya dead beat...Poker? Yeah, I play...Saturday night?......Got nuthin' planned....sure, I'll get Belker and Kite, I'm sure they'd be happy to take ya money, too...you just show up with ya money....Ohh I'm *so* scared, I just wet my pants....Whatever, see ya Saturday, my place, pigeon."

Wilcox hung up the phone and got to his feet as Jason approached the counter. "Jason, how are ya, son?" Wilcox smiled cheerfully. His brows furrowed as he spotted the backpack. "You haven't been home yet? Ya father is gonna murder ya, boy. Why are ya still out and about?"

Jason shrugged his shoulders. "I was playing basketball when the storm came. I stood under the overhang at school waitin' for the rain to stop"

Wilcox nodded as Jason paid him then slid the milk off the counter. "Well, ya better get on home fast."

"I will. I just had to get this milk."

Wilcox quickly rang up the purchase, counted out the youngster's change and promptly handed it to Jason. "Has there been any word at all... about ya mom?"

Jason's shoulders sagged. "No sir, Dad's been callin' the police and all the hospitals every day but no news at all."

"It's gonna be ok, son, right now though ya need to hurry home. Ya father must be worried sick."

"Yes, sir."

"Good boy, now on ya way, and have ya father call me the second ya get there."

Jason nodded and was out the door, off and running. At last, he ran past the familiar mailbox on the corner, took a right and dashed down Latimore Avenue. At the sixth brownstone, the one that his family called home, he dashed up the five sandstone steps, up another four flights of stairs, turned right and speed walked to the second to the last door on the right. Home.

How safe he was, he'd find out after he got inside. Dad must be pissed. Jason knocked and waited, then heard his dad's footsteps coming fast. The door flew open and he found himself face to abdomen.

"Where the hell have you been? You was supposed to be home over an hour ago."

"I know, I'm sorry, Dad. I woulda been home on time but the storm came." Jason walked in, passed the milk to his father as the closed the door behind him. "I was under the overhang at school near the basketball courts."

"If you had started home like you were supposed to, you woulda beat the storm home."

He removed his backpack and set it in a nearby chair. "I know, I know, but we was in the middle of a game. I didn't want to just leave. You always told me never to quit."

He directly found himself nose to Dad's index finger. "Don't get cute, you know what I meant."

"Sorry, Dad. Have you heard any news…about Mom?"

Logan's demeanor softened. "No, but I'll call right now. Hit the showers, sport, dinner's ready."

"Ok, Dad. Oh, Mr. Wilcox wanted you to call him as soon as I got here."

"Alright, I'll call him first then I'll call Detective Richardson again. Now go on and get cleaned up."

"Ok, Dad." Jason turned to leave then paused. "Dad?"

Logan went to his son, hugging him tight. "I know buddy, I miss her too."

When they broke their embrace, he went toward the bathroom as Dad put away the milk.

*****

Taking a seat on the couch, Logan picked up the phone, and started dialing. After informing Wilcox that Jason was home safe, he called the police department. The police operator picked up after several rings then Logan went into his routine. "Detective Richardson, please...yes, I'll hold."

He listened to the Eagles sing Hotel California as the sound of Jason starting the shower reached his ears. It was another couple of minutes before he heard the familiar click.

"Detective Richardson?...Yeah, it's Pearce...We're holding up about as well as can be expected. Have you turned up anything...I see...Yeah, I've called her mother, sisters and all her aunts and uncles. Nobody has seen or heard from her. We're all scared spit less, this simply isn't like her...I know you're doing your best, detective, but there's a lunatic out there, my wife is missing and now I see on the news that you guys found another body. I just want her home safe...Thank you, detective, I really appreciate it...I will, thanks."

Logan hung up the phone, hung his head and leaned back on the couch. Where could she be? Was she hurt or dead? Tears stung his eyes as he ran his hand through his hair. His mind tortured him with horrible images of Marie suffering at the hands of some manic. He sucked in a deep breath, blowing out a long exhale. *Gotta keep it together for Jason.*

Reaching for the television remote, he wiped his eyes clear just as the shower shut off in the bathroom. Jason would be out and ready to eat in a moment. Logan rose from the couch, and started for the kitchen when a knock came at the door. He wasn't expecting anyone. *If it was that super's nosy wife again...* "Just a sec, I'm coming," Logan called out. The knock came again. Whoever knocked, knocked even harder *"Alight*, stop beating on the damn..."He yanked the door open. His jaw dropped open.

Marie.

At least it looked like her. The body and face were right, but everything else... Marie's makeup was generously applied. Normally, she barely wore any at all. Her lips were coated in a hot red lipstick and gloss that almost made her lips look like cherries. He felt a familiar jump in his pants as he took her in. She was decked out in a red, stretch mesh chemise, sheer thigh high nylons and garters with matching high heeled pumps. Her brunette hair was wild and the look in her eyes… it excited and frightened him. She looked…hungry.

"Marie, Oh my God!"

Sweeping his wife into his arms, he held her tight. He was afraid he might break her he squeezed so hard. Marie returned his embrace as she pressed her face to his neck. "Where the hell have you been? We've all been worried sick!" He held her at arm's length.

Marie smiled. For reasons he couldn't fathom, it sent a chills down his spine. "I'm sorry, baby," she said, her voice remorseful.

"You're sorry? I've been callin' every day to the police, hospitals and any fuckin' body else who would pick up a goddamn phone, lookin for you and all you got to say is, I'm sorry?"

"*Mom!*" Jason's came tearing from the hallway, throwing himself into his mother's arms. Marie drew her son tightly against her, placing tender kisses upon his head.

Logan's anger came to a boil. "Marie, where have you been and why are you walkin' around dressed like that? You owe us an explanation!"

"I know. I was out."

"What kinda fuckin answer is that? Out *where* Marie? It's been over a fuckin' week."

Marie kissed the top of Jason's head, caressing his face. "I was fine, I was with Trish."

He was approaching meltdown. It was about to get ugly. *Best to get the boy out of the line of fire.* "Jason, go to your room, *now!*" Jason looked from him to his mother. Logan erupted. "What did I just tell you to do?" As Jason started away, Logan bellowed. "Marie, why the *fuck* are you walkin around in that outfit, where the fuck have you been and who the fuck is Trish?"

"I am. Hi, I'm Trish."

His jaw dropped open. A blonde, stunning, impossibly beautiful, wearing ruby red lipstick and an amazingly sheer, gold lace bustier stood in his doorway. His eyes popped, roaming over the mini skirt which left little to the imagination. He licked his lips as his gaze followed her long legs from her firm looking thighs to the crisscross sandals with their five inch spiked heels.

Trish sashayed into the room; her eyes were stunning, intense, and filled with heat and desire. In spite of himself, his shaft twitched, brought on by the sudden and irrational need to possess this woman.

Logan fought for self-control, but it was flowing away from him like it was carried away by a rapid. He wanted her, needed her, on floor right there. He'd take her in front of his wife and child. Trish wanted that. So did Marie, but… *how did he know that*? With strength of will, he forced the inner beast back into its cage. *What the hell was the matter with him*? Trish looked into his eyes, smiling, as if she knew what he was thinking. *What the…*

There were tips of something peeking from under her top lip. *Fang*s? He shook his head to clear it. His eyes are playing tricks on him. The blonde stood next to Marie. Placing her hands on her hips, Trish studied him, like she wondered what he'd taste like. Where did Marie meet this woman? Trish looked like she'd stepped out of someone's X-rated fantasy. They exchanged looks. She wanted him. He wanted her too. Marie. She didn't seem the least bit jealous of the obvious sexual attraction between him and Trish. No, she seemed excited by it.

He hated to admit it, but he couldn't blame his wife for taking off with this amazing blonde bombshell. Hell, he wouldn't have been able to resist her either. The sexual energy she exuded almost made him forget how pissed he was. Almost. "What did you do to my wife?" he asked with less venom than he actually felt. He was set to blow a gasket a moment ago, now he was mellowing out. Something was wrong, he was calming down way too fast.

Trish's voice grew husky. "Oh, I've done *so* many sinful things to her, haven't I, Marie?"

Marie flushed, literally purring as she exchanged looks with Trish, the air between them becoming charged with erotic energy. Logan blinked. *Who was this Trish that she could do this to her?*

His anger reignited. Throw Trish out was his first thought, but something was soothing him, trying to strip him of his outrage. He was having none of it. "We need to talk, Marie. Alone."

Marie turned to Jason who stood with a death grip on her hand. "Jason, why don't you take Trish, and show her your room while your father and I talk?"

Trish took Jason's face into her hands. "I'd like that very much; I'd love to see Jason's room. Wouldn't you love to show it to me, Jason?"

"Yes," said Jason, lifelessly.

Trish led him away as Logan protested. "Wait a fuckin' minute. You can't just stroll into our home and—"

Marie took hold of Logan's hand. "Shhhhhhh, Logan, we need to talk." She gave it gentle squeeze as Trish continued down the hall with Jason in tow. Logan struggled.

"Baby, wait. Logan, look at me."

"Let go, Marie. Who is she? Where's she taking our son?"

"Baby, shhhhhh, look at me, look at me and it will all make sense."

Logan continued to struggle. He had to get Trish away from him, had to get her out of his house and…Marie, her eyes, so…beautiful. All the fight rushed out of him, as did his will to protect his son.

"Yes, that's right, look at me." Marie leaned in and kissed him passionately, sliding her tongue past his lips. Logan, growled, lost in the fire of his wife's advances. He returned her kiss, wrapping his arms around her. Marie's arms encircled his neck as the sound of Jason's bedroom door closing echoed from the back hallway.

She ran her hands through his hair. Pressing herself up close, she wrapped her leg around his calf. Blood rushed to his cock as she worked her hips, grinding her core against him. Logan fisted her hair, tugging her head back, licking slowly up her neck. She groaned. He growled his approval. He knew his wife. She liked it rough.

All at once, everything shifted. She forced him against the wall with strength superior to his own. An unnatural, feminine growl rumbled from Marie. She kissed him, her tongue exploring. His joined hers in sensual dance. He moaned into her kiss. Her lips were so soft and…*Ow!* He tasted blood. Marie gazed into eyes. They held him, subdued him as she opened her mouth. Her canines lengthened before his eyes.

His breath caught in his throat. She turned his head and struck. Marie sealed her mouth over the wound, as indescribable pleasure flooded his mind. Slowly, she lowered him to the floor, still latched to his neck. Euphoria and disorientation made resistance impossible. But he didn't want to resist. It felt too good. His breathing became labored. His vision began to fail. Terror flashed in his mind.

79

*Jason*!

He was alone with that… vampire. It echoed in his mind as Marie continued draining away his life. Desperately, he wanted to rise, to go to his son, but Marie clung to his neck, like a pit bull. Weakness settled on his limbs. Through the fog, he realized Marie had released him. Droplets hit his lips. A thick, metallic tasting liquid, rained down, sliding past his lips, over his tongue and down his throat.

*Marie*.

She was holding her bleeding wrist over his mouth. Through blurred vision, he saw her licking blood, his blood, from her fingers. He convulsed. His insides ignited, burning him from the inside out. His stomach retched, the spasms jolting his body. He hadn't even the strength the scream. It engulfed him, consumed him in unbelievable torment. He struggled, fought to hang on to life, but the pain…better to give in to the darkness.

"It's ok, baby, let go. Soon, we'll all be a family again. "Marie, or what used to be Marie, beamed at him. She was a vampire, but, there were no such things as vampires. It was his fault. He'd failed as a husband and a father to protect his family, failed to protect Marie from the thing that now had Jason.

His son was in the hands of that monster and he was powerless to stop it. Tears stung his eyes as he cried for his son and the loss of a once bright future now destined for eternal darkness.

# CHAPTER THIRTEEN

"Think about it, Mace, soon we'll be open for business." Vic Mada, vampire, threw out his arms, beaming as they stood on the newly reconstructed front porch. "Medical supplies, refrigerators, cooking utensils, washers and dryers arrive in the morning. All the gas ranges have been installed. Freezers have been stocked with meat and supplies. I've contacted the Drayken, the barber, stylist, and chef I requested are on their way and the fence I ordered is going up tomorrow. Nothing fancy, just a ranch style wood fence. Wouldn't want to draw too much attention to our little enterprise, would we?"

Mace rolled his eyes. This old ass farmhouse turned out pretty good. The remodel was a mind blowin' success. The farm, on which this ole house sat, was an acre and a half of land. And as luck would have it, well off the beaten path. Vic's vision made reality.

The pompous bastard bragged that he got it for a song, he was a real master negotiator. What the fuck ever. All he did was dazzle the owner into agreeing to his very modest offer. The real negotiating came when he presented his dream to the big dawg to green light the purchase. Vic carefully addressed each and every one of boss man's concerns, and answered every question. He'd done his homework, had to give him that.

It still took some smooth talking but, the asshole got the go ahead for the acquisition. According to Vic's master plan, if all this shit went down right, they'd soon be livin' the champagne and caviar lifestyle they all wanted a piece of. But with Vic's clumsy paws on this, he wasn't holding his breath.

"Just in case, I'm having cameras and motion sensors set up all over the property," Vic droned on. "Horace and Jake should be on their way back soon with our first guests. I'd estimate about ten minutes, or so."

Mace checked his watch to avoid looking at the incredible ass wipe and his amazing Technicolor idiot grin. He couldn't take much more of Vic's gum bumpin'. Shooting his ass in the face to shut him up would be fun, but somehow, he didn't think the boss man would be too thrilled about that. On the other hand, nobody actually told him he couldn't cap Vic. And it wasn't like nobody wanted to.

"This is gonna be *huge*, Mace." Vic thumped his chest with his fist. "*My* idea, all me. And you thought it didn't have a chance." Vic grinned at him, slapping him on the back.

His stomach recoiled. He hated to admit it, but it was starting to take shape. It better, given how much jack was goin' into this little venture. And let's not forgot how Vic nearly fucked up the boss' shipment of weapons last month. They were all prepared to receive that consignment when Vic suddenly got a bad case of amnesia about the price he agreed to. Seriously, you try to renegotiate price when you're about to accept the merchandise? Shit started getting' hot. Trigger fingers were twitching. Thankfully, cooler heads stepped in to keep hot silver from fanning out in search of bodies to nest in.

The boss man had to do some fast talking, but he got things patched up. Afterwards, Vic got pulled aside for a little pow wow. When it didn't result in a dusty send off, it came as a bit of a shock, and a big time disappointment. Some mutha fuckas just got more breaks than the law should allow. So, should Vic be on his hands and knees begging the powers that be that this plan of his is profitable? Can we get a hell yeah?

"The chef's a good idea. My skills in the kitchen are limited." Mace wanted it known he was not performing any Michael Symon duties. Wasn't doin' no damn dishes either. It was a UFO, Loch Ness Monster kinda mystery as to why the big dawg chose Vic as second. Watching him work was often like watchin' a train wreck. You couldn't look away but you damn sure didn't want front row seats when mayhem put his feet up and grinned. One thing was for certain though, if the ignorant bastard ever so much as laid a finger on him again, Vic's new handle was gonna be lefty.

Cringing, Mace looked out at the dirt fields that lay in wait for a plow to turn the hard packed earth. As Vic started down the rebuilt porch steps, the stench of manure hung in the air. He was really on a farm. Woo hoo. Nothing but trees as far as his vamp eyes could see. This was bullshit. He hated the country. The air was too fresh, the sky too clear, and it was always too damn quiet. How did Vic ever find this place anyway?

The taskmaster was getting a little ahead of him, so Mace started down the stairs. Better stay close in case the prick needed something checked or done. The instant his foot hit ground, something soft and squishy, spread beneath his brand new loafers.

No.

The rancid stench told him all he needed to know. He'd stepped in it, again. Literally. How stupid could he be? He was on a farm. Always look before you step. He lifted his foot to inspect his shoes. Ugh, whatever unloaded this must have died. Nothing living smelled this bad. But, it still didn't reek as bad as Vic's cologne. Damn it, he was just bought these shoes. Could it get any more fuckin' dandy? After scraping the biological deposit, i.e. the nasty ass shit from his former favorite shoes, he caught up with Vic.

"Go ahead and say it, Mace, I'm a fricken genius, this place is perfect. Just far enough away from the city that we won't attract the unwanted attention yet close enough that we can quickly move and distribute our wares."

He fell into step, wishing he were anywhere but here with Vic. What did he ever do to deserve this gig anyway? The big dawg must really have it in for him. Being Vic's personal gofer? He had half a mind to spray his throat, then eat his .40 cal. It'd be Heaven compared to listening to this asshole.

"So far, so good, Vic but it's still early in the game. I wouldn't start patting yourself on the back just yet." There was still plenty of time for Vic to screw this whole thing up. He had confidence in that.

Vic grunted. "Suck it, Mace. You not rainin' on my parade today, this is gonna work. This time, I'm gonna get the props due to me." Vic's eyes crackled in irritation.

He chuckled. Vic hated when someone even gave the impression they doubted his keen sense of vision and leadership. Until the bastard demonstrated he actually had any, he was gonna continue to hear it from the nay sayers in the peanut gallery.

Mace let his mind drift off to a happy place as Vic fumed. Best to keep any further comments to himself. There was nothing to be gained from it. Plus, Vic would take it as an invitation to keep talking to him. His head throbbed mercilessly. When he signed up with this outfit, he knew he'd draw some fucked up hands, but this… Working for Vic would never do. Padre better make his move and take out Vic soon or it was gonna get done for him. He didn't know how much longer he could put up with the bastard's persistent orders. As they took a turn toward the newly constructed concrete building, they passed a hay stack, a fuckin' hay stack. It reminded him of a song.

"As our business grows, I plan to purchase more land in other areas around the country," Vic lectured on.

*Green Acres is the place to be…*

Vic stopped in front of the unplowed field and pointed out at the land. "In time, I hope to expand the living quarters here. It will be the crown jewel,"

*Farmin' is the life for me…*

"Mace!"

"*What?*"

"Are you listening?"

*Fuck, no!* "Yeah, I was just—"

He was interrupted by the roar of a bus engine and the honk of its horn as it rolled up the dirt drive, toward them. Vic clapped his hands together. "Oh yeah, and so it begins; come on, Mace, let's go greet our first passes to the good life."

He shook his head, following Vic as the vehicle hissed and came to a stop in front of the house, kicking a dust cloud into the air. It was a good thing he didn't need to breathe. All that shit would've choked a horse. The next thing Vic needed to do was get some asphalt laid down.

The door slid open. A tall and lean vamp stepped off the bus. Dressed in a suede jacket and ripped jeans, his medium length, dirty blonde hair was partially covered by a red bandana. He smiled at their approach then turned to the passengers on board. "Welcome to yer new home, folks. Everybody grab yer belongins, step off the bus and watch yer step, please. "His voice was spiced with a pinch of Texas twang.

As they neared the group, the passengers filed off. You actually smelled them before you saw them. How Horace managed to drive with that stink on board was a true wonder.

"Jake, you made good time." Vic strolled up to him, cheesy grin in place, hand extended. The Texan took his hand and shook it, nodding at Mace. Mace nodded back. "Yeah, made a hearty haul too." Jake stepped aside as more bodies climbed off the bus. "Form, two lines as ya exit the bus, please." The new arrivals, obediently did as they were told.

"They're all volunteers, right?" Vic interjected. "If you've dazzled a single one, I want them put back. If they—"

"If they volunteer then we won't need guards to keep 'em from escaping." Vic and Jake faced the new voice as Horace, a medium built vamp, stepped off the bus.

"Relax Vic. We followed your instructions to the letter," Horace said with a smile.

"Good, are there any others on there?" Vic looked over the vamp's shoulder.

"Just one more." The vamp stepped aside and behind him was a diminutive, dirty female. Malnourished, the top of her head barely reached Vic's chest. Her movements were birdlike as her head moved back and forth. She made a beeline to Vic. That was quick, she'd already picked out who was in charge.

"They said you'd take care of me. I need it now, baby. I'm hurtin' bad." She moved in on Vic, running her hands over his chest. "You gonna take care of me aren't cha, daddy? I'll do anything you want...*anything*. "She looked into his eyes and sank to her knees. "Anything, baby, you want ya dick sucked?"

She reached for his zipper but Vic caught her hand. "That won't be necessary, pet." He drew her to her feet and turned to Jake. "Get them cleaned up, fed and settled in. Afterwards, you can begin giving them what we promised. There are a few nurses and techs already on duty. "He smiled down on the tiny woman. "You'll be taken care of, all of you. On that, you have my word. Now go get cleaned up and eat, and then we'll see to your other needs. Then you can begin seeing to ours." As Horace and Jake begin to lead the party away, Vic called out. "Gentlemen, inform the others that our guests are not to be touched. I will inspect them personally on a nightly basis. Let's be clear about this. There will be *no* free samples. If I find so much as a fang scrap, I will hold you both libel. Do I make myself clear?"

The two vamps looked to each other then back at Vic, nodding in acknowledgement, then led the group away. As the new guests were escorted to the house, Vic turned to Mace and smiled. "Still think this is bull shit idea, Mace?" He walked away to join the new arrivals, leaving him alone with his thoughts.

They were definitely breaking new ground. There were already vamp organizations, including them, dealing drugs to the human pop, but there wasn't another crew, anywhere, that could say they could provide this product to immortals. This was a fresh, untapped vein…so to speak.

"Call me a dumbass, but this might actually work. Shit."

# CHAPTER FOURTEEN

Another hazy, suffocating day came to a close as night returned to New Carrollton. Heat stressed motorists, pedestrians, and public transportation riders, worn down by the brutal high temperatures, learned from the five day forecast that three of the next five days would top the ninety-six degree mark.

Mia Foster was one of the lucky ones. She worked in an air conditioned office building and lived in a condo with central air. Tall and lean with long wavy hair she kept in a ponytail when she worked out, she was out on her evening jog. In her sports bra, running shorts, Nikes and fanny pack, she was born to run. Her skin glistened with a sheen of perspiration. The heat wave and the nut job on the loose, dissuaded many of the usual joggers from coming out, but she wouldn't let that stop her from being fit. Besides, after today, she needed to work off some frustration.

Circumstance forced her to finish up her work on the laptop at home. What a drag. Next thing she knew, the sun had set. Didn't matter, late or not, she didn't break her routine. When the work was done, run time. She didn't bothered calling her mother before she went out. She'd only worry. Her mother always worried, but hey, she was a big girl and could take care of herself. A fourth degree black belt in Tae Kwan Do proved it.

Well into her second mile, she got the strangest tingle. Like ants doing a chorus line on her skin. Someone was watching her. She gazed around. There were people milling about, pigeons doing the things pigeons usually did, and the normal ebb and flow of vehicle traffic. None of them seemed to even notice her.

She passed the hot dog vendor, packing up his wares for the night and took the turn into Jasper Park. She really made good time. The second mile went faster than usual. She rubbed her arm. That weird sensation nagged at her like a bratty child. It just wouldn't go away. Turning her head this way and that, she picked up the pace, trying to identify the source of her unease. But all she saw were trees, grass, and the giant fountain she past nightly. Her eyes told her she was alone. Her intuition screamed she wasn't.

As she rounded the next bend and...what? Her breath caught in her throat. A shadow from the shrubs lunged, taking her to the ground. Her heart pounded, rattling her rib cage. On instinct, she drove her hand into the face of her attacker. His hold loosened. She got to her knees. Another body plowed into her from behind, jarring the breath from her lungs.

She fought, but he was on top and had her by at least forty pounds. His counterpart quickly piled on. The thugs forced her arms to the ground. She screamed. A hard fist landed on the back of her head. Her face ricocheted off the ground. Calloused hands rolled her onto her back. She waited for the right moment. With a grunt, she drove a well-placed knee to the groin. An angry howl burst from his lips.

Message sent and received. They had her but she was far from beaten. Retaliation was swift. The angered hood drove his fist into her face. His partner joined the assault.

"Fuckin' bitch. Grab her legs, man," the larger male snarled.

A leather gloved hand clamped over her mouth. Other hands seized her legs. Together, the bastards lifted her up, pulling her into the brush. Mia scratched, and kicked. *Dear God, somebody help*! They dragged her off the jogging path. Her heart thundered in her ears. Terrified, she prayed. The park hadn't been totally deserted when she entered. *Was there no one who saw the attack, no one to help her; to call the police?* Mia struggled as the men carried her toward the creek below. One of them lost their footing on the mossy ground and slipped. As the three of them came tumbling down the slope to the bottom, the hands lost their hold. Her captors down, Mia, dazed as she was, staggered to her feet. Screaming, she started to run but was tackled. "Help me!"

He forced her face into the moist earth. She struggled lift her head, to draw breath. The second assailant dove atop her. They rolled her over. She thrashed and clawed, frantically reaching for a face.

"Hold that bitch, man." Her arms were forced down. Blows rained on her, splitting her lip, gashing her cheek. Blood seeped from her wounds.

"I got her, hurry the fuck up." The glint of a blade caught her eye. Her fanny pack was cut away, the mugger tossing it aside. Her bra strap was next. The bastard yanked it, off exposing her breasts, while the other grabbed her legs. She was out numbered, out classed, and tiring. A violent backhand sent her reeling. Hands tugged at her shorts.

"Yeah bitch, we got yo ass now. This shit's gonna feel good." They laughed. Tears rolled down her cheeks. Another savage fist came down. Her eye was swelling shut. She tasted blood in her mouth. Another blow, her body, battered and exhausted, gave up the fight. She hadn't the strength left to even shield herself.

They stood smiling over her, admiring their handy work. Hands squeezed her cheeks together. Mmmm, look at that body man, can't wait to get some of that." The assailant eyed her lewdly.

"Then let's get this shit started." He stooped down once more, while his partner unzipped his fly.

A tear ran down her face. *Please God, don't let them do this. Oh God, please don't let them...* she felt a subtle breeze. She gingerly lifted her head. She gasped. Behind them, a shadowy figure materialized literally out of nowhere. He moved toward them. His speed; no, nothing could move that fast. The figure grabbed both men and tossed them through the air like a child tossing a softball.

They landed in a heap. Exchanging stunned looks, they got to their feet. Mia propped herself up on her elbows. She couldn't make out this new one in the darkness, but he was huge. The first attacker charged, lunging with the knife. But the figure simply side stepped, catching the thug by the wrist. He knew how to handle himself. A loud snap startled her. The hoodlum screamed, and fell to the ground holding his arm. The other scumbag drew a gun from behind his back. The dark rescuer, for lack of a better word, flashed, she could barely follow him with her eyes.

He drove the heel of his hand into the chin of the gunman, lifting him off his feet, knocking him, flat on his back. He lay motionless.

It was over. One wannabe rapist, down and out, the other clutched his injured limb, weeping openly. The would be rapists defeated, the shadow rescuer grabbed the laid out criminal and dragged him, by the collar, to his partner. Mia watched, afraid to move or scream, as he knelt down and spoke to them. When he finished, he started in her direction. She scrambled away from him. *What was he?* Nothing could've moved like he did.

"Be not afraid. I will not harm you. "His accented voice was rich, soothing. It made no sense. She'd never seen this man before, yet she knew she could trust him. He would protect her with his life. "Are you severely injured?" he asked, his voice slow and even.

She simply shook her head.

Adalius laid the confiscated weapons at his feet, looked about and retrieved her fanny pack and what was left of her bra, and then handed them over to Mia. "Have you a cell phone?"

She nodded and withdrew the phone from her pack. He turned to the attackers. *Was he actually giving her privacy?*

"Summon the authorities," he continued. "I shall remain with you until help arrives."

Her hands were shaking as she dialed, but her nerves were calming and the pain from her wounds ebbing away. She ended the call, barely remembering talking to the police. A strange peace settled over her. It was like she'd swallowed a hand full of valium. She should've been scared out of her wits, but she was as calm as if she were lying on a sunny beach. She blinked repeatedly as a veil fogged over her thoughts. Her memory of the event blurred. Suddenly, she couldn't remember how her deliverer had saved her.

The dark rescuer spoke not another word as he stood watch over her. He didn't even look her way. She was half naked and he didn't try and steal a peek. It was ridiculous, but she almost felt insulted. Meanwhile, her attackers sat expressionless, like they were in some kind of trance. Only minutes passed but it felt like hours while they waited.

Finally. "Hello, Miss Foster? It's the police."

"I'm here!" Mia shouted as she sprang to her feet and ran up the gully. As she reached the top, the officers drew their weapons. Mia stumbled as she ran toward them and into their arms.

"Ma'am, are you alright?" the officer asked.

She took the cop by the arm, leading them toward the scene of her attack. "This way, they're down there. "She led them to the edge of the gully. "They dragged me down there. They were gonna rape me but that man—"

The officer shined his flashlight down. "What man?"

*Yes, what man?* Mia looked but there were just the two thugs. Where did her savior go? "He was just here, Officer."

"Wait here ma'am, don't move. "The police made their way down toward the seated men while Mia waited above. The officers approached the pair, weapons drawn. "Let me see your hands! "They rose slowly to their feet and locked their fingers behind their heads.

"Get on the ground, do it now!" The officers cocked their weapons.

The suspects did as commanded and the police cuffed and led them back up the gully. Once at the top, the officer shined the light in the face of one of the roughnecks. "This one of the men who attacked you ma'am?"

"We tried to rape that woman," the male spoke up.

"Yeah, we should be arrested. We'll cooperate completely," the other chimed in, both their expressions blank.

The officers looked to each other, then back at the whacked out suspects. "Okay, let's all take a little trip downtown."

"Yes suh, we'll go quietly."

"We won't be no trouble."

Mia's jaw dropped. Their change in manner was startling. *What did he do to them?* Truthfully, she didn't care. Those bastards were going to get what's coming to them. She never believed in the hero arriving in the nick of time, too cliché, just like happy endings. Not the kinda thing that happened in real life. But thanks to a man she'd never met, she was now, happily a believer. Her story indeed had a happy ending.

*****

Kyle soared above the rooftops of New Carrollton in search of his evening meal. He still couldn't believe he'd actually made the trip. He'd given Trey the all the intel he had about the bloody sow and her plans to re-establish a nest in New Carrollton, so frankly, he didn't owe the bloomin' tosser anything else. But this was Anna. The hag *had* killed the poor bloke's wife and child and here he was, all by his lonesome, trying to stop the Destroyer. It brought things home a tad bit. He also knew the agony of losing a loved one to a vampire.

So, against his better judgment, here he was in NC pounding the streets hoping to find anything that would be of help to the slayer. Fool that he was, though he hated to admit it, he'd actually become fond of the annoying sod. He wrapped himself in shadows as he swooped down the get a better look at the pedestrian buffet, strolling up and down the boulevard. Any bloomin' neck just wouldn't do tonight. He was feeling a bit randy and wanted a little play time with his meal.

Banking hard to his right, he made off toward the downtown area. Passing over a park, he came across a rather large high rise when he spotted her. The love was absolute candy for the eyes in her sports bra and jogging shorts. Her curly hair was in a ponytail and one of those thingies women used carry their cash and such while they ran, was wrapped around her waist.

"Blimey, stop the presses," he said aloud to himself. "Now there's a neck I'd love to dip my fangs into. What an amazing beauty you are. "He followed her as she started into her run, her pace brisk. "At a way, love, get that heart pumping, nothing better than freshly oxygenated blood." She was heading into her second mile when she began to look about. "Hmm, looks like you got the gift, you can actually feel me watching, can't you?"

His future dinner and sex toy made her turn into the park as Kyle stayed close behind. "Perfect, a nice quiet spot in the park so we can be alone. Wouldn't want anyone interrupting us, now would we? "He started down, than hovered. What the bloody hell, out of the scrubs, a figure attacked and took her to the ground. Kyle's eyebrows arched as the young woman swiftly, landed a haymaker in the chops of the hooligan, rolled to her knees and was promptly tackled by another attacker. His eyes blazed as the young woman was dragged, struggling off the path, down the gully toward the creek.

"Bugger, my dinner's been snatched. "He scanned through the trees below. She was being accosted by two men. No doubt about it, the girl had spirit. Kyle's fangs lengthened. "Bloody rapists, I'll deal with the filthy sods, when I'm done. For now, one three piece meal coming up. Ahhh, fine dining in the big city."

A large figure appeared behind the thugs. Kyle blinked in surprise. "Bloody hell, where did he come from? "The new arrival blurred toward the thugs and their victim, grabbed the muggers, and flung them through the air, where they landed unceremoniously in a heap. Stunned but ever stupid, they got to their feet, but instead of running, screaming from the bloke who'd just tossed them seventeen feet, they decided to go on the offensive. The first hooligan, charged and lunged at the rescuer with a knife, but the new arrival, easily side stepped the jab.

"Way too slow, mate even a newbie could've slipped *that*." Kyle watched as the rescuer grabbed hold and took the attacker by the wrist. Even from his bird's eye view he heard the snap of bone. The thwarted rapist screamed out, falling to the ground, clutching his injured limb. His partner, displaying a similar lack of sound judgment, drew a gun from behind his back. "Oh, you're buggered now, night, night." Kyle began a silent countdown. Before the knob head squeezed off a shot, the figure blurred, and delivered a swift uppercut, sending the gun wielder to the ground. Kyle winced. "*That* is gonna leave a mark. Bastard had it coming though."

The fight over, the figure grabbed the defeated and dragged him to his partner. Releasing the tosser, he knelt down and spoke to the hooligans. "Give them a sound thrashing, now comes the lecture on changing the error of their ways," Kyle chuckled. "I think I like this bloke."

Finished with the thugs, he rose and turned to the woman, as Kyle whipped out his mental note pad. "Alright, mate, you're clearly a vamp. Check. Built like a bloody tank. Check. Decked out in leather, check. Attitude I can feel from up here, check. Maniacal arse kicker, check. And survey says...*ding*! Enforcer. Guess I get to try out that club I've heard so much about, after all. "Kyle took one last longing look at the dinner and fun that could've been. "Maybe next time, love." Shaking his head, he soared off, in search of the immortal's night club and type AB refreshments.

# CHAPTER FIFTEEN

The old jukebox played *Don't Stop Believing* as Anna drained yet another biker of his blood. When the last drops left his body, she let him fall to the floor and stepped over the empty corpse. That one was staying dead. The asshole plucked on the wrong nerve. He called her a cunt. An ugly word she cared for not one iota.

The instant it left his lips, his fate was sealed. She sucked him dry him in seconds. That filthy mouth would never see the next sunrise. A tiny hiccup escaped her lips. She was gorged. Having such a large meal wasn't her plan, but when the muscled biker pulled up next to her and offered her a ride, she figured on having a bite, some fun and making a new child. When he insisted and took her to his motorcycle clubhouse, against her feigned objections, it felt like she'd hit the Irish sweepstakes. The place was filled with tough and delicious looking men and women.

There were fifteen in all. Four of which she had already started the process of turning. The remaining bikers, not counting the idiot who annoyed her, stood lined up around the shack of a clubhouse, totally immobilized by her mental powers. She was undoubtedly getting stronger. Two months ago, she never could've held so many bodies in check with such ease.

Anna ran her hands sensuously over her hips. Her trusted black, stretch mini skirt had come through again. How could it not, it highlighted her best features, her ass and legs. As she strolled across the room, she reminisced about the days before she became immortal.

She was married to a handsome, God fearing man. She loved him with all her heart. She still missed his sturdy arms about her. Theirs was a strong marriage and partnership. He hunted and worked the land, while she cared for their home and prepared the bounty he provided.

She sighed, hugging herself. She truly believed they would last forever. How foolish she was. Life would never allow such happiness to endure. Out of the blue, her beloved took sick with fever. Smallpox was never kind to its victims but it was especially hard on him. It started with the headaches and nausea, and then came that terrible rash that slowly covered his entire body.

Watching him bear such suffering was nearly as torturous for her as it had been for him. The disease ravaged his body and mind. She did all she could do, making him as comfortable as possible. The infection turned her vibrant man into a helpless, rash covered mass of flesh.

She'd prayed long and hard for his recovery. Those prayers went unanswered. First God denied her a child, then turned a deaf ear to her prayers to save her man. She'd believed the words of how much He loved her, how much He cared, but how dare He claim love for her, withhold a child, then take away her beloved husband? As far as she was concerned, God was a myth. A myth she vowed never bend her knee to again.

A tear welled in her eyes. In the end, there was relief at his death. His torment mercifully ended. To her everlasting regret, she never gave him the son he so desired. It wasn't for lack of trying. Her husband, good man that he was, always comforted her, saying it wasn't her fault. But even now a part of her felt guilt at failing to conceive.

Sudden anger boiled to the surface. She clenched her fists so tightly, they drew blood. *No.* Emotions, especially sadness and regret, are the burden of the weak. They were for the mortals she claimed as her victuals. What had they ever gotten her?

Anna casually crossed the room, humming along with the juke box, her heels clicking on the hardwood floor. It was a wonder she could hear music at all with so many hearts in the room beating in overdrive. There were four women left among the living as she took her time deciding who would be next.

The air was thick with the smell of fear, cigarettes, and cheap booze as she picked the eight ball off the billiards table and dropped it into the corner pocket. Tears rolled down the cheeks of the nearest female. *We have a winner*. As she approached the mortal, Anna's fangs extended as a smile spread across her face.

"Your turn, sweetheart." Anna wiped away the tear as she leaned in for a kiss.

"Don't. Touch her and I'll fuckin' kill you!"

Anna turned to the tough looking female across from her and smiled. The tiger was being threatened by the flea. "Is she your woman?" She approached the roughneck woman.

"You fuckin' bitch, touch her and I swear—"

Anna chuckled. "I'll take that as a yes." Anna gripped the woman's cheeks and squeezed. "She was your woman. When I'm done making her scream my name, she won't remember yours. "The bitch spat in her face. Anna's casually reached into her purse, withdrew a hanky and wiped away the spittle. "I admire your courage. You have more than many males I've encountered in my travels." Anna gazed into the female's eyes. "Poor manners however, I'll *never* tolerate." Anna took hold of her head. With a swift twist, she snapped the woman's neck clean. Stepping aside she let the corpse to drop to the floor. Assorted gasps and screams rang out. Anna placed her hands on her hips. "Who else needs a lesson in manners?"

"Oh my God," the male to her left breathed out, his eyes wide and wild.

Her brow arched. "God? There is no God. If there were, clearly He doesn't care for any of you. If He did, how could He stand by and watch me do this?" Anna clasped the man's head and drove her thumbs into his eyes, slowly gouging them out amid his screams and those present. Tearing them free from their sockets, she dropped them to the ground then crushed them, eye whites oozing from beneath her shoe. As he collapsed; dead before he hit the floor, Anna licked the blood from her hands, then turned to her captives and struck a ta da pose. "There, you see, was I struck down by righteous wrath or burned with divine fire? No. There is no God."

Anna eyed them coldly. They were insects to be crushed at her whim but she'd see to it they became gods. As her children, they would be feared, even by the creatures of the night. Humans. To think she'd once been one of them.

*****

That chapter of her existence ended late in the fall of 1690. Mercifully, her humanity was stripped away. While returning home from a late supper with friends, she was attacked by a vampire searching for a mate and ally against a slayer who had pursued him from the old country.

The fool turned her, and then soon after, took her as his mate. The coupling had been intense, violent, driven by need, hunger, and in her case, anger; anger at her loneliness, anger at being a childless widow, anger at having her life stolen by the soulless creature mounting her.

Together, they made short work of the slayer. It was her first kill. It was astounding how her body responded to the new blood. The feel of it rushing past her lips, the sound of the slayer's final breath and heartbeat filled her with warmth and bliss. She felt alive.

As the slayer lay dead at her feet, like an addict, she craved more. More of the sensation, more of the power, she had to have it and cared not where it came. So she attacked and latched onto the only other blood source available, her new found mate.

His struggle invigorated her. The look of surprise and unabashed terror in his eyes delighted her as she drank in his blood. She knew then that she would relish her undead life. She was a god, able to take and grant life at will.

For months after, she fed upon the settlers. They, who were once her friends and neighbors, became prey she hunted without compassion. Boredom at last sent her out into the world in search of new sensations and victims.

A chance encounter with a Lycan introduced her to a new and glorious food source. Lycan blood contained an astonishing energy. Her body demanded more. So, one by one, she hunted them until they became her meal of choice. As time passed, her cravings became more demanding, compelling her to seek out new and exotic forms of nourishment. Demons, elves, ogres, vampires, they all satisfied her needs. She rose to the top of the food chain. Word of her thirst spread throughout the supernatural world, and with it, fear and hatred. Her very name, Anna Longfellow, became spoken in hushed whispers by the living and undead alike. She became known as the Destroyer.

Coming out of her reverie, Anna casually watched the expressions of horror on the faces of the remaining bikers.

"Pl...please, let us go. Please!" Anna turned to the female on her left. Her tears flowed freely and she trembled so badly that she might have collapsed had Anna not been holding her in place. She approached the sobbing female, caressed her cheek then ran her hand tenderly through her hair.

"Shhh, of course I won't let you go. You'll all feed my children when they wake. But worry not, I promise to turn you all, before your deaths become irreversible."

"What the fuck *are* you?"

Anna's brow arched. "Come now, you know very well what I am. It's your narrow-mindedness that prevents you from accepting what you see with your own eyes." She turned to address the throng. "The world isn't a place where the only things that exist are what you choose to believe in. There are all manner of beings and entities watching you, lusting after you, preying upon you. Your arrogance misleads you into thinking that all you need do is declare something unreal and it will simply cease to exist. It shall be humanity's undoing." Anna glanced around at the frightened hostages. "You will all be a part of the new order. You'll see the world as you never have before. Soon, *we* will dictate how things will be done on this Earth. Man, beast, and every creature of the night will bow before us. Enough talk, now sleep, when you wake, you will be as gods." With a wave of her hand, Anna put them all to sleep.

Anna took a seat and crossed her legs. Yes, a new age was coming soon. The day was approaching when those who hunted her, would become the hunted. For now though, she would continue to prepare and grow her nest.

# CHAPTER SIXTEEN

A black '69 Charger pulled next to an old maple tree near a field of wildflowers. A lonely, rural area is where Neal Kimble found himself. The air was warm, inundated with moisture and the fragrance of southern magnolias as he put the car in park. It was a moonless night, only the stars cared to show up and greet him along with the all-star cricket orchestra. It wasn't the worst place his twenty years of hunting fangs had taken him.

He'd followed the blood suckers into sewers, caves, rickety old farm houses, abandoned buildings, and a host of other dirty, smelly places where just the memories of the stench he endured on occasion, made his stomach roll. The rumble from his chrome tailpipes died out as he shut off the engine and headlights. He stepped out of the vehicle; he'd have to go the rest of the way on foot.

"This is as far as you go darlin'. Have to go it alone from here," he said patting the car door. Leaving his pride and joy parked by her lonesome, in the middle of nowhere, sucked lemons. It was best though. He'd spent the last two weeks searching for this nest and he didn't want to blow the element of surprise. A horned owl hooted in the tree somewhere above him as he took in the landscape. It was peaceful, real peaceful.

Taking in a deep breath, he sighed. The air was fresh and clean. Honeysuckle was growing wild someplace close, and from the sound of it, there was a large stream nearby as well. Not bad. This was the kinda place he needed to relax, unwind, and forget that the world was filled with so much damned evil. A real shame vamps fouled this place, but he was here to fix that. His long, stringy, auburn hair swayed with every movement as he shut the car door and made his way toward the trunk.

He reached for the last cigarette in the breast pocket of his denim vest, but thought better of it. Blood suckers might pick up the scent on the wind. Neal looked out over the open field, there was a faint outline of trees in the distance. A flock of geese grabbed his attention as they flew overhead, honking their way toward the west. He could barely make them out as they sailed off in the distance in V formation, unaware of his presence.

The hunter in him sobbed as the fresh game moved out of rifle range. This place was as country as you could get, and what beautiful country it was. He was gonna stick around after he'd finished his assignment and do some fishing. He'd passed an orchard and a small general store that advertised rod, reel, and live bait for sale. This was the sort of place you'd expect to find people named Opie and Aunt Bea, not undead, blood sucking demons from hell.

Shaking his head, he slid the key into the trunk lock and popped the latch. Lifting the lid, he inspected his weapons, the trunk light putting his stash on display. A spare tire, tire iron, jack, large crossbow, assorted guns, automatic rifles, daggers, explosives, and a bevy of other hardware that would turn even the most seasoned vampire hunter green with envy, took up every inch of space the trunk provided.

He leaned in and grabbed a sawed off shotgun, loaded it, then placed a hand full of extra shells in a leather pouch and slipped its strap over his shoulder. Next, he grabbed two .40 caliber pistols, locked and loaded both, and slipped one into his shoulder holster, the other inside his pants at the small of his back. A handful of fully loaded magazines went into the pouch next along with several small glass vials, of Holy water.

Finally, he pulled out a satchel, which contained the pair of night vision goggles he'd won in a poker game, and slipped it on. *These may come in handy.* Quietly, he closed his trunk and started off across the field in the direction of the old farmhouse and barn he'd been told about.

According to the locals, someone purchased the property several weeks ago, but no one had seen hide nor hair of the new owners. They'd made it clear, however, that uninvited guests would be treated as trespassers. Weird, vamps usually didn't have any qualms about having neighbors over for dinner.

He continued on, serenaded by the field of crickets that stopped singing at his approach, then resumed once he was at a safe distance away. He'd neared the field's edge when he picked up the scent of smoke in the air. Staying low, he kept moving as the house came into view through the trees.

The homestead was lit top to bottom, the chimney billowing smoke as he canvassed the area. A few dozen yards to his right, he noticed the barn had been replaced by an enormous, three story, concrete structure. He slipped quietly through the brush, and headed straight for the new construct. Something about that peculiar building made his curiosity meter go bat shit.

It was hard to see, but he could tell the rectangular structure was windowless and as out of place as a lump a coal in a snow bank. Out in front of the farm house, forty yards or so, to his left, he spotted guards seated around a campfire. Why they'd start a fire, he had no idea, since fangs could see perfectly at night and didn't get cold.

He stayed low, circling to his right, away from the undead guards. The last thing he needed was for those goons to pick up his scent. They all rose to their feet, sampling the air. *Shit*! They'd caught wind of something, him most likely. Great, if it wasn't for rotten luck, he'd have no luck at all. Neal kept moving as he cocked a shell softly into the shotgun chamber, the soft clack, clack offering a degree of comfort.

It was a battle he couldn't win. If they attacked, he was out in the open and alone against several hungry vamps, and let's not mention there was no way of knowing how many more were inside the house. He broke out in a sweat as visions of his death notice danced in his head.

One of the fangs tapped the others and gestured in his direction. His guts imploded. Neal's heart went into overdrive. Sweat trickled down his back. *Fuck me all the way to Tuesday*. Their eyes began to glow. He ducked down, unsure if they had spotted him or not. Meanwhile, his adrenaline machine kicked into high gear as his feet made preparation to vacate the premises.

Two of them peeled off, one to the left, the other to the right. They're gonna to try and outflank him. This was getting worse by the second. His muscles twitched as he accessed the situation. In his mind, he played out the coming battle. Unfortunately, the scenario ended with his very unpleasant death.

He dropped to one knee into the high grass, and drew a bead on the oncoming blood sucker directly ahead. *No firing, until you see the points of his fangs. Wait to the last possible second, then be quick.* The other two wouldn't twiddle their thumbs while he reloaded.

Neal braced himself; his finger caressed the trigger as he drew in an even breath. Game on, the undead directly ahead of him broke into a jog. He was closing in. He took aim. Just a little closer. The blood sucker launched himself forward, barreling in as Neal began an internal countdown.

*Three. Two. Oooof!*

The impact drove the air from his lungs. The world went spinning. Neal found himself flat on his back. Through the fog, he heard the thump of foot falls and cries of 'there he goes, don't let him get away! 'He scrambled to his knees, amazingly, still gripping the shotgun. He was still seeing stars as he watched them take down a white-tailed deer. Bambi was most likely the truck that'd run him down.

As they sank their fangs into their prize catch, several others came tearing from inside the house to join in on the feast. He was sickened by the feeding frenzy. There had to be better ways to go than that. On the other hand, better the deer than him.

Movement to his right drew his attention as several more figures emerged from the large concrete building, no doubt drawn by the scent of blood. They rushed to the venison buffet. Neal moved quickly, never one to hesitate when opportunity came a knocking. While the fang squad snacked, he'd go have a peek inside that big building that his instincts found so interesting.

He circled wide and away from the macabre buffet, toward the concrete structure, all the while, keeping a watchful eye on the feeding frenzy. The blood suckers might be occupied with their meal, but too much noise, on his part, might tip them off to the prospect of dessert.

He drew closer to his target, slapping at the other blood feeders on this farm. He hated mosquitoes. The little bastards always found him no matter where he went. Finally he arrived just outside the steel door of the structure and waited. A quick glance over to where the blood suckers were chowing down, told him that they were just beginning to enjoy the spoils of their kill. Good, that should buy him some time.

After making certain his unsuspecting hosts were still dining, he made his way toward the door of the strange building, taking care to disturb the high grass as little as possible. He ducked into the shadows and paused, scanning the area for guards. All clear, he stalked forward.

Across the barnyard he could make out framework for two more structures in the darkness. Oddly, they were building and renovating the farm. This was not typical of vampires. They moved in, but to do home improvement? That's never on the agenda. Just what had he stumbled on to? Curiouser and curiouser.

Spurred on by the behavioral irregularities, Neal carefully made his way to the door, and prayed he wasn't walking into a vamp convention. He opened it carefully and stepped inside. It was at the bottom of a stairwell. He looked about, shotgun at the ready. It wasn't bad inside temperature wise. It was actually pleasantly cool and the smell of prepared food laced the air. The only light came from the stairway to his right. He was wasting time. If he had any plans of nosing around and getting out in one piece, he'd better move.

Carefully, he took the stairs. As he approached the doorway of the first landing, he took a silent three count and ducked into the hall, leveling his weapon swiftly in one direction, then the other. Clear. Doors, maybe fifteen in all, lined the walls, and red, plush carpeting covered the hall floor from end to end. Stylish, but he didn't come to critique the décor, better keep moving. Turning, he continued up the stairs, hugging the wall. His breathing slow and even, Neal neared the top. Light from up ahead grew brighter. The drone of voices filled the stairwell along with the smell of antiseptics and beef stew. Crouching down, he made his way through the doorway; the entire third floor was nothing more than a catwalk which went around the entire perimeter of the building. Numerous light fixtures hung from the ceiling, bathing the area below in a gentle, white light. Neal glanced about, relieved to see no hostiles present. Perhaps they'd all heard the dinner bell.

Cautiously, he lay on his belly and crawled to the edge for a better look at the space below. No wonder the place smelled like a hospital, it looked like one. The space was lined front to back, side to side with cots. On most of them, lay a person giving blood. Medical refrigerators lined the walls where the blood was being collected and stored.

Workers moved about in all directions. Some starting or removing IV bags, others escorted donors to and from cots. There was even a recovery area where donors were fed then led away to be replaced by more donors. The whole damn thing had the feel of an assembly line.

"What the fuck… *is* this?" Neal whispered to himself.

"It's nap time, *home boy!*"

Neal looked up just in time to see the rifle butt streaking toward him, then the lights went out.

# CHAPTER SEVENTEEN

The trip back to the motel was an adventure. Every road not blocked by flood waters, was cut off by fallen power lines, debris, or trees. Dozens of traffic lights were either malfunctioning or knocked out altogether by the storm. At the larger, busier intersections, police officers were stationed to safely direct the flow of traffic. The carnage the storm inflicted on the city was amazing. He'd seen hurricane damage on occasion and while this wasn't nearly as bad, it would still take weeks, if not days, to clean up.

Six reroutes, two gas station attendants, and a police officer later, Trey arrived at the parking lot of the Palace Motel, where he'd rented a room. He parked into an empty space, grabbed his wings, and made his way to his room on the second level. A refreshing blast of cool air and the drone of the air conditioner greeted him, as he stepped inside. Closing the door behind him, he flipped on the lights and laid his jacket across the back of a nearby chair. He grabbed a seat on the bed, boxed wings in hand, and removed the cell from his pocket.

Funny that the thing hadn't twitched the past few days, it was hard to believe Maya hadn't buzzed him. It'd been nearly four days since he last checked in. If she didn't hear from one of her slayers after a day or two, she'd ring their phones. Once she got through, then would come the tirade that would cause third degree burns to the ears of the poor bastard on the other end.

That in mind, every slayer checked in every two days…usually. He'd been so busy with first tracking down Kyle, then making his way to New Carrollton that he'd simply forgotten to call. On the other hand, phones did work two ways. Maya hadn't tried to contact him, so maybe, for once, all was right with the world. Maybe Maya was starting to mellow out and finally decided to treat her slayers more like adults, instead of little brats that needed her constant supervision. Yeah, right. Laying the boxed wings down next to him, Trey whipped out his cell phone and hit the power button.

"Oh shit!"

His phone was off. It'd completely slipped his mind. He turned it off near the Ohio/Pennsylvania border when he stopped to investigate a suspicious looking farm house. It turned out to be abandoned and fang free, but during his inspection, he switched off his phone. It would've been just his luck the place would've been crawling with vamps. And dollars to navy beans, Maya would've picked that moment to ring him up.

Trey's stomach churned as he stared at the cell phone. He had to turn it on. Every nerve in his body pleaded with him not to. He hit the power button. After his phone finished rebooting, it presented him with the great news of twenty-three missed calls from Maya. His head dropped, his eyes squeezed shut. He was in for it now.

She'd no doubt left a slew of colorful messages, cursing the womb that spat him out. The only way to spare himself some of the tongue lashing was to call her back before....the phone vibrated in his hand. He closed his eyes. *Please don't let it be Maya. Please don't let it be Maya. Please don't let it be...*he checked the caller ID.

"Damn." Trey blew out a breath. Time to take his medicine, may as well be comfortable. He fluffed a pillow, laid down, propped his feet on the bed, and accepted the call. *"Helloo?"* His tone was really gonna piss her off but screw it, may as well have a little fun.

"Where the *fuck* you been? I been worried *sick!*" Maya thundered.

So much for being able to hear outta *that* ear again. "Awww, ain't that sweet, she worried about me."

"Worried about you, fuck you, I was worried about my bike!"

Trey smiled to himself. "You mean *my* bike don't you? I won it fair and square. "And he did, in a poker game. It was the one time she shouldn't have called his bluff.

"You cheated me and you fucking know it."

She knew he hadn't, it just galled her that she'd lost her favorite bike. "How did I cheat, Maya? You dealt."

"I don't know how you did it, but I know you did, you thieving bastard."

Sticks and stones might break his bones, but names would never get her bike back. "Mmm, you know it turns me on, when you talk like that. "He didn't have to see her to know that she was smiling.

"Kiss my ass, Trey, the only reason I put up with yo narrow ass is because of your father, may he rest in peace."

Trey rolled his eyes. "As you've told me for the nine billionth time."

"Shut up, boy; now, where are you?"

"New Carrollton."

"New Carrol…Why are you in New Carrollton?"

He expected that reaction. His last assignment was in Nevada, near Vegas. "One of my sources passed it along that Anna was planning on reestablishing a nest here."

"Umm hmm, and by sources, you mean that shiftless little blood sucker you always talk
to?"

"Shiftless, cowardly, little blood sucker, yes," Trey corrected her.

"I don't understand why you haven't already staked that shit bag."

"Because intel like he provides doesn't grow on trees and so far, it's all been on point. "He had her there.

"Alright, point taken. Ok, I'm gonna get you somebody to ride shotgun."

"No need, Maya, I got this."

"No, you don't. I want you to have back up."

Trey could hear rustling paper and Maya muttering to herself. "Ok, Neal is the closest to you. I'll try and contact him, but like another one of my hardheaded slayers, he don't like to turn on his damn phone."

He rolled his eyes. He was going hear about this the next six months. "Ok, Ok, it won't happen again."

"See that it doesn't. Hang on." Maya switched over to another call. Trey tapped his finger on the box of wings beside him. It took a few moments before he heard the line click once more. "Stosh just checked in, he's on his way but he's in Denver. It'll be a few days before he can get there."

Trey groaned. If those people had been bit and were turning, they'd be unalive and kickin' before Stosh could arrive. He couldn't wait. "Maya."

"He's on a bike Trey!"

Again with the fear of flying, Stosh could be such a baby. "He's six foot seven, three hundred fifty pounds. He'll charge into a vamp nest without a second thought, and take on an army of Lycan without hesitation, but won't set foot on a plane?"

"He had a bad experience, ok?"

"I can't wait. The media here reported the cops finding five dead bodies in the past week. I need to find a way into the coroner's office to see if they're vamps in the making." He was right and Maya knew it. He couldn't wait. If they'd been bitten, they had to be put down, pronto.

"Alright, keep me posted. Stosh will contact you as soon as he gets to New Carrollton. I'll keep trying to reach Neal. In the meantime, be careful and don't do anything stupid."

Trey grinned. "You know me."

"That's what I'm talking about Trey. You are one of the best slayers I've ever trained, but you're not as good or as smart as you think you are."

Trey chuckled. It still made him smarter than all the rest of them. "Ok, I hear ya."

"Good, make sure you buzz me when Stosh gets there."

"Will do, boss lady."

Maya's voice rose slightly in pitch. "You better, cause if you die on me, I'm a come to New Carrollton and kick yo ass."

"Yes, ma'am."

"One last thing, Trey, if this checks out and it is Anna, do *not* try go after her by yourself."

Trey sat up on the bed. "Maya. I got this, I don't need anybody's help."

"If she was just your garden variety vamp, and you didn't have such a large stake in this, I'd agree."

What the hell, he wasn't a toddler. "I don't need a babysitter and I don't need nobody lookin' over my shoulder."

"Yes, you do. You let your emotions cloud your judgment when it comes to Anna, and it could get yo ass killed."

"Maya, I'm cool."

"No, you're not! You run way too hot when it comes to Anna. You hide it well from the others but you're too much like your father, you can't hide it from me. I see it in your eyes whenever anybody even mentions her. "Maya let out a long sigh. "She killed your wife and daughter, baby. You don't just turn that on and off whenever you like. Listen, do your thing, but if it is Anna, contact me and we'll all come to New Carrollton. But under no circumstance do you go after her alone, you got that? *Answer* me Trey!"

"Yeah, ok. Alright." Trey ended the call, setting the phone on the nightstand next to the bed. Maya was right about one thing; Anna Longfellow was indeed no ordinary vampire. As if any vampire could be considered ordinary. But Anna was one for the books. She was like nothing any of them had ever seen. Not only did she feed on humans, but Lycan, demons, sirens, gremlins, and Heaven only knew what else.

She even drew strength from feeding on other vamps, which should have been impossible. No life could be drawn from the blood of the dead. Yet somehow, Anna did just that. It made her a threat to everything on earth, living, undead, or other.

Despite hunting her for the past five years, he still didn't know as much about her as he would have liked. Clearly, she'd been feeding on her supernatural counterparts for quite some time and had become a bogeyman of sorts to the things that go bump in the night.

He tried strong arming but the night crawlers seemed far more fearful of Anna's wrath than anything he could do to them. He'd all but given up hope until he met Kyle, his cowardly, shiftless, blood sucking snitch.

*****

*It was in a dark alley, behind a hole in the wall dance club, in upstate New York, that he first met Kyle. He'd just finished a job busting up a nest of vampires who'd been using area residents as an all you can eat buffet. Afterwards, he dropped by the club with visions of cool drinks and warm feminine bodies.*

*He'd partied his ass off, dancing up a storm, getting his drink on and met a fine young woman, who'd offered him a soft bed to lay his head and anything else his dirty little mind could come up with. An unexpected and unwelcome call from Maya however, ended his action for that night. Kennedy checked in to report that she and her lover, Jackson, had stumbled across several vamp nests on the outskirts of Hartford, Connecticut and requested back up. So, thoroughly pissed, he bid his new found friend good night after taking her name and number, then headed out to his Harley parked in a side alley. He was all set to crank her up when he heard a soft moan come from behind a garbage dumpster near the back of the alley. It was a reminder of what he would be missing that night. He paused when he heard the moan again. Something about that second one made his instincts take over.*

*He dismounted, unsheathed the sword from the luggage rack along with a silver loaded automatic handgun and cautiously made his way toward the sound. It was an especially dark night; the only illumination came from a wildly flickering security light mounted on the club wall. Sword in one hand, pistol in the other, he moved past the dumpster and saw the couple to his right.*

*She was pinned with her back against the dumpster and his head was buried in her neck. Trey had been slaying long enough to tell the difference between nibbling on a neck to please and nibbling on a neck to feed. He was interrupting dinner, Kyle's dinner. Seems he was always catching Kyle in the middle of a snack.*

*He'd hit Kyle with all the force he could muster, catching him on the side of the head with the silver plated handle. It'd knocked him clean off of her. The woman dropped to the ground, her eyes glassy, she was out of it. Her eyes blinked as she shook off the vamp mind control. He yelled to grab her attention. "You!" He pointed at her. "Get gone!"*

*She didn't need any more coaxing; she took off like a shot, her heels clicking on the pavement. He covered her escape. Massive retaliation was coming.*

Kyle was just a tad worked up. *"Stupid sod, you've just made your last mistake, mate."* Kyle's eyes glowed angry crimson as he bared fangs. The blood sucker started to close the distance when the light bounced off his blade, making him slam on the brakes. *"Bloody hell, a slayer!"*

*"No shit, you a regular Einstein."*

Kyle threw up his hands. *"Easy, mate, don't hurt me. I'm just gonna back away, nice and easy."*

*"Don't hurt me? Bet that's what the girl said right before you put the bite on her."*

The fragrance of BBQ ribs and French fries from the twenty-four hour rib joint nearby filled the alley as he circled to his right. Studying Kyle, he watched for weaknesses.

*"I swear, I wasn't gonna kill her, mate!"*

*"And when I drive this silver in yo sweet spot, you won't kill anyone ever again."*

*"Easy with that blade, never killed anyone, I have."*

As if he would have believed anything a fang told him. *"Bullshit."* He'd moved in on Kyle, who was smart enough to stay out of sword range.

*"I swear on me mum's grave, I've never killed a soul."*

Trey concentrated on piercing Kyle's heart.

*"In all the years I've been a vampire, I have never taken a life, It's the truth!"*

*"What, you want a gold star for good behavior?"* He'd moved in closer as Kyle backed away.

*"I'm pleadin' with ya, don't do this."* Kyle hands were up in a defensive position as he pivoted, keeping away from the blade's tip.

Trey slid the pistol in his shoulder holster and gripped the sword handle in both hands. *"I'm a slayer, you a vamp, do the math. Now stand still, this isn't gonna hurt a bit. Ok, I'm lying; this is gonna hurt like a bitch."* He closed in on Kyle but he sensed what was coming and threw up his hand in surrender.

*"Wait, I can help you!"*

Trey smirked. He'd have paid good money to see the expression on his own face. *"Damn, almost laughed out loud. How exactly can you*

112

*help me? Make it fast, I'm in a hurry." He was already braced for the mental assault he was sure was coming. Sons of bitches would try to lull you with idle chit chat, before they attempted to overtake your mind. But surprise surprise, he didn't feel the sensation of pressure in his head, the tell-tale sign a fang was trying to push his way into your thoughts.*

*"I can give you information, slayer. I can be your eyes. I can get into places you can't and don't even know about. For instance, there's a nest located on the southeast side of town."*

*He'd managed to back Kyle against the club wall, sliding the tip of his blade underneath his chin. He heard the subtle hiss as the silver burned his skin. Much to Kyle's credit, he didn't flinch.*

*"Nice try, songbird, but I already dealt with that. Looks like your info is just like your life, not worth spit."*

*Kyle wasn't done. "Ok, but did you know about the house on Mulberry Drive? It recently received a rather large shipment of cocaine in the past week. A lot of the trafficking in this region can be traced directly back to that house."*

*He slid the blade a bit further stopping just short of breaking the skin. "Do I look like a NARC to you? Got no love for dope slingers, but they fall just a little outside my job scope."*

*Kyle had actually smirked. "Ahh but the chaps who fund and operate this particular business endeavor, fall very much under your job description. This drug house is run exclusively by vampires."*

*"Get the fuck outta here!"*

*"It's not a joke, mate."*

*The whole thing had sounded like some Believe it or not; fact or fiction bullshit and neck biters, as a rule, could lie their asses off but he could see it in Kyle's eyes. He wasn't lying. "What's your name, lie and I'll know."*

*"Kyle, call me Kyle."*

*"Well Kyle, here's the deal. You're gonna take me to this house so I can have a look see. You telling the truth, you get to work for me. Oh, and if this is some kind of trap, I promise you, babe, I'm takin you out first."*

*"Tell me something I don't already know, shall we go?"*

**113**

*Kyle led him to the house and sure enough, it was crawling with night stalkers wheeling and dealing blow. He contacted Maya, relayed what he'd found and five days later, all the slayers, twenty strong, showed up ready to split wigs.*

*They would have started with Kyle but some fast talking spared him the stake. Another six weeks of watching and learning their routine, then they went in. They dusted every blood sucker in the house. Once the hostiles were put down, they dropped a dime to the feds who took away the product. One vamp drug house shut down. As agreed, Kyle went to work for him, becoming his eyes and ears in the supernatural world. Why Kyle continues to provide info, he wasn't sure. If Kyle decided to ditch him, he didn't have the time to hunt him down.*

*Somehow, for all the pleading in that alley, he got the sense that Kyle really wasn't afraid to die. Maybe he was trying to fulfill some oath he'd made or atone for some sin committed, possibly, before he was born. Most likely, he suspected that Kyle did it because he hated vampires, as hard as that was to believe. There was always a hostile undercurrent coming from Kyle whenever they spoke of them.*

\*\*\*\*\*

Trey rose off the bed and checked his watch. The sun was down for the night, time to move. He had to get to the Medical Examiner's office, find a way inside, without being seen and determine if the victims were being turned. If he was lucky, all he would find would be a bunch of unbitten bodies.

114

# CHAPTER EIGHTEEN

dalius landed on the roof of a brownstone apartment. Reaching out with his senses, a cruel smile spread across his lips. His intuition had been correct, Anna was here. He began to run. Leaping from building to building, he could feel her, hiding somewhere in this metropolis. Ferreting her out, however, was going to be a challenge. Though he still had a residual psychic link to her, it'd been quite some time since he fed from her vein. Their bond wasn't what it once was but it was still strong enough to detect her presence. But with so many immortals in New Carrollton, creating psychic white noise, finding her would be like listening for a specific voice in an auditorium filled with people carrying on conversations. No matter, find her he would, he just needed to get close enough.

Thankfully, he was much stronger than when he last faced Anna. He'd become skilled enough to mask his presence in New Carrollton. He would need every advantage. Anna, being his maker, would always be more powerful than him. The element of surprise was crucial. It would make all the difference in the confrontation to come. Suddenly he got wind of it. He slid to a stop. It was like whisper on the breeze, impossible to miss or ignore and coming from an open window across the street.

Wrapping himself in shadows, he leaped across the distance to the next roof then climbed down where he found the air thick with the scent of fear. The lights were out but he sensed a tiny presence within the room. Silently, he moved closer to the window, stole a glance inside, and saw a little girl sitting up in bed clutching her pillow.

The room was typical for a child of her age. The walls were painted a soothing shade of pink and near the bed, lay a collection of stuffed toys. He entered, slowly revealing himself. The little girl watched wide eyed as he faded into view. Her bottom lip trembled. She was going to scream. He projected safety into her mind. "Be not afraid, I will not harm you. Why are you not asleep little one? " His tone was gentle as he addressed her.

The child's tiny hand rubbed her eyes. "I'm scared."

"Indeed, what has frightened you?"

"There's monsters under my bed," the tiny pigtailed girl replied.

"Monsters under your bed, you say?"

The little girl simply nodded. "Daddy says if I think happy thoughts, the monsters will go away."

Adalius smiled, she was adorable.

"Who are you?" she asked, curiosity overriding her fear.

"I am a monster killer. I'm here to protect you. Would you like me to kill the monsters under your bed? "The little girl brightened and nodded. Her salvation had arrived. "Wait here." Adalius lowered himself onto his knees and peered underneath the bed. As he did so, his eyes began to glow a soft teal which expanded and bathed the room in a gentle light, then faded once more to darkness. When he stood, he beheld to look of wonder on the little girl's innocent face.

"The monsters under your bed are gone, you are safe from them."

"Thank you," she said, a Kool Aid smile lighting up her face.

"Of course, what is your name, little one?"

"Carrie Ann."

"Well, Carrie Ann, you are a very brave little girl. I must leave you now but before I go, I want you to have this. Hold out your hand."

Carrie Ann held out her tiny hand and into it Adalius dropped a jewel. It was given to him by Daius, a friend and lord of a vampire clan, brutal and vicious even by immortal standards. Anyone who possessed one of the jewels came under the protection of the warlord and his followers. Few would dare harm her or her family as long as she possessed the stone.

"The gem is magical and will protect you and your family. Whenever you are afraid, show the monsters this and they will flee from you. Keep it safe Carrie Ann and remember, this will be our secret, ok?"

The little girl nodded and smiled. Adalius leaned down and placed a kiss on her forehead.

"Sleep now, Carrie Ann and be at peace. "He gently tucked the child into bed where she fell into immediate slumber. In the blink of an eye, he was gone.

*****

The bedroom door opened. The parents had come to check in on their child. "I could have sworn I heard her talking to someone," whispered her mother.

"You never had imaginary friends? Come to bed honey, she's fine. "The husband gently took his wife's hand and closed the door behind them.

*****

Adalius continued his dash across the rooftops. The city was alive with the sounds of residents carrying on with their lives, unaware of the invisible hunter above them. He leaped the distance with ease from one apartment building to the next, reaching out in all directions with his mind. He caught wind of something familiar. Stopping in his tracks, he lifted his head, his nose sampling the air. It was coming from two streets over.

He blurred, landing on the roof where the scent was the strongest. One of the windows on the fourth floor is where it seemed to originate. He climbed down like a spider, gathered himself then slipped inside.

Sweeping the curtain aside, he drew a pistol from one of his shoulder holsters, a Glock 31, his favorite hand gun. High muzzle velocity, superior precision, and Magnum like stopping power when loaded with silver bullets, was just what the doctor ordered when hunting Lycan or vampires. He never left home without them.

Leveling his weapon, he scanned the room. He breathed in a sample of the air. There were two bodies in the apartment, both human, both dead, along with the fading scent of two, perhaps three vampires. He paused. There was something...familiar in what he detected. Curious.

He followed his nose past the couch and end table, toward the apartment's front door. On the floor, beneath what he assumed was a family portrait, was the first body. The adult male from the photograph.

*Bad Boys* blasted from the television speakers as he observed the male's lifeless eyes. The tang of blood that sang out to him on the breeze and drew him to this place belonged not the dead male but to the vampire who attempted to sire him. He might have risen soon if not for the gaping hole in his torso displaying an empty chest cavity. His heart was gone. Not a good sign, for more than one reason.

He didn't need to see the other body to know it too had received similar treatment. Things had become complicated. It was the last thing he wanted or needed. There was at least one other player seated at this game table, perhaps themselves hunting Anna. Adalius scowled and headed down the hallway, his trench coat flowing open to reveal a bare, powerful chest, and toned abs. Passing the kitchen, he noted a table set for two and a pot of food on the stove. He continued down the corridor, making not a sound nor even disturbing the air until he came to the first of four doors.

The smell of fresh blood had begun to saturate the stagnant air, causing his fangs to extend involuntarily. He forced them back in place as he pushed the door open. Leading with his weapon, he stepped inside. The room was somewhat unkempt with clothes strewn about. The bed sat unmade with its headboard pushed against the wall to his left. A small dresser with an oval mirror and a wardrobe occupied the space on the opposite wall. This was the parent's room. He left, continuing down the hall.

The bathroom is what he found next. A shaggy oval shaped rug lay at the foot of the tub with a young male's clothes in a pile on top. A freshly used towel hung over the lip. He continued his probe of the residence. The last room was just ahead of him. The stench became more pronounced. The body of the mother or her offspring lay beyond.

Gripping the door handle, Adalius turned it slowly then threw open the door. It was dark and still inside. Glock leading the way, he entered. He didn't sense danger but experience had long since taught him that just because he couldn't feel a presence door didn't always mean one wasn't there. He flipped it on the light switch, instant illumination. Sports memorabilia and posters peppered the walls. Assorted balls, bats and gloves were stored in a large box in a far corner.

Adalius seethed as he saw the lifeless body. It was the mortal child from the portrait. He lay supine on a twin bed, his arms stretched out. His head was turned to expose his jugular. Blood oozed from two holes in his throat. As expected, the young's chest had been opened up, his heart removed. Anna and her followers, for whatever reason, left them behind to go through the transition alone. Someone clearly had other ideas.

One question still remained. Where was the female who completed this family? There were two possibilities. Either she was one of the vampires who committed the attacks or she was taken from the apartment by force to serve as a meal for later.

"Butchers of children, I will end your madness," he snarled. Adalius turned and went back the way he came. As he returned to the living room, he slid his gun back into its holster. He would hunt Anna and her lackeys down and rescue the female, assuming she was still alive and human. If not... Unfortunately, he might now have to contend with whoever removed those hearts.

If they got in the way, he would remove them, if possible, without killing them. Anna was his and he would have her. Anyone standing in the way of his right to revenge would not be tolerated, but first, he had to sound an alarm. The immortals of this city needed to know the Destroyer was back in their midst. *Time to pay a visit or two on some old friends.* He started toward the window when he heard a knock at the front door.

"Mr. Pearce, it's Edna."

The knocking continued as he wrapped himself in shadows and glided out of the window. He could have dazzled Edna into leaving but the victims needed to be found. They deserved a proper burial. This, of course, would create yet another concern. With the discovery of the bodies, mortal law enforcement would become involved. A matter best left to the Drayken. He was nearly a block away when he heard the scream. Edna had found Mr. Pearce.

# CHAPTER NINETEEN

It was a large, unassuming, black brick, windowless structure with no identifying marks or signs. Located in the warehouse district of the city, away from prying eyes, Club Détente was a nightclub that strictly catered to immortals. It was the brainchild of its owner-operator, Kiel, son of the Lycan King, Marseth, the albino. It sat on a plot of land that was once occupied by two warehouses. Kiel had purchased the land, dozed the property, and constructed his dream, paving it with asphalt and sweat.

Kyle crisscrossed the city searching for the club and now, thanks to a helpful succubus, had finally arrived.

"Not much to look at is it?" Kyle said aloud as he touched down, giving the building a once over. "Oh well, I've come this far, may as well have a swallow or two." As he started forward, he noticed the set of five steel doors that led inside. He made his way through the center entrance, which was propped open and was greeted by the club's doorman.

He was half a head shorter than Kyle and sharp in his brilliant red, pinstriped suit, matching tie, and white dress shirt. Everything about him, including his alligator shoes and slicked back hair whispered jazzy cool. From his scent, the spiffy dressed gent was Lycan. As he reached into his pocket for cover charge, the Lycan looked him over shaking his head.

"What is it with vampires and leather, anyway?"

Kyle chuckled. "It's really quite simple, mate. Leather makes us look stunningly hot. Makes the curves nice and randy, ya know."

The doorman nodded, stroking his chin. "Really? Hmmm, there's a leather shop down on Sixth Street. Maybe I'll head down and make an investment."

"Do it, mate. On mum's headstone, you won't regret it."

"I think, I will. In the pursuit of booty, a player must adapt or go the way of the dodo."

Kyle smirked. "You must be Taine."

The Lycan beamed. "The one, the only, the wolf, the legend. Fall down and worship me mutha fucka. Taine flashed his pearly whites.

Kyle laughed out loud. "I knew it. I've heard a lot about you, mate. Not all of it flattering, I'm afraid."

"I'm not surprised. Ignore all that bad press, they just hate me cause I'm beautiful. You must be new, never seen you around before."

"Just blew into town, actually. Heard some nice things about your little establishment so, here I am."

Taine offered his hand. Kyle regarded the Lycan then accepted. "Well, welcome to Club Détente, my blood suckin brutha. For your enjoyment, we serve only the finest and freshest blood and plasma."

"Sounds delish, just what a bloke needs about now."

Taine nodded to a waitress passing by. "So, what's ya name, vamp, if I may ask?"

"Just call me Kyle"

"Well Kyle, for a vamp, you seem pretty cool. We get a lot of blood suckers comin' in here wit they nose so far in the air, it's a wonder they can see where the fuck they goin'."

Kyle nodded in agreement. "I know the type. Arrogant sods. If it was up to me, I'd stake the whole bleeding lot of them."

"Preach it, reverend!"

Kyle's expression hardened. "I hate vampires."

Taine blinked. "Ummm, Kyle, aren't you a vampire?"

"Don't bloody remind me."

Taine cocked an eyebrow. "What did those mutha fuckas do to you?"

"A vampire, a particularly depraved bastard named Bartholomew…."

Taine looked like he'd just drank sour milk.

"I see you've heard of him."

"Hell yeah, I heard of that low life son of bitch. Liked to get his rocks off torturing, screwing, and pimping kids. We served free drinks for two straight days when we found out somebody dusted his sick ass."

"Well, back in 1871, he put the snatch on my son. I never bloody believed in such things, until..." His voice broke.

Taine waited as he composed himself.

"The shock was just too much for his mum, she died in my arms. After she was laid to rest, I went looking for Bartholomew and my son, hunting and staking vampires whenever I found them. In the beginning, I was sloppy. It almost got my bloody noodle taken off, but eventually, I got good at it. Too good, perhaps. My name started circulating in all the wrong places. Wasn't long before I found myself ambushed by an immortal with a rather twisted sense of humor. Just for giggles, she turned me. The sow turned me into what I hated most."

Taine wasn't amused. "The dirty bitch."

"Too right, if it wasn't for the need to find my son, I would have staked myself and ended it all."

"Did you ever find him?"

Kyle swallowed. "I did. Took decades but I found him slaughtering an entire family. Not because he needed to feed but because he loved killing."

Taine shook his head.

"I saw the look in his eyes, Taine. He'd kill again and again, just to relive the thrill. I had to stop him, so, I took this and...."

Taine laid a hand on his shoulder. "Damn."

Kyle choked back a sob. "A huge part of me died with him that day. "Tears stung his eyes, his hands clenched into fists. "Needless to say, I went looking for Bartholomew. When I heard someone beat me to him. I didn't know whether to dance a bloody jig or throw a chair."

"I'm sorry, Kyle."

Kyle's eyes flared an angry red. "It should have been me who killed that..."He wrestled his emotions back under control. "You know, I never told anyone that story, you must be a trustworthy bloke."

Taine waved off the compliment. "You'd be surprised how often people tell me their life stories, must be my debonair demeanor and dazzling smile."

Kyle chuckled. "And let's not forget your supreme modesty, mate. I must say, it was a pleasure meeting you, Taine. Let's get together sometime soon. "After paying the cover charge, Kyle turned to leave.

"Hey, Kyle." As he turned, the Lycan tossed him a poker chip. "When you get inside ask for Tracy and give her that."

"That I will, mate, thank you. "Kyle made his way across the plush red carpet, up the steps, through a set of sound proof doors and into the dance floor area. Once inside, he was amazed to find that the place was so much bigger than it appeared on the outside.

The dance floor was filled to capacity as Kyle wound his way deeper into the masses, weaving in and out of the crowd. The lights were dimmed and the air was spiced with a musky bouquet of liquor, sweat, lust, and sex. In a far corner to his right, a Lycan couple, near the bar, were locked in vigorous coupling while a nearby emotion vampire fed on the pleasure shared by the lovers. Finally, he spotted a server and waved to get her attention.

She smiled warmly as she approached. "What can I get for you, sir?"

Kyle fished in his pocket for the poker chip. "Actually, I was looking for Tracy."

"Well, you found her, sugar, what can I do for you?"

He passed her the chip. "Taine said I was to give you this."

Tracy took the chip and placed it in her apron. "What would you like to order, baby?"

"Double A-positive, if you'd be so kind, love."

Tracy beamed. "Comin' right up, baby, be right back."

Kyle eyed her as she walked off. What a set of gams Tracy had. He'd have to try and sweet talk her out of her phone number. Kyle continued to scan the room as the beat from the speakers slammed into him. Off to his left, two shape shifters mated in a corner. Locked in a mad embrace, the couple cried out in sweet agony as their forms began to flow together. Soon, they'd be a single pulsating mass. It would be days before their mating reached its climax.

The crowd moved in time with the music as fog machines came to life and sent billowing clouds that enveloped the gyrating party goers. Across the dance floor, in the booth area, three nude vampires were engaged in a threesome. One of the males reclined back, the female's head bobbing in his lap while the second male, took her from behind.

"Here's your drink, sir. "Tracy had returned with his blood, carefully lifting the tumbler off her tray and handed to Kyle. With drink in hand, Kyle reached into his trench for some cash but Tracy shook her head. "You won't need that, sir. Tonight, all drinks are on the house, courtesy of Taine."

Kyle blinked. "Blimey, are you serious, love?"

Tracy's laugh was bubbly. "Very serious. Enjoy your drink and if you need anything else, just flag me down." Tracy smiled and disappeared into the crowd.

Kyle took a sip of his blood and just like Taine boasted, it was the freshest he ever had, outside a vein. "Hmmmm, I like this place already. "Kyle stood by the dance floor, transfixed. With so many nude and semi nude partiers, the room was electrified with erotic energy. Everything he'd heard about Club Détente, was true. It was indeed an oasis for immortals. It was also a golden opportunity. With all the vampires here, he was bound to dredge up some intel on Anna.

As he took in the spectacle, a stunning, curvaceous redhead strolled up to him. She had the most extraordinary smile and was completely nude. Her aura enveloped him as she wrapped her arms around his neck. Her kiss was passionate, fiery. Taking his hand, she led him toward one of the booths. He certainly wasn't going to put up a fight. *What the hell, no reason he can't have a little fun while working*. Club Détente, a great place to party and his new favorite place to play.

# CHAPTER TWENTY

A cold tongue on his neck was the first thing Neal became aware of, then the realization that he was flat on his back as he continued the slow climb back to the land of consciousness. That licking was becoming damned annoying. He tried to batting away the licker but found his arms restrained over his head. He was helpless as the bothersome tongue kept at its business.

Finally, his head checked in and brought with it a sumo sized headache. *What the hell happened? Oh yeah, some asshole cracked him on the melon with a rifle butt.* A feminine sigh in his ear drew his attention back to the licking at his neck. He opened his eyes in spite of the pain of doing so and looked upon the woman attached to that nuisance of a tongue.

The brunette eyed him suggestively as she continued with the lapping action. From the coolness of her body pressed against him, she was a vamp. It set his blood a boil as he realized the blood sucker was tasting him.

"Would you please take your cold, nasty tongue off me?"

The brunette simply smiled and continued.

"Get the fuck off me! "He tried to rise but found his legs were also chained to the table he was lying on. He struggled. The chains held fast.

"You not going anywhere sugar, so you may as well get comfortable," the she vamp purred.

"Who the fuck are you?'

The vampire's eyes glittered. "You can call me, Jewel, baby, and I must say you look and taste delicious. "Her peepers flashed brilliant green as her fangs grew right in front of him.

*Hell's bells*! He'd seen that look before. She was in bloodlust. If she latched onto his vein, now, she wouldn't raise up till he was sucked dry. He yanked on the chains but there was no give whatsoever. She smiled without pity and leaned in. She opened wide preparing to strike. Fuck. Only one manly thing left to do, "HEY! SOMEBODY! SOMEBODY, HELP!"

The she-vamp grasped his head, turning it to expose the jugular. The door across the room blasted open. A dark skinned vampire charged through the doorway. In a blur, he streaked to the table, grabbed her by the hair, and slapped her to the floor.

"Bitch, I *said* not to touch him." His fangs extended as he glared at her "Get outta here before I break some wood off in yo ass!"

The Nubian vamp pulled her to her feet, shoved her out the door, closed and locked it behind her. With that done, he turned, grabbed a nearby chair and made his way over to Neal. He set it near the table, took a seat, and put his feet up. The new arrival studied Neal and grinned.

"Sorry bout that, she a good girl, generally, she just needs a smack upside the head from time to time. I'm Mace, and from checking out your little basket of goodies, you a mutha fuckin' slayer, ain't that grand. So, what's ya name, slayer?" Neal remained silent. "Figures you'd wanna be a hard ass about this. Fine, we'll do this my way. "Mace shut his eyes. Neal felt a pressure against his temples. The bastard was in his head.

"Nice to meet ya, Neal. Looks like you're a lone wolf. Won't be long before yo peeps come lookin' for you, though. Beautiful." Mace shook his head and smiled. "This fine fucked up situation is brought to you by Victor, dumb ass extraordinaire. Well, enough about his ass, I'm sure you're much more interested in what we're planning to do with you. Damn good question. First of all, the only reason yo ass still breathing is because we needed to know whether you working alone or not. Plus, whether you live or die is not my call to make. That's on the higher ups."

The strong silent routine was getting him nowhere. Neal needed answers and being a mute tough guy wasn't going to get them for him. "What is this place?"

Mace feigned shock. "Oh shit, it speaks. *This* place, slayer, is our up and growing enterprise. This, believe it or not, is a blood farm." Mace smiled at the question written all over the slayer's face. "I can see you have no idea what I'm talking about. Allow me to explain. For whatever reason, drugs have no effect on immortals, unless it's absorbed through the blood of our prey. Follow me? So, if an immortal wanted to get their buzz on from a certain drug, he'd have to locate and feed on a mortal who had ingested their drug of choice. We eliminate the need to search."

Neal laughed. "You're drug dealers? You gotta be shittin' me."

"Oh, I shit you not. There's cash to be made and we gonna make it. Many of us ain't feelin' the hangin' out in drafty old castles and moldy, damp ass caves. The old heads can have that shit. We been watchin' the mortal game on the drug selling tip. We want in on all of it, the lifestyle, the bling, the women, and slingin' blood bags is how we gonna do it. We gonna have a foothold on the immortal market and we whittling down the competition for the mortal dollar. Pretty soon, we gonna be sweatin' money."

He wasn't sure he wanted to know but best to keep this vamp talking. "Those people I saw giving blood?"

"I'm glad you asked. We've gathered junkies off the streets and made them an offer. We provide all the drugs they want, free of charge. In exchange, they make a blood donation to our little enterprise."

Neal balled his fists so tight his knuckles cracked. "In other words, you've kidnapped these people, holding them hostage while you bleed them dry!" Neal spat.

Mace's voice softened as if he were addressing a toddler. "Nah, nothing like that, everybody involved in this can leave whenever they want. After we do a memory wipe, of course. We take good care of them. Dead bodies don't produce blood so it don't profit us to bleed them out. We're careful about what we take and when we take it."

Neal was incensed. What kind of mad house did he fall into? "Fuckin' lyin' vamp."

"If I'm lyin', I'm dyin', slayer. They can walk they asses outta here, right now. There ain't no fences around, if they want, they could be in the wind. But they stay because, unlike the mortal world, we take care of them."

"Bullshit, you mother fuckers keep them strung out so you can milk them and get your party on."

"Chill slayer, everybody gets something outta this arrangement. Since they've come on board with us, they've gotten the best medical care they've ever had in their lives. Most of them have never even been seen by a doctor before now. They get three squares, their own space and a place to lay their heads at night without getting rousted by the Po Po, but to stay, they have to follow certain guidelines."

Neal rolled his eyes "Such as..?"

"If they wanna ride the white horse, they got to shower, shave and eat. They wanna hit the pipe, then they have to brush their teeth, wash and comb their hair. They want a hit of the chronic, then they have to clean their rooms and get a workout in. *They* are our product and as such, they'll be treated like royalty. We plan to distribute only the best. To do that, we need healthy donors. All they have to do to is give us some of their blood in exchange. We win, they win."

Neal expression soured.

"I know what you thinking, slayer. You wanna look down yo long self-righteous nose at what we're doing. But what does the mortal world offer them besides life out on the streets with nowhere to go and nobody who gives a shit about them, huh? Tell me, mister slayer man?"

Neal had no answer.

"That's what I thought. "Mace slipped out his cell phone. "Well, time to find out what hand life has dealt you. If you lucky, they'll just tell me to shoot yo ass. If they leave it up to me though…mmmmmm, I could use a bite. "Mace hit the speed dial and waited. "Padre, what up playa….S'all good here….nope, but guess what *we* caught tonight."

# CHAPTER TWENTY ONE

Flashbulbs popped as the police forensic team combed the Pearce residence taking fingerprints, hair samples, and anything not nailed down as they collected evidence from the apartment. The body of Logan Pearce was discovered by the building superintendent's' wife who'd come upstairs to check on the father and son. She said she knocked on the apartment door and grew concerned when she got no response. When she used her master key and entered the apartment, the scream she let out was heard throughout the entire building and the next.

The evidence collection continued as Detective Richardson ducked underneath the crime scene tape. He'd been off duty for about an hour and had just stepped out of the shower when he got the call from dispatch.

Richardson noted the body being examined by one of the several NCCSI members. As he got a closer look, his heart sank. It was Logan Pearce, the same man who had come to the station over a week ago, pleading for help to find his missing wife. Now he knew why the address sounded familiar.

Directly ahead of him, seated on the couch, was an elderly woman being interviewed by Arnie and Anita. Arnie waved him over. He got to his feet and walked to meet him as the female detective continued the interview. Arnie looked him up and down and shook his head. "Dallas Cowboys jersey? Say it ain't so."

Richardson smiled. "Super Bowl bound, you just wait."

"Got three words for ya, junior. New York Giants." Arnie got back to business as he moved over to where Logan's lifeless body laid. "We got two VIC's. The other is a nine year old male found in a back bedroom. Did ya catch the name on the way over? It's the family of the missing woman."

"Yeah, I saw Mr. Pearce when I came in. Could this be connected to the McClain Park murders?"

Arnie scowled. "No idea, with the exception of the chest wounds, the MO is nearly identical."

As they talked, the medical examiner strolled up from the hallway. She was medium height with short, curly hair, wire framed glasses and wearing a NCCSI vest.

Richardson nodded to her in greeting. "Don't you ever go home?"

The ME flashed a wry smile. "And good evening to you too, Detective Richardson."

Richardson gave a guilty shrug. "Sorry Rhoda, how are you?"

"I've been better actually. Benjamin's on an anniversary cruise with his wife and of course as soon as he leaves, all hell breaks loose."

Arnie cracked a mirthless smile. "Could be worse, Red. There could be *two* nut cases on the loose."

Rhoda stood near the body, eyeing Logan Pearce. "I should be so lucky. Looks like both father and son died from shock brought on by excessive blood loss, just like the McClain Park victims. The twist here is both VIC's have had their hearts removed. The autopsy will determine if the heart removals were post mortem."

Richardson swallowed hard. "Ouch, you don't think this bastard cut them open while they were still alive?"

Arnie reached into his vest and withdrew a pen. "Yeah, somebody would've heard the screaming right?"

Rhoda met their gaze. "Not necessarily, I once worked a case where a perp immobilized his victims with drugs from a syringe. I'm not saying that's what we have here but…"

Arnie nodded. "Get back to us as soon as you got somethin', Red." Arnie scowled as he looked over the crime scene. As he did so, several techs arrived with gurneys. Rhoda immediately took charge of her crew.

"Load Mr. Pearce carefully, Rick. Johnson, Turner, with me, I'll show you where the other body is." Rhoda escorted the second pair of techs back to where Jason lay dead.

He'd watched Arnie the whole time, keeping his silence. It was counterproductive to break his partner's thought process, best not to disturb the older detective when he started taking his mental inventory of a crime scene. Arnie had an intuition that sometimes bordered on genius.

Arnie sighed out loud as he ran his hand through his hair. He'd concluded his survey.

"You got something Arnie?"

Arnie turned. "Yeah, I think I do, but you're gonna think I'm nuts."

Richardson grinned. "It's long too late for *that* old man. Let's have it."

"Okay, you asked for it. Do you believe in vampires, kid?"

"Vampires?"

"Yeah, vampires. You know, I vant to drink your blood?"

"If you're suggesting that vampires are behind these murders, you're right, I *do* think you're nuts. This is the work of some whack job, Arnie, not some make believe boogeyman."

Arnie held up his hands. "Just hear me out. All our VIC's, including the ones from the murders twelve years ago, have been attacked at night and had all their blood drained away. Little of which has been found near the bodies or crime scenes. They all have two puncture wounds in the neck. After examining our current VIC's, Rhoda thinks they were made by fangs, maybe from some kind of animal."

"Arnie, those punctures could have been made by needles from a syringe."

"Nope, Rhoda says the slight tearing around the wound is not consistent with wounds from a needle."

Richardson's brow furrowed. "Arnie, there is no way you are gonna convince me that a *real* vampire killed these people, the victims from McClain Park, or the people from twelve years ago."

Arnie ran his hand through his hair. "I'm not sure I entirely believe it myself, kid, but it sure looks like *someone* does. Somebody cut the hearts out of these people. I think whoever did, was trying to stop them from becoming vampires."

He wasn't sure what scared him more, that Arnie actually believed all this or that in some nutty way, it was starting to add up. "Come on Arnie."

"Kid, you're gonna find if you do this job long enough, that sometimes what seems like an impossibility is not only a possibility, but a probability."

Richardson threw up his hands. "So should I trade in my weapon for a mallet and wooden stake?"

Arnie glared at him. "Smartass alert, smartass alert."

It did sound nuts, but bloodless bodies were piling up and now someone had started removing the hearts of victims. No, he didn't believe in vampires but maybe he should consider picking up a cross and making a garlic necklace.

*****

It took Trey over an hour to make his way to the medical examiner's office. Many of the roads still remained impassable. That, coupled with the surprisingly high volume of vehicles still on the road, made the trip a much more difficult journey.

Along the way, he passed several city cleanup crews using chainsaws to remove branches, trees, and other debris from the roads while cops diverted traffic safely around the work area. At the last detour, Trey observed workers from the New Carrollton Illuminating Company trying to corral a live wire that sparked and wiggled wildly on the ground. He was more than impressed with how well the crew handled themselves. As far as he was concerned, there wasn't enough money in the entire state that would be enough for him to do their jobs. Fighting vampires was one thing, but fuckin' around with electricity....*that* was dangerous.

When he at last arrived on the 7500th block of Fulton Avenue, he parked his Harley, removed his duffle bag which contained his equipment from the luggage rack, and walked the remaining block to his destination. Once there, he hid among the shrubs near the ambulance entrance watching and waiting for an opportunity to enter the building, preferably without witnesses.

Carefully, he gave the building a once over and noted the positions of all the security cameras, located around the building, including the one which monitored the double doors where the paramedics brought in the new arrivals. As an ambulance pulled in, he crouched into the shadows while two paramedics got out and unloaded a gurney on which laid a body zipped in a bag. He could hear the men talking as they rolled the casualty through the double doors. It seemed someone had doused the poor bastard with gasoline and lit him up like a Roman candle.

"Damn and I thought vampires were vicious," Trey said aloud to himself. He checked his watch. It was getting late, time to lock and load. If the bodies from the McClain Park murders were indeed killed by vampires, it wouldn't be much longer before they'd rise.

Reaching into his duffle bag, Trey removed his babies. The twin Browning SW1911 pistols had served him well during his hunts. They would serve him well again. He slipped several of his electro-darts into to his jacket pockets and loaded a magazine of wooden bullets into each gun.

He preferred silver bullets of course, but wooden bullets were nearly as effective in dealing with vamps. The darts were a product of Maya's pet mad inventor and were surprisingly effective in slowing down vampires. Each dart packed nearly the juice of a stun gun. Neck muncher or not, their muscles tended to react to electricity the same as human muscles. One dart would be enough to slow a fang down enough to escape or buy the time needed to put him down for good. He was armed and ready to go. All he needed now was an opportunity.

# CHAPTER TWENTY TWO

Rhoda sat hunched at her desk, typing out reports, in an office she affectionately nicknamed the coffin. The space had only enough room for her desk, a couple of filing cabinets, a fax machine, a chair, her radio, and her. What a week. With her boss on vacation, she'd put in some major overtime.

Just her dumb luck a serial killer would pop up and make a five body deposit in addition to Mother Nature's three from the nursing home that terrible storm set on fire. And let's not forget the assembly line of bodies coming in from the ongoing gang war. But it wasn't the body count that had her anxiety on the rise. She'd finished the autopsies for three of the five victims of the McClain park murders and the facts were becoming more and more...unsettling.

Vampires.

The word kept popping into her head. No matter how many times she dismissed it, it came back like some stubborn boomerang. She'd seen so many vamp movies over the years; it felt like she was practically an authority on the subject. And she wasn't the only one who was starting to connect the dots. She hadn't forgotten the stories Arnie told her about the bodies turning up twelve years ago. They too were missing their blood.

She'd seen the look in the detective's eyes when she told him about the neck wounds. He was thinking the same thing, whether he admitted it or not. But it was ridiculous. Those poor people couldn't have been killed by a vampire. It *had* to be some sick mind who just thought he was a vampire. That had to be it. *Vampires weren't real. Right?*

The problem was they were now finding bloodless bodies with their hearts removed. Rhoda blew out a breath, and removed her glasses. Rubbing the bridge of her nose, she laid them on the desk.

Bang!

She nearly leaped out of her chair. It was one of the metal lockers outside her office door being slammed shut. "I'm going out for lunch, Rhodie, you want me to bring you back something?"

Rhoda looked up at the young male standing in her doorway. Leo was the best intern she'd seen come down the pike in a long time. Had a helluva nice ass too, not that she'd noticed. "Hey Leo, bring me back a large mocha latte." She smiled cheerfully.

"You got it, be back in a few."

Rhoda watched him go with a lewd eye. Even through his scrubs, she could see he had body that should be bronzed and displayed in a museum of art. He had such a cute baby face that she often found herself caught between the compulsion to feed him milk and cookies and the desire to throw him across her desk and screw his brains out.

Bang!

Rhoda blew out an annoyed breath. She actually jumped again. That's it, no more expressos. "Leo, do you think you could make a little more noise?"

The intern stuck his head in and grinned guiltily. "Sorry." He quickly ducked back out, then tripped and fell as he made his way toward the exit. Sexy as hell, sharp as a razor, with all the gracefulness of an elephant, how could he be so skillful with a scalpel and so awkward with his feet?

Rhoda replaced her glasses and continued typing. The reports needed to be complete before the next shift arrived. There were still two bodies left to autopsy from McClain Park, a Latino male and a black female. Normally, they'd all be done by now but it had been a busy week. The Dragons/ Vice Lords turf war was escalating. The violence and waste of life sickened her but what the hell, it was job security at least. *Ha ha.* Just couldn't beat gallows humor.

Bang!

"Damnit Leo, what are you doing out there?" *What the hell was he doing anyway?*

Bang! Bang!

Rhoda groaned, sat back in her chair and listened. Silence. Suddenly the sound of a crash and glass breaking rang out.

"Leo, for Heaven's sake." Rhoda rose from her chair headed out into the hall. She walked past Benjamin's office to the stainless steel door of the lab. She opened the door. Half the overhead lights were out. She hesitated, looking about the empty room. Goosebumps chorus lined up her arms.

"Leo, are you alright?" No response. She cautiously walked toward the center table. Broken glass and solutions scattered on the floor. No blood on the tile. At least he didn't hurt himself.

"Leo?" Anxiety tightened her chest. Strange. Other than the broken glass, you wouldn't have known anyone had been there and yet.

*"Rhoda."* A whisper.

Rhoda snapped her head around. No one there. Now she was hearing things. *Served her right with all the vampire crap.* This had to stop, she was scaring herself. She went to flip on the remaining lights. What in...the door leading to the refrigeration units was open.

A prickly sensation danced across her skin. A chill ran down her spine and it wasn't because of the air conditioning. Her chest tightened with every step she took toward the doorway. She was trembling. It was getting hard to breathe. Jesus, she was working up to a panic attack. It was all she could do not to run screaming to the exit. But she couldn't leave, Leo may be hurt. She had to find him.

Rhoda made her way through the open door. Silence rang in her ears. It was always quiet in the lab, but there was now something different about the stillness now. She took a deep breath, trying to settle her nerves. Nothing seemed out of place. The autoclaves to her right were open, standing by for use as usual. Everything was as it should be and yet... one of the refrigeration units was open. What happened to the body?

"What the hell?" Rhoda made her way to the open drawer and slid it back into place. "Leo, I swear, if this is some bull shit prank..."

Rhoda whirled about. Her heart hammered in her chest. Someone blew in her ear! Her breaths came in pants. She snapped her head to and fro, backing against the wall. Something... was in the room with her.

*There*. In the far corner, two red, blazing orbs. *Sweet holy mother, they're eyes!*

They started toward her. She shook her head, her eyes wide, her mouth hung open. The eyes stopped. They hovered, watching her, staring. She gazed back, unable to look away. She sucked in breath to scream. Nothing came out. She passed the eyes to the door. She had to get out of there. They moved between her and the exit, as if they knew what she was thinking. Rhoda blinked. A line took shape around the eyes. Substance filled in the lines. It was male. He was tall and lean yet muscular, black hair tied in a ponytail. He wore a gold silk shirt, completely unbuttoned, partially obscuring a smooth chest and washboard abs. A diamond shaped pendant hung around his neck, a crimson jewel at its heart. Black jeans and stylish loafers completed his ensemble.

Rhoda stared in disbelief. The figure came toward her. She screamed. Louder than she'd ever in her life. With impossible speed, the fair skinned figure was upon her, grabbing her by the throat. His smile was cruel.

She struggled. He laughed and flung her across the room. Landing hard on her side, she slid into the counter jarring her glasses from her face. Dazed and in pain, she saw the red eyed attacker closing in. Her scream tore through the air as the figure grabbed her by her neck and arm, jerked her to her feet and forced her against the wall.

"I simply came for my siblings but since you've kindly offered yourself, I accept," It said, its voice soft and laced with menace. The monster leaned in and opened wide displaying dagger like fangs.

Rhoda's eyes widened in horror. *Vampire! It's a nightmare. She was sleeping in her bed at home. So, why wasn't she waking up?* On instinct, she reached into her lab coat, palmed and withdrew the scalpel therein. In one motion slashed the vampire's hand. The creature howled as Rhoda drove an adrenaline powered knee into his groin. His hold loosened, she broke free and ran. Before she was away, the vampire grabbed her ankle. She crashed in a heap.

"You little bitch. I'm going to enjoy ripping your throat out. "The blood made his grip slick but he held firm as he dragged her toward him.

Rhoda desperately sliced the hand more deeply, causing the creature to release his hold. She sprang to her feet and ran screaming from the room. She was almost to the lab door when another figure materialized, blocking her escape. *No fuckin' way!* It was the black female that had been lying in her morgue the past few days.

Her eyes glowed a sunny yellow as she smiled, displaying two lethal looking fangs. Rhoda came to a screeching halt. She backed slowly away. A hiss behind her, Rhoda turned about. Her original attacker, his wounds were closing fast.

The male addressed the snarling female. "You're going through blood lust. I was afraid we were going have to search you out a meal but, low and behold..."

The female growled. Rhoda moved to keep the table between her and the vampires. In a blur, the female dashed around the table and tackled her to the floor.

The male smiled in approval. "*Very* good, I didn't need to teach you that. Now, feed but save a little for me." Rhoda tussled with the she-vampire while the male looked on. She was overmatched. The creature was much stronger, it pinned her arms down. The creature opened wide and struck. Rhoda shut her eyes and wailed as the fangs pierced her flesh. Fiery pain was quickly overtaken by a strange euphoria. The thing moaned in delight.

As the thing sealed its mouth over her wounds, the lab door burst open. A tough looking man in a leather jacket entered, flung something at the male, and fired a shot from the pistol in his hand. The she vamp never stopped. It was draining her, swallowing down her life. She was cold, going into shock. A tear rolled down her cheek. Help had arrived but she'd never get the chance to say thank you.

# CHAPTER TWENTY THREE

The instant the surveillance camera panned away from his direction, Trey made his move. He'd watched a guy in medical scrubs get into his car and drive away. *One less pair of eyes to worry about. Happy dance.*

As he approached the ambulance entrance he noted yet another camera aimed at the doorway. *Better make sure to take all the security discs before he left. Wouldn't want to end up being New Carrollton's most wanted by day break.*

Trey made his way through the automatic doors that opened with a hum. Cool air rushed up to greet him like a long lost love. Just beyond to his right was the guard booth. Empty. Good, no one was watching the monitor. Most likely the officer on duty was either on patrol or on break. Hot damn, he was on a roll. Hearing the door close from within the booth, Trey ducked down then peered carefully around the door jam.

The guard was facing away from him making an entry in a large binder. All of five seven and a hundred thirty pounds, if you added twenty pounds of rocks in his pockets. He looked like a blonde Q-tip. *This* was the security guy? Really? Mofo didn't look like he could punch his way out of a wet paper bag. Okay, maybe he was stronger than he looked. Whatever, sonny boy was about to get a nap.

The guard returned the binder to its place as Trey slipped in behind him. Quickly, the slayer wrapped his forearm around the throat of the guard and applied a choke hold. Startled, the guard pulled at Trey's muscled arm trying to dislodge it. Trey tightened the hold, shutting off his air intake. A quick tug took the human matchstick to the floor.

Skinny bastard *was* stronger than he looked. He almost broke loose. Almost.

He bore down on the carotid artery until twigman's thrashing ceased. He lay silent. Trey released him. "Sorry, slick, if there was any other way, I would have done it." He disarmed the subdued guard and dragged him into a back room.

After disabling the security cameras and taking the DVR unit, he placed it in his duffel bag and started down the hallway, moving deeper into the building. The halls were well lighted, the floor sported a coat of fresh wax, the smell of chemicals hung in the air, and not a soul in sight. It was never a bad thing to move unobserved but something was wrong. It was *way* too quiet in here. Even at this hour, shouldn't there be some kind of foot traffic in a building this size?

Stopping outside a doorway marked 'Lounge', he paused, listening for the sound of voices. Not a beep. Stepping into the entryway he froze as he came face to faces with the evening shift, a baker's dozen of them. Nobody moved. Literally.

It was like looking at a 3D photograph, the bodies were all frozen in time. A security guard caught in mid stride, with bottle of Coke in hand, was directly in front of him. Beyond him, people were scattered about. Some sat at café style tables with food purchased from the vending machines. A cluster of three stood together, near a dollar changer, their conversation interrupted, while another stood in a line, three deep waiting his turn to make his dinner selection. Every motionless one of them wore the same blank expression. They'd been dazzled. *Damn, everything goes to hell from here, doesn't it?*

A woman's scream echoed from down the hall. "Why am I only right when I don't wanna be?"

Trey raced toward the sound of the voice, as he reached the lab door, he heard a struggle going on inside. He dropped his bag and burst inside, drawing a dart and his pistol.

He identified a male vampire to his left and a female attacking a woman on the floor. The electro dart was airborne in a split second striking its target, the voltage sending the creature's body into a macabre electric boogaloo. The follow up wooden bullet fired from Trey's gun pierced the vamp's heart. The male crumbled to dust as he hit the floor.

The slayer whirled on the second blood sucker but the she vamp, already on her feet, knocked the gun from his hand then spun and delivered a roundhouse kick to the side of his face. The slayer hit the wall, rattling every bone in his body and driving the air from his lungs.

His cheek felt warm from the swelling and a galaxy of stars performed a Rockettes chorus line about his head. Trey groaned, forced down a breath of air, and willed his eyes to focus. *Fuck. Me.*

Why did Murphy's Law have such a hard on for him? There had to be a least a million and a half people in a city the size of New Carrollton. Out of all those locals, these ass holes turned an extra from Kung Fu theater.

The coroner was bleeding badly from a neck wound. She wouldn't last much longer. She needed medical attention. Stat.

*Focus!*

Trey forced the rising empathy back where it came from. He had to disconnect from his feelings for the coroner and concentrate on the danger at hand or they were both dead. The female vamp moved in to continue her assault, her eyes sparkling like jewels.

"All this power, strength, speed, I am gonna love being a vampire." She smiled displaying a lethal looking pair of canines.

Trey snorted. "Don't get used to it, you won't be around much longer."

The vampire smirked and lunged, firing a right hand intended for his still throbbing cheek. Trey deflected the strike and launched a right hand of his own. The blow caught her on the side of her head. He threw a second punch, but she blocked it, grabbed hold of his arm then hip tossed him to the floor. He sprang to his feet in time to deflect another round house kick then drove his fist into her face.

As she staggered back, Trey went low and took her down with a leg sweep. They rose, facing each other, circling.

The vamp spit blood from her mouth and smiled. "You hit like a girl."

"Maybe I need practice, slide your face back over here."

She blurred and threw a side kick catching him in the sternum. It sent him skimming backward across the floor. Wetness soaked into his jeans. Momentum had driven him into the blood of the injured coroner.

Before he came to a complete stop, she was on him. Straddling his chest, she backhanded him with such force that his head threatened to divorce his body.

"I'm going to tear your heart open!" The vamp's fangs lengthened in front of him. *Marvelous, the scent of fresh blood was sending her into blood lust. His luck was in rare form tonight.*

Another backhand, this one more violent than the first, it sent spit flying from his mouth. The world spun faster or was it his head? Damn, his IQ dropped every time she connected. Had to end this fast or he'd die a battered moron. Blood seeped into his mouth from his gashed lip. She was on top and as a vampire, was far superior in strength. He had her right where he wanted her.

Taking hold of his head, she turned it to expose his jugular. Her fangs extending even further as the smell of his blood poured into her nostrils. Saliva dripped on his skin, her eyes locked on his vein. *Now or never.* He reached for it. It was in his jeans pocket. Trey tugged. It was pinned underneath him and stuck in his pocket. *Are you kidding me, come out of there, this bitch is hungry.*

Panic tried to slither into his mind but he was his father's son, the son of a slayer. He wouldn't give into fear and he most certainly wouldn't give in to this damned blood sucker. As she was prepared to strike, her weight shifted. An opening. He rolled to his side, taking her with him but her grip was like iron. She held on tight, wrapping her legs around his waist.

He gagged as the vampire shifted her hands to his throat, closing off his wind pipe. But now his ace in the hole wasn't trapped underneath him. All he had to do was…the female leaned in, trying to make eye contact. Trey averted his eyes. If she laid her dazzle mojo on him, it was a done deal. The vamp hissed, frustrated that her meal wasn't being cooperative. Poor baby.

She lunged for a bite. He was so waiting for that. He drove his own head into the bridge of her nose. The crunching sound made bile to rise in his throat. It rendered the desired result though. She recoiled, her head snapping back, blood seeping from an open gash as she fell back. In one motion, he yanked the atropine injector free from his pocket. He'd taken to filling them with his own special cocktail. She was gonna love this.

Not.

The she-vamp roared as he slapped the injector into her thigh. She leaped off him like she'd been burned with fire. Her eyes were wide eyed, body trembling.

Trey winked. "Silver Nitrate. Kills werewolves and it's a bitch to vampires too."

She screamed as the solution began to burn from within. Her skin blistered and smoke rose from her body as she fell to the floor writhing in agony. Trey felt sorry for her. She didn't ask to be turned into a vampire, but she was enjoying her situation entirely too much. She would have killed again without conscience or mercy. She had to be put down.

The vampire contorted. Her body sizzled. The horrid stench of burning flesh tainted the air. With a gasp, she crumbled to dust at his feet.

"Hi ho silver," Trey said as he got gingerly to his feet. He took mental inventory of his injuries. No broken bones, a few lacerations, and a swelling cheek. A few hours sleep, a bottle or three of Percocet and he'd be good as...pain shot through his neck, new.

No time to lick his wounds though, he had to work fast. The coroner needed an ambulance and he needed a sample of the vamp dust, then he could be away before someone came in and got a look at the carnage and his bloody face.

# CHAPTER TWENTY FOUR

Trish and Marie, wrapped in shadows, made their way arm in arm to Marie's apartment. They had to get back to keeping watch on Logan and Jason. After they had set the two males turning in motion, Trish, who was still hungry, suggested that they went out to hunt and return to watch over the pair later.

They left through the open window in the living room and flew off together in search of prey. They had only flown a few blocks when Trish was attracted to another open window by the musky scent of sex.

There in the bedroom of the apartment, they'd discovered a young couple entangled. They'd entered unnoticed and watched the young lovers' vigorous coupling. Marie sensed Trish reach out with her mind and seized control of the hot blooded pair causing them to separate and position themselves at opposite ends of the bed.

The scent of Trish's arousal had been acute as they moved to join them. They sexed them for hours, satisfying their carnal needs while feeding on their blood.

Trish decided not to turn the pair that night. When the time was right, they would come back for them. They could wait. There was still Marie's husband and son to teach when their turning was complete.

After Trish wiped their minds, they dressed and left by the same window they'd entered, flown down to the street below, and started back on foot. Trish preferred flying but she wanted to walk and hold hands. As they neared the brownstone of the Pearce apartment, they were greeted by the dozen or so flashing lights mounted atop the numerous police cruisers, lining both sides of the street. Trish guided Marie into an alley when they spotted the scene.

"Trish, they're in front of our building. Could someone have found them?" Marie's anxiety grew as they glanced around the building corner at the activity going on. Trish pushed Marie back into the alley. "Wait here, my love, I'll take a look."

"Be careful, Trish." Trish kissed her lips, wrapped herself in shadows, and took to the sky. Marie backed in the alley to wait.

*****

Trish glided up to the window. The curtains were drawn. She hovered closer for a better look. Someone did find Logan and Jason. There were police officers everywhere in the apartment collecting evidence, while an elderly woman was being interviewed by a police detective. Toward the doorway where Logan laid, she saw two males and a female conversing while another officer hovered and worked on Logan's body. That was when Trish noticed the large hole in Logan's chest.

*Goddess*!

A shiver ran down her spine and her heart sank. It was a slayer. A slayer found them. She had to warn the mistress. How could she tell Marie? Her husband and son lost. There would be no comforting her.

It couldn't wait any longer, it was time for Marie to meet the mistress. She'd need them all carry on through the grief. She would be there for her mate, for Marie, always. She loved her and would see to it Marie would never be alone. Trish flew off to rejoin her lover in the alley. When she arrived, she found Marie on her hands and knees sobbing bitterly. She knew.

Trish gently lifted her distraught mate into her arms then rose to her feet. Tears flowed from Marie's eyes like a stream. "I knew, Trish! I felt what you felt," she sobbed. "I knew!" Marie rested her head against Trish's chest and wept.

"I swear to you, my Marie, the slayer who did this will die. I will kill them with my own hands. "She kissed Marie's head, shed a tear, and launched them both into the air.

*****

145

Trish flew about with Marie in her arms. She pressed her face to Trish's bosom until the tears ceased to flow. As they descended, she lifted her head and saw their destination. The faded sign on the roof said, AJAX Textiles Plant. When they touched down, by what was most likely the rear entrance, Trish gently set Marie on her feet. She looked about at the broken and crumbling parking lot with its faded park lines and the severely rusted chain link fence that ran around the perimeter.

"Why have you brought me here, Trish?"

Trish took her hand and kissed it tenderly. "It's time for you to meet our mistress. Now that a slayer has arrived in the city, she needs to be warned." Trish started toward a pair of boarded up doors. Marie followed.

As they approached, one of them opened slowly as if by an unseen hand. Trish opened it with her mind. It was going to take Marie time to get used to the idea that she could do that as well. Trish didn't break stride as she walked across the threshold. Marie followed closely behind. The click of their heels echoed as they made their way down a long, dark corridor. The air was thick and stale. Rats scurried away at their approach. She could hear the flutter of a moth's wings as they continued down the hall.

It amazed Marie how much sharper her senses had become since she was turned. There was no light at all but she could see as well as if someone had aimed a searchlight into the hallway. They took a left at a T-section and made straight for a door at the end of the corridor. Trish paused a moment then gently knocked. "Mistress?"

A feminine voice responded in their minds. "Enter, my children."

Trish opened the door and stepped inside Marie stayed in her wake. To her surprise, the chamber was immaculate, spacious, and bathed in a gentle white light. The walls and ceiling were painted bright crimson and coordinated beautifully with the plush carpeting. Artificial trees, resting in large golden pots, lined the room adding warmth and contrast to the red tapestry. Off to left was a stainless steel commercial refrigerator along with a moderate sized mahogany wood bar, assorted café style tables and chairs, and an unmarked door to the bar's right.

"Come, my children." The voice was seductive and tender as Marie followed her lover deeper into the room. They approached a king sized canopy bed, resting on a four stair, marble platform.

As they reached the foot of the pedestal, Marie took in the contemporary sconces mounted along the walls, flanking life sized portraits of a striking woman dressed in the finest clothes from different eras. Though the hair color, styles, and apparel changed from painting to painting, the eyes, those silver grey eyes, never did. It was the same woman.

"My dear ones, welcome." The spoken words drew her attention back to the bed. A hand pulled back the sheer golden material flowing down from the canopy. Marie's jaw lowered like a drawbridge. It was the woman from all the paintings. She was magnificent, completely nude, and unashamed.

Marie licked her lips at the subtle bounce of her mistress' breasts. Her skin was luminescent, without blemish. Her auburn hair fell loosely about her shoulders and her grey, mesmerizing eyes, sparkled like diamonds.

Nipples erect, perfection smiled as she descended the marble stairs. She could sense Trish's desire and the deity's arousal. Her own nipples puckered. The sudden need to surrender herself for the pleasure of this goddess made Marie's legs tremble.

"Dear Trish." Trish was pulled into a passionate embrace, their lips locked in a fiery kiss. Trish moaned, her arm wrapped around the goddess' waist. Jealousy flared in Marie. Not because her mate delighted in the encounter, but because she, herself, burned to taste the lips pressed to Trish's. The kiss was broken, her chest heaving, Trish turned to Marie.

"Mistress, this is my mate, Marie. Marie, this is our mistress, Anna Longfellow." Trish beamed like a proud parent as Anna smiled. Marie's cheeks flushed as Anna slid her arms around her.

"Welcome, Marie." Marie shuddered as blood rushed to pleasurable places. Even Anna's voice was saturated with sexual energy. Moisture pooled between her legs. She was flowing and all Anna did was hug her. Anna drew Marie against her, crushing their breasts together and kissed her. She slid her tongue past Marie's lips swirled it around hers. She welcomed it. Tingling sensations raced across her body and into her core. Tenderly, Anna broke the kiss, leaving Marie breathless and panting.

As she steadied herself on rubbery legs, another female, wrapped in a towel, entered through a rear door. High cheekbones, her brunette hair in a bob, she started toward them, her movement smooth and sensual. She was still human by her scent. A blood doll, Trish told her about them; humans ready and willing to give up their vein to a vampire, in exchange for the promise of someday being made immortal.

She backed into Anna's embrace. The mistress kissed her slender neck while cupping the woman's breast. Anna's fangs extended. She sank them into supple flesh, eliciting a soft moan from the female.

"Mistress, I have come to warn you, there's a slayer in New Carrollton."

Anna withdrew her fangs, her eyes narrowing. "You are certain of this?"

"Yes, mistress. We'd begun to turn Marie's husband and son and left them for a short time to continue hunting, but someone discovered the bodies and phoned the police. When we saw them, I went to investigate. Her husband's heart had been removed."

Anna brow furrowed in concern. "I expected this, but not so soon."

"Forgive me, mistress, it was because of my carelessness that they were lost to us." Trish lowered her eyes.

Anna regarded Trish affectionately and smiled. "The only crime in making an error is not learning from it, Trish." Anna snapped the blood doll's neck. She fell dead to the floor. Anna's eyes sparkled angrily. "You have learned your lesson, haven't you, Trish?"

There was no mistaking the warning. Trish bowed to the mistress and nodded. Marie reached out psychically to comfort her mate.

"What do we do now, mistress?" Trish took Marie's hand.

Anna paused. "We continue to grow the nest but we will do so more cautiously."

"There are more of us?" Marie chimed in.

Anna smiled. "Yes, dear one, there are more of our kind. Soon, there will be many more." They all turned at the sound of the door. A tall Latino male approached them.

148

Marie gasped. He had the most gorgeous green eyes. A large bath towel wrapped around his waist, Marie's mouth watered as he strolled across the carpet toward them. She wanted to run her hands all through his thick, wavy hair. He caught her staring at his smooth, muscular chest. A sly smile creased his lips. He winked. It broke the spell. The room was back.

The Latino came up behind Anna, slid one arm around her waist, took his free hand, brushed her hair aside and placed a tender kiss on her neck.

Anna flushed, reached back over her shoulder, running a hand through his hair. "This is Ricardo." Anna smiled at the effect he was having on Marie. "Ricardo, say hello to Marie and welcome her into our fold." Ricardo eyed Marie while slowly licking up Anna's neck, causing a long sigh to escape her lips. He gently released Anna, and then circled toward Marie. Her fangs lengthened as Marie felt Ricardo' eyes caress her body.

"Welcome, you honor us with your presence."

*Mercy, his voice.* Rich, accented, and oh so sexy. She was pooling. Her breast felt full, her nipples were so hard they threatened to pierce her bra. She was ready to let him fuck her anywhere and everywhere he wanted.

He seemed to sense her thoughts. Ricardo smiled, gently took her hand, and kissed it. She felt feverish. If he didn't kiss her now, she was gonna take him to the floor. Ricardo stepped up and pulled her into his arms. He kissed her with such passion that her blood boiled in her veins. She melted against him as his hands roamed over her body. His scent was dark and spicy musk. Her hands slid up his back, exploring the hard muscles underneath his smooth skin.

Her nipples ached, her panties were soaked. She was ready to be taken. Devoured. Ricardo pulled her tighter against him. The huge erection trapped between them, swelling, hardening even more. She whimpered, grinding her sex on the rigid shaft. Trish moved toward them, her eyes sparkling, fangs extended. She leaned in and kissed her mate feverishly. As Ricardo drew away, he loosened the towel, allowing it to fall from his waist. His shaft now free, it stood erect and ready.

Trish flowed into his arms. "Ricardo," she breathed out.

Their eyes met. "Trish," Ricardo growled.

Their kiss seared the air. While watching them, Marie removed her skirt and blouse. Anna pounced, moving behind Marie, her arms encircling her waist. Marie leaned back into her. She was theirs and they were hers to love and care for. Anna's hand slid to her breasts. Delicate fingers traveled down her body, slipping inside her panties. Marie arched toward the tongue swirling around her nipple. Trish. Moist lips drew in the other. Ricardo. Marie bit her lip as Anna slipped her fingers between her folds, and massaged her swollen clit. Anna nipped her neck as fingers slid inside the top of the lace, slowly drawing them down, they fell around her ankles.

As Marie stepped out of them, Ricardo, growling with approval, scooped her into his arms and carried her up to the bed. In all her life, she never felt more like she belonged. They unconditionally cared for, accepted, and loved her, and she them. Her humanity cast aside, she embraced her new identity. She was Marie Ann Pearce, vampire.

# CHAPTER TWENTY FIVE

Trey made his way, bruised and bloody, out of the coroner's office. He was too late to help the Medical Examiner. The vamp ripped the carotid artery and she bled out while he fought for his own skin. Before he left, he managed to take a sample of the she-vamp's dust, retrieve any evidence of his presence, and get out before he was spotted.

Guilt gnawed at him for not calling someone, but he couldn't risk getting caught. He'd be forced to answer too many unwanted questions. Questions with answers they'd never believe and would only get him an all-expenses paid trip to the psych ward.

The long trip back to the motel was nerve racking. Nothing like riding around blood covered on a bike to make a body all self-conscious. Thank Heaven it was clear when he arrived and pulled into a parking space. Letting out the kickstand, he grabbed his satchel and dashed to his room. Once inside, he stripped off his jacket, tossing it and his carrier onto the bed, then marched into the bathroom to start the shower.

Here's hoping he wasn't spotted when he hopped off his Harley. If anyone had saw him, they would've certainly dropped a dime and he'd be entertaining at least a dozen police officers and their big shiny guns.

The steam started to rise as he went to take a glance out the window. Pulling the curtain aside, he noted a stray dog making a get away with a food wrapper in his mouth and a lone couple walking arm in arm across the parking lot. No cops, though; finally, a good break.

Turning to the bed, he went for his jacket. Trey reached into the pocket, and retrieved the vial of vamp dust he collected, and then inside his duffle bag, took out a small bottle with an eye dropper.

151

Taking a sample of the clear solution, he popped the cap on the vial and added it to the vampire dust. He replaced the cap, the agitated the ampule, mixing the dust and the liquid. As he made his way over to the nightstand, he switched on the lamp. He held it under the light and waited. The solution turned blue, which meant a positive reading. Placing the dropper back in the bottle, he tossed it back into the bag, then held the container again up to the light.

Confirmed.

The vampires he fought were from Anna's clan. She was in New Carrollton, or at least her children were. If he played his cards right, maybe one of them would lead him to Anna, herself. He'd tell Maya what he found, but not yet. All he knew was that Anna's brood was here. *Best to keep nosing around.* It might produce something he could actually use. For now, there was nothing more to be done. *Time to get cleaned up.*

Trey set the vial on the nightstand, finished stripping and got into the shower, letting the water hit his raw, achy body. Feeling heavy, the weight of fatigue settled on his shoulders. He leaned forward, resting his head against the shower wall, images of the dead M.E. played in his mind's eye.

Just like his wife and daughter, Jennifer and Haley, the bastards killed that poor woman. His eyes watered. Their brutal murders haunted his days and nights. It was a life sentence Anna committed him to. His family was dead and he should've died with them.

Reaching for a washcloth and soap, he lathered up and started scrubbing the nightmare of the M.E.'s death from his skin. Rose tinted water continued flowing into the drain as he scoured his flesh. He flinched, more images flooded his mind. They slammed into him like a physical force. Jennifer ripped apart, her intestines lying about like squiggly worms. Haley drained, cold, and lifeless. His hands shook. He dropped the washcloth, trembling as he fell back against the shower wall.

Somewhere within him, the dam burst. His chest heaving in sobs, he sank to the floor. Face contorting, his mouth stretched open in a silent cry. *His wife, his baby girl! Why, why had he been spared?* Trey cried hard and bitterly holding himself until long after the shower ran cold.

# CHAPTER TWENTY SIX

Trey slept well into the next day. When he awoke, he switched on the radio. The M.E. had been found. All Hell was going to break loose now. New Carrollton's finest would be jacked for some big time payback.

*Just what he needed. Not.* It was bad enough dealing with Anna and her blood thirsty jackals, now he had to look out for cops as well. Rolling out of bed, he stretched. He felt a little better. Sleep works wonders when you can actually do it. Walking over to the window, he parted the curtain, and looked outside. The bright sun made his eyes water and blink. No way any vamp was going out in that. He could grab a few more winks. No telling when he'd get another chance. Sleep would come quickly. All he had to do was lay back down and let the Sandman do his thing.

He woke again about 7:00 p.m., ordered a pizza and waited. Once the sun checked out over the horizon, he went out on patrol. The streets were calm and quiet. There wasn't any vamp activity, at least none he ran across. Not surprising, Anna knew to lay low until the hornet's nest one of her children stirred up calmed a bit. She needed stealth to establish her own haunt. The sudden increase in police activity would draw the attention of other curious eyes whose gaze she needed to avoid.

Hours of pounding the streets turned up nothing. No sign of anything remotely vamp related. Riding around was getting him nowhere. There was nothing to do but wait until she resurfaced. He decided to grab a bite when his phone rang. Pulling to the curb, he whipped out his cell, checked his caller ID, smiling he accepted the call.

"Stosh, what up big man, where are you?"

"You not gonna believe it but I just stepped off the plane. I'm here at New Carrollton International."

Trey's eye brows rose. "Get outta here! *You* on a plane, I think I'm gonna faint."

Stosh chuckled. "That's what I said, Tommy. Almost did when them wheels left the ground."

Tommy, Trey hated that name, and Stosh knew it. Even though Thomas was his surname, the big man was only one who could call him that and get away with it.

"So what happened, I thought you were done with planes for life?"

Stosh blew out a sigh. "Hemorrhoids happened, son. No way I woulda made it on a bike. So what's the four one one, have you figured out if it's Anna yet?"

Trey gave the area a quick once over. "I'll tell you everything I know, soon as you get here."

"Outstandin', I'll grab me some rent a wheels and meet ya at your twenty."

Trey's empty belly rumbled. "Got a better idea, Hoss, I'm off to grab some chow. When you get your wheels meet me at a bar and grill called Delany's."

"Roger that my friend. I'll get a buggy with On-star and meet ya."

"See ya there, big man." Putting away his cell phone, Trey pulled off into traffic.

It took a half an hour to make it to the bar and grill. When he arrived Scott had checked out for the night but left him in the very capable hands of the Delany staff. He was seated at a booth and ordered a pitcher of beer. *Might as well get comfortable until Stosh made his big entrance*. It was the only entrance kinda Stosh would ever make.

He'd ordered his wings and was starting his second beer moments before Stosh lumbered in. As expected, everyone paused. With his size, pony tail, chops, and backward turned baseball cap, he'd make any room he entered stop and take notice.

Stosh looked about until he saw Trey stand up and wave him over. The big man smiled broadly and made his way to the booth, his size eighteens thudding on the hardwood floor. The two men embraced. Trey disappeared into the giant's arms. "Good to see you big man." Trey slid into the booth as Stosh squeezed into the opposite side.

"Does my heart good to see yer ugly kisser too, junior." The man mountain beamed.

As they settled in, the server arrived with Trey's order. "Here you are, sir." She smiled, placing the sizzling wings down, along with a stack of napkins. The peppery aroma filled the air as she regarded Stosh. "Would you like a menu, sir?"

"I certainly would, sweet thing." Stosh winked. Surprisingly, she flushed.

"Alrighty, I'll be right back. "The woman moved off to grab another menu as Trey picked up the first of his wings.

"Looks good, Tommy, maybe I'll order me some of those. What are they?"

"Four alarm wings. If you finish the first dozen, the second dozen is free."

"That a fact?" Stosh stroked his chin.

"Sure is, try one."

"Don't mind if I do." Stosh speared a wing and took a bite. His eyes bulged; his hand flew to his throat. He gagged and coughed as sweat broke out on his forehead. Snatching up the pitcher of beer, he started chugging and didn't come up for air until he hit the bottom.

"Holy fuckin' shit, Tommy! You trying to kill me?"

"Come on, they're not *that* hot." Trey smiled wickedly.

"Fuck you, those mother fuckers are *hot*! What is that, Satan kibble? Why would anyone want another dozen of those things?"

"Stop being a baby, and order the wings. It'll put hair on your ches...ok, maybe you don't need any more of that but..."

Stosh grabbed a napkin and wiped his mouth. "Fuck...you! I'm ordering something a little less homicidal."

The server arrived with a menu. Stosh sucked in a breath. "Bring us another pitcher, darlin', if you please? "She nodded and went for the beer while Stosh went to work on what he wanted for dinner. One thing was for certain, it wasn't going to be four alarm wings.

Trey grinned. Once you got to know him, Stosh was cool. He'd pulled Trey's bacon out of the fire more than once. Trey loved him like a brother, though it wasn't always like that. When he had first joined up with Maya's crew, he and Stosh were often nose to nose, but Maya squashed it. She knew how to nip it in the bud.

Months of getting every shit job Maya could come up with, forced them to put the nonsense between them aside and learn to trust and respect each other. Out if it, a strong bond and friendship was born.

He continued enjoying his wings while Stosh poured over the menu.

"I'm disappointed, big man, thought you were a tough guy."

Stosh ignored his friend and continued reading. "Think I'll have the Carrollton Blue Cheese burger meal. I see it comes with a slice of apple pie; haven't had good apple pie in ages."

The waitress strolled up and set down the pitcher of lager. "Ready to order, sir?"

"I sure am little lady. I'm gonna have your Carrollton Blue Cheese burger meal."

"You got it, excellent choice." She smiled and moved off to place the order.

"So, you gonna give me the four one one, junior, or are you just gonna sit there and stuff your pie hole?"

Trey finished off the wing in his hands, lifted up a napkin and wiped his mouth. "It's her. I checked out the M.E.'s office the other night and found a vamp chewing her throat open."

Stosh grimaced. "Damn fangs. You run the test?"

"It came back positive."

Stosh fisted his hands. "You call Maya?"

"Not yet."

"Might wanna handle that, Tommy, you know how she gets."

"I will, but first let's nose around a little more and see if we can locate the nest. *Then* we call in the cavalry. "Even Maya wouldn't bitch about that.

"That's what I like about you Tommy. You think before you move...usually."

Just then the waitress returned. "Your order will be up in a few minutes."

"Thank you, sweet thang."The waitress winked, and made her way into the kitchen.

Trey's eyebrows arched. "I'll be damned, she actually likes you."

"The lady clearly has great taste in men and a keen eye for beauty."

Trey rolled his eyes and chuckled. It was good to have the big man there. As long as he was, Trey knew his back was covered. And when hunting the Destroyer, was never a bad thing.

# CHAPTER TWENTY SEVEN

Adalius landed outside Club Détente's entrance and approached the set of steel doors. His neck muscles tightened. This was the last place he wanted to be. But, if he was right, and he was, the Lycan had to be warned of Anna's presence in New Carrollton. He sighed. Unfortunately, the best way to do it was to speak with his old friend. At least he used to be his friend, but all of that changed so long ago.

It pained him how things now stood between him and Kiel. It was his decision that led to this. Sadly, if offered the chance to do it over again, he would make the same choice. To his eternal regret, the terrible price was paid not by him, but by those he loved. Clenching his fists, he fought the surge of guilt. One day, he hoped Kiel would forgive him.

As he neared the entrance, he was greeted by a kaleidoscope of scents and the revelry of partiers. It'd been a long time since he'd ventured to Club Détente. Aside from a few new light fixtures and a fresh coat of paint, it hadn't changed a bit. As usual, the center door remained open to welcome party goers. Stepping across the threshold, he was immediately greeted by the club's Lycan door man.

"Adalius! You blood suckin' bastard, how are ya doin' man!" Taine was dressed in a stylish mustard colored suit, navy blue silk shirt and tie with matching shoes and a one carat diamond stud in each ear. The tie was boldly embroidered with the golden image of a wolf in mid leap, his fingers were decked out tastefully in diamond rings and his hair was slicked back with not a single strand out of place.

Adalius nodded in greeting as the Lycan strutted up to him. "I am quite well, thank you. It is good to see you, Taine." Adalius offered his hand to Taine who smiled from ear to ear, took it and drew the vampire

THE SANDRIAN CHRONICLES: WRITTEN IN BLOOD

into an embrace. "I see you still man the doors. Surely by now you have earned a promotion with all your hard work in this establishment."

Taine released his grip. "Oh yeah, the boss man offered but fuck that, I'm happy right here."

"Truly?"

The Lycan grinned. "Fuckin' A! Do you realize how much pussy comes through these doors on a given night? Vampires and werewolves and demons, oh my, it's enough to keep this naughty little wolf howlin."

Adalius smiled. "Have a care, little wolf, too many vampires on a social calendar leads to excessive blood loss, a less than ideal situation, health wise, even for a Lycan."

Taine waved off the comment. "Not to worry, my brutha, I slam a hand full of iron tablets a night and eat a river fulla liver a week. I'm no fool, so, what you doin' back here? You know the boss man don't want you anywhere near the premises."

Adalius' manner turned solemn once more. "I need to speak with him on an urgent matter, then I will leave immediately."

Taine shook his head sadly. "I can't believe this, man. Y'all was always so tight, like brothers. What the fuck happened between you two anyway?"

"What happened between your cousin and I is not your concern, little wolf. Perhaps in time what was torn asunder…"

Taine threw up his hands. "Yeah, yeah whatever, you know something; he said some of the same bullshit when I asked him about it."

"Is he in his office?"

"Yeah, he in there."

He paused. "And Lucas?"

Taine rolled his eyes "Yeah, that stupid mutha fucka here too, somewhere. Came back about three weeks ago and been bumping his gums about you ever since. Everyday it's I'ma rip Adalius' throat out. I'ma cut his balls off, I'ma eat his heart out. Blah. blah. blah. blah. blah. blah. Do me and all our bleedin' ears a favor, the next time you decide to fuck him up, yank out his tongue after you done breakin' his limbs."

"I will try to keep that in mind."

"Would ya please, can ya do that for a brutha?"

Adalius simply smiled. "Time is short. I must speak with your cousin. The longer I remain here, the greater the chance of confrontation." He laid his hand on the lycan's shoulder. "It is good to see you again, Taine."

"Yeah you too. You know where I live; don't be a stranger. Ok?"

The vampire nodded. "I will stay in touch."

Adalius turned and made his way across the plush red carpet toward three steps which led to five sound proof, steel doors. Opening the center one, he was greeted by the thump of subwoofer powered techno bass. He stepped inside, the door closing slowly behind him.

*****

Taine watched him disappear into the club when to his left; he spotted Club Détente's chief of security. He'd caught sight of the vampire.

"Oh shit." Taine made a bee-line to intercept him.

"Was that Adalius?" Lucas pointed in the direction of the closing steel door.

"Yes and no."

Lucas glared. "The fuck does *that* mean?"

"It means yes, it was Adalius, and no, please don't go fuckin' with him."

The security chief scowled. "I'm not scared of that blood sucker."

"You should be."

Lucas jabbed a finger at the doorman. "Fuck you Tai—"

"Listen, listen, listen, you're security up in here. I get that and you do a damn good job. The asshole population has dropped dramatically since you took over and you do a sensational good job keeping the customers who come here to party safe. If it comes down to a throw down, my money's on you unless you fightin' Adalius."

"Fuck Adalius, he ain't nobody."

"Oh he somebody alright, he the mutha fucka who broke your nose, three of your ribs and both, count em, both yo legs. Now call me a simple bastard, but maybe, just maybe, you should quit fuckin' with him."

160

Lucas growled. "I ain't got time for this. I want his ass outta here." Lucas went to go around Taine but the doorman again stepped into his path.

"Luke, don't do that." Lucas again attempted to go around but Taine cut him off again.

"Luke, if you got to do this, at least take Jax and Poke with you."

"I can handle this, now get the fuck outta my way, Taine."

"Whatever. Go. Bye." Taine stepped aside and gestured toward the steel doors. "See ya in the E.R. mutha fucka."

Lucas gave Taine the dirtiest of looks then headed off through the center door in search of trouble. As the door closed behind Lucas, Taine spotted a waitress who had just changed into her black lace up stretch bustier, hose, and pumps, the uniform of the waitress staff. "Hey Tracy,"

Tracy stopped and turned at the sound of her name and smiled when she saw Taine making his way over. "Hey Taine, what's up baby?"

"Do me a favor and run down stairs and grab the first aid kit."

Tracy's eyes narrowed. "Why do I need to get the first aid ki...Adalius is here isn't he?"

"Umm hmm."

"And Luke went after him again, didn't he?"

"Ummm hmmm."

Tracy rolled her eyes and sighed "I'm goin' to get it now."

Tracy was off to get the kit as Taine made his way to a wall phone stationed near the club entrance. Lifting the receiver, he punched in a three digit number and waited. "Ulysses, this is Taine, just wanted you to know, we bout to have a situation....Adalius just walked in the club.....why didn't I stop him!?....cause I didn't want him playin' snap crackle pop with my mutha fuckin' legs....Well I'm sorry but getting around without the aid of crutches is hip to me....No, one of the guys went to head him off....*You* know which one....No...I tried to tell his stupid ass to take some back up....ok....Stayin' put is *just* what I had in mind."

\*\*\*\*\*

Adalius entered the dance floor area, his senses seized by the volume and thump of the music. A smoky haze filled the air along with the scent of exotic tobacco and sex. The lights were dimmed to low levels to accommodate the more nocturnal, light sensitive guests in house. A wise decision given some beings tended to erupt in flames when coming into contact with certain illumination.

The place was packed tight, with nude and seminude couples gyrating on the dance floor, mingling or drinking. Fog machines, stationed at the four corners, billowed fluffy clouds of white accompanied by a flickering strobe light above. Directly to his left, a werewolf couple fucked mindlessly.

The male had pinned the female against the wall, his arms hooking her legs drilling her like a machine while she braced herself on his shoulders, head held back, howling like a banshee. He shook his head, Lycan and their libidos. He moved deeper into the club.

Adalius snaked through the crowd, toward the bar, aware of the numerous pointing fingers and whispers of his name. As always, the bar was elbow to elbow with patrons. At Adalius' approach, the barflies parted. The bartender, a blond male vampire, spotted him and walked over. "What can I get for you?"

"Blood, O-Neg."

"You got it." The bartender turned about, grabbing a shot glass. Filling it from a tap, he placed it on a napkin in front of him. Adalius looked about in admiration. Kiel's vision made reality. Nowhere else could vampire, Lycan, elf, and troll sit together and share drink and camaraderie without fear of treachery.

Adalius lifted his glass and sipped his drink casually. The bass from the sub woofers rattled his fangs and the techno music grated on his nerves. He had to hurry with his business. He'd go batty with this noise they called entertainment.

"You got a lotta nerve comin back in here, I think you should leave."

Adalius didn't need to look to know who was hovering just outside his personal space. He sensed Lucas' approach the moment he received his glass. Apparently, he needed another lesson in courtesy.

162

"Ask me if I care what you think." Adalius never turned to acknowledge the security chief as he took another drink of blood. His anger simmered. He was not in the mood.

"I want you gone. Now get yo ass out or I'll throw you out." Lucas stepped closer as the vampire set down his glass, turned, and took a step of his own, bringing the males nose to nose.

"I seem to recall you trying that before." Adalius lowered his eyes to Lucas' legs then up again to meet the Lycan's gaze. "I see your legs have healed nicely." A grin spread across the vampire's face.

"That's it, asshole, you're outta here!" Lucas reached out with his left arm. Adalius caught the Lycan by the wrist, forcing his hand down on the bar top while at the same time, drawing a dagger from beneath his trench coat. He drove it down, through hand and bar top, trapping the Lycan. Lucas arched back, and howled. Adalius reached behind Lucas, grabbed a handful of mane and slammed his head violently down into the bar top. Lucas sagged, stunned into silence by the force of the blow. Screams brought the music to an abrupt halt. Lucas moaned, on his feet, only because Adalius held him upright with a hand full of his hair. The entire room watched in stunned silence.

Adalius leaned close to his captive. "Do not move, I am going to want that back." He released his hair and started toward Kiel's office. Projecting menace as he went, the crowd parted like the Red Sea, the thud of his boots on the wooden dance floor went out ahead of him like a herald. No one dared breathe; those who did breathe that is.

As he neared the office door, it opened and a single male exited, as expected. Adalius detected the Lycan's scent the instant he started toward Kiel's office. Ruggedly handsome, the Lycan was tall and impressively built with long, dark, corn silk hair drawn into a ponytail that was shoulder length. Well groomed, his beard was trimmed, the navy blue, tailor made, silk suit fit him flawlessly. With the matching tie, white shirt dress shirt, and very expensive looking wing tipped shoes, he had GQ cover model written all over him. The wolf had style.

The model approached him, piercing blues eyes locked with his own, while two muscular Lycan flanked him, falling into step. Though part of the club's security force, their primary function was to keep unwanted guests from dropping in on the boss.

163

The larger of the two, the one to the model's right, was a dreadlocks sporting Nubian, wide across the chest and narrow at the waist, as was his equally impressive, spike haired, Caucasian counterpart. Both wore black mesh body shirts, jeans, and Nike's. They all came to a stop. Relaxing his shoulders, Adalius came to a halt, the model and entourage blocking his path. Bowing his head subtly, he acknowledged the lead Lycan.

"You are looking well, Ulysses." The security guards folded their arms across their chests and scowled. "Jax, Poke, it is a pleasure to see you both again as well."

Ulysses' gaze was withering as he addressed Adalius. "You may as well turn your ass around vamp."

"I seek an audience with your alpha."

Ulysses shook his head. "He's not entertaining tonight. Make an appointment and *maybe* he'll see you tomorrow."

Adalius removed his shades, meeting Ulysses' glare with one of his own. "Inform Kiel that I see him now, or I shall begin sending his security staff to the infirmary."

Ulysses weighed his options. A battle with Adalius would lead to loss of lives, and a gigantic repair bill. Not to mention the bad publicity hit the club would take.

"Wait here." Ulysses turned and addressed his security. "Watch him." He headed off in the direction of the office. Jax and Poke continued to scowl as he replaced his shades. Adalius turned to the dance floor area where the still stunned crowd stood in silence.

At the bar, where Lucas remained pinned, he spotted another staff member going to the aid of the trapped Lycan. Sensing the vampire's eyes upon him, the staffer turned. Adalius slowly shook his head. The would be rescuer retreated back into the crowd.

From behind him, he sensed Ulysses approach. "He'll see you now."

He took a step; Ulysses pressed a palm firmly to Adalius' chest. "Hold the fuck up. Weapons, fangboy."

Adalius glared. Ulysses wisely removed his hand. Jax and Poke stepped forward to take any dangerous items from the vamp's possession. Adalius removed his Glocks from their holsters and handed them over along with his remaining daggers.

"That all of it?" Ulysses eyed the vampire suspiciously.

"It is."

Ulysses leaned in and sneered. "You sure?"

"Cross my heart and hope to die." A wicked grin spread across his face.

"Fuck you vamp, come this way."

# CHAPTER TWENTY EIGHT

Plush carpet greeted them as Ulysses opened the door, allowing Adalius to enter. The room was spacious and lined with ten foot floor to ceiling bookshelves, loaded with a collection of literature ranging from Shaw to Shakespeare. A ceiling fan circulated the crisp air, tainted with the scent of old leather and Killian cologne. Steel filing cabinets, three across rested against the far wall.

Ulysses glanced over to his boss seated at an impressive Cherry wood L-shaped desk conducting business on the phone. Behind Kiel hung a life sized portrait of the Lycan king, Marseth, the albino, Kiel's sire. Just below it, sat an enormous aquarium filled with assorted exotic fish.

Setting down the pen he twirled in his fingers, Kiel waved them in. Despite his apprehension, Adalius' spirits lifted at the sight of his friend. He continued in as Ulysses exited, closing the door behind him.

Kiel, owner of Club Détente, heir to the Lycan throne, was a broad shouldered, powerful Lycan. Brutally handsome, he was clean shaven and immaculately groomed. Dressed in a black Armani suit and black dress shirt with the top two buttons left undone, a tie lay neatly folded on the desk in front of him. His long, silky black hair was also in a ponytail and hung past his shoulders. Kiel hung up the phone as Adalius approached.

"Kiel, it has been a long time."

"Adalius, it hasn't been long enough. Please, take a seat." Ever the businessman, Kiel gestured to one of two leather, high backed chairs which sat apart and angled in toward the center of his desk.

"Drink?"

Adalius planted himself in the chair to Kiel's right. "No, thank you."

"Smoke?"

"No."

"Good, now that we got all the pleasantry bullshit outta the way, you can tell me why you're back in my club threatening violence and tacking the help to the bar!"

"Anna is back in New Carrollton."

Kiel's brow dipped. "What makes you think so?"

"Every lead I have uncovered points to her returning here."

The Lycan paused. "Have you informed the High Council?"

Adalius shook his head. "Not at this time."

"Then you don't actually *know* she's here."

Adalius removed his wraparounds. "She is here, Kiel."

"If you haven't informed the Council, it says to me that you just have a *feeling* she's in New Carrollton."

His temper flared but he quickly subdued it. Kiel knew better than to question his senses. The Lycan was simply attempting to 'get his goat' he believed the term was. He would remain calm. The Lycan would get no satisfaction. "She fed from my vein and I from hers. Nothing more need be said."

"Well since you haven't chosen not to alert the Council, we'll take it from here."

Adalius gripped the chair arm rests, keeping his voice even. "According to the agreement made by your father, Anna falls under vampire jurisdiction."

Kiel shifted in his seat. "The agreement was that in the event of Anna's return, we'd step aside and let the Enforcers to deal with her. Last time I checked, *you're* not an Enforcer."

A slow sighed escaped the vampire. "I did not come to debate with you Kiel. I came to warn you so that your people can take steps to protect themselves."

"And I thank you for the heads up. Now unless you're planning to inform the Council, I'm gonna do everything in my power to find Anna and put her down."

"Kiel, I am asking you to stand down. Allow me to deal with her."

The Lycan sat forward, rested his elbows on the desktop, leveling his eyes at the vampire. "Let's be clear on this, I don't give a fuck that you got a hard on for Anna cause she killed your gypsy honey bunny." Adalius' eyebrow arched subtly. "Yeah we know about that. We also know about the spell that makes you sunshine proof. I paid good money to have it removed but whoever cast it, got mojo on steroids, but I digress. Anna killed two of my dearest friends. I plan to cut out her heart, have it pickled, jarred, and then mounted in a trophy case I'm having built."

It was going as expected. Kiel was being difficult as always. He played the one card he had left. It was a long shot but there was nothing to lose. "We were friends once, very good friends. As someone who was once your friend, I am asking you to please leave Anna to me."

Kiel glared, considering his request. The Lycan blew out a breath. "Fine, but if any of my people so much as break a nail because of her,"

The vampire nodded once. "Understood, thank you, Kiel."

"You're welcome. Now, get the *fuck* outta my club, Adalius."

*****

He stepped out of Kiel's office and was promptly met by Ulysses, Jax, and Poke. The security Lycan returned his weapons as the club crowd watched nervously. When he had replaced his pistols into their holsters and secured his daggers, he started off but Ulysses blocked his path.

The Lycan scowled at Adalius. He glowered back. Ulysses took a step forward bringing them nose to nose.

"Just so you understand vamp, if you *ever* come back into this club and harm another staff member, they'll be carrying what's left of you out in thimbles."

Adalius removed his wraparounds, his eyes sparkled angrily. "Threaten me again, Ulysses and the next coat I wear shall be made from wolf pelt."

Ulysses stepped aside and gestured toward the dance floor. "You know the way out."

Adalius replaced his shades and made his way back across the dance floor. Once again, the crowd parted, allowing him passage. Drawing near the bar and the still pinned Lucas, he could hear a voice coming from the direction of the sound proof doors.

"Pardon me. Excuse us, coming through. Would you mutha fuckas move!" Tracy appeared through the crowd carrying a first aid kit, followed closely by Taine. Tracy looked about, spotted Lucas, and moved to his side. Setting the kit on the bar top, she opened it up as Taine moved to join her.

"Well, he still on his feet. That's a good sign. What he do to you this time Lu...*holy shit, medic!*" Taine stared wide eyed at the dagger embedded in Lucas' hand. Tracy slapped his arm. "Stop it Taine and help me pull it out."

"Allow me." Adalius gripped the handle of the dagger and yanked it free.

Tracy smiled as she withdrew a roll of gauze from the first aid kit. "Thank you Ada." Carefully, she wrapped the punctured hand as Lucas groaned in pain.

Adalius wiped the blade clean, then returned it to his trench coat. "Thank you for looking after my dagger, Lucas."

"Fuck you, vamp."

Taine looked from Adalius to Lucas back. "You forgot the tongue."

"Sue me."

Adalius walked away while Tracy doctored the injured Lycan, rolling her eyes. None of this was in her job description. She was so going to ask for a raise.

# CHAPTER TWENTY NINE

The door had barely closed when Kiel picked up the receiver and punched a button on his desk phone. "Wanda, put me through to the mansion….yes, thank you."

Wanda went to work and a moment later the line on the other end was ringing. It rang a fifth time before; at last, it was answered. "You have reached the domain of his highness Marseth. How may I be of service? "It was Wellington the family butler, who'd served his father for hundreds of years.

Kiel was proud to call him friend. "Hi, Welly, how are you?"

"Ahh, Master Kiel, how are you, sir? "Kiel could hear the smile in the butler's voice.

"I'm fine, thanks. Is my father or mother available?"

"I'm afraid not, sir. His highness and your mother are off on a tour of the Mediterranean. I do not expect them back for at least another week."

Kiel snapped his fingers, they had told him about the trip. His mother had been abuzz about the vacation for weeks. "I forgot about that."

"May I be of service to you, sir?"

"Yes, if either of them call the mansion, have them contact me."

"I could relay a message if you like, sir?"

The model of efficiency, that was his Welly. "Actually yes, tell them I need to speak with them ASAP, it's *very* important."

"I will do that immediately, sir."

"Thank you, Wellington. How are you?"

"Quite well sir, I'm preparing the nursery for the new arrival."

The butler always delighted at the thought of an addition to the pack. "You sound almost as excited as my mother." Kiel leaned back in his chair as a tender smile spread across his face.

"It *has* been some time since we have heard the sound of tiny feet in the mansion, sir."

"Well as long as you are running things, my new sibling will be in good hands and have the best friend he or she could ever ask for."

"Very kind of you to say, sir."

"It came from the heart, Welly. Gotta run now, take care and I hope to see you soon."

"I will see to it your message is sent, sir. Good day."

Kiel hung up the phone. Hopefully, his father would get back to him soon. Anna loose in the city again was not good news. He assured Adalius he'd take no action against Anna for now. Still, it was a good idea to alert his father in case the king had second thoughts on how Anna should be dealt with.

# CHAPTER THIRTY

The Metropolitan was one of two new nightclubs that had sprouted up in downtown New Carrollton. Club Met as it came to be known, was adorned with etched glass windows, which lined the front of the watering hole, providing an introductory glance from the street to the festivities within. Upon entering, customers often were met by a charming hostess, greeted by the ambiance of a mature crowd, welcomed by modern décor and hickory wood floors, and treated to fabulous acoustics paired with a state of the art sound system.

The dance floor, highlighted by an extravagant light system, was kept cool by air flowing from large vents above, fed by ducts, leading up to commercial air conditioning units mounted on the roof. The DJ, in rare form from his booth above the dance floor, was giving the crowd their money's worth mixing a smooth blend of the latest hot tracks with classic hits from the past. A giant hand carved, U-shaped oak wood bar stocked to the teeth with foreign and domestic beer and liquors, was the eye catching focal point.

A dining section, filled with chic café style tables, sat opposite the bar separated from the dance floor by a waist level, hickory topped, glass block wall.

The air was laced with the scent of BBQ, hot and mild wings, and an assortment of other finger foods stationed at the rear of the tavern for the late night troop. The overhead lights on the dance floor flashed on and off in time with the music, while the café jumped with the activity of hustling servers and the buzz of conversation.

Detective Sergeant Ross Bricker pushed his way through the throng. He'd spent the better part of two shifts collecting evidence and knocking on doors in the ongoing manhunt. At day's end, he went home and flipped through his little black book. He needed to blow off some steam, make a new conquest. So after jumping into the shower, he shaved, dressed, and here he was ready to sweep the next piece of ass off her feet.

The partiers were packed in tight like sardines, the body heat driving up the room temperature in spite of the air conditioning. The thump of the bass from the speakers rattled the glasses on the tables and the strobe light flickered while Jay-Z's music pumped in stereo. He had *no* idea what these dingy broads saw in the guy, but it never seemed to fail to pack the dance floor. Bricker shook his head in disgust. There was simply no accounting for taste. An inebriated male staggered and bumped into him. The detective fanned the air as alcohol laced breath hit his nasal cavity.

"Watch where you goin' dip shit!" Bricker shoved him as the idiot kept on his way. Holding the set of car keys he lifted from the drunktard in his hand, Bricker slid them into his jacket pocket. Captain Drinkski could pick them up from management after he'd slept it off. One less intoxicated loser behind the wheel tonight.

Scanning the crowd, Bricker checked out the talent, searching for the one who had the look; tipsy, sexy, bored, and not too bright. Reaching a small clearing in the throng, he got a clear view of the clientele seated at the bar. No singles available. Every female appeared to be chatting with, smiling at, or kissing their dates.

Seated to the far right, next to an empty bar stool, was a female who went clear off the Ross Bricker hotness scale; long beautiful legs and hair, simple but sexy little black dress, matching high heeled sandals and half carat seven-diamond Journey necklace.

*What a piece of ass!*

Sitting with her legs crossed, she glanced about, perhaps waiting for someone. He knew an opportunity when he saw one, and this one had real possibilities. But he needed to be patient, had to be sure some husband, boyfriend or maybe even a girlfriend wasn't coming to join her. He had time. If she had a date, her loss, he'd just move on to the next broad.

Ten minutes went by, according to his watch. Nobody'd come to join her. *It's Bricker time.* Acting nonchalant, he came up behind her. She continued looking around. Clearly she was waiting for someone. It was her lucky night. Someone had arrived.

Whipping out his breath freshener, he gave himself a quick spritz, took out his comb, giving his manly mustache a quick grooming, and then made his way over. Bricker ran a finger through his hair, smirk in place. He was gonna make her night, the lucky bitch. He came up and stood by the empty seat beside her flashing a smile. "Well hello there, is this seat taken?"

The woman turned toward Bricker, rolling her eyes. "No."

"Great." Bricker took a seat sporting a cheese eating grin. His eyes roamed over her body, taking in every line and contour. "I must say, you look fantastic."

The woman blew out an annoyed sigh. "Thanks."

He offered his hand. "I'm sorry, let me introduce myself. I'm Lieutenant Ross Bricker, N.C.P.D. Homicide."

The woman brightened noticeably. "Really? Thank goodness. I was just sitting here trying to think of what to say to make you go away. I've just been a little on edge since those murders started up in the McClain Park area." She took his hand.

"Not to worry, little lady, me and my team are conducting a full investigation and I guarandamntee you we will take this psycho down."

The woman closed her eyes and exhaled. "I can't tell you how much better that makes me feel."

He couldn't help himself. Bricker took in her body, starting from her pedicured feet and worked his way up to her very sexy cleavage. "So why is a beautiful woman like you out by yourself?"

The woman shrugged. "Well, to be honest, looks like my date stood me up."

*Hot damn! Hottest skirt in the joint and she was all his.* "No fricken way!"

"Certainly looks that way." The woman fidgeted on her seat averting her eyes.

"Who is this imbecile? Give me a name so I can arrest him for aggravated stupidity."

She chuckled and smiled. "*That* won't be necessary."

"You sure, wouldn't be a problem. I could just…"

"No, really, it's ok."

They shared a laughed as the bartender arrived. "What can I get for you, Brick?" he shouted to be heard over the blasting music.

"Double bourbon and give the lady whatever she's having."

"Coming right up." The bartender cut his eyes at the beauty then turned to fill their order, shaking his head.

The woman smiled. "Thank you, you didn't have to do that."

"It's the least I can do to make up for that moron standing you up."

"Are you always so chivalrous, Lieutenant? "She beamed.

"Call me Ross and yes, I am."

The bartender returned with their drinks, setting them down on a coaster. "That's one double bourbon for you and for the lady, one red wine."

Bricker reached into his back pocket, retrieved his wallet, pulled out some cash, and handed it to the bar tender. "Keep the change."

"Thanks…*Lieutenant*."

He gave the bartender the evil eye, shaking his head as the barkeep moved on to the next customer.

The woman took a sip of her wine and Bricker lifted his own glass to his lips, as 'Blame it' by Jamie Fox erupted from the speakers.

The woman's expression brightened. "Dance with me, Ross, I love this song." She stood and took his hand, leading him to the dance floor.

He felt like he'd hit the lottery. She was even taller than he expected and had a killer body. Some dumb bastard stood *this* skirt up? Must have been a blind date. The sucker's loss was gonna be his gain.

She led him through the crowd until she found a spot on the dance floor. Turning to face him, she was off, dancing in time with the music, and how she could dance. Gave him an instant hard on watching the sway of her hips. No doubt about it, this woman could move it between the sheets. For the next few hours, they partied and danced well into the night.

It wasn't unusual for him to scope out the other action, even when he had a date. But he just couldn't seem to take his eyes off this hottie. It was as if someone else was in control of his eyes.

After last call was announced, the woman picked up her purse, hanging it over her shoulder as she stood. She hugged him. "I had a wonderful time, Ross. Thank you for turning a drab evening into a blast!"

"Yeah it was great. Hey, let me see you to your car or maybe even see you home? There *is* a nut on the loose still."

She smiled slyly. "There is, isn't there. Yes, Ross, I think I'd like very much for you to see me home." She took his arm as they started for the exit.

"Wait, I've had such a great time that I don't ever think I got your name."

"I'm so sorry, Ross. Where are my manners? My name is Patricia but you can call me Trish."

# CHAPTER THIRTY ONE

Serena Espinosa slid open the patio door, making her way out toward her pool into the fading light of dusk. Caramel colored, tall, exotic, and beautiful, with deep blue, almond shaped eyes and high cheek bones, she was an extraordinary Sandrian vampire.

Circumstance had blessed her with being able to go out into daylight, but it came with a price. More than ever, she found herself in the company of mortals. *Ugh*! It was like socializing with dinner entrees.

The sun's slow departure from the heavens left a painted sky of orange, red, gold, and blue in its wake. She sighed, cherishing what many humans took for granted, the warmth and beauty of a sunset. All she need do was tolerate the nuisance that was mankind and in exchange, she got to partake in nature's infinite works of art. It was an equitable trade off.

Rockwell Heights was home, a quiet suburb of New Carrollton where the upper middle class lived out the American dream. Thanks to some prudent investments over the centuries, she'd accumulated a modest fortune which afforded her the comfort she now enjoyed. Blessings be upon the Drayken. They'd guided her through many tough financial straits, the stock market crash of 1929 being the worst.

Looking about at the high, manicured hedges and privacy fence that surrounded her property, she strolled toward the deep end with towel in hand. The golden hue of the deck tiles contrasted beautifully with the blue of the water. The air was hazy and heavy, causing moisture beads on her skin. With a heavy sigh, she wiped her brow. *Blessed Elder, it's still so hot.* It wasn't just the weather. How anyone did without a pool during this horrid heat wave was beyond her. Yet another blessing she would have to count before she turned in and sleep claimed her.

Slipping free of her sheer robe, she laid it across the back of one of the deck chairs of her patio set. Adjusting the top of the silver and black striped G-string bikini, she breathed out a soft moan. The silky material of the bikini caressed and stimulated her skin just the way she liked it.

For days, anything she wore causing the slightest friction sent waves of sensual pleasure rolling over her body. Her cycle was riding her. She'd be going into heat soon. The lights lining the deck and pool walls looked like glowing orbs as she pulled her jet black hair into a ponytail, which was no small feat considering its mid back length.

Laying the terry cloth down near the edge, she dove in, barely disturbing the water. Breaking the surface, she began swimming toward the opposite end. She loved swimming. It soothed the nerves and was good exercise. Keeping a figure like hers required that she stayed active, ate right, and took in plenty of blood every day.

Running was a must to keep her long legs toned and shapely. Sometimes, she envied her undead vampire cousins. They never need worry about the scourge of love handles and cellulite. On the other hand, they'd never be able to savor the sweet taste of chocolate covered strawberries and fine champagne. *No chocolate, ever? She'd throw herself on the nearest wooden stake!*

Tossing the repulsive thought into the backseat of her mind, she kept swimming. Stroke. Stroke. Head turn. Deep breath. Head down. Keep those legs kicking. Stroke. Head turn. Deep brea...a scent on the air, subtle, barely perceptible like the whisper of a whisper. She paused, treading water, her nose testing the breeze. It was gone now.

A heightened sense of smell was one of the advantages of being vampire, if you weren't stuffed into an overcrowded elevator with a bunch of hot, sweaty, city dwellers. She shuddered. Some people seem to think that cologne and perfume were adequate substitutes for soap and hot water.

She inhaled another lung full, her nose sifting the air's contents. *Nothing out of the ordinary.* Carefully, she took inventory of her surroundings then continued on. After the sixth lap, she glided over to the pool ladder. Pulling herself out of the pool, she leaned down, water running off her, and scooped up her towel. Drying herself, she made her way toward one of the deck chairs. Dinner would be ready soon. Till then she could...*mmmmm*. Need flared. Her hand traveled over her breasts then made its way southward. Tender mercies, she needed to head inside and take the edge off.

Her mate had better hurry. Though Sandrian females were faithful partners, Heat cycles, had a nasty tendency to strip away reason. If a mated female went into heat while her mate was away, it's best she be sedated. The drive to procreate would send her storming off into the night, seeking a virile male. If you can't be with the one you love...

Her skin tingled. She stopped. So, she wasn't imaging it. Her eyes darted about. A blue jay sitting on the fence screeched then took off like its tail feathers were on fire. Something frightened him. Her eyes sparkled. *He was getting careless. Better get inside.* Vulnerability was never a good thing when stalked by a predator. Serena made for the safety of her home. Out of the corner of her eye, a blur. Startled, she turned. Nothing. No matter, she wouldn't be deceived. *He's here.*

Her body shifted to defense mode, adrenal glands went into overdrive, heart action was revving up. She looked above and about. From which direction would her *guest* strike? An air disturbance, she whirled around. He was toying with her. Hot breath on her neck. The patio door was just ahead. Her respiration becoming pants as the familiar comfort of home was almost within her reach.

Something huge crashed against her from behind. Powerful arms wrapped around her waist. A gasp escaped her lips. The arms tightened. A hand ran through her hair and grasped her locks. The intruder was swift, powerful, his strength irresistible and his hold like iron.

She sensed... satisfaction. *No. She would not yield*! She twisted. It was anticipated. His weight shifted accordingly. Her body tight against his, a firm pull of her hair exposed her jugular. She resisted. He held firm. *Dammit, she couldn't break free! She couldn't... break... free!*

The aggressor leaned in. The hairs on her neck stood on end. She jerked away. He pulled her back. Closer he came, he had her. *She'd lost, damn him. She'd lost!* Shutting her eyes, she waited for what was to come. A tender kiss on her neck.

Serena purred. "Mmmmm, the set to you, really Adalius, you've been a vampire for over three hundred years and *still* you haven't learned to approach your prey from downwind?" Serena locked her hand in his.

Releasing her hair, his arm snaked around her waist drawing her to him. "Perhaps I wanted you to know I was near," he rumbled seductively.

A tingle danced along her skin. His voice always gave her goose bumps. And his lips....*breathe*! "Rogue, where have you been and how goes your search for 'She Who Tasks You So'?"

Adalius gave her a gentle squeeze. "I have tracked Anna up and down the eastern seaboard. Now it appears she has returned here to New Carrollton."

Serena suppressed a pout. "So it's Anna who brings you back. Did she also prevent you from using a phone?"

He sighed. "You are right, Serena. I am a thoughtless fool. Forgive me?"

She lifted his hand, kissing it affectionately. "You are already forgiven, Adalius."

"I have missed you, Serena."

"Have you truly?"

Adalius nuzzled her neck. "Of course I have."

"Tell me then, which do I owe my thanks for your return: your desire for me or your need to kill Anna?"

Adalius nibbled on her earlobe, she giggled. "Any male worth his weight in soot would sever a limb for but a moment of your embrace."

She blushed. "Flatterer, thy tongue is skilled in more ways than one." Reaching out to Adalius with her senses, her heart sank. *He's so weak. When was the last time he fed?* "Take my vein, Adalius, you need to feed."

"I am fine, Serena, really."

Stepping out of his embrace, she turned. "Your body betrays you. I sense your need."

Adalius shook his head. "I do not wish to burden you."

Tenderly, she took his face into her hands. "You are *never* a burden, Adalius. You're my joy, I'm happy to feed you."

Adalius caressed her cheek. "And for that, I give my thanks. You honor me, beyond what I deserve."

Noble till the end, it was but one reason why she loved him. "It's the very least I could do after what you've done for me."

Adalius kissed her palm. "That was over a hundred and fifty years ago and Carlo deserved to die. He was a blight on us all. Poisoned all he came into contact with. My only regret is I cannot kill him again."

"He was my mate Adalius, no one knows better than I what a bastard he was. The beatings I suffered at his hands, the humiliations…" Serena shut her eyes against the horrific memories.

Adalius caressed her cheek, his outrage rising. Serena, you need not—"

She lifted her chin, squaring her shoulders. "No, it no longer holds power over me. I find talking about it…cleansing."

Adalius gazed deeply into her eyes. "Such a courageous spirit, when you at last find a male worthy of you…"

She stepped closer, sliding her arms around his neck. "I have already found such a male."

Adalius shook his head solemnly. "I am not worthy, Serena. You deserve more than what I now offer. I cannot ask you to wait while I pursue that monster."

"Must I say it again, Adalius? I'm prepared to face whatever the future holds for us, together. What we share is beyond the flesh, beyond life itself. Meyo teh vore."

My love, my life. The vows of the wedded spoken in the old tongue.

Pulling her into his embrace, he kissed her deeply. She melted into his arms, running her hands through his hair. Her blood ignited, pulse quickening as his hands roamed over her body. She missed him, needed him. The comfort of his warm body next to hers, the scent of his skin, the taste of his lips, the power of his thrust.

Adalius slipped free of his trench coat revealing his amazing physique, two hundred seventy- five Sandrian pounds of rock hard abs, deltoids, and pecs. He was a god and she wanted him. For however long, she would cherish it. Life without him was living death.

Her nipples ached for his attention. She was wet and ready to take him. She could wait no longer. Stepping away from him, she bit her lip

181

and went to work undoing her bikini top. Adalius watched her, adoration in his eyes.

Serena's blood sizzled as Adalius licked his lips, devouring her with his eyes. His nostrils flared as he took in her scent. She smiled. Nipples erect and aching, she wiggled her hips, running her fingers along the top of her bikini bottom, sliding them down. She stepped out of them then they fell to the deck.

Never taking his eyes from her, Adalius knelt down, loosened his boots, and kicked them away. Her eyes teared. He was her dearest friend and lover. There would be no other for her. His fangs extending, Adalius scooped her up. She locked her arms around his neck. Carrying her through the patio door, he headed to her bedroom.

The instant he set her on her feet, she molded her body to his. It had been so long. She drew in his scent as Adalius leaned in, covering her mouth with his own. Their tongues intertwined in a delicious heat. Sliding his hands around her, he cupped her ass.

She whimpered at the feel of his lips upon her. The light scrape of his fang on her neck, made her crazy, made her want to give him everything, all of her life blood. She would have his young again and again.

Her breath quickened as he moved downward, his tongue traveling toward the place reserved only for him. She coiled her leg around his, her body moving, surging against him. With a growl, he lifted her up. She wrapped her limbs around his waist. She was like static cling as he laid her down on the bed. The beast had come for its mate, and she'd been waiting. His fangs lengthened further as her arms and legs drew him down. Settling between her legs, he worked his hips as if drawn to the heat in her core. She ran her hands softly over his back as he slipped between her folds and thrust inside. Serena gasped, fisting his hair.

Reaching out with her senses, she touched his mind. He caressed hers their thoughts intermingling, desperate to complete the joining. She arched her back as he pushed deeper inside her. She bowed into him, her muscles drawing him in. Adalius withdrew then slowly pushed back into her depths. She matched his rhythm, running her hand over his back. He arched, taking her, filling her. She moaned, writhing against her mate. Their minds intertwined, joining as their bodies were joined. She whispered his name. They were together again, bonded in mind, spirit, and love.

*****

Adalius kissed her cheek as he slid his arms around her waist. She moved against him, her back pressed against his torso. He nuzzled her neck, as he stroking her senses with his mind. She returned his mental touch, interlocking their fingers, planting a kiss upon his hand. She was whole again. Her mate had come back to her.

"I missed you so, Adalius. My bed has been cold and empty without you."

Adalius gave her a tender squeeze. "I am sorry, Serena, I know this has been hard on you but Anna must be hunted down."

"I don't question that, but why must it be you who kills her? She's dangerous. Even elder vampires fear her."

"Serena, I have shared the story time and again."

"But the gypsy is long gone."

Adalius paused. "Perhaps, but his magic grants my immunity to sunlight. It's my advantage. In exchange, I gave my vow to kill Anna. My oath is intact, it binds me. "

Serena breathed out an annoyed sigh. She turned toward him. "Males and their oaths; even Carlo, as vile and contemptible as he was, was no different. Once he gave his word…"

"You never told me how you came to be mated to such a male."

Serena rolled onto her back. "You knew him. How else did Carlo go about getting what he wanted? Treachery, coercion, deceit, and violence. You are clever in your attempt to distract me, Adalius. You know what I was next going to ask."

Adalius blew out a breath, closing his eyes. "Serena, we have discussed this."

Serena sat up. "No, I have discussed it; you have simply avoided it by invoking your oath to kill Anna. Do you not love me, Adalius?"

Adalius tenderly took her face in his hands. "There are not as many stars in the heavens as there are ways in which I love you."

"Then let us, together, submit to the bonding ceremony. We are already mated in every way that matters. We need only complete the circle."

Adalius gazed deeply into her eyes. "I would without hesitation bond with you but…"

"But what, Adalius?"

"I will not allow you to wait here and worry over my safety."

Serena's eyes sparkled hinting at her rising anger. "Will not *allow* me? I am your mate, Adalius not your offspring!" Fire coursed through her veins. Carlo used those very words time and again to manipulate and control her. Never again!

"Serena…"

She pushed away his hand. *"No.* Will you have me as your mate or will you not?"

"Serena, I cannot ask you to…"

Her anger ignited. "Leave me, Adalius. Her eyes glowed bright violet. "Get out and do not return until you feel you are ready to treat me as an equal!"

Adalius inhaled to speak but she'd laid down the gauntlet. "I know your thoughts. I will hear no more of them. Get out!"

Adalius rose from the bed never taking his eyes from his mate.

She threw out her arm, extended her finger, and pointed toward the door. "I said, get out!"

Adalius left the bedroom.

When the patio door closed, the tears she held at bay flowed freely down her cheeks. Adalius was her soul but, until he recognized her as his equal, they had no future together and a future without Adalius was no future at all. Serena cried into her pillows, her sobs echoing off the walls throughout the rest of the night and on into the next.

# CHAPTER THIRTY TWO

Arnie made a beeline to the coroner's office as soon as he got the call. *Please God, let it be just a big mistake! Rhoda couldn't be dead. She just couldn't be!* His siren wailed as he barreled down Main Street, approaching an intersection. Cars ahead either came to a stop or pulled to the curb, the road opening up like a constricted airway when an inhaler was applied. The huge knot that was his stomach tightened as he eyed the clock on the dash. *Only a couple more blocks to go. Only a couple of minutes and...*

*TAXI!*

He cut hard to his left, going behind the yellow sedan, barely avoiding a major accident. Damn fool was trying to beat the light.

"You *moron*!!" he screamed out the window, laying on his horn. No time to chase that idiot down. He was almost there. The M.E.'s office was coming up fast on the right. *Now*!

Rubber screeched in protest as he fish tailed into the parking lot. His vehicle shuddered, his bones rattled from the boom boom of his tires going over the speed bump near the entrance.

Flashing blue and red atop the multitude of police cruisers flooded the area in a dueling strobe light show as he pulled into the parking space nearest the entrance. Wheels bounced against the curb as he threw the gear shift into park. The engine barely finished shutting off as he all but leaped from the car. He walked with purpose, his steps crisp, heart pumping with dread. Eyes with tunnel vision locked on to the double doors ahead.

Cool antiseptic air rushed in around him, drying the sweat on his brow as he strode through the automatic doors, past the guard's shack where McGee and Anita were interviewing the security officer on duty. Down the corridor he marched, the echo of his steps bouncing off the walls. His heart hammered against his sternum as if demanding immediate release from confinement.

Passing by the doorway of the employee cafeteria, he noted the room filled with the graveyard shift. Many were arm in arm, consoling one another while others who were able, gave statements to detectives. Department shrinks would be doing triple time for the rest of the year from the look of it.

Arriving at the already propped open lab door, he came to a stop as if he'd run into an unseen barrier. Everything moved in slow motion as forensic teams scoured the lab taking pictures and gathering evidence. There on the floor, to his right, was a sheet covered body. Perspiration trickled down on his forehead, a caustic chill raced down his spine. *God, no.*

Forcing down the bile rising in his throat, he stepped across the threshold. His legs were heavy, barely responsive, like they were filled with cement. They trembled, struggling to support his weight. Dear Lord, he didn't want to look. Couldn't bear to face what lay beneath the sheet. But he was compelled. He had to know, had to see for himself.

Captain Williams and Richardson spotted Arnie when he entered. They moved carefully toward him, watching in silence, ready to lend their strength. Good, he was just a flea's eyelash from going down like the Titanic.

As Arnie made his way over to the covered body, voices and the sounds of activity around him drifted a world away. He stooped. His heart palpitated. Richardson kept a respectful distance but close enough to offer support. Slowly, he reached down. His chest was tight, it was hard to breathe. Steadying himself, he blew out a breath and counted to three. He drew back the sheet. A gasp caught in his throat, his heart wailed, his fists clenched, the shock like a shotgun blast to the chest.

Rhoda.

"Awww Jesus, Red..."

Looking on the face of the daughter he never had, he saw the terrible wounds. Her throat looked like it'd been chewed out. He wept silent tears. *Mother of God, it looked like she'd been mauled by an animal.* A

186

portion of her trachea hung loose, still attached only by the slimmest thread of tissue. Tears blurred his vision as his eyes clamped shut.

She was so young. So. Damn. Young.

He'd met Rhoda eight years ago when she was still a bright eyed kid fresh out of college. A real spitfire, all smiles and full of wonder, ready to take on all comers including the ones who told her she'd never make it. She showed them all. Bless her soul.

She worked her tail off, paid her dues, and it *was* going to pay off. With Bennie retiring in a year, it was a foregone conclusion that Rhoda would get the department head promotion. Bernie told him he put in a good word for her personally. She was such a good kid. She'd saved his life.

Tears trailed down his cheeks. When his wife died, Rhoda was there, never left his side. They were the darkest days of his life. She was the light guiding him every step of the way, often sitting with him well into the night, holding his hand, crying with him, laughing with him, and more than once, talking him out of eating his revolver.

How many times did she turn down a hot date to come sit with him and watch old movies till the sun found them both asleep on his couch? She had become closer to him than his own daughter, who had herself, grown quite fond of Rhoda. The two had become like sisters. How could he tell her? How *would* tell her that Rhoda was dead?

*Dear God, Rhoda was dead.*

"Arnie?"

He looked up at his partner's approach then rose to his feet, withdrawing a hanky from his pants pocket. *Pull it together, Page.* Somewhere through all his grief, the voice of the detective inside him, forced its way out through the sorrow, through the rage and anguish. *Have to file this away, time to go to work.* "What do we got, Theo?" his voice quivered.

"Arnie, you need time—"

"What do we have, Theo?!" He was in no mood. Every second gave Rhoda's killer a bigger lead. *Murdering sonuvabitch!* His expression softened as he saw the pain echoed in Richardson's eyes. He wasn't the only one who loved Rhoda. He laid a hand on his partner's shoulder. "There'll be time for that later, kid. Now give me the lowdown. Please."

Richardson ran a hand through his hair and took in a steadying breath. "Ok, but hold onto your hat, old man. This is some Twilight Zone shit. Leo came back from lunch, found the guard unconscious in the shack, then Rhoda, here. In between, he also told us, he found the entire shift in the cafeteria frozen like statues."

Reaching into his breast pocket, Arnie whipped out his pad and pen. This already sounded like something that shouldn't be committed to memory.

"Everyone we've talked to say they're missing time."

Arnie grimaced. "Missing...*time*?"

"They all recall going into the lounge on or about 8:30. They say the next thing they know, it's almost nine and Leo's screaming that Rhoda was dead."

His head was swelling. "Any complaints of lightheadedness or nausea?"

"I think I know where you're going, old man. We've already taken samples of the table tops and counters in the lounge. They're on the way to the lab as we speak. If some kind of chemical agent was used, we'll know soon enough. They seem okay, now, but Cap wants them all taken to Metro soon as we've taken their statements."

Captain Williams was no fool. "Good plan. What about the security video?"

Richardson shook his head. "Nada. Whoever overpowered the guard was smart enough to disable the security cameras and snatch up the DVR unit. Follow me." Arnie stayed on Richardson's heels as they walked to the rear of one of the lab tables where a pile of whatever lay on the floor. "We found two piles of this weird ash or dust. The other is near where Rhoda's body was found. I had samples of each taken and they too are on their way to the lab for analysis."

*Dammit, how did he miss that?*

Richardson stepped back toward where Rhoda's body lay. "Then there's this." He pointed to the streaked blood pooled around the body. "Looks like there was some kind of struggle. Tracks through the blood seem to indicate a barefooted female and a booted male. Thing is, there are two sets of bloody prints but only the boot prints lead out." Richardson threw up his hands. "So where did the female go?"

Arnie ran a hand through his hair.

"Oh, it gets better, old man, seems two bodies are also missing from the morgue."

Cranium expanding. "Missing?"

"Yeah, from the looks of it, they're the only things that are."

Head was going critical mass. "This isn't making any sense, Theo. All of this just to steal a couple of dead bodies. What're they trying to hide?"

"I was hoping that keen mind of yours had some idea."

*Hell, if he could figure all this out, he'd go play the lotto and retire.* "Fuck if I know, kid. I'm stumped."

"The wounds on Rhoda's neck look like they were made by an animal. But of course, *no* animal tracks were found in the blood or anywhere in the building."

Arnie's head was splitting. "First, bloodless bodies in McClain Park, then bloodless bodies missing their hearts, and now this, it's just not making any sense." Somewhere in Arnie's mind however everything was starting to make sense.

"Page, Richardson? "The captain waved them over as forensic teams continued about their business. He already knew what Williams was going to say, may as well beat him to the punch.

"Don't worry, Captain, I won't let my emotions get the best of me, I can do my job so *please* don't take me off this case."

There was sympathy and sorrow in his blue eyes. "I'm sorry Arnie, but I need you both to go check on Bricker. He hasn't reported in and he's not answering his phone or pager."

Richardson shook his head. "Not good. Bricker's a greedy prick. It's not like him to not show up to make a buck."

"Agreed. We'll handle the crime scene. I want you both to go look in on him"

There wasn't time for this. "Captain, surely you can get one of the black and whites to head over. This is Rhoda we talking about here!"

"Arnie, we all loved Rhoda but I need this checked out and frankly, *you* are way too close to this." He waved them to a far corner, away from other ears. His voice lowered a decibel. "We've had sudden influx of missing persons reports filed today alone. Now Bricker is off the grid.

189

The mayor is calling in the Feds and the last thing I want or need is to add a cop's name to the list of the missing." Arnie looked back at the body of Rhoda, grief spiced anger welling up in him like a rogue wave. "Arnie, I promise you, we'll find who did this to Rhoda. I'll *personally* lead the investigation, but for now, I need you both to find Bricker."

Richardson leaned in to the elder detective. "Come on, Arnie, Cap can handle this, let's go see what's doin with this ass hole."

Arnie hesitated looking at the dead body of his friend. "Alright. But I want updates on whatever you find."

Williams placed a hand on his shoulder. "Of course, as soon as I know anything, you'll know."

The captain was a good man, he'd keep his word. "Fine. Alright kid, let's go."

Richardson led the way out of the lab. As he reached the doorway, Arnie turned and looked back at Rhoda's lifeless body. "So long, Red, I'm gonna miss you." A tear trailed from his eye. A tear shed for Rhoda and all the sunsets she'd never get to see. For the lost chance of being the one to give her away at the wedding, she so looked forward to one day. For the lives of the children she would've have had, their opportunities ripped away before they were ever conceived. A tear for a very good friend; lost forever. Gone. This wasn't gonna stand. Someone was going to pay for this. And he didn't give a damn if it was human, vampire, or other.

*****

They arrived at Bricker's apartment thirty-five minutes after they left the coroner's office. Neither said much during the drive over. They were in mourning, each grieving in the privacy of their own mind. Richardson hadn't known Rhoda nearly as long as he had, but everyone who met Rhoda took an immediate liking of her and her genuine charm and wit. To know her, was to love her.

Why was it always the good ones who got killed when there were tons of dirt bags out there to choose from? Pulling into the apartment building's parking lot, they found a spot then got out. The place was just two clicks north of an eye sore. The seven story apartment was littered with graffiti of all types. Naturally, most were gang inspired works of art.

Ballsie.

They either didn't know a cop lived here or didn't care. Figures Bricker would call this *paradise* home.

The basketball courts in the distance were fully occupied and lighted, sort of. Only two of the eight light posts were lit. Lucky for them, each brought the gift of Edison to a court. Two guys, three spots down, worked on a tricked out '72 Malibu, the chrome on the steel wheels gleaming even in the dark. The hood was up, one guy worked while the other passed tools, like an O.R. nurse. All in all it seemed quiet enough, of course, things always were when cops made an appearance.

Richardson took a gander around them. "Don't see Bricker's vehicle anywhere. Let's head up."

He scanned the parking lot as they made toward the building. "After you, Junior" Arnie's mind drifted back the Rhoda as they took four flights of stairs to Bricker's door. Striding down the catwalk, they found the building's superintendent standing outside the apartment. Looked like he was about to knock when he spotted them approaching.

"What's going on? "He flashed his badge.

The super looked it over and responded, "Ross is late with the rent, *again*. He's gonna have to shape up or he's out."

Richardson smirked. "Well, it just so happens, we're looking for him too." The kid stepped past the super and knocked on the door. "Bricker, its Richardson." He knocked again and got the same nothing response. Theo looked to the super who stood back with his arms folded across his chest. "Can you open it for us?"

"Sure." He took out his master key and unlocked the door, then stepped aside allowing the detectives to enter. The air was cool and stagnant with a hint of cigarettes and cheap cologne. The room was unremarkable but somewhat tidy with its dated furniture that looked right out of the eighties and brown carpeting that had seen better days.

A galley style kitchen off to the right hosted a sink filled with dishes. The television was still on. A slasher flick was playing from the sound of the woman's screams coming from the speakers. In front of the dingy upholstered couch was a small, white, oval shaped coffee table. A green glass, star shaped ashtray sat in the middle flanked on one side by a stack of Penthouse magazines and an equally high stack of Car and Driver on the other.

Richardson pointed to the superintendent and then to the door. The man took the hint and made his way back outside. They cautiously made their way toward Bricker's bedroom door.

"Bricker, its Page, you alright?"

Richardson drew his weapon as Arnie reached for his own. He stood to the side. Richardson moved to the other side. Slowly, he reached for the knob, turned it, and threw open the door. When no shot was forthcoming, he quickly ducked his head into the doorway then back. "Age before beauty, old man."

"Bite my ass, sonny." The old detective lunged inside with gun at the ready. The room was dark but not completely without light. He could see a made bed and clothes laid out on the floor. "This *really* ain't good. Those are the duds Bricker was wearing when he left work two days ago." The detectives turned back and headed out the way they came. Once in the hall they spotted the building super who had parked it at the end of the corridor.

Arnie led the way as they went to speak with him. "When was the last time you seen Detective Bricker?"

"A couple days ago. He came home then went back out, looked like he was headed out to party."

Richardson chimed in. "You remember what time that was?"

"I think it was about ten. I had just jumped out the shower and saw him headin' outta the lot."

Richardson reached into his back pocket, withdrew a card from his wallet, and passed it to the super. "If he comes back or you hear anything, give us a call."

The super took the card but didn't seem thrilled with the honor. *He didn't like Bricker either. What a shock.* As they made their way back toward the car, he thought of how Rhoda would have reacted to the sight of Bricker's castle. She'd have run screaming to the nearest Home Depot to pick up a drum of Pine and Lysol.

"Where to now, kid?"

"Bricker likes to hang out at one of the new clubs downtown. If he went there, *somebody* had to have seen him."

"Never thought I'd see the day I'd be worried about Bricker."

As they got in the car and drove off, they took a right into traffic. Arnie's stomach curdled. McClain Park, the murdered Pearce family, the missing Mrs. Pearce, Rhoda, and now Bricker was missing. All of this tied together, somehow. And he had a very bad feeling this wasn't the end of it.

# CHAPTER THIRTY THREE

The click of her heels on the pavement ricocheted off the bricks of the decrepit apartment building as she walked, keeping a watchful eye on traffic. The area was dark and trash cluttered. The street lights were on, the ones that still worked, that is.

It was like a ghost town. None of the other girls seemed to be working tonight. Not Raider's hoes, not Verelli's or even Sweet Dick's. It was just her. The McClain Park killings had these bitches spooked. Never know, the killer could be hiding behind any tree waitin' to get ya!

*Ohhhh, scary.*

Fuck that, the rent got to be paid, psycho or not. Had to watch your back here though, southeast New Carrollton wasn't for the weak. Living here meant often having to roll with force. That war between the Dragons and Vice Lords wasn't helping either. *Now*, as if all that drama wasn't enough, a serial killer was stirring shit up. People were staying inside, doors latched, windows locked. Even though it was happening on the other side of town, there was a whole lot less people roaming the streets, including her usual fuckin' customers.

*Dammit.*

Everybody was staying home. How the hell was a working girl supposed to make a living? The cops needed to nail this freak so things could get back to normal. Barely made enough last week to keep the lights on.

She came up on the lonely strip where Cinnamon usually worked. She was one of Sweet D's honeys. A smile spread across her face. Everybody's favorite pimp daddy, damn, what a fine mother fucker he was. Always dressed in them tailor made suits. Always smelling well...sweet, and from what she'd heard from some of his bitches, he wasn't called Sweet Dick cause his name was Richard.

Mother fucker must really have a gold member. And he damn sure seemed to know how to use it. Once he fucked a bitch, it was like he took they minds, even Cara. She knew her from way back in seventh grade. Thought she was the meanest bitch on Earth. All the guys wanted to fuck her and she knew it. Made all they asses work for it, too. But only a couple ever made it with her. She never, ever gave it up easy.

But Dick not only got them panties off, he didn't spend a dime doin it! Musta really laid it down, too. People say they heard her all down the block.

She even heard Cara been fixing his *Sweetness* pancake breakfasts ever since. Ain't that some shit. She slept over once and that ho wouldn't fix her so much as dry toast. She really needed to try some of Sweet D. Find out what all the noise was about. But, maybe it wasn't such a good idea to be messin' around with Tricky Dickie and his magic wand. She needed her mind.

As a rule, she wore as little as possible when she worked but the heat, along with a lack of cash flow, forced her to dig deep into her closet and drag out her ultra-sheer mini skirt and blouse. She'd tied the ends into a knot, just below her C-cups, to expose her midriff. She worked hard on her abs and showing them off was a must. Competition was steep in this part of town. Usually.

Stepping over a portion of sidewalk missing a large chunk and into the shadows, she caught her heel and stumbled. Thanks to some very quick feet, she caught her balance.

*Fuck.*

She balanced herself against a tree, lifted her leg inspecting her foot wear. If she scuffed these shoes, she was gonna sue this dirt hole city. They never wanna fix shit.

Brushing her heels clean, she sashayed on, hoping some john with heavy pockets and a hard dick would flag her down.

Strolling along, her mind drifting, she passed a vacant lot. As usual, the city hadn't bothered to come and trim back the grass and weeds. Looked like a fuckin' jungle in the middle of the block. Guess tax dollars don't go far as it used to.

A large van rolled slowly by. The guy behind the wheel was checking her out. She made eye contact, winked, and blew the driver a kiss. He smiled but kept on his way.

*Oh well, his loss.*

A prickly sensation flowed across her skin. Out of the corner of her eye, she saw it. Her head snapped around. "What the fuck?" She held her breath. Something in the shadows moved. She stared into the tall grass. Apprehension coiled around her spine like a serpent.

Nothing.

She wasn't crazy. She did see the grass move...didn't she? But if something did move in all that green, wouldn't it still be swaying or something? Her eyes must be playing tricks. Maybe these damn contacts need to....something rushed toward her. She screamed.

A fat rat padded its way out. Waddling across the road, it slithered down a storm drain. She blew out a breath. Fuck, now she was getting' jumpy. Guess, fatty's had it for the night. If things didn't pick up soon, she was gonna do the same th—.

"Hi sexy."

The sudden voice in her ear, almost made her leap out of her heels. Her heartbeat hammered against her rib cage. "Oh fuck! You scared the shit outta me."

The medium sized male dressed in a hooded sweatshirt, jeans, and Reeboks stood, hands in his pockets. She eyed him suspiciously. *Please, don't let this bozo have a gun. And wasn't it kinda warm for all that?* She was used to losers, but this asshat just stood there, leering like he wanted to eat her or something. He was making her a little nervous.

"Sorry, I was just lookin' for some action."

Uh, uh. She knew bullshit when she heard it. He wanted something, alright, but it wasn't sex. A sudden bad vibe told her goin' anywhere with creepy would be a big fuckin' mistake. "Sorry baby, I'm headin' in for the night. I should be back tomorrow, come back then." What a big fat lie. She'd have to do extra Hail Mary's tonight. Blowing him a kiss, she turned on her heels, and walked right into him.

She swallowed a shriek. "How the fuck did you do that?"

He smiled. That's when she noticed them. Two points sticking out from under his top lip. Fear threw her body in reverse, her heart revving up like an Indy car. His smile peeled back. Now she could clearly see his...

*Oh. My. God.*

He smiled and winked. She ran screaming, her heels clicking rapid fire on the pavement. She was babbling. Everything coming out of her mouth led with "Oh God, oh God". One of her heels snapped. *Can't stop. Can't look back.* Whatever the fuck he was, she knew was right behind her. As she hit the corner, her hair got yanked. Pain jolted a yelp from her lips as her head snapped back, her legs flew out from under her. She slapped the ground. Hard.

With a pull, he jerked her to her feet. She turned, desperately gouging at her attacker. His eyes were wild with excitement. She'd seen that look before. He was getting off on it.

"Yeah, I love it when they fuckin' struggle!" He drew back and slapped her senseless.

*Holy fuck.* Nobody ever hit her that hard. Not even her slap happy ex. Her head throbbed as she was dragged down the alley between two abandoned buildings.

Air blasted from her lungs as she was forced her against the wall. The harsh brick scored her back. He pushed her head sideways. "Hold still, now, this won't hurt, much."

She screamed. But, if anybody heard her, would they fuckin' care? Bitches were always screeching out here. Nobody would even bother calling the police. She was fucked.

*****

The black SUV rumbled down the asphalt. Stosh was behind the wheel while Trey, shotgun at his side, rode same. Running his hand over the soft material covering his seat, he breathed out the sigh of contentment. This thing was plush, spacious, and the ride was smooth as glass. He had to get him one of these. Sure beat the hell outta riding on the Harley. Whoever dreamed up this baby, took luxury, style, and comfort, put it on four wheels and name it Ford Expedition.

Thanks to Stosh's contacts, they were loaded to the teeth with vamp snuffing hardware, a whole boat load of automatic weapons, stakes, silver bullets, and other goodies. Wonder how the designers would take knowing their monument to extravagance had been turned into a supernatural urban assault vehicle? If New Carrollton's finest pulled them over…well, he'd heard the scenery around N.C. Correctional was lovely this time of the year.

They took a right and rolled down Penny Street. They'd spent most of the night cruising the city's underbelly. Best place to go when hunting vamps. It was easier preying on the ones no one would miss or even care about.

No such luck tonight, though. Anna was a wily one. She knew a slayer would anticipate that. So now, they were headed for the lower southeast side, the mean streets of New Carrollton's ghetto. Stopping at a light, he noted a corner store. The red neon open sign flickered erratically. The white paint was distressed nearly to the point of nonexistence.

Just a few feet away a young hood chatted on a cell phone. He looked all of sixteen, dough boy most likely, slinging rocks was his game. With a whole lot of luck, the kid might see eighteen. Doubt it though.

The light turned green. The SUV urged forward. Three blocks down, Stosh hung a left. A tall, curvaceous, blonde in a black lacy halter top, Daisy Dukes, fishnets, and heels, waved and blew a kiss.

"*Whoooo weee!*"

He gave the big man's shoulder a pat. "Steady, big fella."

"Tommy, I ain't seen a rack like that since cousin Vance's BBQ."

He didn't lie, the girl had been blessed. Mightily. "Breathe, Stosh. Just keep driving."

"I know, I know, business. But *boy* howdy, I'd sure like to introduce a stimulus package into her economy."

He rolled his eyes. Stosh was always hungry and horny.

It was late. Frankly, he was hungry too, so they stopped at the golden arches and grabbed some sandwiches, plural. Trying to feed Stosh with one burger would be like using an eyedropper on a forest fire.

They drove a few blocks. It was amazing how empty the streets were. All those murders must've really spooked these people. The sounds of Alabama's *Elvira* filled the cab as they drove a block further and took yet another turn. The working street lamps here were few and far between. Shadows were numerous, large enough to hide a number of hungry, bloodthirsty neck biters.

Coming up on the right, a lone woman wearing next to nothing stood staring off into the blackness of a grass covered field. Judging by her outfit, she was a working girl. Out here alone with a serial killer running loose, she had guts. Her head bobbing up and down, side to side, something sure grabbed her attention. Stosh saw her too. He slowed the SUV's speed to a crawl.

She screamed. From out of the brush, plodded a portly rat; damn, couldn't blame her for screaming, it was a big fuckin' rat. But, it wasn't the least bit interested in her. It kept right on by, out into the street and down a storm drain. Once the plump rodent was gone, she turned. Whoa, that guy just popped in out of thin air.

*Gotcha.*

She whirled about as Stosh moved in slowly. Good. If they spooked him, he'd just blur away. As they drew ever closer, the street walker and the vamp conversed. The kiss she blew, a moment later, signaled that the chat was over. When she started away, the vamp blurred. She walked right into him.

Even from where he was, Trey could see she was starting to freak. She was getting ready to...*and* there she goes. But the blood sucker chased her down in the wink of an eye. The bastard grabbed hold of her hair and yanked. The poor girl's legs flew out from under her. She slapped the ground so hard, it made his body ache.

Clenching his teeth, he gripped the shotgun. Sonuvabitch yanked to her feet. The girl was a fighter, though. She went right at him but a vicious slap put an end to that action. Not good, he dragged her into that alley.

Feeding time.

Screaming her head off, she fought the blood sucker like a hell cat. And not so much as one light flicked on, in any window. Baby girl needed rescue. And she was gonna get it.

"Punch it, big man!"

"We're rollin' like thunder, junior." The SUV surged as Stosh jammed his size eighteen down on the gas pedal. Tires screeched as they

199

rounded the corner and roared down the alley. The headlights caught them in its bright beam. The vamp had her against the wall. Another sharp slap across the hooker's face, forced her head back, he opened wide, all set to take a bite, and it wasn't gonna be out of crime. Stosh slammed on the brakes. The big man's door flew open at the exact instant he threw open his. Finally, a chance to split a wig and some fangs.

*****

He slapped her again. She couldn't see anything for all the stars in her eyes. Forcing her head again to the side, he leaned in, opening his mouth wide. His breath was like ice on her neck and smelled like a shit house. She struggled but he was fuckin' stronger than anybody she'd ever seen. She couldn't even wiggle her fingers.

He leaned in, saliva dripped from teeth that looked like ivory knives. She clamped her eyes shut. *Jesus, just get it over with*!

With the roar of an engine, headlights flooded the alley. A huge SUV skidded to a stop, the doors flying open. Hissing, he released her throat and rushed the Ford. She was free, time to go. Her legs wouldn't move. And what the fuck, her voice, she couldn't even squeak. Desperate, she wanted to yell, 'run, it's a fuckin' vampire'! *But who was she kidding? They'd think she was on something.*

The silhouette of one of her rescuers threw something at her attacker. He stopped dead, shaking wildly as the second one, a mountain with legs, dropped the bastard with a fist the size of her head. Mister fangs fell flat on his back as the first rescuer rushed to her side.

"Go. Get outta here."

What a damn good idea. A firm shove in the back got her going. Her feet never touched the ground as she ran like hell, outta the alley. Fuck this shit. She was goin' back to school. Time to get off these streets and get a real fuckin' job, rowdy johns she could deal with but vampires…check please.

*****

The vampire struggled against the silver hand cuffs searing his skin. The blood sucker was flat on his back, arms underneath him, legs shackled. The smell of burning flesh stung his nostrils as Stosh came back from the rental with a small leather case. Scowl on his face, the big man stooped down and grabbed the vamp by his cheeks.

"I figured I'd save myself the trouble of askin' ya nicely, vamp." Setting the case down, Stosh opened it up and withdrew a vial and syringe. Trey kept look out in case sunshine had back up of his own.

"This here is silver nitrate. Just a few cc's of this stuff, for you, would be like chuggin' acid. Stosh plunged the needle into the vial and withdrew a little into the syringe. "Now, I know you one of Anna's cause we tested your blood. So, I'm gonna ask you one time, son, where is she and where's her nest?" The captive responded by spitting at Stosh.

"I don't think he likes you, Stosh."

"I'm all broke up. Well Tommy, I always told you I'd show you how to get answers from these bastards. Looks like this is your lucky night, you get to see how to interrogate a vamp. "He walked over, regarded the vampire and grinned. "Holla if ya need to, Slick. This might hurt a bit."

# CHAPTER THIRTY FOUR

Despair hung on Adalius like an anchor. His hair flew about his head, trench coat tails snapping in high winds that seemed intent on testing his metal. He stood, a lonely sentinel, atop the highest building in New Carrollton. Watching. Brooding. The city below was alive with activity as he scrutinized the heat exhausted metropolis. His spirit mourned. Blessed Elder, to dwell in a city filled with so many, and yet, still be alone.

Serena.

Her name seared into his being, she was his world, his life, as much a part of him as his own hand. Without her, it was hard to comprehend why he need exist. He threw back his head, locking his jaw. *Why couldn't she understand? He wanted only to protect her.* In an instant, he could meet his end hunting Anna and her sycophants. What kind of male would he be to ask her to endure night after restless night, worrying for his safety? How could ask that of her? What right did he have?

The weight of creation fell upon him as he cast his eyes skyward. If only he could go back. He would change all that had come to pass. Undo it all. He would prevent Anna from turning him, and sending him on an odyssey of senseless bloodshed.

Anna.

Her name was like venom on his lips. It all went back to Anna. She was his maker and for so long, his lover. He shuddered at all the lives they had destroyed together, enough to fill a canyon with bodies and a sea with blood. The faces and screams haunted every moment of his existence. The outraged voices of the dead thundered in his soul like an avalanche. There was no respite, no escape. Only remorse at the knowledge that there was no way to change what had been.

His heart hardened. Thoughts of his sire shanghaied his focus. By Hell's heart, he would end her madness. It drove him, denied him peace even in the depths of sleep like a ruthless taskmaster. Recurring dreams of his blade severing Anna's head, and watching her crumble to ash, hounded him as if demanding retribution.

An annoyed growl rose in his throat. Recollections of the night he first encountered Anna on that lonely stretch of beach so long ago, where it all began.

\*\*\*\*\*

*June 15th, 1697, the island of Jamaica.*

*He'd left the dwelling of his brother Kalleal. It was late. Breezy. The ocean had blessed the land, after a brutally hot day, with cooling salt air. He was alone, and so very lonely, as he walked along on the moon lit beach. The stars twinkled peacefully above as he strolled along listening to the gentle sounds of the surf lapping at the shore. A bitter chill engrossed him. The sharp contrast in temperature was like a slap in the face. That was when he saw her. Like a wraith, she took form tall, beautiful, and sleek.*

\*\*\*\*\*

The wind gusted suddenly as if trying to force him from the rooftop. He whirled about, flashing his sword. Body taut, adrenaline flooding his veins, Adalius resonated aggression. Sometimes rogue winds heralded the arrival of an adversary. Reaching out with his senses, he scanned the shadows, trolling for concealed assailants. Eyes darting, blade at the ready, he shifted his stance to defense position. Shadows lay directly ahead. He probed it, his mind like radar. Clear.

More shadows to his left. Pivot and hold. Wait. Listen. Feel. Clear. Once more to his right, as before, clear. Exhale.

The darkness harbored nothing within. Satisfied there was no other presence but his, he returned the sword to its sheath. No antagonist would be forthcoming. Nature was simply flexing its might.

Anna, so evil was she, possessed of an unnatural beauty and persuasive charm, it was understandable how they who serve her are held thrall to her whims. A deep breath, then long exhale, flushed the remaining tension from his system as the past exerted its pull on him once more.

*****

*Anna's hair was waist length, and appeared almost made from moonlight. It moved about as if alive. It fell about her shoulders, partially covering the soft mounds of her breasts. She was completely devoid of clothing, smiling as she approached him. The sensual sway of her hips were hypnotic, her eyes, luminescent. They seized him, drew him in.*

*It was difficult to resolve what frightened him more, that he was losing himself in the depths of her gaze or that he didn't care. All that mattered were those beautiful eyes. Nothing was more important than the delight found there.*

*Each time he tried to look away, it was as if a limb were being torn away. Breath would flee from his lungs. So he clung to her gaze like a drowning man to drift wood. Anna stepped into his embrace. Her lips soft and sweet, her body rose against him as she drew his lips to hers with a fire he had never known. The heat between them was all consuming. Yet her body radiated no warmth. As her tongue slipped between his lips, it was as if something invaded his mind and spirit. Her arms encircled his neck as she deepened the kiss, giving so much, while stealing much more.*

*When she broke their embrace, she called him by name. It nearly broke the spell. He had not told her his name. How did she know? Who was she? From where did she come? Those thoughts were drawn from him as if by vacuum. She whispered to him her name. Anna. Told him that he of all she had encountered stirred her passion. She had chosen him.*

204

*With a will not his own, he took her into his arms. And there on the beach, they made desperate love as time itself seemed to stand still. While deeply engaged in coupling, she smiled down on him, with teeth like daggers. To his shock, she opened wide and struck. Searing pain was washed over by a wave of euphoria. His body weakened while Anna moaned and clung to his vein.*

*Darkness descended on his soul like a veil, coiled about him like an inflamed lover as Anna sank her fangs ever deeper. When she released him, blood trickled from the corner of her mouth. He was helpless. Dying. Closing his eyes, he awaited the end. Instead, Anna made an offer a dying man couldn't refuse. Accept, and he would live forever. Refuse... a lifeline to a dying man. He accepted.*

*The smile he grew to fear, love, then at last despise, spread across her lips. With surprising care, she sank her fangs back into his neck. The world dissolved and he along with it, barely conscious, a thick liquid trickled past his lips, into his mouth. Somewhere in the distance, a fading voice beckoned. Drink. And how he drank.*

*****

His anger yanked him back to the present. Fangs extended to attack position, ready to rend and tear. Eyes blazed like headlights, muscles swelled, ready for action. *Control, must maintain control*! His rage, the demon within, was breaking free.

No.

Assuming a fighting stance, he focused and concentrated on breath control, on forcing the beast back into its cage. Deep breath in. Turn. Slow controlled exhale. Thrust. Deep breath in. Slow exhale. Block.

Smoothly executing his Kata, he focused on his form, channeling his anger into each punch, block and kick. Breathing even and steady, he continued subduing his inner adversary. The greatest opponent he ever faced, himself. Finishing his routine he returned to his original start position, exhaled, and relaxed.

Control was his once more. He was the master of his anger. No longer would he be ruled by it. Mind cleared, he let go and waded again into the depths of history.

*****

*How much time passed? He did not know. But when he awoke, his size strength and size were vastly enhanced. His vision and hearing were more acute. Sounds of the jungle were magnified a hundredfold. He actually heard the beating wings of insects, the thumping hearts of birds flying above, and fish splashing near shore as they fed on hapless insects wandering to close the water's surface.*

*All of it crashed against him. It was staggering, like standing underneath a dam that suddenly burst. But Anna guided him through it. Had it not been for her, he might have gone mad.*

*Taking his hand, she lead him off the island with by far the most unexpected and wondrous benefit of his transition. Flight. For decades they roamed the world. She groomed him. Taught him all he needed to be vampire. Sadly, she also instructed him in the ways of tormenting prey before feeding, by savoring the sweetness of terror as well as their blood.*

*They traveled across Asia and Europe, corrupting everything they came into contact with. Anna transformed him into more than just a creature of the night. He became an incarnate of darkest evil, vile, irredeemable, one of the most sadistic creatures on the face of the Earth. Until that fateful day his humanity was restored.*

*They had been journeying across the countryside of Portugal when he and Anna stumbled across an encampment of gypsies. Wrapped in shadows, they watched them as they danced, ate, and sang around the campfire. That was when he saw her, an alluring gypsy girl named Esmeralda. She was beautiful, graceful with eyes filled with life and mystery. It was as if he had spent a lifetime holding his breath, then was at last was given permission to exhale.*

*It was surreal. For so long, he had only known Anna's depraved idea of love. He had come to believe himself incapable, unworthy of true love, but what he felt for the Esmeralda was magic.*

*As a vampire, light was his greatest enemy. But he would have happily stood in the light of Esmeralda for eternity. Anna felt it. Sensed what had occurred and tested his loyalty. Anna demanded he kill the girl. As his maker, she ordered him to slay the gypsy. He refused. Anna was incredulous. No vampire had ever defied an order from their sire. Like the sun rising in the south, it should have been impossible! Anna, however, would not be dissuaded. She threatened that if he did not kill the gypsy, she would. Her jealousy would not allow a rival for his affection to live.*

*For the first time, they quarreled and fought. He was no match for her. Anna simply overpowered him. When he recovered, Anna stood before him, a mortal heart in hand. Esmeralda's heart. Damn Anna to eternal fire! It wasn't enough to kill Esmeralda, Anna utterly defiled her. With a satanic smile, Anna bit and tore the organ apart. A thousand silver stakes would not have caused him as much torment! Mocking him with her laughter, she flew away.*

*When he journeyed to the gypsy encampment, he found carnage. Anna had been merciless. Not even toddlers or infants were spared. Severely wounded, weeping, and still holding his dead daughter is where he found Esmeralda's father.*

*It was his fault, all of it. He failed to stop Anna, and the gypsies had paid a horrific price.*

*Before death took him, the gypsy astounded him with an offer. In exchange for his vow to avenge them all, he would weave a spell that would make Adalius immune to sunlight. He did not know whether the human was delusional or not but he was fading fast. Hesitation was not an option. Becoming a daywalker would grant him an advantage, a fighting chance against Anna. He gave his word.*

*****

He had pursued Anna around the globe and would not stop until her ashes were scattered in the winds. He drew a dagger. Slicing diagonally across his hand, he watched blood rise and pool. Closing his hand into a fist, he raised it to the night sky. Anna would answer for all the lives she has taken. Vengeance would have its day, for the gypsy, for himself, for all who live and will live, but most importantly, for Esmeralda.

A scream below snapped Adalius out of his reverie. There had been many since he perched atop the skyscraper but none had come close to the stark terror of the new cry. Shutting his eyes, he listened, trying to determine from where the voice had come. Once again, the scream rang out followed by a growl then a crash.

Adalius was airborne like a missile. There was little time. A woman was under attack, from the sound of it, by a very hungry vampire. Homing in on the woman's cries, he spotted them.

She was running as if hell hounds pursued her. Stumbling into cans, crawling on her knees, she kept screaming and scrambling. It made little difference. The vampire was gaining. He dove down as the vampire tackled his prey to the ground. The female struggled frantically but against a vampire in blood lust, she would die if he did not act. When his boots hit the ground, he blurred. The immortal had pinned her wrists to the ground. He was seconds from claiming his prize. Just as the vampire was about to strike, Adalius collared the aggressor and flung him away. He slammed against the brick wall to the rear of the alley.

"Get to safety!" Adalius yelled. Rising to her feet, she ran. As she did, he dazzled her mind. There would be only vague images of being mugged by a gang banger. Instinct compelled him to pursue, to chase down fleeing prey, but he was no longer servant to his impulses. Turning, he strode toward the vampire, who was rising to his feet.

Adalius threw out his hand. The attacker flew back and was pinned against the wall. The vampire snapped, snarled, trying to break the hold, but Adalius was far too strong.

The villain glared, its eyes a fiery orange. "Whadda you want?!"

"You are one of Anna's. I can smell her mark upon you."

"Let me go."

Adalius' expression hardened. "Unlikely. I need information. You are newly turned, a danger to yourself and others. Why have they left you to fend for yourself?"

The immortal snarled. "What do I look like? I'm not a fuckin' pet. I do what I want, when I want. Fuck them mother fuckers! I don't need them."

"You need instruction, there are things you must learn if you are to survive."

"Fuck that, I'm my own man. I don't take orders, 'specially from some vamp bitch with an empress complex."

"Perhaps, but still, you need guidance. If you help me, I will see to it you have the knowledge you require. All you need do is tell me where to find Anna."

The newbie laughed bitterly. "I'm no snitch, mother fucker, kiss my ass!"

Predictable. "I suspected you would be unwilling to cooperate, but I will know what you know. Adalius entered the mind of the newbie.

The vampire flinched. "The fuck are you doing?"

"I am doing what you will be able to do, in time."

The newbie's face contorted. "Get outta my head ya fucker!"

Adalius focused as he probed through the vampire's mind. "I will be but a moment."

The vampire groaned as he attempted to block the mental incursion.

"You waste energy, even if you were versed in your abilities, you are too young to resist me."

"Ahh, get outta my head ya bastard!" The newbie shuddered as Adalius probed deeper.

Anna would need a nest far enough away from the populace that it would not attract unwanted scrutiny, yet close enough to provide ready access to New Carrollton's residents, a structure that would allow her nest room to expand, something large and unattended. Like…that lighthouse! He had seen it when he had flown into the city. He withdrew from the vampire's mind.

"I have what I need." Adalius released his captive from the wall. The vampire fell in a heap. "If you are willing, I will still teach you what you need to know. It is too dangerous for you to wander about uneducated."

The newbie rose to his feet, brushing his clothes free of dust. "Fuck you! I didn't ask for or need your help. Now get outta my way, I gotta eat."

The sound of a thud echoed across the alley. The newbie's eyes went wide as he crumbled to dust.

"I am afraid you will not need any meals henceforth. Forgive me, I could not allow you to roam free unchecked. Rest well and in peace." He replaced the dagger in inside his trench.

209

There was a subtle shift in the air, light as the breeze made by dragonfly wings. He whirled about, pistols drawn. "Show yourself, I know you are there! "Silence. "I will not ask again. Step forth and be recognized."

The outline of a huge figure faded out of the shadows. He was a giant powerfully built, wearing a black mesh body shirt underneath his leather jacket. Undoubtedly, underneath, lay a small arsenal of weapons. An Enforcer.

The blonde crew cut, diagonal scar running across his face and the patch over his left eye, told him all he needed to know. Trouble had made its way to his doorstep.

The Enforcer sneered as he held his hands in plain sight. "Nicely done, half breed, saved me the trouble of finishing him."

Adalius' blood came to a boil. "Kruger."

# CHAPTER THIRTY FIVE

That vampire was a tough nut to crack. It'd taken longer than Trey thought, but before the sliver reduced him to dust, the vamp spilled everything he knew about Anna's nest. It was located near the Colgate Bridge in the old lighthouse, a perfect place for Anna to establish her nest of vipers. Finally, they had a solid lead.

They parked the rental by the side of the road, grabbed their gear, then made their way across a pedestrian bridge which ran parallel and just under a four lane motorist bridge, ninety feet above the river below.

Once across, they stepped off the path and into the tall grass. Strolling up to the front door wasn't an option. They weren't Avon salesmen. Instead, they made their way up a sloped hill, approaching the house from the rear.

The fragrance of honeysuckle and other wild flowers drifted to his nostrils as they traversed the landscape, strafed by numerous hungry insects. A sheen of perspiration covered their bodies. Trey wiped his brow. *Could get any hotter?* Two in the morning and it was still eighty six degrees. The muffled roar of the water, the full moon above, the sound of traffic, and the chirp of crickets kept them company as they journeyed closer to where fangs took refuge.

The lighthouse had seen better days. Boarded up windows, peeling paint, weather beaten wood, missing planks, and shingles, betrayed its age. The long, cracked driveway sprouted weeds and wild grass. Nature was going about its business, repossessing land on which the lighthouse sat.

"This must be the place, son," Stosh said, keeping his voice down, as he drew his Smith and Wesson.

Trey slapped his arm to kill a feeding mosquito. "No doubt. Only a vamp would pick a dump like this."

Stosh checked his weapon as Trey did likewise. Feeling a sting, Trey slapped his neck. Damn blood suckers all alike, going for the jugular.

While watching for signs of a trap, Stosh spied something. "Lookee there, Tommy." The big man pointed to a gaping hole in the light house wall. He saw the jagged, pickup truck sized opening. He didn't like it one bit. It provided the blood suckers inside a king sized escape hatch. A dozen or more could break camp before they could lay wood down. *Shit. Life just refused to be simple. Oh well, being a slayer was a bitch, then you die.*

"No need to check under the mat for a key. I'm just guessin'." Stosh flashed a grin.

Hilarious. If they weren't about to lock horns with vamps who'd happily chew their vital organs out, it'd be a real gut buster.

Trey's eyes roamed over the lifeless structure, he turned his attention above to the searchlight area. "Think some could be nesting up there?"

Stosh shook his head. "I'm bettin' it's lit up from sunup to sundown. They probably stay as far away from there as they can."

That makes sense.

Uneasiness drew his eyes back to the opening in the wall. The hairs on his arms stood on end. The two upstairs windows, along with that ugly hole, gave the house an almost face-like quality. Creepy. It was like the place was inviting them into its maw. A mouth undoubtedly filled with vamp fangs. But damned if that wasn't what they were going to do. What the hell, today was as good as any to get killed. "Let's go big man, but watch your six. We don't know how many there are."

"Roger that my friend."

They proceeded toward the wall opening, knifing through the tall grass. They each took a side of that nasty hole, quietly setting down their duffle bags. Trey reached into his satchel, withdrew a few darts from his stash and placed them in his jacket. Turning, he did a double take as Stosh unloaded a huge battle axe from his bag. A wicked looking thing too. Large curved blade, long spike in the back. It looked like it'd snuffed out more lives than cancer.

Ole Mildred is what Stosh called it. The big man said he'd had it since the day he dusted his first fang. Stosh insisted that if he ever bought it, he wanted Mildred buried with him.

Checking his weapons, he gave the man mountain a quizzical look. Stosh held up his index finger. He needed a second. Reaching once more into his bag, Stosh withdrew a canteen, took a swig, and then returned it to its place. Patting the axe like a beloved hound, he gave the thumbs up. Stosh was ready. Trey nodded. Game on. Slowly, carefully, they crossed the threshold and entered hell's mouth.

The place was covered with a layer of dust you could cut with a butter knife and smelled of mold and rot. Intermittent moon beams peppered the room. Tiny specks danced into then out of the light.

No horrifying screams. That was never a bad thing. They moved with care.

It was best to keep the noise down. If they wanted to keep breathing, that is. Losing the element of surprise could cost them more than just the battle. Vamps could hear a kitten lapping milk from a mile. His muscles tightened. Tension was a bitch. *Breathe. Now, step. Floor creak. Shit!*

The floor groaned once more behind him, pleading for relief. He turned. Stosh's teeth were clenched. He scowled at the big slayer. That's what eight Big Mac's will do for you. A sting pinched his sinuses. *Oh no*. He locked his jaw. A sneeze threatened to blow dust and their cover.

His nose primed to ready to fire. Stosh shook his head, wide eyed, while he engaged in 'No you're not. yes I am.' with his schnoz. The struggle was brief, but it damn sure felt like hours. At last his nose took the hint and disarmed. Stosh blew out a relieved sigh then gestured with his hand. Spread out.

Trey moved carefully to opposite side of the room. Cobwebs hung from the vaulted ceiling like vines as they eased through what was once a cavernous living room. His skin tingled. His eyes flashed around the room, the vamps know, they're there.

"Oh shi-" A blur slammed into him. Air blasted out of his lungs as he driven backward through the nearest wall. The fight hadn't even started and he was a dead man.

# CHAPTER THIRTY SIX

The German was massive. Two inches taller and thirty pounds heavier than the two hundred seventy-five pounds Adalius' own frame supported. Arms raised in surrender, Kruger stalked toward him.

The corners of Adalius' mouth upturned at the sight of the Enforcer's scar. A souvenir he'd given his nemesis from their last encounter. When the Enforcer was within fifteen feet, he sensed it, waves of distortion, a psychic interference. It was Kruger's mental shield. All vampires kept their psychic barriers raised to prevent others from reading their thoughts. But the Enforcer's was so intensified it that it was interfering with his senses. Making it difficult to focus, it was like one radio signal jamming another.

Suppressing a groan, Adalius clenched his jaw at the pressure building at his temples. It worsened with each step his adversary took. This was deliberate; Kruger was hiding something, something important to expend so much energy to conceal it.

Even from the shadows, the contempt was evident in Kruger's remaining eye. The bitter malice matched only by the dark malevolence smoldering in the Enforcer's heart. Adalius sneered, the grip on his pistols tightened.

Monster.

Kruger reveled in inflicting unspeakable torture on those he hunted before passing the Council's final sentence. His brutality gained him notice in political circles and the favor of those in high places. Through that and cunning, he quickly rose to the rank of First Lieutenant. Among the Enforcers he ranked second only to Argus, the First.

Internally, he raged at creation for the indignity that one such as Kruger was one of his brethren. They were both Sandrian but while he had been turned, Kruger was pure bred. He was born Sandrian. A bigot and an elitist, his disdain toward the turned, was renown, as was their hatred of each other.

"Ve meet again, half breed. Now I know vhy this placed smelled of sewage. The whole area stinks of Mohars." Bristling at the slur and Kruger's predatory smile, Adalius leashed his anger. The villain was undoubtedly trying to bait him into doing something foolish.

It nearly worked.

The compulsion to attack was overwhelming. To carve another scar across his smug face would be a delight. But it would be on his terms not Kruger's. "State your business, Kruger," he growled with Glocks trained on the intruder.

The Hessian came to a stop, that sinister eye looked him up and down as if inspecting an insect. "You don't look pleased to see me. I'm vounded." The Enforcer place a hand over his heart feigning injury.

Adalius' eyes glowed teal in warning, if provoked he was more than ready to let loose a volley of hot silver. "State... your... business." His chest reverberated at the power of his own voice.

"My business ist my own, half breed." Kruger lowered his hand, his lone eye locking with his.

"Whatever your business, it is not here with me."

Kruger sneered, his scar shifting with every change in facial expression. "No, not this night anyvay."

"Then be on your way, Enforcer."

Kruger threw back his head, letting loose a belly laugh that echoed off the walls. "Or vhat? You will shoot me? The mighty Adalius, reduced to gunning down an unarmed, helpless opponent."

His lips peeled back, exposing his fangs. "You are many things, Kruger, but helpless you are not. Now, be on your way or kill you I shall."

Aggression charged the air. Adalius' body coiled, ready to spring. His warrior eyes took stock of the alley. The tight quarters were far from his liking. If combat ensured, he'd have to get airborne. The constricted space and Kruger's superior strength would give him the advantage.

The Enforcer glowered, but made no threatening moves. A wise decision, the slightest muscle twinge and the first shot would enter through the only thing remaining between him and complete blindness. Time stood still, frozen between seconds. He waited for the moment Kruger made his move, for the flash of Enforcer steel. Instead, Kruger did the unexpected. He nodded, in approval.

"You seek Frau Longfellow. Interesting, an entire legion of Enforcers struggle to track the Destroyer, yet you manage to do so vith little difficulty. Vhy ist that, I vunder?"

"She is my maker, even you should have little *difficulty* comprehending that." His eyes sparkled, fingers caressing the triggers. Patience was wearing thin with Kruger's games.

"Jawohl, I do in fact comprehend. How is it that you seemingly do not? Perhaps there ist something you vish to remain hidden. Or could it be you truly have not made the connection. Vhich invites other interesting questions, but no matter. You are but a mongrel, but you have courage. Vun day I shall be your slayer. But that day is not today. But there vill be a time. I take my leave of you half breed, for now." With that, he backed away and faded from view.

He did a mental sweep, holding fast to his weapons. Kruger was treacherous, known for lulling an opponent into a sense of false security then attacking when defenses were down. But the pressure at his temples was fading. Kruger had indeed vacated the area.

Stress receded like the tide from a shore. Holstering his weapons, he blew out a calming breath, musing over this latest encounter. Kruger did not come so far from the Sanctuary to confront him, and then simply walk away. There was more to this than was immediately apparent.

It was a conundrum for another time. There were far more urgent matters at hand. He now knew where to find Anna. Kruger could wait. But the day would come when their vendetta would come to a very violent conclusion. One day very soon.

With a thought he wrapped himself in shadows, lifted off and was airborne, streaking westward toward the lighthouse where the sun had set.

# CHAPTER THIRTY SEVEN

**S**tosh heard Trey grunt as the vamp tackled him through the wall. Sweet molasses that was gonna leave a mark. No time to lend a hand. He couldn't see a blessed thing, but he knew what was headed right for him. He swung his battle axe. The blade severed the vampire's head. Dusted before he knew he'd been struck.

Stosh caught a sharp blow to the side of his head. It staggered him. Shaking off the effects, Stosh gathered his wits. A pair of hands clamped down of his forearm. Fangs pierced his skin. Stosh clenched his teeth as a third vampire materialized in front of him.

"You gonna pay for offing Rick, fat man," the new blood sucker hissed!

He drove the butt of his battle axe into the nose of the feeding vampire. The blood sucker cried out, releasing his hold. In a swift move, he swung Mildred in an upward arc, slicing through neck. Poof! That's *two* dust bunnies!

The remaining vampire roared and launched himself into his sternum, knocking the axe free from his hand. He fell backward through a three legged coffee table with the irate vampire still atop him.

A sharp punch connected with his jaw. Blood flowed from his split lip. *Fiddlesticks.* The scent would send the bastard into blood lust, and most likely bring any other blood suckers running.

The vamp rained blows. He avoided some, blocked the others. The ones that did land though were taking a toll. *Gotta hang on. If Tommy was dead or worse, bein' turned, he wouldn't leave him. He wouldn't abandon him to the undead life. Never leave your own behind*!

Stosh received another punch. His face felt warm from swelling. It was hard to think. *Hell, what was his name again?* His arms dropped to the floor, he couldn't take another punch. One play left, if he missed, Mama Milford's baby boy wouldn't be home for dinner, ever. The vamp grinned. He thought it was over. Maybe it was. Extending fangs, he leaned down.

"Time to pay up, fat man!" A gunshot rang out. *God Almighty, Tommy!* The smile on the vampire's face was triumphant. "Sounds like your friend just had his ticket punched." The blood sucker grabbed hold of his head, turning it to expose his vein. His fangs gleamed, saliva dripped from the tips. As the vamp opened wide and went for the jugular, Stosh jerked his head free and spit water into the demon's open mouth.

The vamp leaped to his feet. Choking and gagging, he shook his head from side to side. His mouth sizzled as the water went to work turning his lips into a bubbly goo.

Stosh wiped his mouth on his sleeve. "Ya looked parched thought ya could use a drink a holy water, Sparky."

The vampire glared, then charged. A gunshot! The vamp's head exploded into a plume of dust. He stepped aside as the headless body crumbled to the floor.

Trey.

"Nice shot, junior, you alright?"

Trey blew out a breath, wiping his brow. "Considering I just got planted through a wall, peachy."

"Had me worried for a sec. Thought you might have checked out on me."

Trey smirked. "Not a chance."

"One thing's for sure, if there were more of them, they woulda either come a runnin'"

"Or got the hell outta Dodge." Trey finished his thought.

"Yep, but we still got to clear this puppy so let's get to it." Retrieving his axe, he and Trey scoured the house. Like they suspected though, the other blood suckers split. Satisfied that the dump was vamp free, they made their way back outside.

"You thinking what I'm thinking big man?" Trey asked, digging into his duffle bag.

"It was too easy? Yeah, there's another nest out there somewhere. We can't wait no longer, Tommy, we need to let Maya know."

"I hear ya. Soon as we get back to the rental I'll call her."

They went back inside, placing crosses at every entrance and window, blessed the lighthouse and the land on which it sat, packed up their gear, then headed back toward the bridge in silence. The lighthouse and its property were now useless to Anna. Now it was time to call in backup. They had confirmation. Anna's nest building was in full swing; time to bugle for the cavalry.

*****

They discussed possible strategies as they started across the bridge. Midway, Trey felt a strange sensation running down his back. Like ants down his spine. Something coming up fast behind them! Before he could shout a warning, it slammed into him with violent force. He went flying. It felt like he'd been hit by a truck. Trey landed face down on the hard concrete of the pedestrian bridge, scraping skin from his palms. He momentarily lost consciousness. By sheer will, he clawed his way back from nothingness, and regretted it. Every part of him screamed for attention or just screamed.

Somewhere in the fog draping his mind, he heard a voice crying out. *Dear God, Stosh!* Adrenaline blasted away the remaining cobwebs as he forced himself to his knees. His body protested as he struggled to his feet. When he turned, a brunette female vampire was holding Stosh by his neck, dangling him above the raging river below. Stosh was covered in his own blood. The she-vamp yanked a dagger from his body and stabbed him again and again.

"*Stosh!* He charged. The vampire flashed a look in his direction. She smiled cruelly, then drew the blade across Stosh's throat. As blood flooded from the wound, she released her grip. Stosh dropped from sight.

The suddenness, the brutality, the realization that Stosh just died, in front of him...Raw grief ripped his soul. It was as if the vamp had reached into his body and yanked out his insides. In a blur the female tackled him to the ground, before he reacted. When she took his head in her hands, he saw it, furious rage. She thirsted for more than blood. This wasn't just a vamp going after a couple of slayers. This was personal! This bitch wanted revenge.

He could relate.

"Must be a red letter day for me, two slayers in one day and I bet it was one of you bastards that cut open my husband and son." She extended her fangs. He was dazed but not helpless. He'd managed to slip a dagger of his own from his jacket as he was driven to the ground.

Her family. Apparently, some slayer took down her little hubby and crumb snatcher. And for that she slit Stosh's throat. Stinkin' vamp! He was going to *enjoy* this. When she leaned in to feed, he was going to ram the blade up through her neck. It wouldn't kill her but it would disable her. Then he and *sweet thing* were gonna have a party slayers would talk about for generations!

She stretched open her mouth and leaned in. *That's right, just a little closer.* Suddenly her head jerked skyward. Hissing in fear, she dropped him and launched herself into the air.

She was gone but he got a damn good look at her. He'd remember her face. Oh yeah, damn sure would. He was gonna find that bitch, if it took the rest of his life, he would find her!

He tried standing, but his shaky legs buckled and folded. On his hands and knees, he crawled to the rail where Stosh had been dropped and looked below. There was no sign of him, only the churning frothy river. He was gone. Dear Lord, he was gone! Tears stung his eyes. He wept, pounding the hard ground with a closed fist.

He was dead. Myron "Stosh" Milford, one of the best vampire slayers on Earth and his best friend, was dead. How many times did Stosh save his ass? And, when the big man needed him most…Maya, he had to tell her. Her slayers were all the family she had.

She'll be devastated. With every slayer lost, Maya died a little too. But losing Stosh? Thank God, Seth would be there for her. One day he prayed her spirit would be healed. For him, Stosh's death would become yet another scar on his soul that would never heal.

# CHAPTER THIRTY EIGHT

Rocketing toward the abandoned lighthouse, Adalius' pulse quickened. His eyesight sharpened, temper seething, he focused on stilling his anger. He wouldn't allow himself to be overtaken by emotion. It could make him careless.

Wrapped in shadows, the younger vampires wouldn't be able to detect his approach, but Anna certainly could. He concentrated on shielding his presence, on becoming like the American Stealth Fighter, invisible to Anna's mental radar.

Once on the ground, the new vampires he would eliminate, one by one, preferably without alerting Anna. The tide of battle could dramatically shift, if she unexpectedly joined the fight.

Doubt seeped into his mind like toxic ooze. Was he truly ready to confront her? She had defeated him easily at their last encounter. Like an adult would squash a toddler. But that was long ago. He was still young then, powerful but undisciplined. Not the skilled warrior he had become. No, Anna would find him a far more worthy adversary than the one she first faced. Clearing his mind, he silenced his inner demons.

He had wandered the countryside for years searching for Anna. It was fortunate he did not find her. She would have destroyed him. He simply lacked the skill needed to fulfill his oath. To kill the Destroyer, he had to change, to become more than Anna's child, more than just a new bite rebelling against his sire. He had to become what Anna christened him. Death.

It was sheer chance he encountered the enforcer, Vegas. Vegas, of course, went by a different name in those days. One visit to that city in Nevada, so impressed the enforcer, that he adopted its name as his own.

221

Vegas took him under his tutelage. He became expert in the art of the blade, a master of hand to hand combat, the equal of any enforcer. Vegas even recommended him to the High Council for enforcer consideration. It was unprecedented because he was turned and not pure bred. He was, of course, ruled ineligible. Though disappointing, Vegas had already given him what he needed. The enforcer molded him into a match for the Destroyer. For that he would always be grateful.

The lighthouse came over the horizon as he glided toward it. Scanning the pedestrian portion of the bridge ahead, he spotted a dagger wielding, immortal female dangling a large human male over the river, her intent clearly malicious.

Accelerating, Adalius summoned all the speed he could muster, but he was too far away. Elder's mercy, he would not make it in time. With cold suddenness, the female slit the mortal's throat and dropped him into the raging waters. Turning, she attacked a second human who lay nearby. Outrage fired his blood. The human had one chance. He sent a warning into her mind. *"The human is my prey. Surrender him or die!"*

Her reaction was instantaneous. She released him and flew off. The human was safe. His friend however, if he survived the fall, wouldn't last long in the powerful current of the angry river. If he could reach him in time, Sandrian blood could heal like no other vampire blood.

Adalius dove down into the river. Once beneath the surface, he reached out with his senses, astounded by the strength of the current. As the water shoved against his back, he probed for life signs. Nothing. Even the scent of his blood was washed away too swiftly to home in on. Damnation. He was gone.

With no recourse, he rose from the waters back to the bridge. There, on his hands and knees, he found the human weeping, his fists pounding the hard bridge cement. Anguish burned him, wounded him in ways no physician could heal. The mortal's pain, reached out and up. It enveloped Adalius communing with the wounds within his own heart. The mortal was tormented with feelings of loss, anger, and guilt.

In days gone by, Adalius would have relished his suffering. Fed on it like a contemptible leach, but that being was no more. His humanity restored, he was now capable of compassion, able to feel empathy for the suffering of another. He looked down on the human with sorrow. "Such despair. Dear, blessed Elder, give him peace."

Mingled in the human's despondency were flashes, scenes, playing out in his mind, numerous battles with vampires, demons, and Lycan. His mood turned decidedly dark. They were slayers. The one dropped into the river, they were not just his friends, they were also partners.

This did not bode well. Judging by the visions, the slayer was one of extraordinary skill. Now he was infused with a singled minded hunger for revenge; revenge against his friend's murderer, and Anna herself. This slayer could come between him and his right to vengeance of his own. It had to be addressed.

At last the slayer rose, he withdrew a cell phone from his jacket. Gingerly, he made his way across the bridge, a slight limp in his stride. Adalius followed closely in the event others waited to ambush. Deeper probe of his mind told him the slayer was staying at a nearby motel. Excellent, he would meet him there. They had much to discuss.

His heart went out to the slayer. Grief made them kindred spirits. Kindred spirits or not, however, he would allow no interference. Anna was his prey. He would first try reason with the slayer, try to convince the human to leave Anna to him. However, If the human refused to stand down...

# CHAPTER THIRTY NINE

Something was wrong. She could feel it. Pacing the floor, Maya wrung her hands, her stomach knotted so tight she felt like throwing up, even though she hadn't eaten in hours. Nerves. She just couldn't settle down, but when it came to her slayers facing fang and bite, she never could. They were her responsibility. She swore to Lincoln at his death bed she would lead them, care for them. She'd done her best, training and preparing her crew.

Cringe. It still felt funny calling them *her* crew but they were her slayers now.

Despite best efforts, there'd been losses. There was no preventing it. There were two important rules slayers couldn't break. Rule number one was that in hunting vampires, slayers would die. Rule number two was that nothing could be done to change rule number one.

Thank Heaven Trey hadn't been one of those lost. He was Lincoln's lone son and the only tie left to the man she loved. But special treatment wasn't an option, not when it came to assigning him missions. It wouldn't be fair to the others. Lincoln wouldn't have allowed it, the other slayers wouldn't tolerate it, and Trey would never forgive her for it.

The ticking of her wall clock kept time as she paced the floor like a nervous cat while Seth, her lover, sat nearby with his eyes glued in a book. From time to time she caught him stealing a glance, through those moppy dreads, those beautiful dreads.

They hadn't spoken in over an hour. He'd tried to comfort her, more than once, but she pushed him away. She needed to be strong for herself and her slayers. Thankfully, Seth was an understanding man. He really understood her need to stand alone. Just his being near was enough. Her Seth, words couldn't express how much she loved and appreciated him for his patience.

"Maya?"

She turned to her lover. "Yes, baby?"

He gazed into her eyes. "I love you."

She flushed. "I love you too. "Seth smiled then returned to his reading.

She regarded her man. Boyish good looks and muscular body, she did love him. She loved him with a passion she didn't know she was capable of. A passion she'd never known even with Lincoln. Just a touch from him, made her tremble, the sound of his voice when he called her name that certain way, made her skin tingle. When she looked into those gorgeous eyes, they pulled her in, unable, unwilling to resist.

The sudden ring of the phone shattered the silence. Racing to her desk, she yanked the receiver from its charger. "Talk to me, Trey? What's going on, is it Anna? Did you find her?" *He's taking too long to answer*. "Something's wrong, what is it?...Just fuckin' *say* it Trey."

No.

"Tell me how it happened...I see...I'm fine, Trey, the question is, are *you* ok?" Seth rose to his feet, the unspoken question apparent on his face. She simply held up her index finger. "Ok, I'm gonna make some calls. We're *all* coming to New Carrollton...This is *not* a discussion, Trey. As soon as I get everyone together, we are gonna hunt that bitch down together. Got it? Good. When we get to New Carrollton, I'll contact you. And don't you dare go after her alone!....Just fuckin' do as I say for once god dammit." She hung up the phone and turned to Seth. "Stosh is dead. It was one of Anna's. "Seth move to console her but she threw up her hand like a traffic cop. "No, not now." It wounded him. She could see it in his eyes. But it was her responsibility. It was time to take action.

"Baby, I'm so sorry. Are you..?"

*Stosh is dead.* "I'm fine." Maya hit one of the buttons on the speed dial and waited. "Kennedy, when you and Jackson finish that assignment get back here...Trey just called, Stosh is dead...One of Anna's killed him...I'm fine... I'm calling everyone in on this. It's time to put her down once and for all...Yes, Kennedy, I'm fine, now wrap up your assignment and get back here...Dammit, Kennedy I *said* I'm fine." She ended the call and continued on to the next. After all of her slayers had been notified, she set the phone back in its charger and headed down the hall, toward the bedroom. Neal still wasn't answering his phone. Typical. If that bastard wasn't in trouble, she was going to kick his rotten ass.

"Maya, what are you doing?" Seth followed her into the bedroom as she continued to the closet. Opening the door, she walked inside. Her footlocker was sitting toward the back. She was going to need help getting it out.

"Baby, can you help me with this?"

Seth walked in the closet, bent low and grabbed one of the brass handles. She took the other one, and together, they dragged the chest out into the bedroom.

"What's in this thing anyway?" Seth studied the black leather coffer, flexing his shoulders, as she marched to the dresser, opened her jewelry box, and took out a key.

*Stosh was dead.*

Sliding the key into the lock, she carefully opened it. Seth's mouth fell open. Inside were her armaments, which included two crossbows, bolts, silver plated daggers, a sword, a couple of leather cases, and a pair of leather pants and vest. Reaching inside, she withdrew a crossbow, blew off the dust, and laid it on the bed.

"Holy shit, Maya. You could hold off a vamp army with all of this."

She smiled. A time or two, she had. "What, did you think I always sat on the sidelines directing traffic? "Reaching again into the chest, she pulled out one case then another and laid both on the bed. "These belonged to Lincoln." She opened the first case. Twin .40 caliber handguns rested in a red velvet interior. In the second were two .357 Magnums. Maya pulled the first .40 out of its case, then the second, checked both and laid them on the bed.

Seth watched her cautiously. "Baby, are you..."

"Seth, if you ask me if I'm okay, I will stomp you."

"I'm just worried about..."

There wasn't time for this. *Stosh was dead.* She had one more call left to make. Without a word she made her way back to her desk.

Grabbing the phone, she hit the speed dial. When the line was picked up, she wasted not a breath. "I need all the darts you can crank out…. Just keep making them till I tell you to stop." When Seth caught up with her, she'd tossed the phone down and was shuffling through her files.

"I'm thinking that they all should be here by the end of the week." Her voice was starting to break. "The only one of these bastards that was ever consistently on time was…."

*Stosh. Stosh was…*

She'd never see his silly smile. Or put up with his dumb ass comments. Or look at that old ugly baseball cap he wore backwards on his head. That jackass…He'd never work her nerves again. Never…Never piss her… Her hands shook. All the anger, frustration and pain she ever experienced, exploded in an incandescent fury.

She heaved a breath and screamed to the ceiling, sliding everything forcefully off her desk. It all crashed in a scrambled heap as her legs folded under her. Seth rushed to her side as she sank down. He caught her in his arms as sobs racked her body. "That bitch killed Stosh. Oh God, Seth. She killed him!"

She wept uncontrollably. Tears streamed down her face like water from a spigot. They fell, staining Seth's shirt as she clutched the material in her hands. It was personal now. She wasn't walking away from this. So help her, the Destroyer's account was coming due. As far as she was concerned, Anna was already dust. Dammit to hell, that bitch was already dust.

# CHAPTER FORTY

Trey returned to the motel battered, wounded in ways no medicine could heal. Maya, she said she was fine, but he knew better. She and Stosh went back to when his father first put the team together a lifetime ago. Yet another friend, lost to vamp hunting. Stosh wouldn't be the last.

Death and losing friends were a fact of life for a slayer. Something you never got used to, and if you were lucky, never would. Thank God she wasn't alone. Seth would care for her. She was in good hands. He'd be eternally grateful for that.

*Stosh.*

*Stosh was dead.* The words cut like a straight razor and burned like fire. There was no way to measure the impact his death would have on them as a team and as individuals. He was their big gun. Their right arm in the war against the supernatural. Even when it seemed like their tickets were about to get punched, his wisecracks, Stosh's way of flipping off the reaper, lifted them, encouraged them.

Dragging himself up a staircase that seemed to have gained more steps, he prayed. His mind was on overload. His legs were barely responsive. The bruises on his body had bruises, and the heaviness in his chest, threatened to crush his heart. The cold, hard reality of death fell upon him. The big man left a pair of shoes nobody would ever be able to fill. It was his fault, he hadn't been strong or fast enough, and Stosh paid with his life.

He clenched his fists. Knuckles cracked. He gnashed his teeth in furious anger. Grief threatened to blow the cap off his composure. Anna.

It may not have been her hand, but it was still her doing. He'd make her pay, and all her parasites with her.

His breath became pants. Like a wild tiger, he needed to hunt. *Please God, just put something in front of him to kill.* A target at which he could direct his anger, vampire was the first choice, but any supernatural trouble maker would do.

A stray sunbeam caught his eye. The sun was rising over the horizon, the birth of a new day. A day Anna got that Stosh never would.

Arriving at his room, he slid his key into the lock, and stepped across the threshold. Once inside, he locked himself in; his weary head came to rest against the cool steel door. He needed a drink, lots of them. An ocean of Jack Daniels would be a good start. Had to try and...

"Greetings slayer."

There was movement behind him. Startled, he whirled about, dart in hand and flicked on the lights. His breath caught in his throat. The size of the intruder stunned him.

The trespasser threw up his hands. "Forgive me, I did not wish to frighten you."

One look at his uninvited guest and he knew. "Vampire!" Ask and you shall receive. He snarled, letting fly with his dart.

The vamp plucked it out of the air. Unfazed, Trey launched another dart then another and another. The blood sucker swiftly captured each, one by one and tossed them harmlessly on the bed. "Please, I will not harm you. I wish only to talk."

*Talk. To a two legged parasite? Yeah, that's what he'd do.* "Fuck you blood sucker!" He drew his pistol. The intruder extended his hand. Before Trey squeezed off a shot, the gun flew from his grasp straight to his opponent.

"Be at ease, Slayer. I simply wish to chat." The vamp removed the magazine from the gun, then the round in the chamber, and laid them gently on the bed. Out of the corner of his eye, Trey saw sunlight from the outside. The sun had risen.

"If you please, I mean you no harm." The vampire gestured toward the chairs.

Trey eased toward the drape covered window. If he could just get there, he'd give the son of a bitch a serious sunburn. *Easy, no sudden moves, wouldn't want fang baby goin' all speed demon. It'd ruin the vamp fry. Now take it nice ...and slow, just a step ...closer.*

The vampire shook his head. "I promise not to harm you. Won't you please sit down?"

*Now!* He made his move. "Burn in Hell, blood sucker!" Flashing to the window, he yanked on the curtain cord. The drapes flew open allowing the sun's rays to flood the room, bathing the vampire in its glory. Trey blinked. Not even a sizzle. The vamp didn't even shield his eyes.

*No way he could have gotten it wrong. He knew a fang when he saw one. So why wasn't this one going all crispy critter?* The vamp let out an exasperated sigh, moved around the bed and closed the drapes once more.

"What the fuck kinda vampire are you?"

The intruder again gestured to the chair. "*Now* may we talk?"

He threw up his hands. "Fine, so talk. But I hear just fine on my feet."

He nodded. "As you wish. My name is Adalius and—"

*Knock, knock, knock.*

Trey drew and cocked his other pistol. Never knew his hands could move so fast, funny how fear could motivate.

Adalius threw out his hand. "Wait. That is most likely the delivery man. I was amazed to find a place that actually delivered at this hour of the morning."

*Did he say...*"Delivery?"

"Yes, I took the liberty of ordering us breakfast. I hope you do not mind."

"Breakfast?" *There's a hidden camera in the room, right? He's being punked. That's what this is.*

Adalius went to the door, accepted two large plastic bags, paid the driver, then placed them on the table. Gun trained on the vampire, Trey maintained his distance. Removing a Styrofoam container from one of the bags, Adalius presented it to him. "I ordered you a western omelet with bacon and wheat toast. Is that satisfactory?"

He stepped back, ready to make the bastard dance a hot silver jig.

Adalius rolled his eyes. "Won't you please put away your weapon? It does not take enhanced senses to hear you have not eaten."

The vamp was right, he was hungry. His mouth watered in spite of him as the aroma of the omelet and bacon reached his nostrils. Slowly, he lowered his pistol and cautiously reached for the container.

He had to be dreaming. A vampire was offering food, not trying to turn him into today's special. He'd give a mint for a picture of the expression that must be on his face right now. "You said you wanted to talk, Adalius. I'm listening."

Adalius removed plastic ware from the bag. "To everything there is a time, Slayer.

For now, it is time to eat."

May as well make this easier. "The name's Trey."

"I am honored to meet you, Trey Thomas."

Damn blood suckers. "Stay outta my head, vamp."

"You are right. That was very bad manners. Please, excuse my transgression." Adalius removed the remaining two containers and placed them on the table before him. "You must excuse me. I have not eaten in days. I was told the steak skillet was excellent. I hope that was not an exaggeration." Reaching into the second bag, he removed a two liter cherry Pepsi. "I usually prefer orange juice but I am afraid this will have to do."

*Hell no. There's no way he was going to believe that this blood sucker—* "You eat and drink *Pepsi*?"

Adalius cocked his head like a confused puppy. "You prefer Coke?"

"Yes…no, I'm saying that you, a vampire, eat and drink?"

The vampire blinked. "You do not?"

"Are you fuckin' with me? Vampires don't eat and they damn sure *do not* drink cola."

Adalius cocked an eyebrow. Opening his container, he lifted a fork full of eggs into his mouth, chewed and swallowed. Next, he twisted the cap off the Pepsi and chugged a drink. Air bubbles rose inside the bottle as the cola flowed into Adalius. Finally, he set the bottle down, and belched.

Trey's head swam. All his training, all his instincts told him Adalius was a vampire, but nothing about him added up. Not only did that sunbath not bother him, it looked like he could've laid by a pool for hours soaking in rays. He eats food, cooked food, and let's not forget the cola chug. Vampires just didn't do these things. But if Adalius wasn't a vampire, what the hell was he?

"I am sure you have many questions, Slayer. If you allow me to finish my meal and finish your own, I will indulge your queries."

He regarded Adalius then nodded in agreement. They ate in relative silence. Savoring his meal, he watched the vampire polish off the first steak skillet then start on the second. If they were half as good as his omelet, he understood why. It was the best western omelet he'd ever had. He'd have to get the name of the place from Adalius. He stopped. *Was he actually going to ask a vampire where to find a restaurant with good food?*

After they finished and cleaned up, Adalius turned his chair to face him while he sat on the bed. "Before we begin, allow me to offer my most sincere condolences on the death of your friend. I regret I arrived too late to save him."

"You were there?"

Adalius nodded. "I dove in after him when he was thrown from the bridge but was unable to locate him. He appears to have been swept away by the current. I am sorry. Once I located you again, I took where you were staying from your mind and came here to meet you."

He examined Adalius over from head to toe. "You said you dove into the water after Stosh?"

Adalius, again nodded. "I did."

"But your clothes, they don't even look damp."

"The same power that allowed me to take the gun from your hand can also be used to repel."

Damn, he could only think of about a hundred instances that little power would have come in handy. "So, can you use that to deflect bullets?"

Adalius grinned. He knew he was being pumped for information. "In your experience, has any vampire demonstrated the ability to generate such a field?"

Wasn't the answer he was looking for, but it sounded a whole lot like the only one he was gonna get. "So a vamp's best defense against guns would be don't get shot?"

"Perhaps, but as you are no doubt aware, shooting a vampire is easier spoken than accomplished."

"True that. Ok, you clearly eat and drink. If you're vampire, how is this possible?"

Taking in a deep, even breath, Adalius slowly exhaled. His eyes took on a faraway look, the internal debate on display across his face. When he spoke, it was carefully, as if choosing his words. "I am indeed vampire. You will find that just as there are different types of roses, so too are there are different species of vampire. Our kind are called Sandrians. We eat, drink, have heart beats, and even reproduce. We can have children."

The supernatural he knew, just got blown to the bottom of Hell. Now everything ever imagined was on the table. Exhibit A was right in front of him, a vampire that could eat and make babies. What was that saying about there being more things in Heaven and Earth?

This talk had been very educational. And he was betting this was the watered down version. Still, there was just one more thing bugging him.

"What about your not being affected by sunlight?"

Adalius' eyes hardened. "I am not prepared to discuss that subject, at least not at this time."

No surprise there. Couldn't say he'd volunteer that either, were he in the vamp's place. He had to ask though. "Fair enough. Well, I admit this has been very interesting, but you didn't come here just to have breakfast and chit chat. Killing me doesn't seem like it's on your agenda, so what's on your mind, Adalius?"

Adalius shifted in his chair. "I have come because you and I appear to be hunting the same prey."

*The Destroyer. What the hell, did everything lead back to her?* "You're talking about Anna."

"Indeed. I have pursued her across the globe for over a century. I have sworn an oath to see her evil ended."

He wanted to kill Anna too. Ha! Take a number and get in line. "Well, too bad you're not gonna be able to fulfill that oath. I intend to put some wood right through her sick, depraved heart."

Adalius rested his hands on his knees, his features darkened. "I am afraid I must insist that you back away. Leave her menace, to me."

He stood and shook his head. The kid gloves were coming off. If Count Sunscreen thought he was just gonna waltz into his room and cut him out of a piece of the action, then Adalius was out of his Pepsi swilling noggin. "If that's why you brought yo ass here, then you wasted my time and yours. I'm a slayer. It's what I do and I *will* kill her, bank on it."

Adalius rose to his feet. "Then you will die. She is becoming stronger with each passing day. Soon she may become so powerful that none of us will be able to stop her." Adalius' voice was even. Standing tall and unmoving like a great monolith, he made no threatening moves, but the air about the vampire was charged, the vamp was pissed.

"Well then, it sounds like we need to be workin' this together."

Adalius' jaw tightened. "Absolutely not. I will not place your life in jeopardy with such an action."

Bullshit. This was more about getting Anna all to himself. Nice try though. "First of all, I don't need you to protect me. Second, I'm gonna continue hunting Anna till she's dust in the wind. So, if you think you're just gonna cut me outta this, you can kiss my ass."

The vamp's eyes sparkled, his hands curling into fists. "I could wipe your memory and send you to a nice sunny beach."

He stepped closer, bringing them nearly nose to nose. "You could but, we *both* know it wouldn't last and I'd be back faster than you could say, 'fuck you, vamp'."

"Stubborn mortal!"

He shrugged. "Been called worse. Now, the way I see it, you and I could come at this from different angles and probably wind up getting in each other's way. Anna could end up skipping happily away while we bullshit around in a pissin' contest. But if we work together, I'd be willing to try if it means that bitch gets dusted. It's up to you, Adalius but I *am* gonna continue to track her."

Adalius blew out a sigh, turned, and paced toward the door. The vamp was weighing his options. He waited, slipping another dart from his jacket, in case Adalius decided force was the best solution to their impasse. Slowly, tension seemed to melt from Adalius' shoulders. The vamp turned. "Very well, Slayer, we will work together."

He blew out a sigh of his own, slipping the dart back in its place. "I was hoping this wasn't going to get messy. So what's your beef with her? What'd she do to you?"

Adalius was stoic, only the gleam in his eye betrayed the storm churning within him. "My reasons for hunting Anna are…a private matter."

Before he could form the next question, yet another knock at the door interrupted. They both drew their firearms.

"I take it you didn't order anything else?"

Adalius slowly shook his head and stepped away from the door as Trey moved to answer the knock. "What do you want?"

"Open the bloody door, Thomas, it's me."

# CHAPTER FORTY ONE

Anna lounged in the afterglow of sex with Ricardo and Trish. Ricardo lay between her legs, his head propped on her stomach while Trish lay in her arms, peacefully sleeping. She smiled at her children. She adored Ricardo but Trish... Trish was her golden one.

Nine months after the end of the Second World War, she saw Trish in a diner having a late night meal. To make ends meet, Trish worked for some shipping company. Her husband, like many other Marines, died in the battle to take Iwo Jima.

She recoiled. Mortals weren't the only ones to suffer during that terrible war. Many immortals met their end at the hands of Hitler and his SS. They of course had help. There'd been a traitor, widely believed to have been a vampire, who'd sold out to the Third Reich. Though never identified, the search for the vermin continues, even today.

Anna had strolled into that diner in search of her own meal when she spied the blonde. She'd taken the booth diagonal to where Trish was seated. Even in those dreadfully frumpy clothes, Trish's beauty was astounding. If anyone had taken the time to look, they would've seen a true work of art. And watching Trish was like admiring a Picasso, a masterpiece.

Without thinking, she'd slipped into Trish's mind, and was startled. Beneath the calm exterior, ran powerful currents of wild passion. Expecting a stoic mountain, she instead stumbled onto a raging volcano. The first of what would be many pleasant surprises.

As she lay stroking Trish's hair, she thought of Padre and the proposed alliance with his employer. Mostly, she thought of Padre. Such a dynamic vampire; she was going to enjoy seducing him, bending him to her will. No easy task, she was certain. She read his thoughts, Padre was cunning as a panther, clever as a fox, and possessed a heart hard as titanium. But break him she would, regardless of how long it took. Once she saw his leash holder was safely out of the way, Padre would assume control of their operation. On that day, she'd have a very powerful ally, indeed.

Ricardo stirred but remained asleep. Her gaze fell upon him; her hand lovingly curled a lock of hair behind his ear. He was such an attentive, intense lover, and yet amazingly gentle. She seriously considered making him her consort, but that was before she laid eyes on Padre.

A smile spread across Anna's lips. The nest was growing as were the abilities of her brood. Soon, she'd be able to stand against the council and their lap dog Enforcers. One day soon, the tormentors would be a distant, distasteful memory.

A sudden, sharp pain knifed through her temple. She clenched her fist. Fear. Panic. Something had terrified one of her children. The door burst open with a whoosh. Marie entered in a blur. Startled, they all sat up in bed.

Such an impressive child, Marie was learning remarkably fast. The control of her abilities was a testament to her determination and Trish's instruction. The young one came to a stop, fear etched across her face. "Mistress, the lighthouse nest is gone!"

The shock made her all but leap from the bed. "How? What's happened, child?"

Trish was instantly at her mate's side, taking her hand. "Two slayers, mistress, they were coming out of the lighthouse as I arrived."

She breathed a sigh of relief. Slayers weren't good, but they weren't Enforcers.

"Did they harm you? "Trish caressed her hand.

"No, I'm fine, Trish. In fact I managed to kill one of them and—"

"Only one of them?" Anna asked, descending the marble stairs. The slayer would most assuredly call for aid. More pests to deal with.

"Yes, mistress. I was about to feed on the other when another vampire, an older one, warned me off. I could hear him in my mind. He said the slayer was his prey, and if I didn't let him go, I would be killed."

"How do you know he was older, my love?" Trish kissed her hand.

"Because when I tried to block his thoughts, like you taught me, he forced his way in."

As worry painted Trish's expression, Anna approached the couple. "Did you see his face, this vampire?"

Marie shook her head. "No, mistress, as soon as I heard his warning, I came back here as fast as I could."

The brunette trembled. Whoever the vampire was, he could be a threat. He had to be eliminated. The answer to his identity lay in Marie's mind. "I want to hear the voice of this vampire. Open your mind to me, child."

She went to Marie. Trish stepped aside as she took Marie's hands in her own. Closing her eyes, Anna concentrated. Marie lowered her mental defenses as Anna gently pushed through, into her mind. Her mental discipline was astounding for one so young. She'd become versed in many things in such a short time. Before long, Marie would be a very powerful vampire, indeed. A close eye would have to be kept on her in case ambition grew as quickly as her powers.

A sigh escaped Marie as Anna tunneled into the depths of her mind. Sorting through memories old and new, Anna searched for the voice of he who dared threaten one of her own. Deeper she traveled, witnessing events of Marie's mundane former life until she came across visions of the lighthouse encounter. She watched it all happen through Marie's eyes.

Her focus was on the fat one. Maybe it was he who killed her family. Hand, tight around his throat, the flash of a blade, blood flying from the neck wound, she released him. A scream, his partner's. She turned, then attacked. Rage took her. The face of the second slayer was a blur. She felt Marie's fangs extending, preparing to feed on the slayer. Then, she heard it, a voice from the past, *her* past. The scene evaporated.

In her mind's eye, against a backdrop of black, a pinpoint of light appeared in the distance. Like the headlight of an oncoming train, it swelled in size as it approached. A form took shape. A Skull, no, a face, coming for her, he couldn't be bargained or reasoned with. She threw out her arms to protect herself. Whether she did actually or only in her mind she didn't know. Accelerating, it slammed into her with single minded fury. The force threw her back. Back the way she came. Its violence blasted her out of Marie's psyche. They both flinched.

"Marie!" Trish rushed to her mate's side, catching her as Marie's legs buckled. Anna staggered backward, blinking repeatedly. Goddess, he was in New Carrollton. Her brood, all her plans, imperiled. Whirling about, she headed for the shower. She'd give him one last chance, a final opportunity to come to his senses. He deserved that much.

"Mistress, what is it?" Trish called to her but, she continued on without responding. Adalius' appearance was unexpected but not unmanageable. Nothing in Marie's memories suggested he'd gleaned anything useful from her mind. There were matters that required her attention, but none were as pressing as this.

Once inside the bathroom, she closed the door, turning on the shower. Steam rose from the tub. From beyond the door, she sensed their emotions. They were all confused, frightened, with good reason. She'd comfort and reassure them, after she washed and scrubbed. Anna rubbed her face. Sadly, the same couldn't be done for her mind. Adalius' psychic residue was like static cling. It would be hours, if not days, before it subsided.

She sighed.

Adalius. She loved him still, but if he continued to stand in the way, she would not hesitate to kill him. But first, she had to find him, and she had a good idea where to look.

# CHAPTER FORTY TWO

It sounded a whole lot like Kyle. But in all that sunlight, he'd be ash tray filler. It was a trick, had to be. Well, if some asshole came looking for trouble, he'd found it.

"Hang on a sec," Trey said.

Nodding to Adalius, who took his place near the door, he unlatched it then looked to the vamp. Adalius nodded, he was ready. He mouthed a three count then whipped opened the door. Adalius with unsettling ease, yanked the figure into the room, and threw him onto the bed.

He closed and locked the door as the new arrival let fly with a series of expletives. Moving toward the window, he looked outside, it was bright and sunny. All he saw was a couple loading luggage in an SUV and a stray dog sprinting across the lot with a paper bag in his mouth. If this guy had back up, they weren't put off that their boy had been snatched.

Time to see who came a calling, Joining Adalius by the bed, he took a gander over the vamp's shoulder. Kyle laid perfectly still, Adalius' Glock pressed to his temple.

His stoolie looked up at him. "Maybe I should've said, please?"

It was Kyle alright. "Let him up."

Adalius withdrew his weapon as they pulled him to his feet. Kyle shoved away from Adalius straightening his rumpled shirt. "Now there's a jolly good way to greet a mate."

Trey shook his head. Two sun proof vamps in a day? Was there a convention going on?

"Three questions Kyle. What are you doing here, how did you find me, and why aren't you dust?"

240

Kyle's eyebrow rose. "I'm all tingly to see you too. To answer your questions in the order received, I'm here to give you more information about Anna. I found you because I searched every motel in town until I found your bike, then followed your scent to this room, and lastly, I'm not well dust pan material because of this." Kyle lifted a medallion he wore on a chain around his neck.

Adalius scanned the item. "That is a Markalan medallion. Only the most powerful sorcerers can produce such a thing."

Kyle eyed Adalius suspiciously. "How do you know so much about it?"

"You are not alone in having friends in mystical places," Adalius said matter of factly.

Trey shrugged. "So, what does it do?"

Adalius studied the medallion. "It neutralizes the sun's effect on a vampire. There are those who gladly would slaughter thousands to possess this."

His eyes turned to Kyle. "Have you lost your mind, walking around with something like that? Where did *you* get it?"

Kyle shifted his stance. "Pull your tit out the wringer, granny. There's no way I'd chance this little lovely falling into unsavory hands. It's been crafted to disintegrate in 24 hours. I'm not a bloomin' moron."

He had half a mind to launch a dart in Kyle's eye. "Where, Kyle?"

Kyle folded his arms across his chest. "If you must know, I met an old sorceress friend while I was at Club Détente. Kind enough to whip it up for me, she was."

Adalius shook his head. "He is lying. No mystic would ever produce such an item for a vampire. If caught, the offense is punishable by death."

Kyle's eyes sparkled. "Piss off. Nobody's gonna get executed unless I'm caught with it, and only if I reveal where I got it, which I won't."

Adalius scowled. "Perhaps, but she still would not have simply given you the medallion. She most certainly would have demanded much in exchange."

Kyle looked from Adalius to him. "Who's he?"

"That's Adalius, my new vamp…friend. Don't change the subject. What did you do or give her for it?"

Kyle shuddered. "Trust me mate, you *don't* want to know." Kyle glanced at Adalius then squinted. "You're Sandrian."

Adalius leveled his pistol. "You have a problem with Sandrians?"

He waved his hand. "At ease, Adalius, it's not personal; Kyle has issues with all vampires."

Kyle snorted. "Issues. I bloody hate vampires."

Adalius blinked. "Are you not vampire?"

"I get that a lot." Kyle paused. "Wait, seen you before, I have. You're the bloke who thrashed the knobheads who put the snatch on that girl in the park."

Trey interjected. "Wait a second, you *knew* about Sandrians?"

"Of course." Kyle answered as if asked if he knew the sky was blue.

"You never mentioned them to me." *Limey bastard.*

"You never asked. Bloody hell, Thomas, I'm not a flipping mind read...well, actually I am, aren't I? But you told me to stay outta your head, didn't you?"

He pressed his forefinger against Kyle's chest. "Never mind, but later, we're gonna have a little chat about what other things you know about."

Kyle knocked his finger off. "I been trying to get you to do that for three years, ya flippant sod!"

The stupid grin on Adalius face continued to spread. "Forgive me, how long have the two of you been mated?"

"Fuck you," Trey and Kyle responded in unison. Vampires were such assholes.

Trey glared at Kyle. "We'll talk about this later. Now, you said you had some intel, so let's hear it."

Kyle cleared his throat. "According to the yakety yak, Anna may have a nest in an abandoned bakery on Long Avenue."

He didn't question it. It was a lead. There'd been few since he got to New Carrollton. Whipping out his pistol, he checked it and started for the door. "Let's go, Adalius."

Adalius stepped into his path. "Wait, you should rest first."

*Hell no. Was this vamp trying to mother him now?* "I'm fine. We're wasting time, Adalius."

"You need sleep if we are to face Anna and her minions, not to mention you have just experienced the trauma of losing your companion," Adalius said, his voice even and firm.

Kyle interjected, "You lost a slayer? Who?"

He met Kyle's gaze. "They killed Stosh last night"

Kyle sagged. "Bugger. I'm sorry, Thomas. I know he was your friend. A right fine bloke he was too."

Trey waved off the comment. "Not as sorry as Anna's gonna feel before I'm done."

Adalius met his gaze. "There will be time for Anna, *after* you have slept."

Trey clenched his fists. If Adalius didn't back his muscle bound ass up... "I don't need you to tel-" A wave of Adalius' hand was the last thing he saw before the world went black.

# CHAPTER FORTY THREE

Club Détente was nearly bursting. Most of the supernatural underworld in New Carrollton was in house, letting their hair, fangs, tails, horns or whatever down. It was a busy night. And a busy night meant a fat register, which translated to a happy Alpha. Everything was rainbows and lollipops, until *she* strolled through the main entrance. Anna paused, her eyes scrutinizing every soul present.

Taine suppressed a howl. To say she was hot would be like saying the Antarctic is a little chilly. Her platinum blonde hair, pinned up and stylish, highlighted very high cheeks bones. Her full lips were coated with a blood colored lipstick and gloss that made them look lush and moist. Yum, yum, lips like those begged to be kissed.

Drinking the sight of her long, toned legs, he licked his chops. In that form fitting, off the shoulder chiffon mini dress and matching spiked heeled pumps, she was a wide awake wet dream in white. Mercy Mother Moon, that vamp had it going on, for a blood thirsty, nut job, killing machine.

She commanded his attention, and not just because she was the Destroyer. What a sexy psychopath. She could make a wolf wanna run off and hump a leg. He knew cause he was ready to hump the first limb coming in arm's reach. But sexy or not, Anna was bad news.

She strode toward him, curvy yet sleek. Her walk was graceful and totally feminine. The exquisiteness of her rendered him speechless. Almost.

"Oh *hell* no, you not bringin' yo ass up in here!" He shook his head, waving his arms like a referee signaling incomplete pass.

Her eyebrows rolled up. She was surprised, amused, and a little annoyed. Bet she wasn't used to hearing 'no'. "Really? Let's pretend you could stop me. Why can't I come in? I have money for the cover charge and this *is*, after all, a club for immortals is it not?"

Details, details. "Yes, it is, but your money's no good here and frankly, we can't have yo toothy ass strollin' in here drinkin' up the customers. That shit be bad for business."

Her laugh was melodious. Anna smiled sweetly, but in a 'I could chew your liver out' kinda way. "I see, so you recognize me."

She gotta be bull shittin'. "Hell yeah, I know who the fuck you are. You're the wicked bitch of the west."

Anna studied him carefully. "You have me at a disadvantage, Lycan, what's your name?"

"The name's Taine, but you can call me burn in Hell, eat shit, and die." His legs were trembling and his bladder was on the verge of throwing up in his pants. This neck muncher eats Lycan. No way he was backing down though.

She smiled warmly. "You fascinate me, little wolf. I can smell your fear, yet you wield your tongue against me like a sword. I have killed many for less than a fraction of what you've said to me. Yet here you stand, utterly defiant. You have spirit. Because I believe the world would be far more interesting with you in it, I won't kill you."

And she could, but he'd take a sizable chunk of her magnificent backside with him.

Anna regarded him with a twinkle in her eye. Reaching into her purse, she fished out a fifty dollar bill, placing it into his hand. "Here is the money for admittance. You may keep the rest. TTFN Taine, I *so* look forward to seeing you again." She smiled as she strolled away.

Watching her go, his expression, soured. "Great, why is it I always attract the crazy bitches?"

*****

Anna approached the steps leading to the steel doors of the dance floor when she was intercepted by two security personnel. Eyeing her with disdain, they moved in from her right and left flanks. As she halted, the males came well within arm's reach and stopped. Her mouth watered as their scent drifted up her nostrils. Her fangs extended involuntarily. The urge to drain them was acute. She needed to feed soon.

Her attention was diverted when the center door opened and three more Lycan, two of which were in wolf form, stepped out from the dance floor area. Music and the sound of revelry thrummed with life as they found an out, then was again muffled when said door closed.

The Lycan in human form was flanked by his two werewolf counterparts as they came to a stop. The male leader addressed her. "Uh uh, walk away. You are *not* welcome here."

She clicked her tongue. This must be the security chief, Lucas. She'd heard of him, a grape seed for brains with all the charm of mucus. "Threats and insults, are all your patrons forced to endure such crude treatment?"

"All of our *patrons* don't have death warrants hanging over their heads from the Vampire High Council and the Elfin Senate, to name a couple."

Irritation kindled her blood. Lucas wasn't nearly as endearing as the doorman. Tearing him to bits would be an orgasmic thrill but she whipped the impulse into submission. She'd learned patience over the centuries. On the other hand, ripping out the heart of one tended to adjust the attitude of the others. Diplomacy first though. It'd be a shame to ruin her dress. "It is universally recognized that Club Détente is neutral ground. As long as no laws are broken within these walls, all are to be welcomed."

A vein in his neck swelled. She had him and he knew it. "True, but management still reserves the right to refuse entry to anyone it deems undesirable, and that includes bloody ass fucks like you!"

She gasped audibly. *That mangy mongrel.* Her eyes blazed luminous white. She was through talking. Pity, she was so gonna miss this dress. In a blur, she back handed the guard to her right unconscious, then swiftly pivoted and drove the ball of the same right hand into the solar plexus of the second, forcing the air from his lungs, sending him flying.

As the second guard crashed to the carpet, clutching his chest, the werewolf security guards, made their move. They were fast, Lycan fast. From her perspective however, they moved as if mired in quicksand.

With a mere gesture of her hand, she sent both werewolves sailing into the reinforced steel doors.

Behind her, Taine was trying to join the fight but using her mental abilities, she held him fast. He could only watch as his Lycan brothers crumpled limply to the carpet. The indentations they left behind in the sound proof doors bore testament to the velocity they traveled at the time of impact.

Before Lucas could move, she clamped her hand firmly around his throat nonchalantly lifting him into the air. "*That* was extraordinarily rude and I demand an immediate apology," she said calmly, as if reciting a cookie recipe.

Lucas struggled as her hand tightened. He was trying to bring on his metamorphosis. She could feel it. With a thought, she stopped the change cold. *Naughty puppy, mama spank.*

He knew she preventing his transformation. She could see it in his eyes. Fear. Fear of her and her power. Blood pooled around her nails as they started breaking skin. Coughing and gagging, Lucas clawed at her hand. He was losing consciousness. No matter, if she couldn't have her apology, she'd have his life. Not even the Council would charge her given the grave insult hurled at her as witnessed by those present. Matters of honor were taken seriously. Latitude was generously given when defending it.

Lucas slumped. He hung limply as she increased the pressure. She had him. No one would dare intervene. His life essence began to ebb away when from somewhere beyond, a voice boomed.

"*Anna, put him down*! "Kiel had arrived, his lieutenant and right arm Ulysses at his side.

"Not until I have my apology. "She never took her eyes off the dangling Lucas. He wasn't dead...yet.

"On behalf of Club Détente's management and staff, I offer my most sincere apology for the way you've been treated this evening. Now, if you please, let him go."

Ok, she got her apology; this little doggie gets to live after all. "As you wish, apology accepted. "She dropped Lucas in a heap. Additional security staff hustled the fallen safely out of harm's way while Taine joined Kiel at his side.

"What type of club are you running here, Lycan?" She placed her hands on her hips. "I have never *seen* a more discourteous staff. First, I'm insulted by your adorable doorman, then I'm threatened and further insulted by that ogre of a security chief."

"Who the fuck are you callin' adorable?"

"Taine," Kiel warned his cousin.

"There, you see? How you manage to remain in business with such insolent, brash, uncouth-"

"Why are you here, Anna?" Kiel wasn't bothering to hide his annoyance.

"I need to explain why I feel the desire to go to a night club?"

"Don't play games with me, Anna." Kiel's voice took on a dangerous edge. Incredible hostility flowed from him.

"I don't need to read your thoughts to know what you're thinking. You hate me and wish me dead."

"Fuck, who don't?" She knew Taine couldn't resist that one.

"Taine." Kiel shot him a look. That little Lycan was cute, but seemed to have no concept at all as to when to shut up. It appeared though the message finally got through. Taine scowled but buttoned his lip. Good, this was between her and the Alpha.

"You murdered two of my dearest friends, Anna. Is it any wonder I harbor ill feelings about you?"

*Goddess Moon, had he not gotten over that?* "Really Kiel, it's long since time you put it behind you. Your *friends* tried, literally, to rip the meal from my mouth. Because of them, my prey escaped into the night. They cost me my nourishment. I insisted they reimbursed me for my loss and saw to it they did. So, tell me, oh pure and righteous Kiel, what would you have done in my place? Club Détente has achieved a reputation abroad as a place where all species are welcomed regardless of who they are or what they've done, where all bias, hatreds and vendettas are left at the door. Tell me, Kiel, is this the truth of Club Détente or a seductive lie aimed at generating revenue until the time comes when you can be more selective about who is desirable and who is not."

Kiel regarded her as if coming to a decision then made it. "Welcome to Club Détente, we will do our best to serve you and see to it that you enjoy your time with us and we hope you come again soon."

Ulysses could be silent no longer. "You can't allow—" Kiel silenced his protest with a wave of his hand. Taine rolled his eyes in resignation, returning to his post at the door. The Alpha had spoken.

"Well, that's more like it," triumph laced her voice. "I knew you had far too much savvy to allow personal feelings to influence how you conducted your business. It's been lovely chatting, gentlemen. Have a pleasant evening. "She turned to head for the dance floor.

"Anna? "She stopped. "Be aware that if you so much as nick a guest in my club, we will chain these doors and we will finish what was started here. Do you understand me?"

"Perfectly, Kiel, now, if you'll excuse me, I would like to go and enjoy the company of my own kind."

"There *are* no others of your kind."

"Why thank you, Kiel. I will take that as a compliment. But I can most certainly assure you, there are."

# CHAPTER FORTY FOUR

Her smile made a chill cascade down Kiel's spine. Suddenly, he was starring in his own version of *Finding Nemo,* because this must have been how Nemo's dad felt when Bruce, the shark, spread his lips and put those razor Chiclets on display.

With a wink, Anna went up the carpeted steps. As the door closed behind her and the music returned to muffled levels, Ulysses spoke his mind. "I can't believe you let that….monster in the club."

Neither could he, but like it or not, Anna was a guest. "Easy, Ulysses, I'm sure you've heard of keeping friends close and enemies closer. As long as she's here, we can at least keep an eye on her," Kiel said, his stomach jumping like water on a hot griddle.

"Ok, we know where she is, what now?"

"Tell Miguel and Paytor to change into their civvies. Have them watch her and tail her when she leaves. I want reports on her movements. Get Yvette to join the in-house surveillance. I want that harpy followed into the restrooms as well. Tell them to be careful. Anna's no fool; she'll expect us to try something."

Ulysses' gaze was sharp. "Got it."

"Not sure why she's here, but maybe we can gain some advantage from it. See to it, Ulysses, I'm headed to my office."

"I'm on it." Ulysses went off to carry out his instructions as Kiel made his way toward the dance floor area. Stopping to examine the damaged doors, he studied the indentations left behind by Poke and Jax. Taking a rough guesstimate, he blew out breath. Replacing those doors was gonna cost, big time. More troubling, he had a fairly good idea how much force it would've taken to launch Lycan their size fast enough to cause the damage before him. Anna was far stronger than when they last met. He stroked his beard. It could be his imagination, but she also seemed…bigger.

Kiel entered through the steel door to the thump of techno music. Pushing his way through the mingling crowd, he passed the bar surrounded by thirsty customers, across the dance floor packed with bodies dancing, making out, feeding, or mating, and continued toward his office.

As he exited the dance floor, he caught sight of Anna. She'd made herself at home at one of the booths that lined the club walls. She was being entertained by Cam, a Nubian male, an amazing physical specimen of Lycan masculinity. Anna stood, bent over the booth table, her dress hiked up to her waist. While she grasped the table edges, Cam, with a hand full of her platinum blonde hair, drove his hips into her again and again. His long dreads swayed in time as he took her like the alpha wolf he was.

Nudity was not only allowed at Club Détente, it was encouraged. Cam was one of the many who dared to bare. Far from being just a pretty face, Cam was a highly skilled fighter, one of the few Lycan ever known to have fought an Enforcer to a standstill.

At last reaching his office, he stepped inside. Striding to the desk, he picked up the phone receiver, punched one of the line buttons and waited. "Wanda, put me through to the mansion…yes, she's here, but there won't be any trouble, I've taken care of it." He took a seat, grabbing one of the pens lying on the desk. Twirling it in his fingers, he waited; his mind doing wind sprints over Anna's veiled revelation. She'd been creating others like herself. Adalius better move fast. Promise or not, there was no way he could sit on this for long.

Pressure built at his temples. His head felt like it was in a vise. Stress. No surprise there. The Destroyer was in the house. It's a wonder there wasn't a mad stampede to the exits. Obligation demanded he report her appearance to the High Council, immediately. If not for giving his word to Adalius, he'd already be making the call.

The weight of burden sat heavy on his shoulders. Why was Anna here? Certainly not just to have a good time. He was missing something. The hairs on his neck stood on end, his instincts screaming warnings that refused to be ignored. Dammit to hell, Anna walked into the lion's den. So, why did it feel like he was the one who was trapped? At that moment the line began to ring. After the fourth ring, Wellington picked up. "You have reached the domain of his highness Marseth."

"Hello, Wellington."

"Good evening, Master Kiel. How may I be of service, sir? "He could hear the smile in the butler's voice.

"Have you been able to relay the message to my father?"

"I'm afraid I have not spoken with his highness directly, though I have passed your message on to his royal guard. Do you wish me to try again?"

"No. But, if either he or my mother calls the mansion, have them contact me immediately."

"Very good, sir."

"Take care, Welly."

Hitting a new line button, he made a second call. Adalius had to be warned. Anna was back in the minion making business. It took only a few rings for the vampire to respond.

"What is it, Kiel?" Adalius' voice was smooth, rich and even.

"Looks like your instincts are still good. Anna just strolled in the club."

"Anna is *there*?"

"My sentiments exactly, walked right in like she owned the place. Word of warning, looks like she's begun nest building, again, you need to end her, fast. Don't know how long I can keep a lid on this."

"Understood." The line clicked ending the call. After wrapping up the conversation with the vampire, the phone rang the instant he laid the receiver down. Reclaiming it, he hit the last blinking button.

"Go, Ulysses."

"All the injured have been treated, debriefed, and released. Miguel, Paytor, and Yvette are all keeping watch on Anna, as instructed. As for Lucas, he's freaking out. He says he needs to speak to you immediately. Better hurry, Kiel, never seen him like this before."

"Sit tight, I'm on my way." His stomach curdled while his headache tightened the hammer lock it had on his skull. What the hell was bugging

Luke? He tended to be a bit dramatic sometimes, but he wasn't the kind to…well, cry wolf. If he's agitated, there's likely a damn good reason.

Rising from his seat, he headed out of his office, bound for the medical bay. Once in the club area, he took a quick visual scan of the dance floor. Anna, exercising her clothing option, had slipped free of her attire with the exception of her diamond necklace, earrings and spike heeled pumps. Down on all fours, she and Cam had taken their sexual coupling to the next level. Good. That would give him time to speak with Lucas without stressing over Anna's whereabouts.

Approaching the red steel door near the bar marked 'Staff Only', he entered. Down a flight of steps, he padded to a brown security door, Kiel keyed in the code on the pad on the wall, and let himself in. Cool, antiseptic air flooded his nostrils as the entry clicked softly shut behind him. The lock reengaged.

To his left, was a long corridor which led to the medical staff locker rooms and lounge. Ahead of him, was the doorway to a hall which led to the medical bay. To his immediate right was the doctor's office.

His head was screaming like a banshee. Problems were piling up. First Adalius makes an unexpected and unwanted return, then Anna waltzes back into town, pops in out of nowhere, announcing she had a new nest brewing, Lucas, was apparently going ape over who knew what, and to top all it off, his father, the king, was on the other side of the world.

No point in asking if things could get any worse. Somehow, he knew that's exactly where this little joy ride was headed. Stepping into the doctor's office, Kiel stopped in his tracks. *Mother Moon.* One look at the worried expression on Ulysses' face was enough to send him to the medicine cabinet. May as well beat the rush and grab some TUMS, water, and a Motrin or six.

# CHAPTER FORTY FIVE

"Just so you know, vamp, when this is over, we gonna go for that sleepy time shit you pulled at the motel. "Trey was crouched next to Adalius as they looked down on the abandoned bakery from a rooftop across the street.

Adalius grinned. "So, you slept well."

"Kiss my ass, Adalius," he growled.

"You are welcome," the vamp replied with a smirk.

He could take those wraparounds and ram them down his neck biting throat. Business before pleasure though. First, Anna gets hers, then Adalius gets his. The visual of the vamp hacking up his shades was interrupted by the electronic ringing of a phone. Adalius whipped the cell out of his trench coat and took the call.

While smartass talked to whoever reached out and touched him, he took the opportunity to scope out the bakery. The mouth of the spacious parking lot was roped off with a heavily rusted chain. A large, wooden gazebo sat crumbling to the rear. All entrances and windows of the factory were boarded up, the aging plywood sporting assorted urban artwork. Most likely some gang marking their territory. He squeezed his hands into fists, cracking his knuckles. Busting banger skulls was tempting, but they'd leave the small fry to local law enforcement. Tonight, they were after big game.

Eyes moving on to the second level, he spotted a metal catwalk. From what he could see, it ran around the perimeter of the building, leading to a ladder which dropped to a side alley just off the street. Finally he found what he was looking for. A lone window draped in shadow, free of obstruction, easy access for all manner of vermin; couldn't ask for a better place for a vamp nest.

Adalius closed the cell phone, his eyes brows dropping behind his wraparounds.

*Uh oh.*

"Spit it out," Trey said, his eyes never leaving the bakery.

The vampire slipped the phone back into his trench. "Anna has appeared at Club Détente. It is believed she is again growing her nest."

Shit. Good news must've taken a holiday. "She's not wasting time."

"So it would seem." Adalius tensed, the air about him crackled with energy.

"Wait a sec, I'm fairly familiar with the nightlife in New Carrollton. I'm positive I've never heard of a Club Détente."

"You would not have. Club Détente is a night club for immortals."

"No shit. So, what's her angle? Wouldn't showing up there generate the kind of attention she's been trying to avoid?"

Adalius scowled. Apparently, it crossed his mind too. "Anna never does anything on a whim. Rest assured, her being there is intended to provoke a desired response."

"Oh, she's about to get a response alright." Trey rose to his feet, checking his weapon.

"Indeed, first we destroy this nest, if truly it is a nest—"

"Then we roll into this club of yours so I can take this bitch out."

Adalius rose to his feet, facing him. "No."

"No? What the fuck you mean no?"

"Club Détente is neutral ground. I cannot legally kill her there if she has broken no laws within club walls."

He turned to the vamp. "Who said anything about you killing her?"

Adalius interrupted. "Anna is mine, slayer. I will not allow you to deny me my right to vengeance."

Clenching his fists, he rolled up on the vamp like an angry storm front. "Fuck you and your vengeance. This ain't got a damn thing to do with what you'll *allow* me to do. When I suggested this little team up, I never said I'd step aside and let you do the honors. I got my own personal stake in this, so let me spell it out for you. The first chance I get, I'm breakin' some wood off in her sweet spot. The only way you gonna stop it is to kill my ass."

Adalius removed his wraparounds and took a step, closing the space between them. "I do not need to kill you to stop you, Trey Thomas, but if you force my hand…"

They stood eye to eye, the tension between them, explosive. This alliance was a powder keg, and they were both striking matches. "Guess we have an understanding." He stared unblinking into the eyes of the vampire.

"We do indeed." His lips peeling back, revealing the tips of his fangs.

"Ok, then let's quit bull shittin' around and get to work."

"After you." Adalius gestured to the open air and the drop which separated them from their target.

He glanced at the long way down. "Think I'll take the fire escape. "He replaced his pistol and made his way to the rear of the roof top.

"Light weight." Adalius grinned.

"Fuck you," he responded, the corners of his own mouth curving upward.

*****

The air was thick with the stench of filth as they entered the bakery through the second story window. Adalius went first, he was close behind. Armed with handguns and assorted weapons, they silently dropped to the floor from the window sill. Withdrawing his pistols, he took off the safeties as Adalius reached back over his shoulder and slid his sword from its sheath. The vampire paused, as if listening for some distant sound. "They are here. I can sense them."

"I'm betting they've set up shop somewhere on the factory floor."

The vampire nodded. "Agreed. When we strike, we must move swiftly to prevent any of their numbers from escaping."

"Now you talking my language, vamp."

They made their way across what was left of the rotting office carpet, into a long darkened corridor, stretching out in both directions.

Rubbish and debris left behind by squatters littered the hallway along with several rodents who scurried away.

Trey glanced from one end of the corridor to the other, noting stairwells on each end. "Two stairwells, two of us, we should split up and hit them from both sides."

"Very well, when you are in position, I will give the signal. Then we attack."

Adalius turned about and started toward the far stairwell.

"Wait." Adalius came to a halt. "How are you gonna know when I'm in position?"

The vamp glanced over his shoulder. "I will know."

"Fine, but you didn't say what the signal would be. How am I suppose know when to move?"

Adalius grinned. "You will know." The vampire made his way down the hallway with sword in hand, and disappeared down the stairs.

"Jerk." Heading for the opposite stairwell, he started down. It was hot, muggy, dark, and reeked of urine, feces, and he didn't care to guess what else. Claustrophobic was the operative word. The walls seemed to close in as his stomach shifted to spin cycle. Why couldn't these bastards ever camp out in a nice, clean penthouse?

Breathing through his mouth didn't make the slightest difference. He could practically taste the muck at the back of his throat. One step at a time, he continued down into the darkness. His spirits lifted at the sight of lunar light, coming through a doorway. Arriving at the bottom, he quietly cocked the hammers on his pistols, crouched, and moved out onto the factory floor.

Moonbeams shone down through a huge sky light. The glass long ago shattered, it allowed enough illumination to prevent him from stepping on or bumping into anything which would betray his presence.

In the distance, came the sounds of muffled conversation. *Pay dirt.* Staying low, he crept toward the sound of two, maybe three voices ahead. There were a multitude of crates stacked two high, littering the floor. Sticking to the shadows, he moved from one stack to the next. No telling how many there were. Stealth was best till he knew what they were dealing with. Good thing there are so many of these…wait a second.

*What's with all the crates?* he thought, replacing his pistols into their holsters, he drew a knife. He slipped the tip of the blade underneath the lid of the nearest crate. Keeping a lookout, he silently worked on the lid, opening it enough to peer inside. Raucous laughter erupted. He whirled, drawing a pistol. He was alone. His chest rising and falling rapid fire, he waited. While his heart got its drum solo on, his finger caressed the trigger. He steeled himself for the sound of footfalls, his eyes darting about. *Damn, too many angles to cover. If they found, and rushed him...*

The voices resumed their idle chatter. He blew out a relieved breath, swallowing down the grapefruit sized knot in his throat. Producing a penlight from his jacket, he flicked the tiny switch, then shown its beam into the opening.

"What the fuck?" There were assault rifles inside, ten across. Did the vamps walk in on an arms deal, whack the dealers, and decided to keep the merchandise for themselves, or did they buy all this outright? But, that made no sense. Why would vamps need this type of hardware? Screams and staccato gunfire exploded from the area beyond. That sonuvabitch started the party without him. "So much for letting me get into position."

Trey charged toward the combat area. As he burst on the scene, the combatants could barely be made out as they moved in and out of the intermittent moonbeams, shining from above.

Locating Adalius, however, wasn't a problem. The vamp with flashing sword was a whirling dervish, sending one vamp after another to his final dust laden resting place. The sound of rifle bolts snatched his attention to a pair of vampires drawing a bead on his partner. Quickly, he reached into his jacket pocket and withdrew two electro darts. Letting them fly, he dashed toward them. The projectiles found their marks. One lodged in the arm of the first vamp, the other in the chest of the second.

*Boo ya!*

Electric current, tore through their systems, wreaking havoc on their muscles. The gunman shook uncontrollably, dropping their weapons. He opened fire. The vamps disintegrated to dust. That's one that bastard owed him.

Approaching footsteps heralded the coming reinforcements. Good, he would've been pissed if

Adalius didn't leave him any. Drawing his second pistol, he joined the sword wielder. Back to back they fought, Adalius with his blade, he with his pistols. When his last magazine spit out the final slug, he drew his blade. Fighting like a hellion, he matched Adalius body for body. Vamp dust swirled about like the clouds of some whacked out fog machine. Out of the corner of his eye, he spotted a shadow speeding away. "We got a runner!"

Before the echo of his shout faded, Adalius drew a dagger from his trench coat and let it fly. The blade tumbled through the air, lodging in the back of the fleeing vampire. Its heart pierced, the vamp cried out, falling forward. As he hit the floor, its body crumbled to dust, scattering on the breeze.

They waited, braced themselves for the next wave of attackers. None came. He let out the breath he'd been holding. Awww, no more to play wi-

pop, pop, pop, pop.

Muzzle flashes. Plink, plink, plink, plink. He ducked down. *No, Adalius did not just deflect those bullets with his sword*! The vamp drew his own pistol. The gunmen froze. Trey couldn't see their faces but they had to be just as floored by what they'd seen, as he was. Adalius squeezed off two shots. One vamp silhouette flinched. The other, let out a groan just before both forms disintegrated away. *Damn.*

Adalius was one of the most dangerous vampires he'd ever seen. If Enforcers were anything like him, slayers could find themselves on the endangered species list if the High Council ever decided to eliminate vampire hunters.

The battle won, he filed away his awe, remembering how pissed he was at that saber toothed jackass. Adalius slid his sword back into its sheath.

"What the hell happened to waiting for me to get into position, vamp? "He stopped. That blade, it wasn't Adalius' broadsword. It was a katana, the weapon of samurais. It then occurred to him, the individual, though roughly the same height and definitely a vampire not only lacked Adalius' long locks but was also wider across the back. His grip on the knife tightened. He took a step back. As his *partner* turned, an unfamiliar face sporting different shades, snarled.

*Oh shit.*

As the dark skinned vamp stepped into a moon beam column, he noted a clean shaven face. His high tapered fade cut was crowned by a flat top that would give an aircraft carrier an inferiority complex. The vamp looked down and growled.

"Slayer," the rich bass voice rumbled with malice. The vampire fired a right hand. *Whoa*! He barely managed to sidestep that punch. If that one had connected, it would have turned his head into a maraca. Trey slipped inside, delivering a two punch combination to the vamp's midsection, followed up with a violent right cross that forced the fang's head a quarter turn. The back hand that caught Trey came in too fast for him to react. It launched the slayer off his feet, knocking the blade free from his grasp. Landing hard, the blade rattled away as Trey slid across the floor picking up glass shards until coming to a stop.

His head throbbed. Vision blurred, Trey made out the six blood suckers closing in. Shaking his head to clear it, the six vamps coalesced into one. Rolling away, Trey attempted to get to his feet but his adversary was upon him. A huge hand closed around his throat, the vamp's grip was like iron. The fang forced Trey to the ground. The slayer's throat locked down, breathing became an issue. Dammit, the backup blade was in his boot, outta reach. No darts left to stun the brute either. Trey gagged as the grip tightened. If he didn't shake this gorilla's hand off, Maya would soon be shopping for a headstone.

"It's over, slayer, die. "The vampire sneered.

It was hard to focus. His limbs became heavy. A miasma like darkness nibbled away the edges of his vision. Needed oxygen was getting harder to come by. Calls from all over his body, flooded into his brain from his central nervous system, vital organs demanded he breathe. He couldn't. The hand continued shutting off his wind pipe. He was exhausted, with no strength left to draw on. He couldn't fight if he couldn't breathe. Nothing left to do but die.

A blur sailed into his fading vision, striking the vamp on the side of the face. The hand lost its grip. Not wasting the opportunity, he rolled on his side and sucked in a gulp of air. Dusty, stale, funky, sweet, wonderful air. His assailant staggered back, but quickly recovered. His eyes, ignited in fury. That's when a leather clad angel stepped between them.

Adalius. *About damn time*!

Drawing his sword, Adalius assumed a fighting stance. The vampire drew his katana, the invitation to combat, accepted. Moving closer, blade ready for bloodletting, flat top growled. Getting in air was coming along but not fast enough.

His lungs still burned. Then there was the matter of the stand order his brain sent his legs. They weren't responding. Either the order hadn't been received or his limbs were still trying to reboot. He was gonna have to sit this one out. The good news was he had a great seat to watch the vamp fight. An all-out, no holds barred, battle to the death with him and his collapsed trachea, the grand prize. Talk about a buzz kill.

The combatants circled each other. Then with a clash of steel, the battle was joined. The factory echoed with the clang of blade meeting blade. Sparks flew from the metal on metal action as each probed for weaknesses in the other. The vamp deflected what would have been a fatal strike from Adalius, then raised his own sword, swinging it in an arch meant to slice off his opponent's head. As if reading his thoughts, Adalius countered, then parried a second strike as the titan quickly whirled and struck at his left flank.

Sensing an opening, Adalius fired and connected with a hard right cross. It staggered flattop. Moving quickly, Adalius lunged to press his advantage. This time however, it was the giant who saw opportunity. Recovering his bearing, the vampire brought his blade swiftly across his body. Adalius moved. But not fast enough. The blade sliced his abdomen. The wound was superficial, but seeping. First blood had been drawn. Even from where he lay, Trey felt the rage. Adalius' eyes blazed teal as flattop once more assumed a defensive stance, his own eyes glowing like golden suns.

The tips of his fangs appeared from beneath his top lip as Adalius raised his sword. "Prepare thyself, Death has come for you. "It was on now. The safeties were off. Adalius was done fuckin'around.

Upon hearing the threat however, Flattop lowered his sword a fraction, cocking his head. "Ada?"

"I am Adalius, speak and identify yourself."

The titan lowered his sword. "Surely it hasn't been so long that you have forgotten the voice of thine own brother?"

# CHAPTER FORTY SIX

"How are they, Ulysses?" Kiel swallowed the Motrin, chasing them down with his cup of water.

"Lonnie's got bruised ribs, Jax and Poke just had the wind knocked out of them, and Ramone has a major concussion. Doc sent him to our med facilities uptown for observation." Efficient and concise, never once had he regretted hiring Ulysses.

"And Luke?"

"Doc's checking him out now. The others said they didn't notice anything unusual with Anna. But Lucas, something's *really* got him spooked."

He nodded. "Alright, let's go see what he has to say." They made their way out of the doctor's office, toward the medical bay. Half way, they ran across the on duty nurse.

"Is the doc done examining Lucas?" Kiel asked, half not wanting to know what was on Lucas' mind.

The nurse smiled, hugging the clipboard she was carrying. "He'll be out to see you in a moment."

"Thank you, nurse." She smiled, and continued on her way. Before she was completely out of sight, Dr. Roman appeared at the doorway, placing his stethoscope in his lab coat pocket as he approached.

Tall, youthful, lanky, and frail with fair skin, and sandy blonde hair, Roman always struck him more like a teenaged surfer then a two hundred and twenty year old doctor of supernatural beings.

"What's the verdict, Doc, how is he?" Kiel asked as Ulysses fidgeted. His right hand man was a nervous Nelly when it came to hospitals.

The physician let out a subtle sigh. "He's got some moderate lacerations and some bruising on his neck. He's still quite agitated but otherwise, he's fine."

"Can we talk to him now?" Kiel asked, his concern rising like a baking soufflé.

"Anytime you're ready. He can go home when you're done."

"Thank you, doctor." He offered his hand. Doctor Roman took it, gave it a couple of shakes, and then continued on to his office.

Kiel paused before stepping into the medical bay. Even through all the antiseptics, he could smell Luke's extreme anxiety. Very bad. Lucas wasn't to type to scare easily. This was gonna be every bit as unpleasant as he thought.

Lucas looked up when Kiel slid the curtain aside. He entered while Ulysses remained in the aisle.

"How ya feeling, Luke?' He gently laid his hand on the Lycan's shoulder.

Lucas actually flinched. "Like someone tried to twist my head off, but I'll be ok."

No point prolonging this. "I understand you have something urgent you wanted to tell me."

Lucas looked up. He could see it in his eyes. Fear. "Hell yeah, I do. Anna, she can block our ability to change."

Kiel blinked. "Pardon…did you…she can what?"

Lucas drew in a deep breath. "When Anna had her hand around my throat, I tried to shift, but I couldn't. The whole time, she was looking into my eyes, smiling. She was stopping it, and she wanted me to know it."

"Goddess moon," Ulysses exclaimed.

Lucas tried to hide his trembling, but couldn't. "I know what it sounds like, but I'm not crazy. She can stop us from changing. What *is* she Kiel, even the oldest vampires can't do that?"

Ulysses whipped out his cell phone and began dialing.

*What indeed.* Up until now, Kiel always believed Anna just a souped-up vampire. But if what Luke was saying was true, Anna was a far greater threat than anyone realized.

Lucas locked eyes with his. "We have to kill her, Kiel. Whatever she is, we have to kill her if we can."

"I agree."

"I can't reach Paytor or Miguel." Ulysses shook his head, worry lacing his voice as he put away his cell phone.

Kiel's heart sank. *Mercy Mother Moon.* Miguel, Paytor. They were in epic danger. It was his fault. "We have to find them. They have no idea what they're dealing with, both of you, with me."

They hustled from the medical bay, burst through the brown steel security door, and dashed up the stairs out to the dance floor.

Frantically, he scanned the area. Anna was gone. Sifting through the sea of faces, he spotted Cam. Slipping on his shirt, he was whispering in Tracy's ear. But wolf's bane, where was Anna? Turning, Kiel made his way toward the lobby. His eyes fixed on the exit, he ran into Yvette who'd sauntered up to him. "Yvette, I'm sorry, are you alright?"

He barely managed to catch the server as she bounced off him. "Fine, I think."

"Where is Anna?"

"She took off about five minutes ago. I saw her pulling out as I was coming back from break."

"Yvette, did Miguel and Paytor go after her?" He somehow managed to keep the panic out of his voice.

"That's what they said they were told to do. They took the SUV."

*Oh no.* "Their cell phones, tell me they took their cell phones."

She nodded "Of course, Miguel's mate is pregnant and Paytor is such a ho, he's too scared he'd miss a booty call."

"Thanks, wrap up your shift then take off."

"Yes, sir."

Yvette headed off toward the bar as Kiel turned to his friend. "Ulysses, have my car brought around and keep ringing their phones. I'm going after them."

"It's a good thing we had those GPS trackers installed. You should be able to home in on them with no trouble."

"Are you talking about these? "He and Ulysses turned. There stood Taine with GPS trackers in hand. "I found them lying in the parking lot."

*Goddess Moon.* "Ulysses, keep trying to reach them. Lucas, Taine, come with me."

Ulysses headed off in the direction of Kiel's office while he, with Lucas and Taine in tow, made a beeline toward Cam. This was going to require Cam's special skills. It was going to require muscle. He didn't bother with pleasantries as he approached. "I need your help."

Cam, as usual, was all business. "What do you need, Kiel?"

"Your brother-in-law may be headed into a trap, follow me."

"Miguel? What—"

"No time, this way." Kiel was off, snaking his way through the crowd, out to the front of the club.

Five minutes on the nose, Ulysses arrived with his vehicle. "I still can't get a hold of them, Kiel. I *really* don't like this," Ulysses said stepping out of the vehicle.

"Neither do I." Taine and Cam piled into the running car. "Don't stop trying Ulysses, we've got to find them." Kiel slid into the driver's seat, yanking the door closed behind him.

Ulysses leaned down, nodding to the rear off the vehicle. "I had hardware and silver placed in your trunk."

Kiel nodded in acknowledgement as put the car in gear. "Good. If you can't reach them, get a hold of Javier. Maybe he can track them using the GPS in their phones."

"Got it, boss."

Yvette came running out of the club, stood next to Ulysses, pointed to the south and shouted. "They went that way, toward Hill Street!"

Tires screeched as he slammed his foot down on the accelerator.

*****

"She's an unstoppable, bloodthirsty, psychopathic freak job *and* she can block our change? Why the fuck didn't you tell me this shit *before* I got in the car!?"Taine sat forward in the backseat passenger side.

"Because I needed you to get in the car," Kiel shouted as he weaved in and out of traffic, desperately searching for his friends.

"I'm gonna fuck you up for this, cousin. I'ma fuck you up and gnaw on yo hind legs." Soon as Kiel pulled this little black wagon over it's gonna be wolf on wolf violence.

"Shut up, Taine and show some fuckin' courage." Cam turned toward him from the passenger side front seat.

"Fuck you, Cam. Annette says she needs to talk to you, she's pregnant. "Instantly, Cam's face lost expression, color draining away. Frantically, he began ripping at the phone in his pants pocket. Taine smirked. Ha! That sank his battleship. "What's the matter, Casper? You lookin' kinda pale. Kiel, I think we need to take a detour and go see the wizard. Cam needs some more courage. The courage he had just jumped the fuck out the window!"

# CHAPTER FORTY SEVEN

Paytor and Miguel continued tailing Anna as she drove thru the downtown area. Paytor, at the wheel, kept a discreet distance but stayed close enough to keep her in sight. The first rays of dawn streamed into the cab, bidding a sunny greeting to them and the commuters of the morning rush hour. Shielding his eyes, Miguel folded down the visor.

"What the fuck, isn't she supposed to be a vamp?" Paytor said aloud, as he drove through another intersection following Anna.

"Supposed to be, yeah," Miguel responded, reaching into his pants pocket to retrieve his phone, it was time to update Kiel.

"Well she must be wearing some *serious* sun block. There's enough daylight right now that she should at least be smoking," Paytor said, taking left following Anna.

"She's sucked down so many different kinds of blood, no telling how it's affected her." Freeing his cell, he checked it.

"Still no signal?"

He could hear the anxiousness in Paytor's voice. He was getting nervous. Frankly, so was he. "Naw, man, the provider must be having satellite issues."

"Look, she just took a right at the light." Paytor put on the turn signal then mirrored Anna's direction change. Anna kept a leisurely pace. If she was aware of being tailed, she did a helluva job hiding it. "Where's she going?"

"I think I know. If I'm right, she'll take the next left, then head toward the river front."

"The Dunbar Arms?"

"That's what I'm thinking."

Paytor nodded, keeping his eyes on the road. "It *would* be a great place for a vamp nest."

The Dunbar Arms apartment complex, was supposed to be a huge part of the city's plans to develop the riverfront with nightclubs, restaurants, and casinos. But, in the middle of construction, support and funding for the project collapsed leaving the Arms an empty, boarded up shell.

Anna put on her turn signal, taking the left turn, as predicted. Paytor smiled. "There she goes. You called it, man."

Miguel tapped his phone against his leg. "Yeah, but I'd feel a whole lot better if somebody knew where we were headed." Once again, he checked his phone. "Que? Still no signal." A knot formed in the pit of his stomach, he was starting to get a bad feeling about this. And an oncoming headache wasn't making it any better.

"Should we turn back?" Paytor asked, throwing off acute anxiety.

"Just a couple more minutes, compadre, the Arms is just a quarter mile ahead. We've come this far, I don't want to lose her. In the meantime, I'll keep an eye on our rear, to make sure we're not being tailed."

Anna came upon the Dunbar Arms driveway, and drove in.

"I need to carry yo ass to Vegas, Miguel. You're right, again."

While Anna continued on, he glanced at the side mirror. As far as he could tell, they weren't being followed. The road was packed, but it seemed to be just a bunch of humans headed in the same direction.

"Drive down a little farther, P, then we'll double back." Anna rolled toward the rear of the Arms, kicking up dust as they passed the driveway entrance. Continuing on for another quarter mile, they parked by the side of the road. Miguel checked his cell phone once more then looked over at his partner. "Still no signal, hombre. This is damned peculiar."

"So, what do you wanna do?" Paytor asked, keeping an eye on passing traffic.

"Let's go scout the place, but if we get a bad vibe, we out. If it turns out to be her nest, we report back to the boss, he calls the Vamp Council—"

"And they send in the Enforcers to deal with this. Ok, I'm down, let's go. "He was already out of the vehicle as Paytor closed his door, then locked both with the remote.

"Fuck, man, my head's killin' me." Paytor had a headache too? Must be stress, they were after all, dealing with Anna, the Lycan killer, not the Easter bunny. Their adrenal glands must be unloading.

They started back on foot. The rising sun had already chased away the shadows of night. He and Paytor moved in across the field separating their destination from the road. Taking cover behind a rise of earth and weeds, they searched for a possible way into the dead building. The doorways and windows were all boarded up. The once planned crown jewel of the riverfront development project, now stood empty and hollowed out, like an enormous concrete skull.

He wrung his hands, perspiration rolling down his back. Paytor fiddled absently with the gold cross tucked inside his shirt. Stomach churning, nerves tight like piano wire, Miguel rolled his shoulders. Slowly, he took in a lungful of air, forcing himself to breathe normally.

Carefully, they approached the Arms, and crept toward the rear. Anna's ride sat parked next to a gaping hole in the brick exterior. Moving to opposite sides of the opening, they knelt down and waited. Dare they go in? If this was Anna's nest, the blood suckers inside could be hibernating or wide awake and ready to receive visitors.

Miguel's nostrils flared as he sampled the stale air within the Arms. "They're in there alright, I can smell them. Paytor stared into the blackness, then glanced up. "Let's go give Kiel the four one one."

"Bet." Miguel started to rise when a new scent drew his attention. "Wait, you smell that?"

"Smell what?"

"Take another whiff, P."

Paytor inhaled another sample of the air, his eyebrows rising. "There's a human in there too."

"Yeah, a human female."

Miguel rose off the balls of his feet and started into the Arms when Paytor grabbed him by the forearm. "What are you doing man?"

"We gotta get her outta there, hombre."

"Are you outta your fucking mind? I am *not* riskin' my neck for some human bitch."

"Think about it P, if we rescue this female, not only do we steal a possible soldier from Anna's army, but we gain a pair of eyes that's seen the inside of this nest. Who knows, if she has enough information, maybe we can take out Anna for good."

Paytor's expression was that of someone who'd bit into a peanut butter, jelly, and sauerkraut sandwich. "And if she doesn't, we'd be doing something hugely stupid for nothing."

"It's a big risk, I admit, amigo, but I'm prepared to take it."

"And what the fuck am I supposed to tell your mate if you don't come back?"

His temper simmered. That was below the belt. "You think I wanna do this, hombre? Hell no. But I don't want my little chiquita growin' up in a world with Anna in it. Look, I'm not gonna ask you to take the gamble with me. Wait here. If I'm not back in ten minutes, get outta here and bring back the boss."

"Don't be an idiot! I'm not letting you go in there alone. If you go in, I go in." Their eyes met and they fist bumped then slowly rose to their feet.

"Ok P, we go in, but the first sign of trouble, we break out."

"No argument from me."

"Ok, let's go, hombre."

"After you, my captain." Before they entered, Miguel whipped out a vial and sprayed himself all over then turned it toward his friend.

Paytor threw out his arms. "Whoa, whoa what's that shit?"

"Essence of coyote piss. We just can't stroll in there without masking our scent. They'd be all over us in a second."

"But won't they still come after us? Coyotes have blood too you know."

"True, but if they were hungry enough to eat a coyote, don't you think they would've eaten the human by now?"

"Okay, you got me there. "He aimed the vial toward Paytor, who still held up his hands defensively. "Wait, before you spray that, this stuff washes off easily right?"

"Come on, P, I got a pregnant wolf bitch at home with a nose and hormones in overdrive. If this didn't wash off, do you really think I'd be spraying it all over me?"

"Fine, spray away."

He sprayed his friend from head to toe. Paytor grimaced. "Alright, lead the way. Sure hope you know what we doin'."

They entered the Arms. It was still and not nearly as dark as it appeared on the outside. The entire first floor was open and empty save for dust, trash, cobwebs, and creepy crawlies. He snorted at the stinging in his nose as foreign particulates invaded his nasal cavity. Aside from the support beams, they were the only things present to welcome them, so far, so good.

Following the scent of the human female, they came to a cement staircase, one of the few things completed in the Arms before the money ran dry. Silently, they went up. Winding their way past an empty second floor, they approached the third. The smell of rot, blood, and sex was overwhelming.

Miguel flinched at cluster of nude vampires in a far corner tangled together in hibernation. The blood feeders were clearly spent after an apparent vamp orgy. It took a few moments for their noses to sift through the kaleidoscope of smells dominating the area but they once again locked onto the scent of the woman. They continued upward.

Swallowing down the knot in his throat, Miguel stared into the darkness. Growing more imperceptible with each step they took, it was as if the gloom was urging them to turn back.

The scent of the human was sharp as they approached the fourth floor. They'd found her. It was as murky as the armpit of night. Had they not been Lycan, they would've needed flash lights to safely navigate in the sea of blackness. The hairs on his head and arms stood on end. It didn't feel right. Suddenly, going alone in a dark, abandoned building loaded with vampires with no way of letting anyone know where they were, was starting to feel like a very bad idea.

Looking about, they noted several vampires in hibernation along the far wall. Paytor tapped his shoulder, to get his attention, then gestured to the right. There, lying on the floor bound and gagged was the victim. Her legs were tied together at the ankles, her arms bound behind her back.

They moved in closer, and were greeted by the sight of several bite marks on her neck and thighs. They'd been feeding on her. They edged closer. The smell of fear rippled from her like heat waves off a radiator. She was awake. Miguel shook his head in disgust. What had these parasites been doing to her? He glanced about, his apprehension seeping into the air. Something wasn't right.

The ease of getting this far and no resistance of any kind, it was all too easy. And where the hell was Anna? This was beginning to feel a whole lot like a trap they'd walked into. The quiet rang in his ears. Kneeling down, the Latino slowly but firmly, slid his hand over the female's mouth, clamping it shut as Paytor pinned her legs. "Don't be afraid, we're gonna get you out. Make a sound, and we're all dead. Do you understand? "He whispered into her ear. The female's eyes, wide and wild with terror, nodded. "Don't move. "Miguel produced a hunting knife and cut through her binds then helped her to her feet. "I know you can't see so you're gonna have to trust us to lead you out. "She nodded as Paytor removed her gag.

"Ok, let's get outta here," Paytor said.

Click.

The entire floor flooded with light. The previously sleeping vampires, now wide awake and snarling, surrounded them. Paytor looked about wildly. "They have power? How the fuck do they have power?"

Thirty strong, the vampires closed ranks, cutting off any hope of escape. "Get behind me!" Miguel commanded as he pulled the female behind him. Without warning, the woman latched onto to his arm, whirled him about, extended her fangs and backhanded him to the floor.

"My hero." Marie grinned as several vampires seized him. Paytor flattened the first vampire who attacked him with a sharp blow to its temple before being tackled to the floor and subdued. They struggled. Desperately, Miguel willed his body into change. Paytor's transition was already underway. Then as suddenly as it began, the process reversed. Their features returned to normal. A frigid sensation raced through his veins. Nothing but the Lycan himself, could reverse the change once it had begun. They looked to each other in disbelief.

"Uh, uh, uh, bad dogs, there'll be none of that. "From beyond the circle of vamps came the click of heels. "To answer your first question, we have power because I was fortunate enough to have turned one of the hard working men of the New Carrollton Illumination Company into one of us. "The click of the heels grew louder until at last the circle of vamps parted to reveal Anna, arm in arm, with a sexy blonde. Marie smiled and went to join them.

Paytor shouted at Marie. "How? How could you be a vamp? I...your scent."

Anna smiled deviously. "Allow me to explain. The scent of the human female you detected, I planted into your brains. You smelled what I wanted you to smell."

A realization slapped Miguel in the face. "The headaches, that was you digging around in our heads." He paused, another unsettling epiphany dawning on him. "The cell phones, that was your doing too?"

Anna smiled like a proud mother. "Very good, Lycan."

"What the fuck are you? Vamps can't do that! Paytor shouted.

Anna strolled over to Paytor and caressed his cheek. "I am the future, Lycan, hunted like an animal, but very soon, all of you shall bow befor— "

"You *really* like to hear yourself talk don't you? Paytor interrupted.

"Yes, please, spare us the super villain rant. Cut to the chase. What do you plan to do with us?"

Anna clicked her tongue and rolled her own eyes. "I was ranting wasn't I?I cannot believe I actually did that. "She left Paytor, moving toward him, her heels clicked with each step. "I'll get to the point. My children must be fed properly to allow their abilities to develop to the fullest." Anna looked into his eyes. It was like being swept up in vortex. You could neither escape nor resist. Her smile was hypnotic as she trailed a finger down his neck to his shoulder. "That's where you two come in. Your blood will expedite the development of their powers. But worry not, many of your brethren will join you in sacrifice." She turned, breaking her hold. It was like being dropped to the ground from a rooftop. Anna went to rejoin Trish and Marie, the sensual sway of her hips was as entrancing as her gaze.

Miguel's mind raced. There were even more vampires entering the room, at least forty, in all. There was no way to escape, to warn the king.

Trish and Marie stepped into Anna's arms. Turning, she smiled shaking her head. "I hear your thoughts. Soon, Marseth will be no more of a threat to me than you are now. My heartfelt thanks to you both; your blood contributions are appreciated. "She looked about at her brood of vampires. "Feed my children, and become strong." The vampires flowed toward him and Paytor, fangs growing longer before his eyes.

"I've never had Lycan before, Anna," said the blonde as she turned to kiss Anna's neck.

"Nor have I. "Marie leaned in to nibble on Anna's ear lobe.

Anna breathed out a sigh. "You're all in for a treat. Lycan are succulent and the taste, pure ambrosia. For now my daughters, allow our soldiers to feed. Your time will come. Now, take my vein, feed from me." Anna threw back her head as Trish sank her fangs into her mistress' neck. She and Marie gently lowered Anna to the floor. Once there, Marie moved into position, her own fangs piercing the soft flesh of Anna's inner thigh.

Hands pulled at Miguel's arms and legs. Fangs, like daggers, plunged into his body, seemingly everywhere at once. He barely heard Paytor's screams over his own and Anna's pleasured cries. A hideous swan song as his spirit left his body, bound for a better place.

# CHAPTER FORTY EIGHT

The figure manifested from the shadows, into a column of moon light. Eyes widening, Adalius' jaw went slack. It was an apparition, a cruel prank played upon him by the demons of his mind, or a vengeful adversary bent on tearing at his sanity.

"It...cannot be...Kalleal?" the stunned whisper left Adalius' lips before realizing he had formed the words. Removing the wraparounds from his face, his arms fell. Absently, he held the shades pinched between his fingers, afraid to move or breathe lest the vision disperse like the wisps of a fading dream.

Robbed of the power of speech, his eyes and mind raged back and forth, locked in conflict. His eyes were insisting reality, whereas his mind was rejecting the assertion. The shades slipped from his grasp and clattered at his feet. Drawn forward, he took a step, his legs moving of their own accord. Feelings of denial turning hopeful, he took another step, then another, and another. The vampire moved toward him, seemingly at the whim of legs taking liberties.

They stopped a mere foot apart. Staring into a face familiar, yet alien, he took in the vampire's scent. Dearest Elder, so much like his own! Against his temple came gentle pressure; an invitation and a request. With care, he lowered his mental shield. Normally, such action would be insanity, but he sensed no treachery in the vampire's motives, just a need, like his own, to know the truth. His mental barrier was completely down as the vampire followed suit. Reaching out, their thoughts intertwined.

A myriad of screens raced by like the lines on an interstate, moments of life captured on the film of his recollection. With a sudden flash, he was a child again, being chased on the beach, laughing the laugh of innocence. Cool salty breeze off the ocean, warm sun on his face, this was home. He was reliving a cherished memory, as he had many times before, but, this was different. This time, he experienced it through the eyes of two minds. At once, he was the pursued and the pursuer. Zigging and zagging along the shore line, he tackled and was tackled from behind. They struggled. He pinned and was pinned. Into his vision of a clear blue sky came the face of his brother. Simultaneously, he gazed down into his own smiling face.

In an instant, he rocketed, up and away. His younger self, brother, the ocean, and the beach shrank to a pinpoint of light. The screens of life raced by, becoming streaks of light as their minds returned to where they belonged. With a jolt, the connection was severed. Hit by a wave of disorientation, Adalius struggled to steady himself. The world faded back in, his vision coming into focus on the only other soul who could have that exact memory.

Kalleal.

He dropped his sword. A tear streamed from Kalleal's eye, his own sword landing at his feet, moonlight bouncing off the blade. No doubt remained. They surged forward, coming together in tight embrace. Strong arms wrapped around him, while his own encircled his brother. Adalius held his sibling at arm's length, his eyes drifting to Kalleal's wrist. The Sandrian emblem, as it was on his own wrist, was tattooed there. Kalleal was Sandrian. Confirmation reached his ears in the form of a beating heart. Adalius' spirit soared. It was Kalleal, his fraternal twin. It did not matter how or why. They were together again, brothers, reunited.

"I thought you dead long ago," he breathed out.

"And I you, my brother. I.. I have many questions. "His twin gave him a squeeze.

"As do I." He held Kalleal at arm's length, taking in the sight of his sibling.

"Don't mind me, I'll just lie here and try to breathe," Trey interrupted as he gingerly attempted to get to his feet.

They turned. Kalleal growled. "A moment, my brother, while I deal with this vermin." His twin retrieved his sword. With malicious intent, he stalked toward the slayer.

Adalius caught his fraternal by the arm. "Wait, Kalleal, he is with me."

Kalleal looked from him to the slayer and back. "He...the slayer is with you?"

He nodded. "It is a long story."

Kalleal arched an eye brow. "Of that, I'm certain. I very much look forward to hearing this story."

"Soon, for now..." He led Kalleal to where Trey struggled to rise. Bending, they each took an arm, and pulled the slayer to his feet. "This is Trey Thomas. Slayer, this is my brother, Kalleal."

Trey pulled free of their grasp and stepped away, glaring at Kalleal. "Wish I could say it was a pleasure."

Kalleal sneered. "I hope I didn't hurt you too badly...slayer."

"Fuck you, fang face, I'll be fine."

"Mind your tongue, it's only because of Ada, that I don't kill you, though the night is still young."

"Bite me, tiny." Trey massaged his aching neck. "Forget I said that."

Adalius suppressed a grin, a poor choice of words.

Trey eyed Kalleal with contempt, while he went to retrieve own sword. "What the hell took you so long, your brother here, almost ended me."

He sheathed his blade, rejoining his comrades. "Forgive me, they had taken hostages. It took time to defeat their captors, sweep clean the minds of the prisoners, then lead them to safety."

Trey started off in the opposite direction. "Whatever. You need to see this." They followed the slayer into an area filled with crates, straight to one pried open. Trey gestured to it. "Have a look."

Adalius stepped forward. With his bare hand, he ripped the lid from the crate and examined its contents, while Kalleal went off to conduct his own investigation.

Trey eyed Adalius' brother as he walked out of sight. "Could Anna be behind all this or did these blood suckers stumbled onto a black market arms deal?"

He considered the question, looking about at the multitude of crates. "I do not know. Anna has resources, yes, but this…"

"I believe I've found a clue." They turned toward Kalleal's voice. He approached, carrying a small crate in his arms. Setting it on the floor at his feet, Kalleal busted open the lid. It was loaded with unmarked, cardboard boxes. Lifting one out, he opened it and removed a bullet, a silver bullet. "There are many more crates like this against the far wall."

Trey looked to Kalleal, then to him. "When did vamps start using fire arms? Fangs I've run into tend to use their powers or more personalized forms of combat."

"The Enforcers use them. I use them and I am fairly certain Kalleal does as well." Kalleal nodded, flashing a .44 magnum resting in his shoulder holster.

Adalius examined the silver bullet in his brother's gloved hand. "The implications of this are unsettling. It appears someone is preparing for war."

Kalleal grunted in agreement. "But who's preparing for war and against whom do they plan to wage it?"

"So what do we do now? We just can't leave this shit lying around for Anna or some wannabe warlord to collect," Trey said looking about.

"Leave that to me." Adalius took out his cell phone, punched his speed dial and waited. "I have a favor to ask. Bring a ton and a half truck and all the able bodies you can muster to the abandoned Pennywise Bakery on Long Avenue. Bring pallet jacks and dollies. Move swiftly, I will await your arrival. "He ended the call, returning the phone to his trench coat. "Now we wait."

*****

Nearly an hour passed when a hooded figure lurked out of the darkness. Looking about, he approached cautiously. Over a foot shorter than himself, the individual sported an oversized grey hoodie, baggy cargo pants, and Nike Air's. He spoke not a word as he glanced from Kalleal to Trey and back with his unspoken question.

"They are with me." Adalius met the gaze of his newly arrived friend. "I need you to remove all of these crates." The individual raised his arm and snapped his fingers. Out of the darkness, marched dozens of tiny movers dragging dollies and pallet jacks. They were everywhere. Despite the multitude of movers, he knew there were far more in the shadows watching, waiting.

"They're....children," Kalleal said as he observed them at work.

"Be assured my brother, they stopped being children, long ago."

Trey stepped out of the way of a rolling dolly. "Who are they, Adalius?"

"They are called The Lost. Children abducted by the vampire, Bartholomew. I liberated them when I slew him. I have taken responsibility for them, seen to their needs for their protection and the protection of mortal kind."

Within minutes, the workers cleared all the crates out. When the last of them had been removed, he turned to his hooded associate. "I need information. Lean on your sources, if you must, but I need to know where these weapons came from. Contact me when you have something. For now, keep them safe." After a fist bump, the hooded figure turned about and snapped his fingers. He and his crew blurred and were gone in a blink of an eye.

# CHAPTER FORTY NINE

**W**aiting is a big part of what a slayer does. So, when Adalius asked he and Kalleal to wait in the motel till he returned, it was business as usual. Lying on the bed, Trey passed the time watching the Matrix, while Kal checked his phone, for the nineteenth time. It was starting to work a nerve.

It'd been hours since Adalius stepped out. In the meantime, the sun had risen. Kalleal was a nervous wreck. Drawing his weapons, he checked them...again. Mentioning Adalius was sun proof wasn't on the agenda. If Kalleal didn't already know, then Adalius would have to let his brother in on that, himself.

"Kal, chill man, you're starting to make *me* nervous."

Kalleal holstered his weapons, eyeing the door like it was gonna to do a magic trick.

"He's been gone for far too long."

"I haven't known your brother for very long, but after watching him with that sword, I'd say he can take care of himself."

Kal nodded in agreement. "Indeed, his skills are superior to many I've faced. Still, the sun has ris—"

"I'm sure he's fine. When he's done with whatever he's doing he'll be back. Now take a load off."

Kalleal blew out a breath. "It appears I can do little else." The vamp began pacing.

Trey rolled his eyes. He propped himself on his elbow. Maybe if he engaged the neck muncher in a little conversation, he could get Kal's mind off things. "So, I take it you're Sandrian as well?"

"Yes." Fang face never looked in his direction.

*Annnd, we're off to a flying start. Tight lipped bastard.* "Adalius says Sandrians can have children. Can you also turn humans, like other vamps?"

Kal turned and scowled. "You ask many questions, slayer."

"I'm inquisitive like that. So, were you made or born vampire?"

Kalleal's expression darkened. "The interview is over."

The motel door unlocked and opened, Adalius entered carrying several large shopping bags, placing them on the table. "Forgive me, for keeping you waiting," he said closing the door behind him.

Kalleal's eyes widened, his face ashen and devoid of the scowl he'd come to know and detest. *Now, there's a 'what the fuck' look if he ever saw one.*

The vamp reeled about. "Ada, you... you are Torlume? But, I thought they existed only in myth?"

Adalius laid a hand on his brother's shoulder. "I have encountered no other like myself, in my travels."

"But how is it that you..."

Adalius met his brother's gaze. "I shall answer that question. Later."

"Yes," Trey interjected, "Wouldn't want the slayer," he made quotation marks with his fingers, "In on the big secret, now would we?" Adalius opened his mouth to respond but Trey cut him off, holding up his hands. "I get it. I'd do the same thing. So, what's in the bags?"

The vampire nodded. "They are medical supplies."

"What're these supplies for, my brother?" Kalleal said, asking the very question on his mind as well.

"By giving you my blood, I believe I can pass my sun resistance onto you."

Trey threw up a little in his mouth. "You're gonna try to make Kalleal a daywalker like yourself?"

"If possible, yes."

He sighed, rubbing his face with his hands. *Great. Two sun proof vamps. Was he actually going to sit still for this bull shit? Good thing slayers didn't have a union. They'd yank his card for this.*

"So how much blood do you think it'll take?" Kalleal asked.

Adalius paused. "Truthfully, I am uncertain. It will require trial and error."

Trey eyed the vampire suspiciously. "And what if it requires more blood than you have?"

"Then I will need to feed to replenish myself."

Uh huh, that's what he thought. "Like hell, you will. I'm a fuckin' slayer, remember? I'm not gonna stand around, with my thumb up my ass, while you snack on civilians."

Kalleal rolled toward him, like a storm cloud, his massive size blocked Adalius from view. "And if we decide to drain this pathetic city of all its blood, how would you stop us, little man?"

He took a step of his own, glaring into the eyes of the vampire. "Don't let that little encounter at the factory go to your hat rack, mutha fucka. Try it, and I'll dust you and your brother too."

Kalleal arched his eyebrows and looked to his brother. "I begin to like this human."

Adalius grunted. "He does tend to grow on you."

"Yes, like fungus." The vamp's expression was as close to amusement as he had seen the bastard come.

"Fuck you both very much." Cripes, vamps out the ying yang in this city, and he winds up with Ren and Stimpy.

Adalius smiled as Kalleal rejoined him. "Be at ease, slayer. No one will be permanently harmed. We will begin transfusions immediately. But first..." He looked to his brother.

Kalleal took a seat in one of the motel chairs. "Of course, we both seek answers."

Adalius sat on the bed across from his twin. "How long have you been in New Carrollton and how did you come to be at the Pennywise Bakery?"

This looked like it might take a while so Trey grabbed a chair and took a sit down.

Kalleal rested his hand on his knees. "I arrived here several days ago. I've been tracking Anna for some time. Her trail led me here, to this city. Hours after I arrived, I stumbled upon a dwelling where I discovered a human male and his young in the process of turning. I detected the Anna's scent on them, so I removed their hearts."

Adalius nodded thoughtfully. "So, it was also your scent I detected in the apartment. I also discovered the bodies. Apparently, after you had completed the task."

Time to jump in. "What bodies are you talking about?"

Adalius shifted his gaze to Trey. "Recently, while hunting, I discovered a male and his young with their hearts removed. I had believed a slayer's hand at work but clearly it was Kalleal."

Adalius returned his gaze to his brother. "Who turned you Kalleal. Who is thy sire?"

"Have you not guessed it was Anna who turned me? It happened two years after you vanished. I searched for you nightly on the beach where you were last seen. One night, she appeared, seduced, and then turned me."

Adalius' brows furrowed. "In all the years we were together, she never mentioned that she had turned you. She knew of you, she admitted as much." A change in Adalius' expression signaled a thought dawning on him. "Kalleal, your wife and children, what happened to them?" Kalleal's expression hardened as he rose from the chair and paced away. "Kalleal, what happened to your family?"

"It's not a matter I care to discuss, Ada."

"You are my brother, my twin. Please, let there be no secrets between us."

Maybe Adalius was a little foggy about this, but a picture was forming in Trey's head.

"It's Anna. She did something to your family, didn't she?" Trey sneered.

Kalleal stood silent and unmoving like a monolith.

Adalius rose. "Kalleal. Is that true, did Anna murder your family?" Kalleal remained silent.

"Kalleal?"

"*No!*" Kalleal whirled, eyes ablaze, fangs extended long as daggers. The vampire drew in a breath. Tension melted away from his shoulders. His expression softened, eyes and fangs returning to normal. "At least, not directly."

"Explain," Adalius said, his voice turning gentle.

Kalleal paused if gathering his thoughts. He clenched his fists so tightly, his knuckles cracked. Reliving this was obvious torment. Whatever happened to his family was really fucked up. "While I lay unconscious, undergoing the change, Anna spirited me away to a cave, where she kept chained for days. The thirst, it robbed me of pride, strength, and reason. I begged, but she refused to allow me to feed. Kalleal swallowed hard, his eyes misting over. "When I'd been reduced to a mad, snarling animal, she dragged me to my home... and turned me loose... on my family."

Silence.

Kal choked back tears. "My wife and children," he said, his chest heaving. "They pleaded.... I couldn't." Tears flowed down his cheeks. "I laid them to rest underneath a shady tree overlooking the ocean. When the sun rose, I allowed it to sear my skin, to remind me, never to forget. I will hunt Anna down for what she's done."

This hit way too fuckin' close to home. Anna took Kal's family, just like she'd taken his. "Is there anybody that sick bitch hasn't hurt?"

Kalleal snarled. "I will kill her, slowly, for what she did to my family."

Adalius nodded. "It appears we all have a debt to repay Anna and pay she shall. For now, let us start the transfusions. Kalleal wiped away his tears, then took his place on the bed while Adalius prepared for the transfusion. "Before we begin, my brother, I have one last question."

"Of course, Ada."

"I was interested in knowing who taught you to wield the katanna?"

"It was the Enforcer, Tanaka."

Adalius' eyebrows flew up. "Truly?"

"Yes, why?"

"I once offered him a thousand pieces of gold to instruct me, but he refused."

Kalleal grunted. "I also offered him a hefty sum for his tutelage only to be rebuffed. He agreed only to settle up on our wager."

"You had a bet with Tanaka, on what?"

"It was on an American Football championship game. I only did so because one of the player's guarantee of victory. The mortal's name was...Namath, I believe."

He laughed out loud. "You got combat sword training because of one of the greatest upsets in sports history?"

"Yes, I was fortunate. Tanaka is a supremely skilled swordsman. It was an honor to be his student. I was most proud."

With that, Adalius set to work finding the vein in Kalleal's arm. Once the needle was in place, Adalius assumed his place on the bed. Trey took it from there. Heaven knows, in his line of work, he'd enough practice. With a nurse's skill, he inserted the needle into Adalius' arm then took a seat in one of the chairs. While he waited, he grabbed the television remote. The late news was already in progress with a report of a John Doe discovered along the river banks.

*Stosh.*

Soon as possible, he'd go and identify the body. The big man was gonna get a proper burial, if he had anything to say about it, a final gift to a friend.

They continued transfusions over the next three days. When it was needed, Adalius went out to feed and replenish himself. They kept the diner delivery man jumping with large orders for breakfast, lunch, and dinner. After sunset each night, they went out on patrol but found no evidence of Anna's activity so they bounced back to the room for another transfusion. When the sun rose on the fourth day, Adalius faced his brother. "Are you prepared, my brother?"

Kalleal, took a deep breath. "As prepared as I'll ever be."

He cast an eye toward the window. The sun was rising, if Adalius was wrong...

"I sure as hell hope you know what you doing, Adalius."

"As do I, slayer. We will do a small test. Kalleal, when I open the door, simply slip your hand outside."

"I understand. I'm ready."

"Very well." Adalius pulled the motel room door ajar. Kalleal carefully avoided the sun beam which peeked in through the crack, steadied himself, and slowly slid his hand out of the door. He didn't scream. That was a good sign. The vamp looked to his nervous brother and nodded, a slow smile spreading across his lips. "I feel no pain. There's no burning at all."

Adalius breathed a sigh of relief. "Excellent. Now, between the three of us, we stand a chance of destroying Anna."

Kalleal drew his hand back into the room as Adalius closed and locked the door. It was then that Trey noticed Kalleal's knitted brow. So did Adalius.

"Tell me what troubles you, Kalleal?"

"Have you not considered the ramifications of this? Your blood has the ability to grant vampires immunity to the sun's rays. Can you imagine if word of this spread? There—"

"Would be war, yes. Immortal would rise against immortal and I would become the hunted. My body and blood coveted, I would become the prize all would seek for themselves. Indeed, I have considered it. That is why my secret remains with but a select few." Adalius' phone rang. Withdrawing it from his trench pocket, he answered without delay. "This is Adalius...how did you get this number....what has happened...I see...we shall come immediately." Adalius put away his cell phone. "We depart this instant for Club Detente."

He knew bad news, even when he didn't exactly hear it. "What's doin', Adalius?"

"Anna has struck. Two of Kiel's Lycan have disappeared while tracking her."

The Destroyer had made her move. They grabbed their coats and jackets and raced to the place where nightmares went to play.

# CHAPTER FIFTY

aya grabbed the case containing her twin .40 calibers. Walking over to her dresser, she collected the remaining magazines, placed them in the satchel hanging from her shoulder, and headed for the door. Stopping in front of the full length mirror, she inspected her reflection. Her pony tailed head bobbed in approval. Decked out in her leather bustier, hip hugger pants, and spike heeled boots, she could still make tongues wag. And had a very sexy ass, if she did say so herself.

Running her hand along her hip, she tugged at the pants. They seemed a little tighter around her thighs than she remembered. *Better lay off the butter pecan ice cream for a while*. With a whimsical smile, she looked over her prized boots. Lincoln always said that he could never figure out how she ran in those heels. She exhaled a sigh.

It dawned on her that the last time she'd worn this outfit, was when she and Linc battled that master vampire. They'd almost got themselves killed. Only Lincoln's fast thinking saved their asses. After giving toilet breath the wooden send off, they went home, cracked open a bottle of bourbon, got naked, and did things she'd never admit to. A tear escaped her eye. Even now...

Cancer. Fucking cancer!

For a mother blessed year, the disease ripped away at him like no vampire ever could. Then one day, he was just gone. For weeks, she laid in bed. The unfairness of it all, Illness took the only man she ever loved. Now, Stosh was gone, too. Dear Lord, Stosh was...Maya wiped her eyes. It was time to go.

Slipping a couple of daggers in each boot, she marched out of the bedroom. The familiar smell of pipe tobacco danced in her nostrils as the click of her heels went out ahead of her. Smoky haze greeted her as she found a man, long and lean, with a ten gallon hat, seated in a chair in the living room. Pipe in his teeth, feet up on her desk, legs crossed, he winked. With that weather beaten face, squinty eyes, and old Winchester rifle, he was everything she imagined a cowboy should be.

"Don't you look purdy," Squinty said, his voice dripping old west.

She blushed in spite of herself. Gil Malone, her mentor and friend. He'd always been more of a father to her than that sperm donor to her mother ever tried to be. He taught her and Lincoln everything they knew about how to fight and kill fangs.

Crossing the room, she leaned down and planted a kiss on Gil's cheek. Eyeing the rifle, she rested her backside against the desk. "When you gonna retire that old thing?"

Gil patted the weapon, caressing it like a lover. "Darlin', this rifle's been in my family since my great grandfather bought it in 1868. My father passed it on to me, and when it's time, I'm gonna be passin' it my own son."

She smiled. Every time she heard that Texas twang, she felt the urge to rope a steer. "I can't thank you enough for coming, Gil."

"Hey, none a that. Told you long time ago, if you ever needed me—"

"I know, *still*..." She fidgeted.

"Listen to me little girl, ain't nothing I wouldn't do for you. Remember that."

She shook her head. "So, how did Nessa take it when you told her you were doing this?"

Gil smiled. "Why don't you ask her yerself?" An older woman wearing jeans and plaid blouse marched in from outside. "Gil, we're missing two magazines. You sure you packed them all?" Nessa's expression turned somber when their eyes met. The older woman opened her arms. As if pulled, she stepped into Nessa's embraced. "I'm so sorry, baby."

She gave Nessa a squeeze. "Thank you both for coming. I'm sorry for bothering you, I know you're both retired."

"Shush, we're family. Of course we were comin'. Soon as you told us what happened."

"Yeah, we loved the big fella too," Gil chimed in.

They broke their embrace as Seth, Kennedy, and Jackson entered the room. Seth placed a kiss on her cheek, taking her hand in his own. "There's still no sign of Neal."

She looked to over to Kennedy, the worry on the slayer's face, a reflection of her own. "And nobody's heard from him?"

"Not a word." Kennedy said taking hold of Jackson's hand. Maya picked up her cordless phone and dialed Neal again. Just as before, the line rang then went to his voice mail. No point in leaving another message. Instead, she returned the phone to its charger and looked to her slayers. "I don't like it. Neal's gone off the grid before, but not this long and never without contacting *someone*. Kennedy, Jack, I want you to go after him." Maya tore free a sheet of paper from a notebook on her desk, grabbed a pen and began writing. When she'd finished, she handed the paper to Kennedy. "This is the area where Neal said he'd tracked a vamp nest. Find him. If he's alive, bring him home." She took a calming breath. "If a fang killed him, you know what to do."

Kennedy nodded. "Dust him and the whole damn nest. We'll find him, Maya." She and Kennedy embraced then she hugged Jackson. The couple exited the room.

Gil was on his feet, rifle in one hand, Nessa in his free arm. "Where is Trey now, little girl?"

"He's in New Carrollton, hopefully *not* going after Anna alone. I know him, Gil, he probably blames himself for Stosh's death. That's why we have to get there before he does something stupid."

"Then let's mount up and ride, darlin'."

She grabbed her jacket off a chair as Seth led her outside, followed closely by Gil and Nessa. They exited out onto Maya's front porch where her slayers waited. Some lay out on her lawn, others sat atop of their vehicles or loitered near the house. She could see Jackson's Blazer rolling off in the distance, dust flying up as it rolled toward the main road.

When the slayers saw her, they all rose to their feet and gathered at her front steps. She looked them over one by one. All wore the same pained but determined look. Stosh was their friend. Each of them owed their life to the man-mountain's strength and courage. Drawing in a breath to steady herself, she squared her shoulders. Her slayers needed answers. It was time to provide some.

"I know you're wondering where Kennedy and Jackson are off to. Neal's gone missing. They're going to search for him. *Our* focus must lie elsewhere. Anna, took one of our own. She murdered Stosh. Now, we are gonna kill that fuckin' bitch once and for all!" The slayers all shouted or whistled in approval. Maya waved them all quiet and continued. "A message has to be sent. Take one of ours, and we kill every fucking one of yours. So, *every* last fang in New Carrollton gets dusted. I don't think I need to tell you some of us aren't coming back. But, we're slayers. It's who we are. It's what we do. You're my family, all of you and I'm proud. Linc, if he were here, would be just as proud." She paused to allow her words to sink in. "Alright, game faces on. Get to your cars, move."

The slayers all scrambled to their vehicles while she, Seth, Nessa and Gil all headed toward Gil's pick up. As the others pile in, a voiced called out.

"Maya,"

She turned.

Sam.

He was as close to a brother as she ever had. His stubbornness not to let her give up after Lincoln's death, saw her through the darkest days of her life. The slayer approached, anger smoldering in his eyes. "Why are you leaving me out of this operation?"

She laid a hand on his shoulder. "Someone has to lead this pack of misfits in case I'm killed. They all trust and respect you, Sam. They'll follow your lead."

Sam slowly shook his head. "This is bull shit. I don't like gettin' left out, but I'll do it cause ya asked. Just do me a favor, don't get killed. I don't know the first thing about how to lead these sons of bitches."

"Neither did I when Linc passed leadership to me. But of all of them, you're the best man for the job."

Sam's expression softened. "Whatever. You just watch ya back, ok?"

"I will." They embraced then she got into the truck.

"Maya?" She looked out of the window to her friend. "Put one between her eyes for me."

She nodded. "I'm gonna do it for all of us. Let's go Gil." The pickup rolled out onto the dirt drive followed by a host of trucks and Harley's. She waved to Sam who stood out on the lawn, shotgun at his side. He waved back as the small convoy, followed them. At the end of the drive, Gil hit the gas and took a left bound for the interstate and New Carrollton.

# CHAPTER FIFTY ONE

Kiel sat waiting at his desk, staring off into infinity. There was nothing else to do. He'd called in every favor owed to him organizing a massive search for his missing Lycan. He drummed his fingers, eyeing the phone which sat silent on his desk as if mocking him.

It'd been three days with no word. Three days since Anna outfoxed him. He tried contacting Miguel's mate to reassure her that all that could be done would be done. But she refused to take a call. Not surprising, her mate was missing. No words would ever be enough.

Rubbing his face in his hands, he tried to clear his head. He'd barely eaten or slept, let alone showered or shaved and felt every bit as crappy as he undoubtedly looked. His body groaned as he stretched. His eyes, sore and red from fatigue, ached and burned. But it didn't matter. He'd wait for news, any news. It was his responsibility. He was the one who ordered Miguel and Paytor to follow Anna. Whatever happened was on his head.

He slammed his fist down, rattling the items on his desk. Adalius. He never should've listened to that son of a bitch. He should've followed his first instinct, and contacted the High Council the instant he learned of Anna's return. They would have dispatched Enforcers to deal with her. Knowing how those killers operated, they wouldn't have bothered asking for help and his friends wouldn't be MIA. Taking in a breath, he slowly exhaled, this was getting him nowhere. Now wasn't the time to second guess himself.

A knock on his office door interrupted his thought process. Before he could respond, it opened and Ulysses entered. "What is it Ulysses, have you heard—"Ulysses stepped aside and knelt as the door slowly swung forward to reveal the Chief of the Royal Guard, flanked by two subordinates, followed closely by his father, King Marseth, the Albino. The two guards took up positions on each side of the door as the chief fell into step with the king.

Marseth stood over six feet four inches. His angular features and slender frame belied his strength. Many a foe had made the fatal error of underestimating him, only to become a broken casualty of combat. The magnitude of his father's spirit, ever present in his azure eyes, hinted at the enormous might and power of the Lycan king.

His were eyes well acquainted with loss, but never had it stripped him of the willingness to impart wisdom on the young and those in need of guidance. To his enemies, Marseth was a brutal adversary, a cunning warrior, and ruthless killer. Kiel knew him only as the father who always had time to listen and council.

Rising to his feet, Kiel circled around his desk, and took a knee. Marseth, whose snowy, corn silk hair fell about his shoulders, wore a long flowing, white robe. The king came forward, delight shown in his eyes. "Rise, my son," Marseth said in a voice ancient as the pyramids.

With a smile, he rose to his feet. "Honored father, welcome."

Marseth clasped his shoulders. The warmth of his pater's smile drove away the chill clutching his spirit. "My son, child of my loins, joy of my heart, pride of my life, vhat troubils thee? I see een thine eyes, unrest."

"You didn't receive the message to contact me?"

"I received the message yes, it is vhy I came immediately."

Kiel's eyes drifted to the door. "Where's mother?"

"Your mother, against dey vishes of her doctor, has gone to partake een her favorite past time."

"She's gone shopping."

"Yes."

Not surprising. His mother, to his father's chagrin, was a notorious shopaholic. "She already has several walk in closets full of clothes she's never worn."

Marseth waved away the comment. "Yesss, she does. End I find I must expand the mansion further to accommodate the clothes she continues to acquire."

"Father, why don't you simply tell her that she has to stop? Surely you can reason with her?"

"If you feel so inclined to tell your mother vhat she ken and kennot do, I vill be happy to allow you dey honor of doing so."

"I think I'll pass on that."

Marseth nodded. "Truly I have raised no fools. Your mother vith good reason is known as dey demon. Now, tell me vhat troubils thee."

"It's Anna, she's returned."

Marseth's gaze hardened. "You are certain of thees?"

He met his father's eyes. "Yes, my father, we've all seen her."

Marseth's brow furrowed. Anna's appearance bound him in a way which left him powerless to address the threat head on…for now. "You have contacted de Vumpire High Counsel?"

No, sir."

"Vhy?" There was that glint in his father's eyes. The king released Kiel's shoulders. Father was not pleased. He better make this good. "I gave my word to Adalius that I would leave Anna to him. It was a huge mistake, my father. Forgive me."

The king's expression soured. "Your actions have compremised our agreement vith dey vumpire."

"I'm sorry, my fa-"

Marseth raised his hand. "I have made many of mine own errs in judgment, my son."

"I fear my mistake may have cost the lives of my friends."

Marseth looked upon him, his gaze that of understanding. "Leadersheep can kerry a hevee burden. Many are de lives I have sent to die in de field of battle."

"But, it was stupid of me to trust such a matter to Adalius alone."

"You have much trust in your friend de vumpire. Do not undair estimate such things."

Kiel's own eyes hardened. "He's *not* my friend."

"Kiel, vhen dey time comes and thy rage hast burned itself out, you vill come to understand, dey vumpire vas not at fault. You share an undeniable and uncommon friendsheep. Never geeve up on dat. Now, tell me vhat hast happened."

He forced himself not to react to the provocation of his relationship with Adalius. "Anna walked in the club a few days ago. I sent two of my Lycan to follow her but it appears she expected it. We installed GPS devices in all our vehicles, but she had her children remove them while she held our attention. She outsmarted me and appears to have led my friends into a trap."

"Kiel?" The rich baritone voice of Jax interrupted the conversation. Jax upon seeing the king thumped his chest with a closed fist. "Forgive the intrusion, my king. Kiel, Adalius has arrived. He's requested to see you."

"Tell him I am on my way."

Jax bowed to the king. "Sire." Jax exited.

"What the hell does *he* want?"

"Let us go end find out, shell ve?"

Kiel led the way out of the office followed closely by Marseth, his entourage, and Ulysses. All the patrons bowed as they made their way across the dance floor toward the steel doors. The club's security staff opened them wide at the king's approach and bowed as Kiel, the king, and his staff filed through.

As they walked down the carpeted steps, Kiel saw Adalius and two others he didn't recognize along with Taine, Tracy, Jax, and Poke standing among the throng, near the exit. One of the newcomers was a vampire, the other was human. He recognized the look. The human was a vampire slayer.

*Adalius, keeping the company of slayers? Truly, a sign of the times.*

When the king entered the lobby, all present bowed with the exception of the human, who removed his shades and nodded to Marseth.

"Please rise, I am honored," Marseth said with a nod.

Kiel went to meet Adalius who'd stepped away from his companions. "What is it you want, Adalius?"

"I heard you have missing Lycan. I have come to offer my aid."

"I appreciate the offer, but I don't need your help. I don't want *anything* from you."

"You need all the help you can get. We must locate them soon to have any chance of finding them alive."

"I *said* I don't want your help."

"Kiel?" Yvette pushed through the club entrance carrying a medium sized box. "I found this outside. It's addressed to you."

"I'll take it, Yvette." She handed him the package then took her place among the onlookers. Whipping out a switchblade knife, he began opening the box.

"Have a care Kiel, it may—"

"You think I don't realize this is probably from Anna? Stand away, and let me open it." The vampire withdrew two paces. Carefully, he opened the box. He half expected it to explode in his face. Thankfully there were no such fireworks, just a box packed to the gills.

Kiel sensed the crowd withdraw as he removed several wads of paper, dropping each to the floor as he dug into the box. *What could that harlot have sent that she'd go through the trouble of...* "Dear...Goddess Moon!" He stood, unable to look away.

"Vhat is it, my son?" came his father's voice, seemingly from another continent.

From a place outside his body, he watched himself, sink to his knees, the box falling from his grasp. It hit the floor and tipped over, its content spilling out onto the carpet. Startled gasps and assorted shrieks rang out across the crowded lobby. It was a head.

Miguel's head.

They were dead; His fault, all his fault. Because of him... He felt a hand on his shoulder.

"I am sorry, Kiel."

*Adalius, that bastard.*

He sprang to his feet. Violently, he knocked the vampire's hand away. Nose to nose, he faced the Adalius, growling dangerously. "Don't *ever* touch me, Adalius. *Don't.*" He whirled and pushed his way through the crowd followed by Jax, as Poke went to gather up the head of his dead friend and replaced it in the box.

Ulysses took charge. "I'm sorry. The club is now closed. Please gather your belongings and make your way to the exits. Thank you for your patronage and we welcome your business again soon."

\*\*\*\*\*

297

Adalius dearly wanted to go to his friend's side, but Kiel needed others now, not a reminder of another loss. Anna sent the head to torment Kiel. It was working. Kalleal and Trey moved to his side.

"What was that all about? "Trey asked.

"Indeed, his animosity is misplaced. It's Anna who killed his friend not you."

"It is not important. Finding and destroying Anna is."

"Vumpire?"They turned to the Lycan king.

Adalius bowed his head at Marseth's approach. "It is good to see you again, your highness."

"Indeed, it hess been a long time."

"Permit me to introduce my companions. This is my brother, Kalleal."

Marseth's browed arched subtly. "Forgive me, but did you not tell me vonce that your brother vas dead?"

"One of many times Ada has been wrong, your highness," Kalleal interposed.

Adalius ignored his brother and continued. "This is Trey Thomas. He has joined me in the hunt for Anna."

Marseth looked over Trey with interest. "You are a vumpire slayer, are you not?"

"Yes, your highness."

"Are you from dey line of Lincoln Thomas?"

"He was my father."

The Lycan nodded. "Even among my people his name is vell known. A fine varrior he vas."

"Thank you, your highness."

"If you vill excuse me, I would like to speak vith your companion een private."

"We'll wait outside, vamp. "Trey and Kalleal headed for the exit leaving the pair alone.

"I know he hates me still for what happened. I came only to offer assistance."

Marseth nodded thoughtfully. "He steel grieves vumpire. Geeve him time. Dey day vill come vhen you and he vill heal dey vounds that exist and you vill be as brothers again. I have seen vith mine own eyes, dey friendsheep you shared. Never has there been such between Lycan and vumpire. Our people live separated by an unstabill peace. Another bloody var vill someday come, unless our peoples, yours, end mine, learn trust. I believe dat you and mine son, in time, vill show us dey vay."

"I wish I shared your confidence. I fear I may have lost my friend, forever."

"Trust me, vumpire. I know mine own son. Vhen his anger cools, he vill come to see fault lies not vith you. Now, if you vill excuse me, I must attend to my son."

"Before you go, may I ask a personal question?"

Marseth's expression was unreadable. "You may proceed."

"How long have you been with your mate?"

"I mated Sarkayla just before the beginning of the second Lycan-vumpire var nearly fifteen hundred years ago."

"I am aware that you, yourself, personally fought in that war. How did your mate take it?"

Marseth heaved a sigh. "It vas hard on her, but she accepted that being my mate meant spending lonely nights vorrying for my safety. They are strong, vumpire, and rarely need our protection." Marseth smiled knowingly. "Now, go to your mate and bond with her. A male vill always be stronger vith his mate then vithout. I know you vish to spare her the agony of vaiting vhile you hunt dey Destroyer but allow her the right to choose if that is vhat she vants. There is a human saying... let the lady decide."

He bowed to the king and his wisdom. "Thank you, your highness."

Marseth laid a hand on his shoulder. "Of course." The king made his way toward the sound proof doors, while Adalius went to join his companions. Outside, he found Kalleal, standing, arms folded, eyeing club patrons as they blurred, flew, and drove their separate ways. Trey rested on the balls of his feet, conversing on his cell, most likely with Kyle.

As he approached, Kalleal concluded his observations while the slayer ended his call.

"So, what's our next move, vamp?" Trey asked, rising to his feet, putting away his cell phone.

"You and Kalleal head back to the motel. There is something I must do. I just pray it is not too late.

# CHAPTER FIFTY TWO

Kiel stormed into his office followed directly by Jax. Resting his fists on the desk, he leaned forward trying to catch his breath. *How would he ever be able to tell Miguel's mate? Anna had to die. She had to die and he needed to kill her. She'd outsmarted him again.*

He howled to the heavens, violently sweeping everything off this desk. "I'll find her and when I do, I'm going to tie her to a spit. And after I've charred every strip of flesh from her bones, I'm going to spread her remains on the pavement and piss on her ashes." He roared, his eyes alive with fury.

"There are many who'd gladly help you," Jax said.

Then, something occurred to him. "Wait a minute, how did Adalius know we had Lycan missing? Someone contacted him. Assemble the staff. I want to know who it was."

"There's no need, Kiel, it was me."

His gaze hardened. "You? Who authorized you to do so?"

"Our friends were missing. You'd mobilized every resource available, except Adalius."

"We didn't need his help."

"We needed all the help we could get," Jax said, his voice rising.

He pointed his finger like a weapon. "That wasn't for you to decide. You had no right—"

"I had *every* right. Miguel and Paytor were my friends too. That you would refuse to call upon Adalius, whose contacts could have made all the difference, because of your vendetta, is inexcusable. Now our friends are dead because you were too filled with pride and hate to ask for his help."

"Don't presume to lecture me, Jax," Kiel rumbled.

Jax took a step closer. "No, you need to hear this. I'm your friend, and as your friend, I must tell you that you can be a pig headed, self-righteous, insufferable ass. You're continuing to blame the vampire for what happened is wrong."

Kiel met the glare of his friend, trembling with anger. "You don't know fuck about what you speak, Jax."

"I know everything, you forget, I was there." Jax' voice softened, "He's not responsible, Kiel."

His voice rose an octave, his hands curling into fists. "You dare defend him to me and call yourself my friend?"

"You know me, Kiel. I have no love of vampires. If left to me, we'd stake the lot of them and watch their dust blow away in the wind. They're contemptible creatures."

"Yet here you stand, defending one."

"He's worthy of defending. There is something honorable, even noble about that vampire."

Kiel scowled at his friend, rage approaching critical mass. "His so called honor and nobility led to disaster. I warned him not to become involved. That pack of blood suckers were slaughtering humans. Humans. What care we for homo sapiens? "He spat the words like they were poisonous.

"He gave us the option of leaving. We chose to remain, or had you forgotten that?"

"There *was* no choice," he fired back. "Can you imagine what my father would've said had he found out I abandoned a friend in battle. And what would she—" Kiel stopped, yanking the sentence from the air.

Jax' expression softened. "Kiel, it wasn't his fault."

Kiel regarded his friend with a sneer. "You think so highly of Adalius, one might get the impression that you're in love."

The air about Jax shifted. His lips peeled back. "Do not use our friendship to take liberties, Kiel. Friend or not, I *will* give you the ass kicking you so desperately need."

Kiel surged forward, closing the space between them. "Think you have the fang for it, Jax, indulge yourself."

"*Enough!*" The air reverberated. Startled, they turned. Marseth flowed into the room. It was as if the very air moved aside to allow him passage. The king regarded them, his eyes moving back and forth. His father's gaze shifted to Jax. "I vould to speak vith my son, leave us."

Jax bowed his head and thumped his chest with a closed first. "My king." He gave Kiel a sideward glance then made his way out of the room. When the door closed behind him, Marseth regarded him with an icy glare.

"Father I—"

"Be still; I vish to speak vith dey vumpire king, make dey call."

"Father—"

"Do it." Marseth's voice was barely above a whisper, his gaze without warmth. It was best not to argue. When father spoke in hushed tones, it meant he was but an instant from lashing out.

Kiel picked up his phone from the floor and hit a line button. "Wanda, put me through to the secretary of the Vampire High Council." Kiel waited as Marseth eyed him silently. Finally, the line began to ring. "Yes, King Marseth wishes to speak with King Vaughn....thank you very much. "Kiel looked to his father. "I'm being put through."

"Geeve me dey phone." Kiel handed over the receiver. Marseth waited several moments and at last... "Greetings vumpire, I trust you end yours are of good health end spirits.... I am vell, life has been kind to me, Sarkayla vill geev birth next month eeef doctors are correct....I am told it vill be a female. I intend to spoil her rotten, I believe dey saying is." After a pause, Marseth got down to business. "I am afraid dis call is more than my desire to exchange pleasantries. Dey Destroyer has returned to dey city of New Carrollton. As per our agreement, I am formally requesting dat Enforcers be dispatched to deal vith this matter.....very vell, ve vill offer any aid dey require.....I also look forward to our next encounter. Peace be vith you vumpire." Marseth hung up the phone.

"Father, you can't be serious about turning Anna over to the Enforcers after she killed—"

"Still thy tongue, I have given my vord and have kept it. However, until dey arrive, dey Destroyer is ours to deal vith. I intend to crush her, but first, ve must find her."

"I have every contact at my disposal combing the streets and so far we haven't turned up squat."

Marseth looked upon him thoughtfully. "To defeat your opponent, you must first under dare stand them. Vhat are their needs? Vhat motivates them? Tell me, my son, vhat does Anna vant?"

Kiel gave it consideration. "She wants to make more of her kind, but she needs to stay off the grid while she does it."

Marseth, nodded. "Good, now, vhat vill she need to make that happen?"

He thought for a moment. "She'll need space, lots of it but in places where there'll be few, if any, regular vampires to tip off the Enforcers." He looked to the scattered items on the floor. Reaching down, he picked up a remote, aimed it at his back wall and pushed one of its many buttons.

Slowly from the ceiling, a wall sized map of New Carrollton descended. They strolled over to the atlas. "She's going to need multiple places scattered about so not to have all her brood in one place." Kiel studied the map carefully. "There are several such places around New Carrollton that would fit the bill. There's the old lighthouse by the mouth of the river and the abandoned Pennywise Bakery to name a couple. If we hurry we should be able to check some of them out before the Enforcers arrive."

Marseth was beaming. "Very good, now you are using dey brain your mother end I gave you."

Kiel went over and pick up his phone, pressed a button and waited for an answer. After the third ring, he got one. "Taine, if Ulysses is still there, have him assemble two teams of security and meet me in my office." He hung up his phone and looked to his father, who nodded in approval.

"Vhen dis is over ve vill talk more about dey vumpire, Adalius and your conflict vith Jax. Kiel knew that tone. They were going to talk about it whether he wanted to or not.

# CHAPTER FIFTY THREE

She was ovulating, and merciful Elder, it was riding her. Serena lay back on her chaise lounge with book in hand, took a sip of wine, and fidgeted. She'd just read the same line in her novel for the sixth time. Frustrated, she closed the hardback, laid it in her lap, and gazed out at the still waters of her pool.

Exhaling a breath, she crossed her legs, trying to ignore the heat blooming in her core. The scent of dark cinnamon spice rose from her body, saturating the air with invitation. She'd have to head inside soon. The fragrance would ride the gentle wind and before long, attract a vampire male looking to claim the in heat female, that being her.

Sandrian females tended to ovulate twice a month. Nature's way of preserving a species, hunted mercilessly for centuries. Of course, the senseless carnage ended ages ago when Sandrians came of age, but unfortunately, Nature never received the memo.

A surge of desire rolled through her body, milking a tender moan from her lips. What a time for her to be at odds with her mate. Naturally, the cycle went full on not long after she threw Adalius out several nights ago. It wasn't her time, but stress had been known to trigger unexpected fertile periods.

Now the flames of desire, the drive to procreate swelled inside her like an inflating balloon. Before long, instinct would drive her to mate. She shuddered. Females in heat weren't particular about partners when the madness overtook them. And with each passing moment, a portion of her self-control slipped away. If Adalius didn't return to her soon, she'd have to make way to the nearest Drayken safe house, so she could be sedated. She'd be damned before she allowed her cycle to strip her of her dignity.

*Adalius.*

Her eyes misted over. She missed him, always did when he was away, but this time there was no way of knowing whether he would return or not. Serena hugged herself as a new wave of desire surged. Blood flowed to all the right places. Clenching her fists, she gazed skyward, hoping to spot a lone figure, coat tails flapping in the wind, streaking her way. Sadly, there was only clear sky.

A tear trailed down her cheek as her hands traveled down her body. She had to take the edge off or she'd go mad. Her hands slid inside her bikini bottom as she thought of her male. *What he was doing? Did he miss her? Did he need her the way that she so needed him now?* She froze. *Or had he already found comfort in the arms of another?*

A growl rose from her throat. Her fangs extended into attack position as she visualized another female's hands upon him. She shook off the image. Forcing her canines back into place, she looked at the phone lying on the table next to her. She longed to hear it ring, have it be Adalius, telling her how much he loved her. The receiver called to her, but calling him wasn't an option. Until he was ready to treat her as a mate and not a youngling, it would be a waste both of their time.

Serena sat forward and stretched. She'd been by the pool for hours now. Restlessness demanded she got up. Rising from her seat, a rogue fragrance caught her attention. Her heart skipped a beat. She paused. Dearest Elder, let it be... It was gone. Her shoulders sagged, just her imagination. Her nose simply telling her heart what it wanted to hear.

Her chest heavy, she got to her feet. Heat flashed from her core, tearing a gasp from her. Dearest Elder, soon she'd be willing to mate a bull if it came near. Where in creation was Ada—

"Serena?"

Startled, she whirled about. The sight of him took her breath away. Her nipples peaked. Magnificent. She flushed, her body temperature rising. As her eyes travelled down Adalius, from face to his sculpted chest and tight abs, the spiced cinnamon scent intensified, as did the sparkle in her eyes.

Adalius' eyes ignited. He sensed her arousal. Subtly, she shifted her stance. Legs, with a will of their own, moved slightly apart. Her fragrance reached out to him, called to him. His nostrils flared, the bulge in his leathers rising, she smiled to herself.

"Am I interrupting?" Adalius moved toward her and she toward him.

Her breath fled. There was no fighting it. She didn't desire to. "No, I was simply reading." She said swallowing the knot forming in her throat. "Are you well, do you need to feed?" She nearly collapsed at the thought of him at her vein.

"I am well, Serena. I came to see you."

She felt the warmth in her cheeks. "Have you truly? And why is it you want to see me, Adalius?"

"Because I missed you, because I missed the warmth of your body and spirit," He moved closer still. She was trembling, nearly in tears. "I missed you the instant I left your home." Adalius reached for her hand.

She immediately took it and placed a kiss upon his palm. "I missed you as well. I'm so sorry, Adalius. I should not have pressured you the way I did, but I meant what I said. You cannot continue to treat me like your young. I am a full grown female and—."

"You are right."

She blinked like someone had thrown cold water in her face.

"I was treating you like a youngling. You are the strongest, most capable female I have ever met. I realize that now." With that, Adalius went down on his knees. "I am under your spell. My mind overflows with thoughts of you. My heart sings in your presence. My spirit is at peace only in the comfort of your love and light. I am ever yours, Serena. If you find me worthy, will you consent to be my bonded mate?"

Tears welled up in her eyes. She could barely breathe let alone speak. She smiled happily and nodded. "Yes, I will have you. Oh yes, Adalius, yes!" she choked out when she at last found her voice. Adalius rose from his knees, reached out and drew her into his embrace.

She fell into his arms as his lips claimed her own. Her body came alive as their kiss deepened, the spicy sweet aroma of cinnamon encircled them. As their lips parted, he held her at arm's length, gazing into her eyes.

Visions of their life together, of the many sons she'd give to him flooded her thoughts. One day, she'd be a grandparent, spoiling little faces and—

Her body flinched. Adalius' face was covered in a spray of blood. The world fell away from beneath her. Darkness closed in. No time, must get it out.

"I love…" was all she could…

\*\*\*\*\*

Joy.

Adalius was in a sea of it. The sunlight seemed brighter, the skies so much bluer, the scent of the flowers were sweeter and the birds in the trees sang with a beauty he never before heard. His love, his Serena, had consented to be his bonded mate.

A tear fell from his eye as he held her tightly. They would soon be of one mind, one spirit, one heart. Releasing her, he held his love at arm's length. He wanted to lose himself in the beauty of her…a dull thud reached his ears; a spray of blood peppered his face. Serena lurched in his grasp. Her eyes widened in shock. Adalius followed her gaze down to a wooden stake protruding through her chest. "Serena?"

"I love…"She fell into his arms, the light fading from her eyes.

"*No*, Serena, stay with me!" Psychically, he reached out to her, desperately trying to buoy her spirit with the force of his will, but it was like trying to grasp smoke. She slipped away. He dove after her. There in his mind, he could see her plummeting into the void. He accelerated, reaching for her hand, but darkness enveloped her, swallowed her whole.

No. *No!*

She was gone. Forever lost. His scream stabbed out at the void as he was cast back to the world of the living.

Serena's eyes sunk in on themselves as she crumbled in his arms. Adalius roared. It was as if limbs were torn from his body. His lungs had nearly emptied when a sudden pressure closed in around him. His body seized, arms going out, as if unseen hands were pulling them opposite directions.

He groaned his eyes blazed bright teal. Unable to resist, he rose into the air. As he fought, the lines of a form took shape. Long legs in high heeled pumps manifested, followed by torso, neck, shoulders, and arms. Then long auburn hair formed, followed by lips and silver grey eyes.

Adalius shook with rage. The thing he hated most in the world came into focus. "*Anna!*" He snarled. She'd masked her presence, but how? Even cloaked in shadows, he should've detected her. "What manner of witchcraft allowed you to escape my notice?"

She smiled wickedly. "That would be telling. But needless to say, it allowed me to hear what you were planning after your little chat with Marseth. You were actually prepared to bond with that?" She gestured to Serena's dust. "I will not tolerate rivals, my love. Did the death of the gypsy teach you nothing?"

"*Murderer*, you killed her."

"And I'll kill any female who dares touch my mate."

"Vicious harlot, I am not your mate. I underwent the Sotirin ritual. I am free of you." Adalius struggled. For an instant he was free, but only for an instant.

She arched an eyebrow. "You've become powerful. I won't be able to hold you for much longer. As for the Sotirin, do you really believe some antiquated ritual can break our bond? You are mine, until I release you. When I'm queen—"

Adalius flashed his fangs. "You will be dust long before you *ever* become queen. I swear it."

"So head strong, it's why I love you. Together, you and I could've destroyed the Council and rang in the new age as consorts."

"You know *nothing* of love. You are an abomination that must be destroyed."

Anna looked upon him with sorrowful eyes. "It saddens me. Still you insist on hanging on to that silly sense of humanity. I must strip away whatever keeps that flame alive in you. Even if I must kill everyone you love until you come to your senses." She shuddered. "I can feel my control of you slipping away. It's time to take my leave. But worry not, my love, will we see each other again, very soon." Anna turned to fly away.

"Anna."

She paused.

"Know that I will kill you for this."

Anna levitated. Gliding up to him, she tenderly caressed his cheek. "I know that you will try, my love." She faded from sight.

Adalius broke free. He looked to the skies. Anna was long gone. His gaze fell upon Serena's remains. Falling to his knees, he scooped up her dust in his hands. Icy cold gripped his heart. Frigid air swirled about him, as the air temperature bottomed out. His rapid breaths burst out in fogs. Fangs extended. Hands clenched. Knuckles cracked. The pool water began churning as windows in Serena's home rattled in their panes.

His chest heaving, he watched his love's remains blow away in the winds. Through gnashed teeth, he drew in a huge breath and roared. Water erupted skyward. Windows exploded, glass flying in all directions. He launched himself into the night time sky. Anna killed his mate. The Destroyer and her brood would pay a terrible price. Their deaths were assured, a certainty already written in blood.

# CHAPTER FIFTY FOUR

Arnie took a right on South Street, rolling with the flow of traffic. Richardson rode shotgun, and Hal was in the back seat. A light sprinkle of rain peppered the windshield as they drove through West Concord Village toward Hal's apartment. Richardson rubbed the bridge of his nose. His head was screaming. Nothing that eighty years of shut eye wouldn't cure.

It was 2:30 a.m., after Hal wrapped it up with the sketch artist, Arnie offered him a ride home. Once copies of the mystery lady were made up and distributed throughout the precinct, as well as faxed to the other districts, the captain gave him and the old man an update on Rhoda's murder investigation, then ordered them home to get some sleep.

He snorted out a breath. Some days it didn't pay to get out of bed. There was a serial killer on the loose, some whack job killed Rhoda, then for reasons unknown, stole two bodies from the morgue. The number of reported missing persons was continuing to climb, Bricker among the missing, and now the cherry on top of it all was the joy bringers from the government were coming. *Sister Mary Sunshine, why couldn't life come with a reset button?*

Richardson and Hal jawed back and forth while Arnie sat buttoned up like a clam. He knew Arnie well enough to know the ole man was pouring over every detail in his head, about Rhoda's murder. There'd be no peace until the guilty was brought to justice.

"I sure appreciate you guys taking me home," Hal said, fanning himself as if it made the slightest difference in the awful heat.

"Not a problem, Hal. Arnie and I are happy to serve as well as protect." They rolled to an intersection and came to a stop. As the traffic light turned green, Richardson leaned forward, peering at two women standing under a street light ahead.

"Pull over, Arnie," he said, jabbing a finger at the working girls.

"You moonlighting in vice or you looking to score some action?" Arnie replied putting on his turn signal, pulling to the curb. The street walkers spotted them and began to saunter away.

Richardson stuck his head out of the window and whistled. "Lynda, its Richardson."

One of the women kept on her way, while the other stopped in her tracks and turned. Looking carefully, she made her way back. Arriving at the car, a smile spread across her lips. "Theo. I thought you was vice."

"Nah, they workin' Upper Concord this week. I thought I told you to get off the streets. There's a psycho on the loose."

She brushed a lock of hair behind her ear. "I know, but my deadbeat ex shorted me on child support again. I had enough to cover rent, but not enough for food."

"How much you need?"

"Theo, you already done more than—"

"How much, Lynda?"

The hooker looked about as if others were eavesdropping. "A hundred should hold us for now. My sister said she'd help out next week."

Richardson reached into his pocket for cash, a counted out the money, then handed it to her. "Consider it a loan. I expect to be paid back."

She leaned in close, tears welling in her eyes, and kissed him on the cheek. "God bless you, Theo. I'll pay it back, every dime of it. I promise."

"Ok, now go home and don't let me catch you out here again."

"I'm going. Thank you. Thank you so much, Theo." She turned and walked away. Richardson watched her go as they pulled away from the curb.

Arnie gave him a sideways glance. "What, are you a social worker, now?"

"I busted her husband three years ago for assaulting her and the kids. The son of a bitch liked to gamble. A lot. When he lost, he'd come home and play family handball. She's a good woman. She just can't seem to catch a break, so I help when I can."

Hal's smile was genuine. "You're a saint, Detective Richardson."

"I just know what it's like to be used as a sparring partner. When I was a kid, my ole man used to hit the bottle pretty hard and when he was done doing that, he'd hit me even harder."

They were passing a local deli when he glanced down the alley next door. There was a couple. Every alarm in his head went ape shit. "Hey, go back," he said, his voice tight.

"What is it kid, what ya see?" Arnie took a U-turn, eliciting numerous horns and expletives from other drivers.

"In there." Richardson pointed to the alley. Arnie took a sharp left a left. He grabbed the dash to steady himself as they entered the alley. Their headlights fell upon the couple. It looked like a hot romantic encounter except the woman was totally limp.

As they approached, lover boy turned. His eyes, they reflected the headlights back at them! The asshole was wearing some jacked up contacts. Dropping his prize, he fled. The brakes squealed as they jumped out of the car, weapons drawn, and raced to the woman's side.

"NCPD, stop where you are!" he yelled out, as the suspect sprinted away.

Arnie reached her first and checked her pulse. "She's alive."

He started off in pursuit. "Get an ambulance. Hal, stay with Arnie."

Arnie's voice faded as he went tearing down the alley with the radio from Arnie's glove box in hand. He raced after the suspect. Son of a bitch was fast. The perp took a left, out of his line of sight. Richardson raised the hand radio to his lips. "Home one, this is unit four in pursuit on foot of a white male, wearing a beige blazer running west on Cortland Avenue. Requesting back up. Code six."

"Copy unit four, black and whites are in route," came the response from dispatch. Richardson rounded the corner. The suspect was already half way down the block. No way, the bastard must have turbo charged feet. He took off in pursuit, while the voice of dispatch broadcast from the speaker. "All units, be advised, suspect may be armed. Approach with caution."

Up ahead, fleet foot took a left down Hill Court. It was a dead end. Game over. Richardson raised his radio. "All units, this is unit four, suspect just ran down Hill Court. He's cornered. I'm going in."

"This is unit sixteen, we copy, unit four. We're five minutes from your location," came the static laced response.

He approached Hill Court. Arriving at the corner, he hooked the radio to his belt and pressed his back against the brick apartment building. Counting to three, he quickly ducked his head around for a peek. Along with a few assorted cars, there was a huge dumpster parked on the side of the street, toward the rear. It was part of the Mayor's 'Keep New Carrollton Clean' project. There was no sign of the perp, but he was in there. This was the only way out. Wait. That sound. Tiny squeals and scratching on the pavement snagged his attention. It was coming from down the alley.

He stopped. Rats.

He grimaced. A dozen or more came scurrying out, scrambling in all directions. Something spooked them. Something they wanted no part of. Discretion and procedure dictated he wait for backup, but this was his collar. Fuck whatever was in there with fleet foot; he was bringing that loser down. That could have been his wife laying in back in that alley.

Leading with his gun, he drew in a breath, and stepped into the alley. Rain continued to sprinkle down as he slowly, carefully, made his way in. His eyes darted back and forth. *Two cars to the right, one on the left.*

Step. Eyes left. Step. Eyes right. Shadows danced along the walls, headlights from passing cars. Goose bumps rose on his arms. Step. Listen. Wait. He reached the rear of the first car. Quick glance, clear.

"Police, come on out, hands behind your head. "Not a sound. It was too still. The silence was like a warning. *Continue at your own risk.* Exhale. Didn't realize he was holding his breath. Easing forward, he passed the rear bumper of the second car. Something moved, on the left. He turned, raising his weapon.

Clear. But he could have sworn...

"Theo." A whisper. He whirled about. *Shit. Now, he was hearing things.* A pebble stuck him in the back of the neck. He snapped around. A chill from behind, he felt a presence. He whirled about. There was some kind of…mist fading away. He blew out a shaky breath. Suddenly, coming in here alone, started to feel like a very bad idea.

"You're cornered, come out, hands in the air," he said with as much authority as he could muster. Nothing moved, everything was as still as…death. *Why do they always insist on doing this the hard wa—*

*Shit!*

He literally jumped. It felt like a finger running down his spine. Aiming his weapon, he caught a glimpse of more of that funky fading mist. His blew out a series of short breaths. *Mother Mary, what the hell's goin on?*

"I'm coming out, don't shoot."

Behind him. That voice. He trained his gun on the dumpster. "Come out, slow and easy, hands in the air." As instructed, a figure emerged from behind the dumpster. He tightened the grip on his side arm. His hands were clammy and shaking. "On the ground, face down." The figure kept coming. He swallowed the knot in his throat. "On the ground, I said, do it now." Richardson cocked the hammer on his weapon. The suspect kept coming. It was like asshole was daring him to shoot

"It's never a good idea to go after a cornered suspect without back up, Theo."

The figure stepped into the light of a street lamp. "Bricker?" Ross Bricker. He'd found him. So, why didn't it feel like a good thing?

There was no humor in Bricker's smile. "I wish I could say it was nice to see ya Theo." The detective strolled forward, hands in the air.

Richardson's heart rate revved up and sweat ran down his back. Something in the way that jerk looked at him was scaring the shit out of him. And he was the one holding the gun. "What did you do to that girl, Bricker?" he asked, his thoughts on where the hell his backup was.

Bricker shrugged. "I was giving her a fuckin' kick ass gift, nothing special, just immortality."

*Immor…great, Bricker was fucked up on something.* He leveled his gun at the advancing detective. "Stay… where you are. Back up will be here shortly, then we'll see about getting you some help."

Bricker snarled. "I don't need your fuckin' help and I'm done taking orders from your kind."

*Your kind?* Sweat rolled down the side of his face. "Stop where you are, not gonna tell you again. "He struggled to keep from trembling. His knees were practically knocking. And it was a good thing his bladder was empty.

Bricker stopped in his tracks, placing his hand on his hips. "You know, Theo, there's a whole world out there we never knew existed. I would've considered making you one of us, but I just can't give up the chance to fuckin' end you." Bricker waved his hand before him. "Sleep, Theo."

Richardson felt himself dropping off. He squeezed off a shot. The bullet caught Bricker in the chest, causing him to stagger backward. The spell was broken. He was awake and alert again.

*Sirens, about damn time.*

Bricker glowered. "You shot me, you prick." Bricker charged. Richardson fired two more rounds. Hit in the torso, Bricker stumbled backward, but instead of falling, Bricker righted himself and grinned. *Sweet Mary and Joseph, what the fuck was going on with Bricker's teeth!*

The sirens grew louder. Bricker smirked as he backed away. "We'll finish this later, Theo baby." He threw out his arms.

Richardson was knocked backward off his feet. It felt like he'd been hit by a bus. Landing with a thud, he clutched his chest, trying to force air back into his lungs. From where he lay, he watched Bricker climb the side of the fuckin' apartment building, like a spider. With a wave, he pulled himself over the top and was gone.

Richardson collapsed on his back. The screeching of brakes and the opening of car doors reached his ears as back up finally arrived. He heard numerous voices about him.

"Theo!" Footsteps. Several officers arrived at his side. "Are you hit? Where is the perp? Can you stand?"

"I'm ok, Sully." *Like hell, he was. What just happened?*

"Help him up!" Richardson felt hands pulling him to his feet. "Where is he, Theo; what happened?"

"He got the drop on me. He's long gone."

"You get a look at him?" the officer asked.

*Yeah, got a damn good look at him.* "No, it happened too fast. The girl?"

"On her way to Metro. She's lost a lot blood but I think she's gonna be ok." Richardson steadied himself, staring up at the building Bricker scaled as easily as he could walk across a floor.

"You sure you're ok, Detective?" Sully gave him a quizzical look.

"Yeah, fine, Sully. "He rubbed the back of his neck. Arnie was right. He'd run into something he couldn't explain or rationalize away. And that something looked a helluva lot like a vampire. *A vampire that threatened to come after him again. The question now was, what was he going to do about it?*

# CHAPTER FIFTY FIVE

Kalleal and Trey waited in the motel room for Adalius' return. While Trey checked in with his superior, he cleaned his Magnums. Thanks to the full volume of her outbursts, he learned she and other slayers were in route to New Carrollton and would arrive within days. When the slayer finished his call, he turned off his cell phone, sighing aloud.

"Her language is most colorful," Kalleal said, loading his weapons.

"You should hear her when she's pissed." The slayer tossed the phone on the bed.

"She reminds me of an associate from my days as a mercenary."

Trey chuckled. "He must have been a laugh a minute."

He scowled. "No, he was not."

The door burst open, a rogue windswept in, like an uninvited guest. Guns cocked, they leapt to their feet as debris from the outside flew about the room. Adalius strolled idly through the maelstrom, which ceased with the slamming of the door behind him. Without a word, he stalked over to the bed and sat down.

They lowered their weapons.

"Are you outta yo fuckin' mind? We coulda shot you," Trey bellowed.

Adalius remained silent, expressionless and unmoving on the bed. Something was tragically wrong. The faraway stare in his brother's eyes, Kalleal had seen before, on the battlefield after violent, bloody combat. He mentally reached out to his brother, but found only a void. It was as if Adalius was but a projection. His anger morphed to concern. Holstering his guns, he locked the door.

The slayer moved toward the bed cautiously. "Adalius, are you alright?" Trey laid a hand on his shoulder.

In his mind's eye, Kalleal saw it, an upsurge of psychic fury from within Adalius, streaking toward him like a wall of fire. Before he could shout warning, his sibling sprang to his feet. Eyes ablaze, Adalius roared, seizing the vampire hunter by the throat.

"Adalius, what...the fu..." Trey croaked out.

Kalleal's hands flew to his temples. *Elder's beard*! Waves of pain and anger slammed into his senses. It was like nothing he'd ever experienced. Raising his mental shield, he suppressed a dry heave as he steadied himself.

Adalius mercilessly gripped the struggling Trey Thomas' throat. With a backhand fling, he sent Trey pinballing off the rear wall, breaking the lamp and nightstand, wood splinters springing into the air.

Trey groaned as he struggled to get to his knees. Adalius charged like a rabid animal. Flipping over the bed, he yanked the slayer to his feet. Stunned, Trey dangled in the vampire's grasp like a lifeless doll. Throwing back his head, Adalius stretched open his mouth. His fangs extended to attack position.

Damnation.

"Adalius! Release him, now!" Kalleal's voice thundered across the room as he projected same into his brother's thoughts. But there was no Adalius to hear him. Only a mindless creature, whose only instinct was killing.

His eyes flashed gold. He had to act swiftly or Trey Thomas would be dead before his body hit the motel floor. Kalleal blurred. Catching hold of Ada's arm, he pulled the slayer free. Trey collapsed to the floor.

"Adalius, stop what you're do..." Was all he managed. Adalius' elbow landed in his sternum driving him back against the dresser. His chest ached and burned like flame as Adalius whirled about. He scowled as he beheld his sibling. His face was a mask of unadulterated hate. Adalius started toward him like a predator, his hand going for a weapon in his trench coat. Kalleal's muscles swelled, his own fangs extending involuntarily.

Adalius snarled as a dagger flew from his hands. It streaked toward him, eye level. He batted it away. Fists clenched, Adalius exploded toward him. Kalleal threw himself aside as a hay maker meant for his face, blasted through paint and drywall. A combat boot raced for his head. Blocked. Right cross, sidestepped.

A follow up left hook, caught him across the cheek. The world spun. A side kick sent him backward. Stumbling over the overturned bed, Kalleal landed on his back. "Adalius, hold; have you gone mad?" he shouted, his cheek throbbing wildly.

The slayer flew into his vision. Adalius's head recoiled a half turn as Trey landed a solid right hand. Adalius growled and countered with a swift backhand. Kalleal sprang to his feet as his fraternal forced the mortal against the far wall. A head butt dazed Trey as Adalius enclosed his hands around the slayer's neck. Adalius roared, gnashing his teeth, as he clamped down on the human's windpipe.

With speed that surprised himself, Kalleal was at their side. Taking hold of the tensing arms, he pulled, but Adalius bore down. He'd focused all his strength, the very power of his being into killing the soul in his hands. Kalleal's mind raced. A sensation, a long forgotten sensation, one he hadn't experienced in over a century, took hold.

Desperation.

He sensed the human's life force ebbing, fading like the fog of a dream. There was but one chance, only one. He had to try and break through. Try to snatch Adalius back from madness. Still clutching his brother's arm, he slipped into Adalius' mind, diving past the aggression, around the rage, toward the center of his psyche. Calmly, he projected into his sibling's mind as he spoke in the old tongue, keeping his voice steady.

*"I have seen into thy heart and mind, my brother. Thou seekth not only the Destroyer, but, also redemption. Redemption for the lives thou hast taken. For all the souls thou have tormented. In thine hands, before thee is another. Wilt thou add another life to thy debt? Another spirit to be atoned for? Release him, Ada. Spare him. Let no more mortal blood stain thine hands. Please, my brother, release him."*

Adalius's lips pressed together in a tight grimace. His brows drew in. Nose wrinkling, he blew out in rapid breaths. Shaking his head, a low growl droned from his throat. Kalleal waited anxiously as reason and insanity warred for dominance. His neck cording, Adalius snapped in a sharp inhale. With an angry scream, he let go.

Trey fell to his knees clutching his throat, air intake resuming. Kalleal bowed his head and gave thanks to the Elder, the muscles of his own body uncoiling. His breathing harsh, Adalius turned away.

"What the fuck is your problem?" the slayer wheezed, rising to his feet, rubbing his neck.

"Yes, Ada, what *was* that about?"

Adalius remained silent, looking about the room as if searching for something.

"Ada?" Kalleal said trying to keep worry from his voice. It was if his brother were sleepwalking. He had to snap Adalius out of it. "Ada!"

Adalius shook his head absently. "I… have seen Anna,"

"Tell me you killed that bitch."

"How did you find her?" Kalleal exclaimed, hoping and dreading, at the same time that Adalius had killed Anna.

"She found *me* and no, I did not kill her. But if I could have killed her…she was wrapped in shadows among the crowd when we arrived at Club Détente."

Kalleal stiffened. "That's not possible, Ada. Even wrapped in shadows, we or any number of the other vampires present would have detected her."

Adalius was ashen. "So much precious time, wasted."

Incredible. After being nearly overwhelmed by Adalius' emotions, he was back to barely sensing his brother at all. He kept his voice even. "Ada, you are certain Anna was at the club?"

After a long pause, Adalius nodded absently. "She admitted as much, my brother."

Kalleal suppressed a chill. "How? Even if she were a vampire several hundred years our senior-"

"I am afraid it is true. She can now evade our detection. I sensed her not, until…" Adalius clenched his fists, seemingly on the verge of another violent outburst.

Kalleal readied himself. "Until what, Ada?"

Adalius stood silently rubbing his arms. Once more waves of pain and sorrow rippled out from him.

Kalleal's brows drew together. "Ada, until what? What's happened?"

Adalius drew in a breath. "It is… a personal matter."

Kalleal hesitated. Given Ada's condition, pressing him was not wise, but… "I'm your brother, lean upon me. What has Anna done to you?"

Adalius bristled. "It is not your concern, Kalleal."

"Not my concern?" he asked, the cords in his own neck beginning to twang. "Was it not you who spoke of family when it was me who bore the burden of pain? Now when it's you who—"

Adalius turned. "It is not your concern, Kalleal," he said, his eyes cold and hard.

He stormed into Adalius' personal space, their faces a baby's breath apart. "No, you don't get to do that. You don't get to barge your way into my private pain with talk of family and oneness, then shut me out with a wall of your precious pride. Now stop being so damnably pig headed and tell me what in Hades Anna has done-"

"She killed my mate!"

Kalleal's jaw went slack. It was as if Adalius slapped him across the face. "You have—"

"Had, my brother," Adalius corrected him.

"Hold up a sec, you never mentioned that you had a mate," Trey said, still massaging his neck.

"I have many dangerous enemies. Concealing her existence was best to ensure her safety," Adalius said, his tone flat and lifeless.

Kalleal subtly bowed his head. "I'm deeply sorry for your loss. I am…all too well acquainted with the grief you must feel." Kalleal paced away. "Anna's power is growing. I must kill her quickly, while I still can."

"What the fuck you mean *you* must kill her quickly?" Trey erupted.

Kalleal glared at the slayer. "Impertinent child, I swore to destroy her over a century before your birth."

Trey Thomas stalked up to him, fists clenched. "Fuck you, canines. You think I'm just gonna step aside and let you do her?"

His eyes ignited. "You dare!" He jabbed a finger at the human, who promptly grabbed his arm and hip tossed him to the floor. Cold steel pressed into the side of his face, the click of a gun hammer. Trey Thomas had skillfully taken him down, and now his weapon was poised to vent his left cheek.

"Don't you fuckin' move, Adalius." The slayer's eyes drilled into his own. "As for you, twitch, and you not gonna have to pucker your lips to whistle. Now, here's how this is gonna play out. If either of you mutha fuckas ever again so much as look at me cross eyed, I will dust both of yo asses. We clear?"

Adalius nodded, his hand on his own weapon. "We are."

Trey gave his cheek a subtle jab. "Nod ya head if you understand, Kally,"

He bobbed his head.

"Okay, I'm gonna let you up, then we can continue our discussion like men and vampires. Alright, don't fuck with me canines, play nice." The slayer rose to his feet and backed away, his weapon still cocked.

Gingerly, Kalleal got to his feet. He'd grossly underestimated the vampire hunter. It wouldn't happen again.

Adalius gave him a questioning glance.

Kalleal nodded. He was ok.

Adalius stared at Trey Thomas, his eyes laced with dark intent. "Anna has killed loved ones of us all, but from me, she has taken love not once but twice. It shall be *my* hand that slays her."

Kalleal flashed his fangs. "You are not alone in suffering the loss of a mate, Adalius. Anna has stolen from me a wife and family."

"And from me," Trey added.

Adalius' voice rose an octave. "It is I who will force Anna to answer for her crimes, and satisfy our family's honor."

He was incredulous. "You?"

"I am the elder brother," Adalius stated matter of factly.

Kalleal exploded. "You would presume to invoke rank?"

Adalius sighed, his expression softening. "I meant not to trivialize either of your loses. But I swore an oath. I am honor bound to see Anna destroyed."

He leveled his eyes at his brother. "Your oath is no more important to you than is mine to me, Adalius."

"Fuck your oath, Anna is mine…period," the slayer added, his eyes intense like fire.

Suddenly there was banging at the door. Kalleal growled. He could hear a male's voice outside. "Will you guys keep it down, I'm tryin to sleep."

Sleep? For interrupting, the fool was about to get many blissful hours of unconsciousness. He blurred to the door, fangs extended, yanking it open. "What do you want!"

The short, balding man's eyes bulged, then he fainted away.

Trey joined him at the door. "What did you do?"

He glared at the slayer. "I did nothing. This… puny mortal fainted."

"I wonder why?" Trey said, holstering his weapon.

"What are you implying slayer?"

"I'm not implying anything, tiny. I'm *saying*—"

"Gentlemen," Adalius interrupted, "Perhaps your energies would be best served attending to the issue of the fallen mortal at your feet. Kalleal, if you would be so kind, please return him to his room, then erase all memory of his ever getting up."

He hesitated. Ada always had an annoying tendency to dictate orders. In this case however... "Your reasoning is sound. Very well, I shall do as you ask."

*****

While Kalleal attended to Captain Courageous, Trey carefully approached Adalius. "You alright now, vamp?"

"No, but I will be," Adalius said with an edge.

The motel door opened. Kalleal had returned the poor slob to his room. Closing the door, the vamp stood waiting, arms at his side, the aura about him anything but relaxed.

Adalius offered his brother a chair. Kalleal shook his head.

The vamp gestured for him to take a seat on the bed, then leaned against the nearby wall. This looked like it might take a while, so he planted his backside on the bed as asked.

Adalius eyed them carefully. "There must be an understanding. We have all sworn to see Anna destroyed but, her power, she subdued me with what appeared to be little effort."

Kalleal scowled, folding his massive arms across his chest. "But how? How could she have become so powerful in such a short period of time?"

Trey had a theory. "They say you are what you eat. Maybe it's because of what Anna's been chowing down on."

Adalius nodded in agreement. "The fact that she feeds on such a wide range of prey would seem the best explanation."

"If that's true, then the mixture of blood could be mutating her, but into what?" Kalleal mused.

Adalius stroked his beard. "I do not know. But I will face her."

"No. If what you're suggesting is true, none of us can stand alone against her."

Adalius leveled his gaze at Kalleal, then Trey. "Then it should no longer matter who kills Anna as long as she meets her end."

Trey rubbed his face in his hands. "Five years I've chased Anna across the country and back. Now, I'm supposed to just step aside because you—"

"No one is suggesting anyone step aside, but we can no longer afford to fight against each other in hunting Anna. In the end, it may take our combined efforts to kill her," Adalius countered.

Trey snorted. Maybe he didn't make himself clear. "No fuckin' way. That skank dies and it's gonna be *me* who—"

"Dies needlessly unless we begin using our heads, it is why we all have failed to stop her. She taunts us into acting irrationally, carelessly," Adalius interrupted.

Kalleal nodded in understanding. "Agreed. I will take this new oath to see Anna fall."

Adalius turned to him. "What say you, Trey Thomas?"

From deep in his mind, an inner voice nagged at him. Adalius had a point and he knew it. Maya had been trying to tell him the same thing for years. Maybe, it was time to listen, at least for now. "Alright, but if I get the chance..."

Adalius nodded. "Fair enough."

As they stood, Adalius held his hand out before him, then he laid his hand over Adalius', Kalleal covered his. As Adalius looked from Kalleal to him, the vamp's jaw tightened. "From this day forward, we pledge the death of Anna to be our one goal. Let the hand that slays her, be the hand that slays her for all."

"Damn right."

"So be it." Kalleal eyed his brother.

He got the same vibe. Adalius' all for one, one for all spiel was bull shit. He still planned to be the one to killed Anna. No shock there. Few things were more cunning and treacherous than a vampire seeking vengeance for a lost mate. Kalleal probably had the same agenda. Neither of these fang mouthed bastards could be trusted.

Once again, a knock at the door. "Thomas, it's me, open up,"

Kalleal opened it.

Kyle strolled in. "Did a lot of digging and...crikey, what the bloody hell happened in here? Had a party without me, did you?" he asked, taking in the carnage.

Trey snapped his fingers. "Kyle, focus. You did a lot of digging and..."

Kyle blinked. "Right. I did a lot of digging, and found you a lead, I have. The yakety yak is Anna's flop house is in an abandoned textile factory on the city's southeast side called AJAX."

Kalleal scowled. "And how reliable are your sources?"

Kyle watched Kalleal as he closed the door, then faced him and Adalius. "Who's he?" Kyle asked, jabbing a thumb at Kalleal.

"Kalleal, he's Adalius' brother."

Kyle rolled his eyes. "Blimey, Thomas, it's not a good sign when a slayer starts *attracting* vampires."

Trey felt a smile tug at the corners of his mouth. "You're just worried about job security. Alright, we'll check it out. In the meantime, take this." Trey handed a slip of paper to Kyle. "If anything happens, contact Maya, she'll know what to do."

Kyle looked suspiciously from the paper to Trey. "Why don't *you* tell her?"

"Because if I call her, I'll have to replace my phone and my eardrums, I just don't have time to debate this. Now, head back to the club and keep your ears to the ground, in case this turns out to be a waste of time."

"Right then, do keep your head down, all of you. I'd hate to have to buy a suit for any funerals. "Kyle turned. Kalleal opened the door for him and nodded as Kyle went by.

"Nice to meet ya, mate."

As Kyle exited, Kalleal closed the door and grabbed his trench coat. "Who was that vampire and how reliable is he?"

Trey retrieved his phone and checked his pistols. "Kyle's been workin' with me for years. Trust me, if he gives you intel, it's money, more often than not."

Adalius nodded. "Then we go to this textiles factory but first we make a stop for more weapons and ammunition."

He cocked an eyebrow. "You've been holding out on me, vamp. Ok, where to?

Adalius retrieved his daggers. "I have a townhouse on the outskirts of town. All we need will be there.

Trey blinked. "You have a townhouse?"

Kalleal's glare was withering. "You think we reside in caves and sleep in coffins like the vermin of Dracul?"

Trey slipped on his jacket and grabbed his keys. "Never actually gave it any thought before now, fang face."

Kalleal opened his mouth to respond but Adalius cut him off. "Enough, let us be off. But have a care, this could be a trap."

Kalleal smiled coldly. "We can only hope."

*****

Trish, Ricardo, and Marie waited anxiously for Anna's return. Her abrupt exit had left them all in a state of confusion. Marie resisted the urge to bite her nails as the minutes turned to hours, hours with no word from Anna. She felt the need to do something. They all did. Anna ordered that they wait so wait they did. Trish gently massaged her shoulders and neck, working out the kinks anxiety knitted in her body, as Ricardo returned from the refrigerator with three glasses of blood on a tray he'd warmed in the microwave.

Trish finally took a seat next to her as she rolled her relieved shoulders. Trish's hands worked wonders on her body but had done little to ease the grip of uneasiness on her mind. Ricardo passed the first glass to Trish, then one to her, taking the last for himself. They drank in silence, the same question consuming their thoughts. Who had Anna heard in her mind and what did it mean for them?

"We should do something. She's been gone too long," Marie said breaking the silence.

Trish took her hand. "No, my love, we were told to wait here."

Ricardo ran his hand through his hair. "Have you any idea at all who the voice belongs to, Marie?"

She slowly shook her head. "No idea what so ever, I've never heard it before."

Trish's tender mental caress comforted her. "Whoever it is, I'm sure the mistress can deal with them. I just wish she would contact us."

The door burst opened. Without overture, Anna swept into the room, concern painted all over her face. They rose to their feet. Marie sighed a breath of relief, but one look at Anna, brought the tension back with a vengeance.

"We must prepare ourselves, my young ones. A foul wind blows on my plans for our future," Anna announced rubbing her arms.

Marie stepped into Trish's embrace. "What is it, mistress? Is it the one whose voice I heard?"

Anna ran her hand lovingly through Marie's hair. "His name is Adalius."

Trish's eye brows rose. "You've spoken of him. He was your mate, the one you nicknamed Death."

Anna paced away, stopped, then faced them. "Yes, he was my mate and death he was; A magnificent god of terror and agony. He was my greatest creation.... and greatest failure. "Anna's face contorted into a sneer. "That gypsy girl, before I knew it, he had actually come to care for her. "Anna's eyes began to glow white. "He actually *cared* for her. I was his maker, his queen. His every need, his every whim, I fulfilled. I would have slaughtered nations with just a word from him. While she... she was nothing more than cattle and yet..."

Ricardo stepped forward. "Allow me to kill him, mistress."

328

Anna's eyes returned to normal as she smiled lovingly at her child and lover. "Dear Ricardo, if only you could. I'm afraid Adalius is beyond any of you. We must destroy him together. Trish, I want you to summon the others. We must make ready for his coming."

Marie felt the knot in her belly tighten. "You truly believe he'll find us?"

"Oh yes, my child, I've seen to that. You see, I killed his mate. He'll seek us out and will discover where we are, and when he does, he most certainly will come."

# CHAPTER FIFTY SIX

The AJAX Textiles factory sat before them dark and foreboding as they surveyed the property, downwind, from a nearby hill. The factory grounds, barely illuminated thanks to overcast skies, were fragranced by a bouquet of wildflowers with a faint hint of metallic chemicals. Like a rotting carcass, the plant's innards seeded the air with its decay.

Trey crouched low while his vampire counterparts hovered close by wrapped in shadows. Thanks to his night vision binoculars, he could see everything. Adalius and Kalleal, on the other hand being vamps, had no need of gimmicks to see everything perfectly.

*Bastards.*

A lone raccoon scurried across the pavement of the dead factory's parking lot while nearby, several red wolves fed on the remains of a deer. Beyond the night critters and vegetation, the property seemed devoid of life. Frankly, even if Anna and her brood were inside, there still wasn't any life in there.

He wiped his brow. "Nothing. I don't see squat. Can you at least sense anything?"

Adalius nodded as he and Kalleal faded into view, the intermittent moonlight bouncing off their sword handles. "They are here. I sense a strong presence that can only be Anna herself. We have found her."

"I concur." Kalleal drew his Magnum.

Trey drew his pistol and slid a magazine into place. "Then what we waitin' for, let's do this."

Adalius laid a hand on his shoulder. "With caution."

330

Kalleal grunted. "Agreed. We may be expected. Perhaps it would be best to attack from different angles. The slayer will have to fend for himself."

Trey bristled. "The slayer can hear you. I don't need you neck peckers to hold my hand."

Adalius nodded. "Very well. There are several entry ways we can gain access." He pointed to the factory rooftop. "That skylight is big enough to allow any of us to enter."

"I'll take that entrance, my brother," said Kalleal.

Trey interjected. "I'll take the window on the second floor near the fire escape.

Adalius checked his weapons. "Excellent, that entry way is yours."

Trey looked over his shoulder at Adalius. "What about you? What are you plannin' to do?"

Even behind the shades he could see Adalius' eyes sparkle. "I, my friend, am taking the direct approach."

"You gonna walk right through the front door?"

"Indeed I am."

"That's hard ass, stupid, but hard ass. They won't be too thrilled with you barging your way in."

"Then we shall all be unhappy." Adalius snarled.

Kalleal stepped into his brother's path. "Surely you have more in mind than simply waltzing into the destroyer's lair?"

"The plan, my brother, is to hold Anna's attention while you and Trey destroy her brood. We must kill the body as well as the head."

Trey rose to his feet. "Bad plan, Adalius. You're the one who said we had to work together. If she's as powerful as you say, how are you gonna last?"

Adalius clasped Trey's shoulder. "Worry not, I will last. Anna undoubtedly will try seduction before she attempts to kill me. That should buy you the time you need to eliminate her minions then aid me in her destruction."

Kalleal shook his head. "Absolute madness, you would be placing your life—"

"Into the hands of you and Trey, I trust no others more. Now, let us be off. Anna must die this night."

Kalleal grimaced, he didn't like this shit one bit. His jaw tightening, the vamp gave his brother one last glance, then wrapped himself once more in shadows. The flap of his trench coat tails, the only indication of his departure.

Trey looked to Adalius. "Good luck, vamp. Save some of that for me."

"Be at ease, I am certain there will be more than enough for us all." Adalius faded from view.

Trey affixed a silencer onto his weapon. Time to get his game face on; deep breath. Exhale. With that, he was off toward the plant keeping low as he went.

*****

The room was spacious, acrid, and covered in thick layers of dust as Trey slid through the window being careful not to slice himself on the jagged shards of glass that still remained in the pane. *Can't afford any mishaps.* The fresh scent of blood would sing out to the vampires below. Silently, he dropped from the ledge and looked about. Broken glass littered the stained and torn carpet. Strewn about were numerous pieces of dated furniture and tables. He suppressed a sneeze as he took in a breath of stale dusty air.

Pausing, he held his breath, listening for the sound of footfalls. Vamps could hear a cat lap milk from a mile away. He waited. All quiet. He exhaled.

Silence really was golden sometimes. Moving on, a step at a time, he penetrated deeper into the room. On the far wall ahead, he noted a life sized portrait of a man dressed in 1930's attire. The painting hung slanted, partially covering a plaque which read 'Lionel Binks, our founder.' In one hand, between thumb and forefinger, rested a fat stogie, the other was tucked inside his jacket underneath the lapel. A hard stern look, cold steely blue eyes, slicked back hair, and a mouth that looked incapable of smiling, dollars to navy beans, the bastard was an asshole's asshole in his day.

Trey, with pistol in hand, withdrew several darts from his jacket as he started toward the doorway directly ahead. Halfway there, it hit him.

The tingling sensation he got when he was being watched. He stopped, his eyes darting side to side. Visual scrutiny told him there was nothing there, but eyes couldn't always be trusted when hunting fangs. Instincts, on the other hand, rarely lied.

The air got still and so did he. He tightened his grip on his pistol. It was like ants crawling over his skin. No doubt about it, he wasn't alone.

\*\*\*\*\*

Kalleal set down on the roof top without a sound. The cloud cover all but subdued any light the moon provided as he looked about. Dropping to one knee, he used his senses to probe the factory below. Slowly, the floor plan took shape in his mind's eye. The area provided plenty of places for ambushers to hide, but the shadows were empty. The activity of minds grasped his attention. Anna and her fiends were definitely here.

Another quick scan of the roof confirmed he was still alone. He rose into the air and carefully descended through the broken skylight. Concentrating on the darkness, he touched down and drew his blade. His brow furrowed. Low level psychic interference was making it difficult to scan beyond his immediate area. Not entirely unusual. Such static could sometimes be caused by poltergeist.

Structures this old tended to contain numerous spirits unwilling or unable to move on to their final destination. Wrapping himself in shadows, he continued his search for Anna. The massive shop floor was littered with the skeletons of what were once big machines. He could almost hear the ghosts of AJAX past hard at work.

He stepped over and around trash and debris, his eyes focused, as instincts led him to…. a minute shift in the air. Silence rang in his ears. He paused, tightening his grip on the sword handle. Someone or something was watching him, studying him for weaknesses. He focused. they could hide from his eyes, but not from his mind.

A ripple of air coming from his left, movement; Kalleal swung his katana up and across his body. Sparks flew as blade met blade. Swinging the sword back, he deflected another blow meant for his jugular. He assumed a defensive stance and waited. He sensed his enemy back away.

"You are predictable and rely too much on your strength. Show yourself!"

Nothing.

Kalleal growled. "Reveal yourself, coward. Face me."

A form faded into sight as did the sword he wielded. When the materializing was complete, it revealed a male whose height and bulk rivaled his own. Kalleal sneered in contempt. "You are Sandrian!"

The buzz cut male grinned. "You're smarter than you look."

The vampire's mental shield snapped into place, but he didn't need to read his thoughts to know who he fought for. "You whore yourself for that harpy."

"Better Anna's whore than King Vaughn's bitch."

Kalleal's eyes narrowed as he looked upon the traitor.

"What, you think I'm alone in my thinking? There are many others who feel like I do. We're sick of having to sit back, watching man walk about ruling, while we crawl around on our bellies in darkness. The humans are our food, yet our so called leadership would have us live next to them, work with them, be like them. "The male spat on the ground in contempt. "Many of us are tired of being led by a spineless king and that court of jesters on the council."

Kalleal's eyes glowed white hot. "You know the penalty for treason."

"Death, yes I know. So who will be my executioner, you?"

"Pray it is I who kills you."

"You don't have the fangs to kill me. Funny you should mention killing, though." The trader lowered his sword as from a hall to his right, a dozen vampires armed with assault rifles took their place behind the smirking male.

Kalleal growled.

"Don't worry, you and your buds are gonna have plenty of company. The revolution is coming. Too bad it won't be televised. Not that it matters, your bitch ass won't be around to see it. Kill the prick." The vampire stepped aside as his minions opened fire.

Kalleal lifted his sword, bracing himself for the hail of hot silver death.

*****

Trey scanned the floor around him. There were three strange anomalies in the dust, one to his right, one ahead of him, and the other to his left. In rapid session, Trey fired darts in the direction of the anomalies. As he heard the crackle of electricity, he aimed his weapon and fired once in each direction. Male forms appeared and disintegrated in one motion, leaving him and his smoking gun alone.

Trey shook his head at the piles of dust. "Come on man, I couldn't see you, but I could see the tracks you left in the dust." He started toward the exit. The world exploded in white hot pain. He'd been struck on the back of the head. Darkness sucked him down, as carpet rushed up to greet him.

*****

"I *told* them that. Thank you for proving my point." A pair of feet in high heeled sandals faded into view, followed by calves, thighs, skirt, arms, blouse, and long haired head. Marie smiled down on the prone Trey Thomas. "Hello, slayer, nice to see you again."

# CHAPTER FIFTY SEVEN

Kyle knocked back the last of his gin laced blood. A bad case of nerves had him leaning heavier on the spirits than normal. Were he still human, his stomach would be rolling like an ocean wave. Thanks to his tip, Thomas and his new mates were headed into Hell's den.

While tracing his finger around the mouth of his glass, directly to his right, the source of his info gulped down another plasma spiked bourbon. It was sheer luck he ran into Finn here. The bloke was the CNN of the supernatural world. They'd been chums for over two centuries.

Sort of.

Good ole Finn. Actually, not so good ole Finn, the wanker lived a most unsavory life and that was before his maker put the bite on him.

Kyle focused on trying to relax. In an aces establishment like this, it should've been easy, but till he heard from that knob head slayer of his, he was gonna go bloomin' crackers.

His eyes drifted to the dance floor. Counting the heads bobbing in time with the music, he added all the noggins that had come and gone since the moment he first walked through those sound proof doors. Blimey, he'd give his left fang for a piece of this action. The place was a gold mine.

A hand slapped his back.

Good ole Finn. "Ad me fill a the tap tonight, why don't yer join me an' de lads. We're pisser for somethin' a bit more fresh."

Kyle waved him off. "Pass, learned my lesson hangin' out with you fucking tossers."

Finn laughed out loud. "Yer still oldin' Paris against me?"

He snorted. "You bloody led that slayer right to me."

"Yer got away, didn't yer?"

He jabbed a finger at Finn. "Not the bloomin' point."

Finn's smirk was as slimy as a snail's trail. "So feckin' sensitive, let me make it up ter yer laddie. Whaen we make de catch, yer get the first nibble." Finn slid an arm around his shoulder. "Whadda yer say?"

He shrugged off Finn's arm. "Not bloody likely. Sod off, Finn, I'm busy."

"Ohh so yer too jammers ter 'obnob wi' stoney broke Finn, are yer? Bet oy knew why. Seen yer go all googly eyed over de red head. Not dat I'd blame ya, I'd love ter sink more than me fangs into dat gran' beauty."

Dropping his glass, Kyle was in motion before he or Finn realized he'd moved. Fisting Finn's collar, eyes bright like searchlights, he held the bastard off his feet. Fangs extended, he hissed. "If I were you, I'd watch my bloody tongue."

A roguish grin spread across Finn's face. "Well feck me, wouldn't 'av believed it if I 'adn't saw it meself. You're al' sweet on de lass aren't yer?"

"That's not your bloody business. Find another way to get your jollies or I'll end you. Clear enough?"

Finn grinned. "Perfectly. Nigh if ya don't mind, put a body down, you're makin' a scene."

Kyle looked about. Several pairs of eyes had indeed begun to take notice. Best to throttle back the aggro. Wouldn't want the Lycan bouncer chaps lurking about to come along and give him the heave ho. His eyes returning to normal, he lowered Finn to the floor.

Finn shrugged free. "Much better. Yer really nade ter work on dat impulse control, boyo."

He jabbed a finger at Finn. "You just remember what I said." A delightful tingle shivered down his spine. That meant one thing. He turned.

Dressed in a gold silk dress that hugged her body like a passionate lover, Donella, glided toward him, the sway of her hips locked his attention in a vise. Her walk was that of refinement, stirred with a heavy dose of heat. Tall, curvy, and magnificent with her high cheekbones, perfect knockers, and firm round arse. The wildest wet of his life come true.

She smiled.

He flushed in spite of himself, his kisser splitting in a broad grin. If he'd a heartbeat it'd be hammering in his ears.

"Hey, love." He planted a kiss on her lips, nipping her.

She purred. "Did you miss me?"

"Indeed I did." Kyle pulled her close.

Finn cleared his throat. "Ain't yer gonna introduce a body, Kyle?"

Kyle scowled. "No."

Finn stepped around him. "De name's Finn lass, nice te meet ye." He reached out and placed a kiss on her hand. Donella subtly recoiled, her expression that of someone who'd just sampled spinach ice cream. "Kyle an' me been mucker for centuries nigh. Judging by the way yer man looks at ye, I'd say ya 'ave a fair chance a makin' an 'onest paddy of 'imself."

Donella studied Finn, then cocked an eyebrow. Kyle sensed the change in her aura. She withdrew her hand. "Pleased to meet you...Finn," She looked to him. "Dance with me, Kyle?"

*Like she ever had to ask.* "Course, love, lead the way."

Finn chuckled. "Well, oy don't nade ter be run over by a street car. I'll be on me way. De pleasure was mine, lassie.I'll be in touch, Kyle, gran' noight ter ya both."

Finn made off for the exit as Donella led him to the dance floor.

As they pushed their way to the center, the mood and music shifted. It was hold 'em close time. *Jolly good timing*! He held out his arms and she walked right in. Did she ever feel right. Everything about her felt right. Donella in his arms felt like home. He leaned in to whisper in her ear. "You look lovely tonight"

"Kyle, listen to me. Finn is playing you; he's working with the Destroyer. It's a set up. Your friend, the slayer, is in grave danger."

Kyle froze. "I've no idea what you're talkin' about, love. I've got no slayer-"

"I know, Kyle. I knew from the moment we met. You're working with a slayer to find and kill Anna."

The jig was up. "How did you—"

"You're good, very good actually. Even a much older immortal wouldn't have detected you were hiding something let alone discover what it was. My compliments, your mental discipline is remarkable for one so young, but as skilled as you are, I'm better." There was that twinkle in her eyes, that'd stolen his heart.

"Bugger, Finn is powerful bloke, how'd you slip into his noggin so quickly and apparently without him knowing it?"

She pressed two fingers to his lips. "I'm four hun…I'm older than both of you. Finn may be a strong vampire but as minds go…well to be kind, his is rather simple."

"Please, tell me you haven't told anyone else about this."

"No, of course not."

"Then you don't care that I'm working with a slayer, why?"

"Well, I'm not thrilled, but you're trying to kill Anna. For that, I'd fund your quest myself. Look around you, Kyle. There isn't a body here that wouldn't pay you both good money to kill that monster. That's why and because… I really like you." Her cheeks flushed.

He kissed her lips. "You're the bees knees, love."

She grinned. "I know. Now go warn your friend, he's headed into a trap."

Without a word, he blurred through the soundproof doors. First, to warn Thomas, then he'd find Finn and pull his guts out through his nostrils.

# CHAPTER FIFTY EIGHT

Kiel and Marseth studied the wall map as reports filtered in from his security staff. Arms crossed, Kiel looked to his father. Marseth, eyes glued to the map, stood in the same fashion.

Kiel smiled. Like father, like son. "Father, it wasn't necessary to have the general wait in the lobby for the Enforcers. I have people who could've handled that."

Marseth snorted. "Dey general needed another task to focus upon, end I needed heem to do so. It becomes tiring being vatched over like a newborn pup."

Kiel smiled openly. Father never cared for being guarded and hovered over but he was the king. It came with the territory. Placed on the map before him, were pins to keep track of where they'd looked and where they had yet to look.

Marseth studied the map, his eyes hard like steel. Father hadn't moved a muscle as the search for Anna's nest escalated. He knew that look all too well. That intense, far away gaze the king got just before he went off into battle was the only thing that ever frightened his mother.

The desk phone beeped. He hit the speaker button. "I'm listening, go."

"This is Poke, here at the Pennywise Bakery. We've checked this place top to bottom. There were vamps here but they're gone now. From looking at the mess, I'd say there was a battle. There's vamp dust everywhere and a lot of rectangular spaces in the dust. Could be they were storing something in this dump."

Kiel stroked his chin. "Is there any clue at all as to whether it was Anna's nest or a regular vamp nest?"

"Can't tell for sure, but there were definitely fangs here."

"Alright, begin setting up surveillance cameras. Whoever it was, I want to know if they return."

"Copy that. We'll handle it." The line clicked.

Kiel sighed, frustration setting in. "We're running out of time and places to look. The Enforcers will be here before long."

Marseth said not a word but continued to gaze upon the map. His brow knitted in concentration, he scanned it top to bottom, as if trying to memorize every nuance and line.

Once again, Kiel's desk phone rang. "This is Kiel, go."

"Kiel, this is Jax, we just arrived at the old lighthouse. This place looks like it's been hit by slayers recently. There's vamp dust all over, and crosses placed at every window and entrance. We also found two sets of fresh footprints leading to and away from the property. If Anna was here, she definitely won't be coming back."

Kiel clenched his jaw. "Dammit. Alright, head to the next location on your list and contact me when you arrive."

"Got it, we're rollin'." The line clicked.

Kiel rubbed his temples. The hunt for the Anna wasn't going well. But he knew it wasn't gonna be easy. She had plenty of practice covering her tracks. His office door burst open. Cam stormed in, thumped his chest with a closed first, and knelt before Marseth.

"Forgive the intrusion, my king."

Marseth nodded. "Rise young vun and be at ease."

Cam rose to his feet. "Thank you, my lord. Kiel, I know you're hunting Anna. I want in. I will kill her for what she's done to my sister. Since Miguel's death she won't eat, even though she is with young. She won't even speak to anyone. It's like she's lost the will to live. She's dying, Kiel and there's nothing I can…" Cam bowed his head.

Kiel's heart sank, yet another soul suffering because of Anna, because he allowed her to beat him again. "All of this is on my head. I sent them into Anna's hands."

"There'll be time to assess blame later, Kiel. The only important thing now is finding Anna and killing her."

Kiel placed a hand on Cam's shoulder. "Come, take a look. "Kiel gestured toward his map as Cam fell in step. He indicated the pins placements. "The black pins are where we've looked, the red where we haven't."

Cam inspected the map. "Looks like you've covered a lot of places already. I have Lycan, weapons, and plenty of ammo. I'll take my crew and begin searching the southeast side of the city."

Kiel took out a phone from his desk and tossed it to Cam. "Good, keep in touch with that and I'll coordinate from here. Between all of us we may be able to find her before the Enforcers arrive."

"Enforcers?"

"Yes, it's the agreement father made with the vamp—"

"Here, vhat is dis place?"

He and Cam turned to the king. Marseth had a finger placed atop one of the pins. Kiel made his way over with Cam close behind. His highness removed his finger from the pin.

Kiel gave it a once over. "That's the old AJAX plant, you think she's there?"

"She is dere."

"How can you be so sure, my father?"

"Trust me, my son, learn to rely on your instincts. I know how dey vumpire thinks. Call it a…vhat is dey vord?"

"A hunch?"

Marseth smiled. "Precisely."

"I got nothing better. "Kiel hit the button on his phone. "Attention all units, drop whatever you're doing and head to the AJAX textiles factory immediately."

"This is Poke, we're rolling."

"This is Jax, we're in route."

Kiel retrieved a nickel plated .40 from his wall safe and loaded a magazine into it. "Get your people ready, Cam, I'll meet you outside in a moment."

Cam nodded to Kiel, saluted his king, then left the room.

Kiel tucked the weapon in at the small of his back. "I'll contact you if we find anything."

Marseth placed his hands on the shoulders of his son "Be safe, my son, for your muther's sake end for mine. I vill vait here for the Enforcer's arrival."

"Good, I was hoping you'd say that. If Anna's there, we'll find her and kill her."

"Let thine heart and mind be clear of anger. Emotion een battle can make a varrrior careless."

"I will heed your advice, my father. "Kiel hugged his king who returned his embrace then left the office.

*****

Marseth watched him go. For the first time felt the fear his mate must have felt each time he himself had gone off into battle. Fear was oppressive as any enemy he'd ever faced. "May dey goddess moon vatch over thee, my child. May she vatch over us all."

# CHAPTER FIFTY NINE

An angry gale descended upon the grounds as Adalius faded into view. Leaves swirled about him. The bottom of his trench coat whipped around his ankles. Drawing out dual submachine guns, he stalked toward the back entrance, his hair blowing freely in the furious gusts generated by the force of his will. With single minded concentration, he focused on the double doors. They tore free from their hinges and flew out of his line of sight.

Stepping through the entrance, he sensed them, at least twenty in all. Anna's children were wrapped in shadows, armed with automatic weapons and swords. His expression twisted into a snarl. Their existence was at an end. None would escape his detection nor his wrath. He surged forward. Those who had rifles raised them.

Focusing, he channeled the gale down the corridor toward his enemies. The force of blast lifted most off their feet while blinding the others. He raised the MP5K's, and fired. Hot silver lanced out. The screams many as the rounds tore through flesh and bone. One by one, weapons dropped as vampire remains were swept away.

His weapons empty, only a handful of sword bearers remained. Adalius cast the smoking guns aside. He charged, drawing his blade rom its sheath. Two of the surviving vampires lunged with their rapiers. Blocking the first, he parried the second. A side kick knocked the second assailant to the deck. As the first attacker gathered himself, Adalius threw out his hand. The vampire sailed back against the wall. Before he could fall, Adalius hurled his sword. The blade split cartilage and bone, embedding into heart muscle. The night walker was dust before the echo of his cry died away.

Advancing on the remaining vampire, he ducked underneath the blade meant to sever head from neck. Momentum carried the vampire off balance. Grabbing hold of the attacker's head, Adalius gave it a quick twist.

*Snap!*

The vampire dropped to the ground, completely immobilized. Screams in the distance, snagged his attention. Two more rounded the corner at the far end of the corridor. Their war cries only further infuriated him. He dashed toward the rampaging vampires, and dove between them. Tucking into a roll, he ended up on his feet, behind the duo. As they turned, Adalius fired a right hand. His fist blasted through the chest plate. Grabbing hold of the aggressor's heart, he crushed it in his hand. The attacker disintegrated.

The second vampire froze. It cost him his undead life. Adalius brought his dust covered arm back across his body, blocking the punch meant for his jaw then drove the heel of the same hand up into the vampire's chin, the blow raising his opponent off his feet. The vampire came crashing down, his weapon clattering to the floor.

Adalius reached out. The sword flew to his hand. With a twirl, he drove the blade through the vampire's heart giving the hilt a quick twist. The body crumbled. Adalius cocked his head cracking his neck.

Through a haze of vampire dust, he went to retrieve his blade. Yanking it free from the wall, he marched to where the powerless attacker lay. Sliding the weapon into its sheath, he knelt down. His face expressionless, he regarded the injured before him.

"Pl...please...please don't kill me." The immortal said, his voice trembling.

Adalius picked up the sword used to attack him. "I cannot kill that which is already dead."

"You *know* what I mean, man, please."

His gaze hardened. "The moment your mistress killed my mate, all of you became forfeit." He studied the sword in his hand. "I believe, this is yours." He drove the blade in, lodging it in the floor. The vampire's eyes and mouth went wide as he crumbled.

Rising to his feet, he retrieved his weapons, reloaded them, and returned them to their place under his trench. Without a backward glance, he made his way down the corridor following his senses as they led him to where Anna most likely awaited.

At the end of the hall, instincts took him to the left. There was a simple wooden door. She was in there. Advancing on the door, he kicked it in. The room was spacious, decadent in its furnishings. Just the sort of place he would expect to find Anna.

Out of nothingness, a dagger streaked toward him. He captured the projectile, snapped the blade from its handle and tossed it aside. As he approached a large canopied bed, blonde female solidified.

"Stay where you are, Adalius." She snarled, pointing her finger like an accuser. He was tackled from behind. Both he and his attacker went crashing through a nearby table and chairs. Rising to his feet, Ricardo landed a right cross. Adalius staggered. Pressing his advantage, the ambusher moved in driving a closed fist into Adalius' solar plexus. He groaned as air was forced from his lungs. A violent left from the Latino connected, robbing him of equilibrium. He went to the ground. His adversary stood back admiring his handy work.

"We were supposed to be afraid... of *you*, puta? You're nothing," the vampire laughed.

Outrage flooded his mind. *He dares! After what his mistress has done*? His eyes ignited, heart hammering, blood searing in his veins.

The world warped and shifted. He found himself back at the pool, Serena in his arms. Everything moved in slow motion. Gazing into Serena's lifeless face, it began. Blood, pouring from her eyes, up through her nose, her mouth, her pores, rising up from the very grout of the pool tile. It dripped from the branches of trees like a crimson shower. The pool churned and overflowed red as blood rain fell from the sky. Flowing toward him, it filled the patio. Rising over his boots, up his ankles, and calves. Serena. Her face disappeared into the crimson.

No.

She was lost to him, gone forever; laughter, Anna's laughter. Once more she had murdered his heart, his love, his life. Coming from everywhere, it mocked him, taunted him, growing louder as the bloody deluge rose. Gore enveloped the patio, the furniture, and his limbs. It covered his shoulders, rising to his throat, up to his chin. Teeth and fists clenched. The fire in his soul detonated. Grief consumed him. Drawing in a deep breath, he threw back his head and screamed. The image shattered like glass.

The vision was gone. As was his rage. Only a sense of purpose remained, a sense of clarity, a lust for retribution. His respiration and heart beat slowed to the rhythm of a killer, a predator.

Laughter. Not Anna's.

The Latino vampire.

He rose to his feet. Removing his shades, he folded, then placed them inside his trench coat. His eyes locked on his assailant, he spat blood from his mouth. "I think I would like some more, please."

Ricardo smiled. "Sure, you can have all you want, ese."

Ricardo blurred toward him. Batting away the anticipated punch, Adalius delivered a counter with such force, the blonde female covered her mouth to stifle a scream. Blood flowed freely from the staggered Latino's mouth. Without mercy, he connected with another blow and another, sending blood and spit airborne. Ricardo dropped to one knee, lurching forward. Adalius caught him by his arms. He wasn't done yet. Pulling his bloodied opponent to his feet, Adalius rammed his forehead into the Latino's nose. He heard the muffled crunch of broken cartilage.

As the vampire arched backward, Adalius tugged him back and fired an immense uppercut that lifted him off the floor. Whipping his leg about, his boot caught Ricardo at the temple. The kick sent him backward, where he slid across the floor and laid motionless.

Facing the blonde, he extended an open hand toward her and closed his fist. The female went rigid. "You are Trish. I saw you in Anna's mind when she attacked me. You are one of her favorites," He sensed her terror. She had good reason. "Where is your mistress?"

Trish struggled. "I'll tell you nothing. You'll just have to kill me, Adalius."

"That was assured the moment I arrived. But first…" He forced into Trish's mind. She resisted the mental incursion. He sneered, a waste of precious energy. With brutal ease, he bludgeoned through her mental barriers.

The sound of nearing staccato gunfire broke his concentration. A rear door burst open depositing two vampires carrying automatic weapons. He drew a dagger and launched it. The gunman screamed as the blade struck home. The vampire crumbled to the floor. The door blasted open, kicked in from the outside, Kalleal burst in, sword in hand. The remaining vampire raised his weapon, his last act. Kalleal severed his head. His brother held a defensive stance, saw him, and lowered his katana.

"It is good to see you alive and well," he said, tightening his hold on Trish.

"I too am glad to see you are unharmed, my brother. Anna's brood are many but if she truly hopes to start and win her revolution, she needs to better prepare her foot soldiers," Kalleal said, crossing the room to join him.

"Indeed. Where is Trey Thomas?"

"Trey Thomas?"

"You have not seen him?"

"I've seen only vampires intent on my demise." Kalleal turned his attention to Trish. "So, who's the bitch?"

Drawing his sword, Adalius swung. Kalleal deflected the strike. A loud clang rang out. Slowly the vampire backed away.

Adalius glowered. "A better question would be who are *you*?"

Kalleal laughed. His body and face distorted. Shifted and changed. When the metamorphosis completed it was not Kalleal who stood before him, but another. *Anna*.

"I'm impressed, you saw through my deception. Where did I go wrong?"

"You overplayed your hand. Who's the bitch? Kalleal would not speak thus." Then it dawned on him. He looked to the piles of dust.

Following his gaze, she smiled. "My children are prepared to die, whenever it's required."

His fangs slowly extended. "Where are Kalleal and the slayer, what have you done with them?"

Anna simply shook her head. "You should concern yourself not with what I've done but what I'm *going* to do." Dropping her sword, she blurred toward him. Before he reacted, Anna caught him by the arm and backhanded him through the air. He collided with a support beam. Pain forced him to cry out before darkness overtook him.

\*\*\*\*\*

Adalius lay motionless. With his focus gone, Trish fell to her knees, gaping at Anna. Staring at her hand, a slow smile creased Anna's lips. She giggled to herself, then laughed out loud. Her growing strength and power were making her nearly godlike. Turning to the door from which she had entered, she snapped her fingers.

"Bring him!"

Several vampires emerged, dragging the unmoving Kalleal into the room. The rogue Sandrian followed them in, came and stood before her. Their eyes met. He growled lustily as Kalleal was laid at her feet. She flushed. Pulling her into his arms, he kissed her passionately. She purred, hooking her leg behind his calf.

Breaking their kiss, he licked her lips as he drew away. "He's a fabulous warrior, my queen. He used his sword to deflect bullets which would've been fatal. Injured as was, he still eliminated seven of our numbers before we finally subdued him."

She looked down on the prone Kalleal. "Imagine my surprise to learn you were here, my Kalleal. So, the brothers have reunited. How touching."

"Mistress." All heads turned as Marie entered followed by two vampires dragging a body. "I caught this slayer sneaking in through a second floor window. He killed three before he was captured."

"Bring him. Show me the face of the slayer." The vampires laid him beside Kalleal. Using her foot, she rolled the slayer unto his back.

Her brows arched. "Trey Thomas. You're truly here as well. "She pointed to Adalius. "Bring him hither." Two vampires dragged Adalius and laid him next to his companions.

"Well, well, all of my men here, in one place. So, you've joined together to destroy me, have you? "She looked down on Adalius. "That's going to be a bit more challenging now, isn't it, lover?"

# CHAPTER SIXTY

Kiel cursed creation for not giving them the cover of total darkness. On the other hand, vampires had such excellent vision that they would see them coming even if there were no light at all.

As they made their way toward the plant, adrenalin coursed through his veins. His senses sharpened. The need to run, chase, and kill was overwhelming. The wolf within burned to be let loose, to hunt; the lunar body shining above undoubtedly contributing to the increased feeling of aggression.

It was a common misconception that the moon brought about their change, as they could change at will. The moon only served to open the door to their more base instincts, hunt, feed, mate. The human side ruled the body unopposed throughout the month but during the full moon, the wolf staked its claim.

They'd passed a black Explorer parked on the side of the road along the way. After it searching it, a pair of armed staffers were left to guard the vehicle while the rest continued on. Kiel sensed the excitement of his squad. They were all invigorated. The hunt was mother's milk to a Lycan.

Over forty strong, they formed a perimeter around the plant while he led a dozen and a half of their number toward the plant entrance. Passing two steel doors laying in the crumbling parking lot, they readied their rifles.

Kiel clutched his M-14 as they reached the now wide open entrance. The scent of gun fire tainted the air. His chest tightened, insides quivering as he sensed the heightened tension of his Lycan. Pressing his back against the door jam, Kiel cautiously peeked into the corridor.

No gun fire.

Nodding to Cam, he silent counted to three. They moved, weapons at the ready through the opening. Crossing the threshold, they stepped into a long passage.

Carnage. Vamp dust, spent rounds, numerous swords and weapons littered the hall. There'd been a major battle. Heartbeats pounded in his ears like dueling percussions. Sweat trickled down his back. His breaths came out in puffs. Arriving at T-section in the hall, they looked in both directions.

Cam tapped his arm, pointing to the door at the end of the left corridor. It looked like it'd been kicked in. Motioning for the lead Lycan to take point, they crept down the hall. When they reached the damaged door, the point man, on his fingers, counted to three. Two stormed into the room. Five went in directly after. Moments passed.

"Clear."

Jax and Poke led the remaining team into the room followed by him and Cam. He took in the room furnishings as the crew spread out to cover the entrances and check behind doors.

Poke whistled. "I'll say one thing for the bitch, she got style."

Jax nodded. "Style and the luck of the fuckin' Irish. Looks like we may have just missed her, Kiel."

Kiel's expression soured. Removing his phone from the clip on his belt, he hit the speed dial.

"Father, we've arrived at the plant. She's gone. Looks like we're not the only ones hot on her heels though. We found a Ford Explorer about a half mile from here, rented out to a Myron Milford. From all the gear in the back, I'd say he's a slayer."

"Is der any sign of heem?"

"No, but from the looks of things, he may have walked into it. There's a boat load of spent rounds out in the corridor along with vamp dust and swords. If he went down, it wasn't without a battle. Have the Enforcers arrived yet?"

"Not at dis time. Dey vill arrive soon enough."

"Alright, keep me posted. In the meantime, we're gonna check out the rest of this hole, just to be sure."

"Be careful, my son. If Anna ees gone, make sure dey plant ees made unusable to her. It seems unlikely she'll return dere but best to make certain."

"Yes sir. We're moving out, I'll check in every ten minutes."

"Do that, I vill contact you dey moment de Enforcers arrive. Good hunting, my son."

Ending the call, Kiel clipped the phone to his belt. He was about to give the order to move when one of his Lycan approached. "The area is secure. One of the guys found this." The Lycan handed Kiel a cell phone.

Cam shook his head. "That's not a good sign."

Kiel grunted. "I don't think so either." Kiel hit the power button. There were ninety missed calls from someone named Maya. "Alright, let's start our sear..." The cell phone began to vibrate. No name on the caller ID, just a number. He hesitated, looking to Cam who shrugged. He answered it.

"Get out Thomas. The hag knows you're coming."

"Who is this?" Kiel responded, his brows drawing together.

"You're not Thomas, where is he?!"

"There's no one here, answer my question."

There was a brief pause. "You're that Kiel bloke, the owner of Club Détente."

"How do you..."

"If you have his phone that means...bloody hell. I will cut that bastard a new smile."

"Who... is this?"

"I work with the slayer, mate. And right now, I need to move fast if I'm to find him in one piece. Hang on to that phone. I'll be in touch."

"Who the *fuck*..."

"Call me Kyle. I'll contact you again when I find the sod who's going help us find Anna and Thomas. Till then." The line clicked.

Kiel's brows furrowed as he drew his .40 cal. "Alright, we're gonna search this place from top to bottom and if we don't find Anna, then we see to it she can't use this place as a base ever again. Teams of five and *nobody* is to go off on their own; I want updates every five minutes. Move." The Lycan formed teams as reinforcements arrived.

Cam gestured to the phone, "What about—"

"He said he'd get back to us. For now, we handle our end of things." He stared off into the distance.

"What are you thinking, Kiel?"

"I'm thinking Anna has to go down, for everything she's done."

Cam nodded. "She will, but first we gotta find her."

"I got a feeling that Kyle, whoever he is, isn't gonna rest until he finds who he's lookin' for. Apparently, he thinks that person will lead us to Anna. "Kiel stood waiting alongside Cam as additional reinforcements arrived. A showdown with Anna was drawing near. He was ready and he'd see to it his Lycan brothers were as well.

# CHAPTER SIXTY ONE

She was lost and had no idea how it happened. Okay, the window shopping probably had a lot to do with it, but she'd only gone a few stores. Alright, fine, it was a few blocks with a few turns here and there. And look what it got her, wandering around, alone downtown, at night, like a tourist. A lost, scared, robbable, tourist. Great.

The last guy she talked to said to walk three blocks this way, take a right, follow the sound of the jazz band, then walk a quarter something north, and dammit, she had no sense of direction. Which way was north? The smart thing to do would've been to ask, airhead.

The smell of sizzling steak and fried onion rings from a restaurant patio she passed, tickled her nostrils. A fresh reminder she hadn't eaten an issue to be remedied as soon as she found her way back to the hotel. The short hairs on her neck stood erect. Her eyes darted around. It felt like she was being watched. Sighing out a breath, she kept walking. Now, along with being tired, scared, and hungry, she was becoming paranoid.

Arriving at the curb, she stopped when the traffic light changed. She scanned about. Nothing looked familiar. Screw that guy and his directions, she was even more lost than ever.

Reaching into her purse, she retrieved her cell phone. She hit the button. The screen remained black. *Geez, forgot to charge it again.* As the light changed, she slipped it back into her purse and stepped off the curb. Her feet were killing her. Who knew how long she'd been walking. Every step she took seemed to lead further into nowhere. Pedestrian traffic had thinned out. She had no idea where she was and was trying hard not to let it show.

The click of her heels on the pavement echoed. There were less people and cars around to absorb the sound. The number of street lights dwindled. Tall buildings were replaced by run down brownstones and vacant lots. Her nose wrinkled at the pungent stench of burning refuse. Shadows darkened the streets and sidewalks.

"Wrong way, this is the wrong way. I don't remember any of this." Her respiratory system was moving into high gear. And though there was no else around, she couldn't shake the sense of being followed.

Stopping in her tracks looked about frustrated and frightened. Up ahead, a man approached from the opposite direction. Her skin crawled. Trusting her gut feeling, she immediately turned around. She picked up her pace. It seemed best to put some distance between her and that man.

"Yer seem lost, lass. Can oi be av some 'elp?" His breath was cold on her ear.

She jumped. Her heart did likewise. She whirled about. Impossible. Nothing human could've covered that much ground. She eyed the stranger. "No, I'm fine, thank you." She backed away. Turning, she bumped into him.

Though his smile was pleasant, she never felt more threatened. "Yer sure look loike yer cud use some 'elp ter me. Yer looking a bit lost."

"No, really, I'm...I'm fine. Excuse me please." She started off but the stranger stepped into her path, leering.

"Nonsense, me friend an' oi wouldn't dream av lettin' yer walk alone through this neighborhud. It jist isn't safe"

What friend?

"We couldn't 'av that."

She was startled by yet another male behind her. Looking from one to the other, she withdrew from the pair. "You're both very kind but really, I'm fine. I need to go now. Good night." She started off. Once again the first man blocked her path, his friend moved close behind her.

"We'll 'ear none of it. Tis not a 'assle at al' for us ter walk yer safely home."

He reached for her arm. Don't look into his eyes. Seizing his wrist, she hip tossed him to the ground then whirled about like a dragon whipping its tail and delivered a kick to the head of the other, knocking backward.

The first male's eyes blazed cherry red as he got to his feet. "Ye bleedin' tick!" He charged. His partner rose as she threw out her arm before her. The corners of her mouth lifted at the muffled thud. The vampire crumbled to dust. Clutching the silver dagger in her hand, she faced the second vamp.

"Holy Mother, a slayer!" Slapping her to the ground, he sped away and down an alley. Blood seeped into her mouth. The bastard split her lip. Now she was pissed. Rising to her feet, she lit after the fleeing vamp.

"Maya!" A voice called out from behind her.

Rounding the corner, she spotted the vamp. Gil's Winchester was inches from vamp nose. One neck biter bagged and tagged.

The old cowboy cocked the hammer on his rifle as she ran up, the glint in his eyes hard like steel. "I know what ya thinkin' son. You thinkin' he's a slayer but he's lookin' a little long in the tooth, so you bettin' my reflexes ain't up to specs and you right. They ain't what they used to be. But before ya do somethin' stupid, I'd take a gander at your right arm. Do it nice and easy like. "The vampire looked. There was a glowing red dot on his forearm. Slowly, the vamp returned his gaze to Gil. "Good, now that I got your attention, that red dot is just one of a dozen. The other eleven are trained on your noggin as I speak. Now, take a whiff of the barrel." The vampire sniffed. His eyes widened. "Yep, pure silver, got a friend with a mine up in Colorado. Now, you gonna play nice or is this gonna get messy?" He raised his hands in surrender. "Sound strategy. You alright, little girl?"

She responded by yanking the blood sucker around and dropping him with a sharp right cross. "*Now* I'm alright."

"Ouch, that's kinda hard on the knuckles. Bet it hurt as much as it looked."

"Bet it hurt him more." She displayed her hand, wiggling her fingers. On each was a silver ring. "Told ya if I played little lost kitten long enough, one of these puss bags would come and try to put the bite on me." Reaching into her purse, she withdrew a syringe, and injected the solution into the vamp's shoulder. The pussy cried out as the drugs flowed into his body. The syringe empty, she withdrew it then grabbed him by the jaw. "That's so you don't do something we'd have to dust you for."

The vampire wheezed and coughed. "Will ye be 'aving sumthin' from me?"

Maya looked into his eyes. "Answers blood sucker. Cooperate we might not stake yo ass but don't get ya hopes up."

Seth rushed up pulling her into a hug, his kiss tender. "Maya, you ok, baby?"

"I'm fine, Seth, really. I told you I would be."

Seth started toward the vampire. "Fuckin' leech, I saw what you did."

Maya caught him by the arm. "Not now, baby, we need some answers."

Seth nodded, drawing a large hunting knife from his belt. "You better tell us everything we want to know or I'm gonna skin you inch by inch."

She went to kneel at the vamp's side. "One of ours is missing, vamp. I'm bettin' you might know where he is."

Finn paused, a grin creasing his lips. "Missin' a slayer are ye? And what makes yer think oi'd be knowin' anythin' aboyt that?"

Maya jabbed the silver dagger into his shoulder. She twisted the blade. "You'd better, otherwise there's no reason not to dust yo ass." Maya began moving it in a sawing motion. The vamp screamed. "But I think you do know something. Now, once more, where is he?"

"Oi....Oi 'eard...aboyt a slayer. No, two slayers. One was killed, the other, Oi don't knew."

She grabbed his neck, twisting the dagger slowly. "I know that's not everything."

"So it tis, so it tis, Oi swear."

"Where is my slayer? What have you bastards done with him?" The dagger slid in deeper, the smell of burning flesh beginning to permeate the air.

"Alright! Alright, Oi 'eard they's been taken captive. Anna captured dem all."

"Where, blood sucker?"

"Oi don't bleedin' knew."

"Oh you know alright and you're gonna tell me. You're one of hers aren't you?"

"*No…*Oi'm not…Oi swear."

Maya looked over her shoulder at Seth. "Baby, get the kit from the truck. We'll test this piece a shit and see if he's telling the truth." She turned to the vampire. "If that test comes back positive and I find you been lying to me, baby, it is gonna get ugly."

"That won't be necessary, love." All eyes turn to the sound of the voice. Out of thin air Kyle appeared. "He is most certainly one of hers." Kyle cast his eyes to Finn. The Irishman's mouth fell open. "Oh yes, mate, I'm just a little cross with you." Kyle blurred snatching up the wounded vamp and held him aloft by his neck.

"Wait, Kyle, if you kill him, we may never find Trey."

"Not to worry, Maya. I wouldn't think of staking my pal here till he pukes up some intel. You'd love to do that for me, wouldn't you, mate?" Kyle closed his hand tighter around the vampire's neck. "In the meantime, why don't you all come with me, I know a few other chaps who would love to hear our song bird here sing."

"Oh no, this bastard is mine."

"And dibs are still yours, love. It's just, if we are gonna rescue Thomas, I have a feeling we're gonna need a lot of back up. Now if you please, let's get going. I can't wait to see if this sod is in good voice."

Maya hesitated. "Alright, you heard him, everybody to the truck. Gil, signal the others, looks like we're goin' to a vampire concert."

She walked over to Kyle. Glaring into Finn's eyes, she thrust the dagger slowly into his groin. "You better sing fuckin good. This better work, Kyle."

As Nessa pulled up, they piled into the pickup and let Kyle lead them to meet with other lovers of undead song birds.

# CHAPTER SIXTY TWO

Kiel angrily shoved a book off his desk. Where the hell was she? They'd tried every location in the area where Anna might hide, but their efforts had yielded nothing. His outburst, of course, did nothing to penetrate the concentration of his father. Unmoving like a Sphinx, Marseth continued his map study, while Cam sat twirling his pistol.

They'd poured over the city and were running out of ideas as to where else to look. Ulysses had taken a crew out, trying another method. So far, however, beating vampires to a pulp hadn't loosened any tongues. The vamps were simply too afraid of crossing Anna, even if noncompliance meant being staked.

The desk phone rang, breaking the silence. Marseth turned from his map scrutiny as Kiel picked up the receiver. "What do you got Ulysses?....Uh huh…No, the Enforcers haven't arrived yet…Uh huh…Ulysses, just spit it out....What…Hang on, I'm gonna put you on speaker." He hit the button. "Ok, say again what you just told me." Kiel sat forward in his chair.

"I said, word is the Vampire High Council is going to be holding a hearing to decide what to do about the growing number of, I shit you not, vampire drug cartels."

Cam blinked.

Kiel looked to his father.

Dumbfounded, Marseth shook his head. "I know nothing of dis."

The Lycan's voice rose once more from the speaker. "Not surprising. I doubt anyone who isn't a vampire knows about it. It seems there are no vampire laws against it but with the rise of these cartels, there's concern that war for territories could erupt and spill out into the immortal general pop. They're deciding whether to outlaw it all together."

Kiel's brow furrowed. "This ain't good. I can't see these vampires giving up what could be a very lucrative enterprise, whether the Council approves of it or not. If the VHC drops the hammer, things could turn nasty in a hurry." Kiel rubbed the bridge of his nose. "Is there reason to believe Anna is mixed up in this?"

Ulysses paused. "At the moment, I would say no but we underestimated her once."

"Point taken. Alright, follow that lead as far as it takes you and get back to me if you turn up anything."

"I'm on it." Ulysses hung up.

Cam holstered his pistol. "What the fuck, Kiel, now it's drug dealing vamps?"

"No shit." As if Anna wasn't bad enough. Kiel leaned back, massaging his temples. *Is Anna involved in this, somehow? What will the cartels do if the Council outlaws their little business venture? Could this drug dealing nonsense possibly touch off a vamp war? And if so, can his people and others avoid being drawn into it? Wolfs bane!* His headache was gaining weight by the second.

The office door burst open. Taine. "Kiel, we got company. Whole mess of vamp slayers just walked in the club and—"

"One side, puppy dog, let a lady through." A chocolate skinned woman with long braided hair, along with several individuals shoved past Taine.

He and Cam rose to their feet as the doorman opened his mouth to protest. "It's alright, Taine, I'll see them."

"You pushy bitch, you turn me on! "Taine grinned.

She rolled her eyes as the Lycan left the room closing the door behind him. The female, flanked by a male sporting his own braided hair, a Texas Ranger wannabe and a leather clad vampire with a hammer lock on another vampire, continued forward.

She eyed him carefully. "You're in charge here?"

His inner wolf growled. "You barged your way into *my* office, who are you?"

"I'm Maya." She gestured one by one to her companions. "The fine gentleman to my right is Seth, the handsome cowboy to my left is Gil, the leather trench wearing vamp is Kyle and the vamp he's holding is fucked if he don't tell us where to find Anna. And yes, we're vamp slayers."

"This is my club. I'm Kiel and this is Cam." He gestured to his friend.

She nodded to Marseth. "And the long haired hippie over there?"

The Texas Ranger nudged her in the back. "Mind yer manners, little girl. We're in the presence a royalty"

"What are you talking about, Gil?"

"I know I taught you betterin' that. How many Lycan do you count in this room?"

"Three."

"Uh huh, and how many albino Lycan with ocean blue eyes have you ever heard of?"

Her eyes widened. "Marseth. But...I thought you were just a legend."

Father actually smiled. "I assure you, my dear, you are not dey first to make such an assumption. Now, please tell us vhy you are here."

"Anna killed one of our own and is holding another and possibly others hostage. Kyle told us you were looking for her too. Maybe, if we pooled our resources, we can rescue them and end her for good."

It suddenly dawned on Kiel. "Wait a sec." He fished the cell phone they'd found from his pocket, pointing to the screen. "You're this Maya aren't you? And you, you're the Kyle I spoke to."

"That I am, mate."

Maya stared at the phone. He passed it to her. "This is Trey's phone, where did you get it?"

"We found it at one of the locations we searched looking for Anna. Unfortunately, it was the only thing we found."

Maya slipped the phone to Seth. "Kyle, if you please."

Kyle forced the vampire forward. "This sod is Finn, thief, liar, cad, and all around swine."

Cam rotated the chair he'd been sitting in a half turn, stepping aside as Kyle forced his captive into the seat. "Sit tight. But do try and make a break for it. Then I'd have an additional excuse to break your bloody limbs."

Kiel reached into his lower desk drawer, withdrew a black leather case and tossed it to Kyle. "Put those on him, they'll keep him stationary."

Kyle opened up the case. Silver hand cuffs and anklets. "Hello, look at these lovelies."

Kiel walked around his desk. "From time to time we get very unruly types who don't behave themselves. Silver does wonders as an attitude adjuster."

"I'll bet. If you don't mind, love, as much as it would thrill me to shackle our chum here, I seem to be somewhat allergic to silver myself, would you do the honors?"

"My pleasure." Maya removed the anklets from the case.

Kyle gave the vamp a dark look as Maya went to work. "If you so much as twitch, mate, I don't mind telling you that it would be a race to see which of us does you first."

Gil cocked his rifle. "I won't kill ya, son, I'll just put the bullet where you won't go all dust bunny on us."

Seth rested a hand on his blade, his glare arctic.

Maya slipped the anklets on. Finn flinched as the silver contacted his skin. Next, she placed the handcuffs snug on his wrists. The vamp groaned as the silver burned his flesh.

She smirked. "Hurts huh? Good."

Kiel leaned back against his desk. "So you think he knows where to find Anna?"

"Oh, he knows alright." Kyle grabbed a handful of the vampire's hair and yanked his head back. "You're gonna sing your pretty little head off or we'll carve you into bite sized nuggets and serve you up as hors d'oeuvres."

Cam leaned down. "Mmmm, my friends love fresh clipped meat."

Maya groaned, annoyance radiating from her pores. "We're wasting time. Is somebody gonna ask that bastard something pertinent or are we just gonna keep pussy footing around?"

"Right you are, love." Kyle cupped the vampire's chin in his hand. "Please, pretty please, tell us where to find Anna?"

362

The vampire glared back. "Go feck yourselves, all of yer. Oi'm not tellin' yer pot lickers anythin'." He spat.

Kyle growled through clenched teeth. "Oh I was *so* hoping you'd say that." His eyes ignited like a stove top as he clamped down on jaw bone. Finn screamed. Bowing off the chair, he babbled incoherently as Kyle bored through his mental shields.

With a mental yank, Finn's defenses gave way. The bloodsucker's earsplitting shriek was like nails on a chalk board. A slow grin spread across Kyle's lips. Pulling Finn's guts out with meat hooks wouldn't be as excruciating as what he was doing to him now. Finn wailed, clutching the chair arms. Twisting and convulsing, he pleaded as Kyle took hold of his head.

Kyle sensed swelling pressure. A psychic push back. Finn. The bloody bastard was fighting back. Good, now, there'd be no holding back. No remorse when he did this... the Irishman lurched with a howl, his eyes bulging in their sockets. Finn writhed in torture as his soul was ravaged. At last, he slumped in the chair with a slow exhale.

Blood ran from his nostrils, spittle dripped from his mouth. He'd been dragged into Hell. What remained had returned.

*****

Kiel recoiled. He'd allowed torture in his club. After he'd worked hard and long establishing the club's rep as a place where all could be assured of safety. Damn Anna, he'd compromised himself and all he worked for, because of her. When it was all said and done, her skull would take its place on his desk as an ashtray.

Kyle released Finn, his eyes returning to normal. The vampire's head dropped limply. "Sorry, mate but you don't get to die just yet." Kyle turned to Maya. "You wanted answers, love, here they are. Anna is holed up in a place called AJAX. It's her main nest in New Carrollton."

Cam shook his head. "Can't be, we tore that place apart. It's where we found your friend's phone. There's nothing there. Try again Kyle, he's gotta be lying."

"Not likely. I ripped every lie from his mind. Anna is at AJAX."

"No way man, it can't—"

"Hang on a sec, Cam." All eyes turned to Kiel.

"You hev a hunch my son?"

"I think I do. AJAX owned multiple businesses and properties in and around New Carrollton before it went belly up. We checked them all, except one." Kiel made his way over to the map. "The old AJAX Arena. I'd completely forgotten about it." Locating the arena, he circled it. "I have got to be the dumbass of the year. It's perfect, fifteen miles south of the city, abandoned for years. All that wooded area and no neighbors for miles. She could build an army out there and nobody would be the wiser."

Maya stepped forward. "Then that's where we go. Here's what we're gonna do."

Cam growled. "Who put you in charge?"

Maya met the Lycan's glare. "How many nest raids have you led, mutha fucka?"

Cam remained silent.

"That's what I thought. Anyone else?"

Marseth spoke up. "Very vell, ve vill defer to your experience."

Maya looked to the king and smiled. "Thank you, your highness."

"Of course, you remind me of my mate, head strong vith very sharp teeth."

"Ok, you're callin' the shots, little girl. How do we proceed?"

"We're gonna walk up to the front door and kick it in."

Kiel smiled. "I like this plan already."

# CHAPTER SIXTY THREE

**P**ain rushed up to greet him as he ascended from the depths of unconsciousness.

"He's coming to." A rich, accented, bass voice to his left. Kalleal.

"Are you alright, slayer?" said a smooth baritone voice from the right. Adalius.

Trey groaned as he opened his eyes. He found himself and his vamp partners hanging bare chested, by their arms, in what appeared to be an old arena. He blinked. The area, illuminated by a single light source, was apparently once a box seat section, with the seats removed. Opposite them, the lower bowl was fairly visible through a thin veil of grey shadow. Darkness completely obscured the upper levels, as if staking its claim. The only other light was provided by three other light fixtures suspended above the arena floor.

Trey swallowed. "What happened, where are we?" *Damn, his throat was as dry as the stale air in this place.*

Adalius tugged at the chains that held him. "We have been captured by Anna. I believe this to be her main nest."

Trey looked about. A hanging beer advertisement caught his eye. He licked his lips. What he'd give for one of those right now. "How long have I been out?"

Kalleal yanked at his chains. "I'd estimate you've been unconscious for approximately four hours."

Four hours and he hadn't checked in. That meant Maya and Kyle were looking for them. And explained why every muscle in his arms screamed bloody murder. "Where's Anna?" Trey asked.

"I haven't seen the treacherous harpy in all the time we've hung here." Kalleal growled.

"We will not have to wait much longer. She just touched my mind, she knows we are awake." Adalius gave his chains another tug.

"Good, I hate being kept waiting," Kalleal rumbled.

Below them, on the arena floor, a metal door click clacked open. Anna led a party which included a blonde, some Latino vamp, and that brunette bitch who killed Stosh, up a set of stairs to their right.

While the others moved off to each side, Anna came and stood before them. Looking them over one at a time, she placed her hands on her hips. "I'm glad to see you're all awake. No thanks needed for the blood we provided to heal your wounds. On the other hand, we did inflict them, so consider us even. Unfortunately for you, Trey, your body will have to heal itself. In the meantime, I hope you're not too uncomfortable."

Trey eyed her with contempt, his jaw clenched tight. "Well to be honest, my arms ache. How bout you let me down so I can rip out your heart?"

Anna simply smiled. "I can't tell you how grand it is to have my men all together. It's exhilarating having you all pursue me, makes a girl feel special."

Kalleal's lip curled into a snarl. "Enough, tell us why you've dragged us here?"

Anna's gaze travelled down Kalleal's body, from his muscular arms and chest, to his tight abs, down to the large bulge in his leather pants. She purred seductively. Striding up to him, she ran her hands over his chest. "You were always so impatient, my Kalleal, always wanting what you want, when you want it. For you, waiting was never an option. I especially loved that about you when you wanted me. Knowing that you would kill any male who dared come between us...oh wait, those feelings were for your wife, weren't they? Pity they didn't stop you from murdering her and your children."

Anna turned, moving on to Adalius as Kalleal roared in rage. "Adalius, my love, the greatest of all my children. I have never seen a vampire more vicious when it came to hunting and feeding." Her gaze became distant, her demeanor turning somber. "Together, we could've destroyed the High Council and their Enforcers." She ran a finger through his curls. "I would have laid at your feet as your queen." Fisting his hair with a yank, Anna's eyes flared. "It would've been glorious, but for that gypsy girl. Then, as if that foolish act weren't enough, you mate that…female."

Adalius gnashed his teeth. His eyes ignited then as suddenly, returned to normal. He blew out a frustrated breath.

Anna shook her head like a disappointed parent. "You think me a fool, Adalius? We didn't give you nearly enough blood for you to use your full abilities. Even if we had, those chains will hold even you."

She turned from Adalius, eyeing Trey. Moving toward him, she caressed his cheek. Trey jerked his head away from her cool touch. "*You,* my dear, Trey, are special in your own right. We are bound in a different way, you and I. I've tasted your blood…indirectly. I wonder if yours is as sweet as your daughter's."

He lashed out, swinging a kick, but Anna simply stepped aside.

"You should be proud, my Trey. She was brave, much like her father. Your mate was equally valiant. Were she vampire, she might have actually defeated me. You chose wisely. Yes, ours is a different bond. Unlike Adalius and Kalleal, you don't carry my blood inside you. I intend to remedy that this instant."

Trey's eyes widened as he realized her intent. "You stay the fuck away from me!"

Anna grasped his head in her hands, turning it to expose his jugular.

Kalleal twisted, trying to break free. "Release him, Anna. Let him go."

"Stand away from the mortal, Anna, now," Adalius roared.

She looked to Adalius. "You are in no position to issue orders, my love. Neither of you are. You are both mine and now Trey will be mine." Her incisors lengthened. Stretching open her mouth, she struck.

The sting heralded a wave of intense sensual pleasure. Anna slid an arm around his neck. She surged against him, snaking her leg behind his calf. He moaned, his shaft swelling as Anna worked her hips against him. His head spun as euphoric weakness overtook his limbs. His breathing became labored as Anna slid her arm around his waist, coiling around him.

She swallowed, her moans sensual as she fed from his vein. His heart hammered in his chest. Anna was stealing his life, but it didn't matter. Nothing mattered but her at his vein. *Yes, take it all. Please.* The fog of unconsciousness enveloped him, dragging him downward. He didn't

care. He was ready, ready to give himself to Anna, to death. She withdrew her fangs. It was sudden, like a slap. The pleasure was gone. His body sagged, up held only by the chains binding his wrists. *No, just a little longer?*

Anna licked her lips. "Come, Ricardo, hold open his mouth. "The Latino did as instructed. Tilting Trey's head back, Ricardo opened his mouth. Anna bit into her wrist. Blood flowed from the opened wound.

"Stop what you are doing Anna." Adalius' eyes sparkled.

She ignored his protest. Positioning her wrist over Trey's mouth, the blood trickled down, into his throat. His neck tingled. It and his other injuries were healing. His strength surged. And wait, that sound? Funny he hadn't noticed it before, a pounding, no, more like a thumping; heartbeats. He actually heard the beating hearts of Adalius and Kalleal, and even the blood surging through their veins.

Anna pulled her wrist away, her own wound closing. Her eyelids fell as she hugged herself. Licking her lips, she opened her eyes. Her irises glowed like twin stars. He looked upon her. She looked back. She sensed it in him. He saw it in her. Desire. Need. She was beautiful. Sexy. Aroused. She ran her hands over her hips, her breaths coming in gentle pants.

Conflicted emotions beset his mind and body. He wanted to cut out her heart. Yet a huge part of him burned to take her, to thrust fast and deep, to join with her in a dance ending in incandescent climax. *Damn Anna to hell, what did she do to him?*

The smile of the wicked creased her lips, her fangs peeking from beneath her lips. "Let it be known, these three, belong to me. Anyone who touches them without my permission will die. They are mine, mine to keep, and if I so choose, mine to kill.

# CHAPTER SIXTY FOUR

Maya took point as she led her crew and Jax through the wooded area toward their objective. Looking over her shoulder, she threw up a closed fist. Head to toe in black camo, they each took cover among the foliage.

Pride bloomed in her chest. Sons of bitches, she'd trained most of them herself. She knelt in the high grass as the faces of friends, slayers long since lost, rose from the mists of her memories. They were grim reminders that training, no matter how extensive, wasn't always enough.

Those damn slayer rules. Nothing could change them. No matter how hard they fought, many of these slayers had seen their last sunset.

She shook off the foreboding thoughts. Forcing back the angry tears welling in her eyes, Maya whipped out her night vision binoculars. The things were a gift from heaven. They turned darkest night bright as high noon. Scanning the area, she grunted, this place had seen better days. The faded parking lines and crumbling asphalt sang a sad song of neglect and abandonment.

Movement caught her eye. Several dozen yards to her left, a lone vamp trudged along on patrol. A shadow flashed across her vision. The blood sucker crumbled to dust.

Kyle.

Thanks to him, they'd taken down a number of Anna's sentinels, so far, before any of them sounded an alarm. Luckily, Anna didn't seem big on technology. None of the vamps had radios on them. But when you could communicate with a thought, why bother?

Maya unhooked her radio from her belt. "We're nearly at the arena and not so much as a dirty look. I'm impressed, Kyle. I see why Trey likes having you around."

"You're gonna make me blush, love. Think that's all of them but I'll keep…hello, two more hostiles at the front entrance."

Maya lifted her binoculars. She spotted them. Both were armed with assault rifles, chatting casually. "I see them. Stand by, Kyle." Maya waved to Nessa. She crawled forward cradling a high powered rifle equipped with a night scope and silencer. "You're up, Nessa."

Nessa smiled broadly as Maya pointed to the arena entrance. "It's about time, young lady. I thought you was gonna let your vamp friend have all the fun." She positioned the rifle and peered through the scope. Maya glanced once more through her binoculars.

"Think you could pick one 'em off?"

"Shoot, from here, I could take the tips of his fangs off. All I need is the go ahead."

"Take the one on the left. Leave the other to Kyle."

"Anythin' you say darlin'."

While Nessa locked and loaded, Maya spoke into her radio. "Nessa's got the one on the left, Kyle. Wait for the signal and the other is yours."

"Jolly good, moving into position."

Maya scanned the vampire guards as they laughed and chatted. "On my mark, Kyle, stand by." She looked to Nessa. "You got him?"

Nessa took aim with her rifle. "Yes, ma'am, I do."

"Take em." Maya spoke into her radio. "Now, Kyle."

Nessa fired. The vampire's head exploded into a dust cloud, his body collapsed directly after. His counterpart, followed suit, his head dropping from his neck, courtesy of Kyle's blade. Touching down, Kyle gathered up the rifles.

Maya waved her team onward. The slayers and Jax dashed out of the brush, across the parking lot toward Ajax Arena. The amphitheater sat atop a pedestal like granite staircase. Even in its run down state, it was an impressive facility. It must have been a source of civic pride, once upon a time.

Ascending the stairs, they assembled in the entrance way. Kyle passed her one of the rifles, removed the magazine from the other, and laid it against the building. "That's all of them, love. So far, I've managed to keep them from detecting us, now what?"

Maya hung the rifle on her shoulder by the strap. "We go in through this entrance, find Trey, and kill that bitch," she said reaching for, then taking the safety off her crossbow.

"Sounds lovely, ladies first?"

She rolled her eyes. "What a man."

They moved toward the boarded up doors when she noticed Jax moving away from the group. "The rest of you, wait here. We'll join you shortly." Maya walked around the side of the arena to find the Lycan undressing. "Hey, wolf boy. What are you doin'?"

Jax turned. "When the shooting starts, I want to start snapping and biting, not stripping."

She let her eyes roam over his powerfully built chest. "Still no word from your boss, sure hope he can be relied on, Jax."

"Kiel will be where he said he'd be, when he said he'd be. Relax, slayer. Now, if you don't mind, a little privacy."

She moved not an inch. No way she was missing this striptease.

Seth came up, took her by the hand, and led her away. "Let's give the nice Lycan some space, shall we?"

Maya slid her arm around his waist, kissing his cheek as they went to join the others. "Jealous?"

"Bet your round ass. Now, when this is over, I gotta do all kind of freaky bondage shit to you. Looks like you need a reminder of who you belong to."

Maya grinned wickedly. "Ohh, I *love* it when you get jealous."

As she and Seth joined their team, Kyle reached for a board. "Alright, you chaps might want to stand clear and give a bloke room to work." The slayers stood aside. Grabbing hold of the plywood, he yanked. The door opened easily.

Kyle blinked. "Well that's convenient. Easy access, love, shall we?"

"As soon as Jax joins us, we move." As if on cue, the Lycan rounded the corner.

Her breath caught in her throat. Easily one of the largest Lycan she'd ever seen, his thick, black coat glistened with a wet-like sheen. Maya backed away at his approach. Enormous and powerfully built with claws like razors, Jax stalked toward them. His muscles rippled under his skin. He was a predator, capable of killing quickly and efficiently.

Maya swallowed and gathered herself. "Alright, we're going in. Let's go get Trey and dust these blood suckers. For Stosh." There was a chorus of muffled acknowledgement and gun bolts being pulled back. Maya loaded her crossbow, nodding to Kyle. They were ready. Kyle held open the arena door, and one by one, they filed into the belly of the beast.

# CHAPTER SIXTY FIVE

Adalius focused on summoning his strength. Trey recovered from the attack as Kalleal scowled.

Anna stood hands on her hips, mocking them with her smile. "I've provided some entertainment for you." Anna double clapped her hands and the arena door, below, clacked open. A multitude of vampires, at least a hundred in all, paraded in, taking their seats in the sections around them.

Adalius' brows drew together. "How have you kept them fed?"

Anna sauntered up to him, stroking his cheek. "Do you really believe I'm the only one tired of King Vaughn's foolish vision of peaceful co-existence with humans? Blood donations arrive daily from across the country. There are those who long for the change I intend to provide." She gripped his jaw. "And provide it, I shall."

Adalius' eyes sparkled. "You and your sympathizers will be hunted down and destroyed. I intend to start with you."

"Yes, yes, yes, you are bound to avenge your mate. I'm well aware." Anna turned about. "For now, bring her!"

The vampire crowd cheered wildly as Anna stepped aside, allowing them a view the arena floor below.

As the crowd roared, Trey groaned. His heartbeat was strong and steady, thank the Elder. Trey turned to him. "Adalius, tell me you didn't let that bitch turn me."

"Be at ease, slayer. You did not ingest enough to be turned, but she managed to bind you to her through the blood you exchanged. There are benefits. For a short time, you will have enhanced strength and will be able to sense her as she now will be able to sense you."

Out of the door beneath them, the Sandrian miscreant who attacked Kalleal, led a human woman in chains and two more of Anna's brood out to the center arena floor. The woman, covered in bruises, had been stripped down to her under garments. There were bite marks on her neck and legs. They had been torturing her.

Despite her swollen cheek and split lip, hair dirty and tangled, she held her head high, her demeanor, defiant. She was shoved from behind to herd her forward. Trey looked from the shackled woman back to Anna. Kalleal glared, his fangs extending below his lip. Adalius simply watched.

He needed to concentrate.

"I know what you're thinking, my love. Relax. Enjoy what I've prepared for you," Anna said, still facing the arena floor.

"What are you planning to do to her?"

Anna ignored his questions and addressed the entire audience. "Behold the slayer, Tia Johnston. She and her former partner have been a bothersome thorn in my side for far too long. Her partner has paid for his sins, now its little Tia's turn."

"Fuck you, Anna," Tia spat.

Anna clicked her tongue. "Very unbecoming a lady don't you think, Kalleal?"

Kalleal's growl rumbled in his chest.

"Let's see if we can silence that insolent tongue, shall we? Let the entertainment commence."

The two vampire guards took their place at the door below out of sight. The Sandrian bowed to Anna and met Kalleal's glare in challenge. In a blur of motion he back handed Tia. The slayer went airborne, landing violently to the ground. The crowd roared approval. Tia barely came to rest before the Sandrian was upon her again, driving his fists into her body and face. The battered slayer covered her head, as the assailant landed a blow after blow. She lay unmoving.

The Sandrian threw up his arms to the roaring crowd. As he turned, Tia drove the heel of her foot into his groin. The vampire folded. Tia sprang to her feet. Going low, she leg swept the Sandrian. He went down, hard.

The crowd groaned, booing as Tia rose to her feet and went on the offensive. While the slayer fought for her life, Anna turned to her captives. "I do hope you're all enjoying the entertainment."

Trey trembled incensed. "I will kill you even if I have to die myself!"

Adalius immediately chimed in. "Indeed, there is no price too high to see you ended."

Kalleal yanked at his chains. "They speak for me as well vile harridan."

Anna clicked her tongue. "You don't find my show enjoyable? After I've gone to such great lengths?"

The crowd's roar drew their attention back to the arena floor. The Sandrian had wrestled the slayer to the ground, his weight pinning her down. A head butt dazed the struggling Tia. Grabbing hold of her hair, vampire fired his fist repeatedly into her face. Tia went limp. The crowd went wild. The Sandrian rolled the beaten slayer onto her belly, grabbed her by the hair and drove her face into the arena floor. Adalius recoiled.

The vampire stood over the slayer, sneering. Reaching for his pants, he unfastened them. They fell revealing a raging hard on. The combat had been but foreplay. Adalius feared what would come next. The applause was thunderous. The vampire looked to Kalleal in challenge as he knelt down ripping away her panties.

Kalleal eyes blazed like golden fire, his fangs extended to attack length. "I warn thee, touch the female and with my last breath…"

The Sandrian smirked. Straddling her body, the vampire went down on his knees.

"Don't you do it, mutha fucka," Trey yelled, pulling at his bindings.

Adalius' muscles swelled as he frantically struggled but the chains held him fast.

With an arch of his back, he pushed into her, glaring at Kalleal, while the crowd cheered wildly.

The monster ravaged the unconscious slayer, his eyes never blinked as he stared at Kalleal. With a final thrust the vampire threw back his head, roaring to the rafters. His chest heaving, perversion complete, he rose to one knee. Grasping the slayer by the head, a wicked smile spread across his lips. He took hold of her head.

"*No!*" Kalleal thundered.

Snap. Dead.

The crowd's roar was deafening.

Anna applauded.

"You are dead, mutha fucka," Trey yelled.

The vampire rose to his feet and spat on the slayer as he was serenaded by the hoots and whistles. He smiled to his mistress. Anna blew him a kiss.

The murderer raised his arms triumphantly above his head. His body pitched. The crowd went silent. The vampire staggered. He cast his eyes to the arrowhead protruding from his chest. His rictus grimace crumbled away as his body collapsed to dust.

Silence.

They focused on the shadows. A female with crossbow in hand, faded in from the blackness, followed by the silhouettes of others behind her.

Anna bristled. Slayers.

The female slayer gestured to Tia. "See to her."

One of their numbers checked on the prone slayer, searching for a pulse. He shook his head.

"Maya," Anna said, with a cool edge.

Maya stepped forward. "I'm here for mine, bitch. Let him go...now."

"Where's Lincoln? You were inseparable as I recall." Adalius sensed Anna reach out to Maya's mind. "I see, done in by cancer." Anna shook her head bitterly. "I should have been the death of Lincoln Thomas not some ridiculous disease."

Maya ignored Anna when she spotted Trey. "Trey, are you alright?"

"Get me down so I can kill these mutha fuckas!"

"It'll be just a sec. We got a *lot* of dusting to do first."

Anna laughed out loud. "You can't believe you're simply going to waltz into my lair, kill me and my children then skip your way out."

"Actually, yes I did. Why, is this a bad time?"

"Not at all, in fact, you're just in time for dinner."

"I hope there's enough to go round." All eyes turned to the new voice. The vampires around them rose to their feet. On the second level walkway stood Kiel flanked by Poke and Cam.

"Kiel. Did you enjoy the little gift I sent you?" Anna's smile was malicious.

"In a moment, I'm going to personally show you how much it was appreciated."

"You're angry with me, I'm hurt," she said with a pout.

"Not yet, Anna but I *promise*, you'll hurt plenty before I let you die."

"We're gonna put yo crazy ass to sleep, you sick bitch!" Maya called out her anger on the rise.

Anna shook her head, her smile dipping not in the slightest. "You actually think you can stop me with a hand full of slayers and four Lycan?"

Kiel growled. "Oh we're not alone Anna, not by a long shot." Kiel raised his phone to his lips. "Hit the lights, Taine." All at once the entire arena was bathed in illumination

Anna looked about. Lycan, a hundred strong, stood lining the second level walkway. She and her children were surrounded.

"Nowhere to run this time, sweetheart, you're gonna die for what you did to my sister," Cam said his hands curling into fists.

Anna's smile was satanic. "What makes you believe running is what I had in mind? You're all so predictable. Do you truly believe your pathetic efforts to locate me is what led you here? You're here because I wanted you to be. My children's full abilities cannot mature without the blood of immortals. I need Lycan and plenty of them. So instead of hunting you one at a time, I lured a host of you to my nest. The fall of the Lycan begins with you."

Cam ripped his shirt off and flung it angrily to the deck. "Then let's go, bitch, you and your little blood babies are gonna find us hard to digest, the odds are even!"

Anna's eyes blazed brightly. "Are they?" Anna tilted head, looking skyward. Everyone followed her gaze to the arena rafters. Elder's beard. There were hundreds of them, eyes ablaze, fangs extended. Anna's nightmare brood and they were hungry!

# CHAPTER SIXTY SIX

"**M**adre de Dios!" exclaimed a voice from over her shoulder. Maya swallowed back the lump climbing up her throat as the mass of vampires looked down on them. Curses, in three languages flew out in all directions. She couldn't blame them. In all of her years, she'd never seen so many together in one place.

Gil leaned in close. "Does the Alamo mean anything to you?" Gil's down home way of saying they were fucked.

She laid down her crossbow and reached for her assault rifle. "Steady, weapons at the ready. Fire only when I give the word."

Jax growled, his muscles coiling.

Anna broke the silence. "You all believed I was moving from place to place, trying to evade pursuit. In actuality, I was playing the part of a snowball rolling downhill. Turn a child here, two over there until....well, you can see for yourselves. No more talk." Anna looked to her brood, throwing up her arms like a toddler reaching for its parents. "*Feed, my children. They are my gift to you!*"

At once the vampires launched themselves into the air. Maya raised her rifle as the cloud of the undead descended. "Light em up!" Hot silver streaked out as the blood suckers swooped in. Lycan and slayer alike were taken to the ground.

Gil fired his rifle this way and that with laser precision, while Nessa protected his rear. Jax tore flesh and snapped bone, vamp remains covered him from head to toe. Maya fired staccato bursts turning vampires to dusty memories.

She'd lost track of Kyle in the initial wave of vampires. The last time she saw him, he had waded into the advancing horde with sword flashing.

A large vampire dropped from the air. Fangs extended, it charged. She pointed and squeezed. The empty weapon clicked. *"Shit!"* She reached for her sidearm and took a vampire in the chest for her trouble.

*****

Anna looked on with satisfaction. She'd lost many of her children but it was to be expected. They were learning to kill, to survive. They would need this experience for the upcoming conflict.

"Mistress?"

Anna looked to Trish and Marie who stood arm in arm. Trish looked at her quizzically. Anna nodded. "Yes, of course my daughters, go, find nourishment. Become strong." She looked to Ricardo. "You may also indulge yourself, dear Ricardo." They beamed as they took to the air.

Anna took in a breath. The smell of blood was irresistible. She needed sustenance as well. Anna turned to the remaining vampire. "Keep watch on them. After I've fed, and returned, you may go."

The vampire bowed low. "Yes, my mistress."

Anna propelled herself to the carnage below.

*****

Trey struggled against his binds, but found no give. "We gotta do something. They're being slaughtered."

"I'm open to suggestion, slayer." Kalleal tugged. The chains held fast.

The vamp guard groaned, went rigid, then crumbled around a sword blade. Out of nothingness, Kyle appeared, dust covered sword in one hand, a dagger in the other. "I have one. "He stooped down and fished a key from the vampire remains, stood and held it out before him. "How bout I unlock your shackles and set you chaps free."

"It's about time you showed yo ass up."

"Bloody good to see you too, Thomas," Kyle hurriedly unlocked Kalleal's chains. Once the Sandrian was free, he went to work on Trey's then Adalius' chains.

"Much thanks, Kyle." Adalius massaged his wrists.

"Save the thanks for later, mate, for now, I have something for each of you." Kyle removed the extra swords that hung from his shoulders and passed one to each. Adalius and Kalleal regarded the swords like they had been reunited with an old friend.

Adalius drew his blade from its sheath. "Take Kyle and assist Kiel, my brother. Come with me, Trey Thomas."

Without debate, they charged toward the second level to join Kiel. Adalius leaped over the rail before him followed closely by Trey. Adalius looked about, then roared. "Your time has arrived, death has come for you all!"

\*\*\*\*\*

Maya struggled as the demon tugged at her head, trying to expose her jugular. She was pinned and outclassed. The vamp's first punch she deflected, but the next connected, driving her head a half turn. Dazed, she tugged at the .45 pinned beneath her thigh. With a yank, she pulled it free. She raised it. The vampire slapped the gun from her hand. His laughter stung her ears as his eyes took on a yellow hue. "No ya don't, now lie still, this won't take long." The vampire forced her head sideways and stretched opened his mouth.

Maya cried out.

As the vampire launched toward her neck, the monster's weight was yanked from her body. She heard the vamp scream then bones break and trachea crunch. She sat up. There was a Lycan atop the vampire ripping away chunks of flesh. Not Jax.

This one was smaller than but no less ferocious as he attacked the blood sucker. When the vampire turned to dust, the Lycan looked back and….did he just wink at her?

Taine. That little Lycan doorman from the club, it had to be him. Maya grabbed her pistol and shot an advancing vampire. Taine and Jax took position on her flanks. As she got to her feet, Ulysses arrived. Together they fought tooth and nail as waves of vampires closed in.

*****

Gil fired his last round. The vampire exploded into dust as he dropped to his knees to reload. Nessa covered him. "I'm almost out, honey, you?"

Nessa fired another burst from her rifle. "Two mags left, baby, we can't keep this up much longer." She fired another burst. Two more fangs dusted.

He drew his hunting knife and launched it into the heart of another. Loading the last bullet, he snapped the tumbler into place as Nessa was tackled to the ground. Gil took aim. Nessa knew what he had in mind. She kneed the vampire in the groin causing him to rear his head. Good girl. He pulled the trigger. Nessa covered her face as vamp dust rained down. He pulled the Mrs. to her feet.

"Thank you, baby, I didn't see him until it was too...*Gil*!" Wide eyed, she shoved him aside. The blade meant for his back lodged in her chest. He rolled onto his side and fired a shot. The slug pierced the vampire's heart reducing him to dust. He turned to his wife. The hunting knife was hilt deep in her chest.

"Nessa!" He threw himself by her side. God o'mighty, so much blood. It poured from the wound. Tears stung his eyes. She wasn't gonna make it. His voice broke as he looked into her eyes. "Fool woman, what were you thinking?"

Nessa looked lovingly into his eyes. "I was...protectin'...what's mine." Her eyes rolled back, her last breath expelled in a bloody gurgle.

" *Nessa!*"

"Awwww, did we kill your little country bit..." The vampire's head exploded to dust before he finished. Gil's Colt smoked at the barrel. He ran a finger through his beloved's hair. "Wait for me, baby, I'll be with you soon." Gil gently lowered Nessa down and rose to his feet. He drew his remaining revolver from its holster and fired. One blood sucker after another, crumbled as he unleashed his bullets. His grief. His hate.

A blood sucker armed with a battle axe charged. Gil used his last bullet to dust him. The heavy axe landed at his feet with a loud clang. He dropped his empty pistols. Clutching the axe, he removed his hat and tossed it aside. He heaved a heavy sob. Nessa. Nessa was gone. Fuck living. Hell awaited and tonight, he was its usher. He was shovin' all these sons of bitches in, and when he was finished, he'd put a bullet in his own head.

# CHAPTER SIXTY SEVEN

Centuries ago Anna nicknamed Adalius 'Death'. And death he was as he dealt it to one vampire after another. He and Trey had gotten separated in the battle. Now, he stood alone as the bloodthirsty horde tried to end his rampage.

Adalius deflected the blade meant for his heart, whirled and parried a strike from a second attacker. Leaping into the air, he somersaulted over his opponent. As the vampire turned, Adalius lunged and drove his sword into neck muscle, withdrew the blade then severed the attacker's head.

As the vampire crumbled to dust, Adalius launched a dagger into the eye of the other. Reaching for the blade, the vampire cried out. Before he dislodged it, Adalius blurred. Swinging his sword in a downward arch, he sliced through from shoulder socket to waist. Blood flowed from the wound as the vampire's upper body slowly slid apart and disintegrated to dust.

Adalius twirled his sword as a new adversary, stepped into his path. This one, a head taller, had him by at least forty pounds. Taking in the newcomer's scent, Adalius' nostrils flared. This one was a ghoul. The biggest he had ever seen.

The ghoul moved in cautiously. Adalius readied himself for attack. The giant lunged, swinging his blade. Adalius deflected the blow. His eyes igniting, Adalius let loose with a series of counter strikes, forcing the ghoul into a back pedal.

Adalius bared his fangs. "What have you to do with this madness, ghoul?"

The ghoul growled. "The humans are our food. Our king, like yours, would have us work with them, play with them. I'm not one to play with my food." The ghoul lashed out once more.

The rapid clang of blades rang out. The ghoul disengaged his attack, nodding with approval. "You're as an accomplished a warrior as I've heard, Sandrian. Even among my people, your name is spoken of in hushed tones. I'll be exalted when I slay you."

Adalius' gaze hardened. "Better than you have tried, ghoul."

The ghoul charged, sword overhead. The creature swung. Adalius deflected the blade upward, whirled and slashed open the soft flesh of the ghoul's belly. Green mucus erupted from the wound. The brute fell to his knees, holding back his innards.

"Thy end has arrived. Death has come for you!" He swung. The severed head toppled as the dead husk fell to the floor. The ghoul dispatched, Adalius turned. He paused. His next opponent awaited him.

Anna.

Adalius's eyes glowed teal. "It is over, Anna. It all ends here."

"Only for you, my love," Anna's eyes ignited.

Adalius assumed a defensive stance. Anna raised her sword. He stopped when he heard it, a high pitched whistle. A sound that had haunted many soldiers on the field of battle.

All around, the combatants disengaged, looking about as the whine grew louder.

Maya lowered her weapon. "*In coming!*"

Slayers, vampires, and Lycan scrambled at the sound of collapsing steel. A portion of the ceiling came crashing down.

A fiery projectile slammed into the arena floor throwing dirt, and debris into the air. He and Anna were thrown from their feet. The dust cloud was thick, visibility was nil. Only few of the overhead lights still functioned.

Within the swirling dust, an obscure figure could briefly be made out then was swallowed once more from view. The cloud spun faster, shrinking in size. At last twin blue white pinpoints of light cut through the haze.

Eyes, eyes cracked with electrical energy. As Adalius rose to his feet, two figures emerged from the swirl. One of them held out an open hand, lifting it like a minister calling for his congregation to stand. The spinning dust rose in a funnel, up and out of the gaping hole left in the ceiling above.

Now, an enormous snow white Lycan with ocean blue eyes, stood next to a golden blonde male, sporting a Van Dyke beard, leather jacket and spiked gloves. Argus, The First, lowered his hand and drew his sword as Marseth looked about, drew in a long breath and roared.

# CHAPTER SIXTY EIGHT

The power of Marseth's voice reverberated in Anna's chest. Her blood jelled. This was totally unexpected. The Council hadn't sent *an* Enforcer, they'd sent *the* Enforcer. Argus, the First, head of the Enforcers League had arrived.

Anna called out to her brood. "It's Argus and Marseth. Kill them!"

The battle resumed.

Argus blurred from one vampire to the next. With his passing, heads tumbled from shoulders, bodies crumbled to dust. Marseth ripped flesh and crushed bone in his jaws as he tore into her children. Many fell like toys to the raw speed and power of the Lycan King.

She noted Adalius still lay stunned. Hit by debris from the impact, he had yet to recover. She saw opportunity. When it knocked, one should never hesitate. "First I'll kill *you*, my love, then your beloved brother and the slayer." She stalked toward Adalius. Fangs extended, eyes blazing, she raised her blade. She swung.

CLANG!

It was deflected by a sword wielded by Kiel. "As much as I'd enjoy seeing Adalius get his, we have unfinished business."

Rage exploded in her head. *That son of a jackal.* "Damn you, Kiel, *no one* gets between me and my true love." Anna charged swinging her blade like a thing possessed. Kiel fought back but she read his thoughts. Her speed and ferocity caught him by surprised. Kiel deflected her back swing. On her periphery a shadow closed in.

Argus.

As The First's eyes ignited, he was tackled to the ground by one of her children. Another joined its counterpart then another and another. "Flee, mistress, we will cover your escape."

The tide of the battle turned because of Argus and Marseth. The day was lost. They had to withdraw. Anna threw out her arm. Kiel was knocked off his feet. She called to her brood. "Escape, my children. Fly away." Anna blurred down a darkened corridor. The battle was lost, but, the war...

\*\*\*\*\*

Marie was lost in the arena corridors. During the battle, she'd gotten separated from Trish. Now, she probed for her mate while searching for a way out. At last, she came across an emergency exit. Marie paused. Trish. She sensed her. Her mate was coming.

Marie blew out a relieved breath. She went to the steel door as the click of Trish's heels grew louder. With a shove, she threw open the door.

BLAM! A shotgun blast.

Marie screamed, pressing her hands to her middle as she was thrown to the floor. Her insides burned. Silver, she'd been shot with silver.

A huge shadow lumbered into the doorway. It cocked a new shell onto the chamber. "Hiya, sunshine, remember me? Cause I *damn* sure remember *you*." Stosh glared down. Marie shook her head. It couldn't be. She'd killed him. Why wasn't he dead?

\*\*\*\*\*

Trish heard the shot. Terror coaxed more speed from her legs as she heard Marie's cry. When she arrived, she found Marie in a large pool of her own blood. A huge mortal loomed over her with a shotgun. Trish screamed in spite of herself.

The human mocked her with a falsetto scream. "Awwww, is she your squeeze? Well, come to papa bear and I'll see to it you two bitches are together forever and ever."

Trish threw out her hand but the slayer remained standing. He laughed at her surprised expression. "You not thinking fast enough darlin'. I figured one of you would try that. It's why I picked up a little somethin' that's gonna keep me from being tossed around by your mojo." He leveled his shotgun at Trish. "Now, where were we?"

Trish blurred and tackled the slayer to the ground. Before he could recover, she got to her feet dashed to Marie and scooped her up into her arms. Marie cried out painfully as Trish lifted her up.

The human sat up. Trish flashed her fangs and flew through the open doorway, into the night.

*****

Stosh got to his feet, shotgun still in hand and rushed to the door. He spotted the pair just as they cleared the treetops. "Y'all come back now, ya hear." He turned and headed deeper into the arena. There were bound to be more of those blood suckers in there. A slayer's work was never done.

# CHAPTER SIXTY NINE

nna crashed over a table, dropping her sword. She'd run into a pair of Lycan prowling the corridors. They'd surprised her with the suddenness of their attack. Were she a mere vampire, her continued existence would've come into question, but she was the Destroyer.

She sprang to her feet. As the first Lycan leaped, she threw out her hand. The beast froze in midair. She visualized the Lycan's windpipe imploding, its neck breaking. She heard the crunch. The sound of caving cartilage and neck bones snapping. The Lycan's eyes bulged. She released her hold. The werewolf fell dead. It didn't discourage the other; the Lycan closed in, snarling and snapping.

She smiled. "Come, little Lycan. Come embrace your death."

The beast obliged. Roaring, it charged. Anna's fangs extended. Her smile savage, she ran to meet its advance. They collided, falling to the floor. She locked her legs around the Lycan. Grabbing hold she sank her fangs into its flesh. The creature yelped. They thrashed about. The creature cried out again and again as Anna tore away chunks of flesh. She struck vein as razor claws scored deep wounds in her back. She laughed. Sinking her fangs in, she drank greedily.

The Lycan's claws gouged her back, tearing her open, but her injuries closed with every gulp of the beast's blood. The Lycan became sluggish. Anna tightened her hold, drawing the werewolf against her. The Lycan exhaled then lay still. Good and dead. With a last gulp, she released it. Standing, she looked down on its body, licking her lips. "Your generous donation was greatly appreciated." She removed her tattered blouse. Her bra fell to the floor.

Stepping over the Lycan, blurred down the corridor, she'd prepared for this possibility. The locker room, once used by New Carrollton's professional basketball team, was her way out.

The floor tiles were cool as she stepped inside. She'd lost her heels during the battle on the arena floor. They were her favorite pumps. She could slaughter them for that alone. She rounded the corner past what was left of the urinal stalls, into the section holding the team lockers. Amazingly, many were still intact. The emergency exit was just ahead. She reached for the door handle.

"You're not thinking of leaving before we've finished our dance, are you?"

Anna whirled about. Kiel, with sword in hand stood there.

Her eyes sparkled. "You challenge me, alone? I'll send your drained corpse to your father."

Kiel sneered. "Paytor was my friend, Miguel, a father to be, and you murdered them both. You're gonna pay for them, and every life you've taken."

Anna's eyes glowed white. She threw out her hand. Kiel went rigid, his sword drifted from his hand into hers. His arms pinned to his side, she mentally lifted him off the floor. He hung suspended. "You threaten one you should be on your knees worshipping?" She closed her hand into a fist. Kiel groaned as the unseen force constricted around him.

He fought to take in air. She didn't allow it. Like a python, she kept his chest from expanding. "Your abilities are infantile." She gripped the sword handle. His shirt buttons popped off as she flicked them away with the sword tip. She pulled open his shirt, and dragged the blade down his chest. "I'm going carve you open and pull out your organs, one at a time." She concentrated, increasing the pressure. Kiel groaned his remaining breath. She squeezed tighter. His ribs creaked. Kiel's eyes bulged. Anna continued to squeeze. She wanted to see them pop from their sockets. Kiel slumped, as he blacked out.

"Anna, release him."

Adalius.

She swept her arm across her body. Kiel flew across the room, hit a set of lockers, and lay unmoving. Adalius leveled his sword. Making his way toward the prone Kiel, he checked the Lycan's pulse. The vampire's relieved expression revealed Kiel's condition.

"He's alive. Pity, I *so* wanted him dead."

Adalius stalked toward her. "It is just between us now, Anna."

"It's always been between us, Adalius." She charged, her sword raised above her head. Adalius blocked her strike. He countered, his blade aiming for her right flank. She deflected the blow then delivered a strike. Adalius barely got his sword up in time.

They circled each other, looking, waiting for an opening. She threw out her hand, Adalius extended his. He blocked her attempt to grasp him! Adalius had become formidable. Her lip curled. "Impressive, you're no longer the precocious child I remember." She lashed out, swinging the sword across her body. Adalius ducked. The blade smashed wall tile, sending dust and shattered tile flying. She threw a side kick, when he touched down, catching him in the chest. It threw him off balance. She swung for his throat. He blocked it. Anna lanced at his sternum. He deflected it once. Twice. Thrice.

Her anger rising, she swung at his shoulder. He moved aside. The sword sliced into the metal lockers, leaving a jagged gash. This time, however, she anticipated his maneuver. She whirled, delivering a roundhouse kick. It caught him at the temple. It spun Adalius around. She lunged. Adalius grabbed her wrist and drove his sword into her abdomen. Agonizing pain took her as blood rush up her esophagus. The sword slipped from her hand, clattering to the floor.

Adalius' eyes sparkled, a satisfied grin flowed across his lips. He was too skilled to have missed her heart. No, he wanted to savor her suffering. Adalius released her wrist and slid his arm around her waist. Looking into her eyes, he caressed her back. His teeth clenched, Adalius forced the sword slowly into her body.

She groaned. Her body folded in his arms. With a grunt, he shoved the sword deeper. The feeling in her legs departed. The sword had severed her spine. Blood flowed from her mouth. Adalius lowered her to the floor, yanking the sword free.

A tingle danced over her body, the energy of her power. It wiped away the pain of her wounds. Feeling began returning to her legs. She wiggled a toe, then two, then three. Feeling returned to her arms, then her hands.

Adalius gripped her cheeks. "I am going to rip you apart. Slowly. When I've finished, I am going to devour your heart, as you did Esmeralda's."

Her eyes burst alight. "Oh, I think *not*, my love." She threw out her hand. Adalius went sailing, his sword falling from his hand. He came crashing down to next to the unconscious Kiel.

Her wounds nearly healed, she rose and stood above Adalius. She reached for Kiel's sword. It came to her like a faithful pet.

Adalius' brows arched.

She raised her blade, eyes blazing. "And so it ends. I will always love you, Adalius." She swung. Adalius reached for his sword. It sprang to his hand. She smirked. Way too slow.

*****

Adalius reached for his blade. It leaped to his hand. Too late, no time to deflect Anna's strike. Anna tensed, muscles coiled to strike. A shot rang out. Anna's hand exploded. The sword clattered to the floor. She staggered away screaming, shaking her arm. Blood sprayed from her wrist.

An enormous human rushed to his side, pulling him to his feet. "Name's Stosh, son. You alright?"

"I am Adalius. Further introductions should wait."

"Agreed, we gotta finish her while we…"

Anna's laugh echoed with power unlike he'd ever heard. She turned and stretched out her arm. Bone, tendon, vein, and muscle, grew out of her wrist. Flesh formed around a new developing fingers, rapidly became a new hand. She regarded them demonic mirth.

Stosh's jaw dropped."Awww, fiddlesticks."

Adalius' eyes widened. "Beard of my ancestors, what... are you becoming?"

Anna's eyes blazed, her voice echoing. "Something beyond all of you, now, my love, I've tired of our game. It's time to die."

392

Stosh stepped forward. "You first, honey pot." Reaching into his vest pocket, the human lobbed a small orb. It exploded into golden white light. Anna screamed, covering her face, one side of her badly burned.

"Ha! How did that taste, sweetheart? How's about I give ya another. I brought plenty." Stosh reached once more into his vest. Anna shrieked, launching herself through the emergency door, tearing it from the hinges.

Adalius and the slayer ran to the doorway. They spotted Anna streaking away before she wrapped herself in shadows.

"I got these babies from a sorceress named Sylvia. She said to give you her best," Stosh shouted after her.

Kiel groaned; he was coming to. They headed back into the arena.

He and Stosh pulled the Lycan to his feet. "Are you injured, Kiel?"

Kiel jerked away. "Get your hands off me, Adalius."

Stosh scowled. "Don't know what the 411 is, son but I think this fella here, just saved your bacon. Ya might wanna show a little appreciation."

Kiel turned to the slayer. "*You* might wanna keep your big fat nose outta my business." Kiel turned and staggered away.

Stosh regarded Adalius. "Maybe ya shoulda let Anna have *one* little bite before ya saved him."

# CHAPTER SEVENTY

**M**aya lost many of her slayers. She almost lost herself. She tended to her wounds as Marseth paced nervously awaiting news on his missing son. Gil sat alone on the floor holding Nessa. She didn't have the heart to disturb him. None one did; Nessa was his life. A tear rolled from her eye. It was all her fault. They came to help her.

When she spotted Adalius and Kiel, she called out to Marseth. Wait, there was another. That walk, that girth, that stupid, nasty ass baseball cap.

"*Stosh!*" she screamed, dashing toward him.

Every head turned including Trey. Whistling and cheering, they raced for the huge slayer. Maya leaped into his arms, throwing her arms around him. Tears streamed down her cheeks as the remaining slayers tackled them to the ground.

*****

Kalleal, drawn by the commotion, spotted Adalius and rushed to greet him. "Are you alright, my brother?" Concern knitted his brow.

"I am unharmed, Kalleal," Adalius said clasping his brother's shoulder.

"What of Anna?"

"Escaped, she remains at large. Her power... we must kill her Kalleal, and soon or I fear we will not be able to kill her at all. "

"We shall find her."

"Indeed, for now, it is time to bury the dead and mourn."

394

Argus made his way toward them. Adalius extended his arm, Kalleal followed suit. Argus grasped Adalius' forearm in greeting, then Kalleal's.

Argus bowed his head and spoke in the old tongue. *"Forgive me, I would have arrived sooner but I came across a most unusual scene. Vampires, young against old, were engaged in a fierce gun battle, it had to be quelled."*

Kalleal's brow arched. "Most strange,"

Adalius chimed in, "To say the least."

Argus grunted in agreement. "My instructions are to find Anna and her nests and destroy them."

Adalius shook his head. "I'm afraid Anna has escaped, for now."

"We will hunt her and her followers down. Please, excuse me, I must now confer with the Lycan King." The Enforcer turned to leave but Adalius had more.

"Argus, be forewarned. Anna has acquired new and frightening abilities."

"Indeed? Then we shall soon discuss it further." Argus left them to speak with Marseth.

Adalius brooded. First, an unknown buyer has begun gathering assault weapons, now vampires are engaging in a gun battles. A bad omen. And he feared it was only the beginning.

*****

The slayers helped Stosh to his feet. He was bombarded with questions but it was Trey's that got his attention.

"I saw that vamp cut your throat and drop you from that bridge. It had to be a seventy foot drop. How did you survive?"

Stosh smiled down. "Vamp blood, son. I always keep a few vials of the stuff on me. When it comes to healing wounds and giving ya a pick me up, it's betterin Popeye's spinach. I managed to get one vial in me before I hit. Took all I had left to heal those other wounds. Still didn't keep me from almost drownin', though."

Maya slapped the back of his head. "Ok, so why then did you let us think you was dead, you bastard?"

"I am sorry about that, sis, but when I finally made it to shore, I wasn't in the mood to be told to hang out till the cavalry arrived. It got personal, if ya know what I mean. I decided to let the ole hag think she'd offed me. Figured it might make her careless if she thought she only had one slayer to deal with."

"Yeah, I understand." Maya grabbed him by the shirt. "But if you *ever* do that shit to me again, I'll beat all the fat off you!"

"*Yes*, ma'am."

*****

Kiel stood with Ulysses while his father and Argus talked nearby. As they spoke, Adalius and Kalleal approached. Adalius called out to Kiel as they drew near. "Kiel, it is my understanding that is was you who saved me from Anna's blade, on the arena floor."

Kiel turned his back to the vampire. "Call it a weak moment, Adalius."

"I care not what it is called. I simply wish to thank you."

"Don't thank me. You save me, so call it even…almost."

"Kiel, I am sorry. I have apologized in every way I know how. If I could change what happened, I would, but I cannot." Adalius sighed frustrated. "I do not expect forgiveness. I simply wanted to show my gratitude." Adalius offered his hand to the Lycan.

Kiel whirled about and dropped him with a violent right hand. Kiel glared down. "Fuck you and fuck your apology. You don't get off with a simple 'I'm sorry', you son of a bitch."

As Kiel turned and walked away with Ulysses right behind. Kalleal bared his fangs. "Mangy dog!"

His sibling went after Kiel but Ulysses turned and stepped into his path. The two were eye to eye and ready to throw down, fang and fist.

Adalius rose to his feet. "Kalleal. Let them go."

Kalleal glared at the Lycan. "There *will* be another time."

"Anytime you want, vamp." Ulysses walked away.

Kalleal faced his brother. "We *will* discuss what it is between you and the Lycan."

"Kal…"

Kalleal pressed a finger to his chest. "We *will*... discuss it. End of conversation." He left to lend aid to others. There was still much to do before the sun rose. Bodies needed to be buried and injured needed to be tended to. Anna was still out there. Killing her had taken on new importance, but for now, she would have to wait.

# CHAPTER SEVENTY ONE

Padre made his way back to his vehicle, envelope in hand. He'd just made the first collection from the new territory. Normally, this would be handled by one of his soldiers but, the first pick up, he always handled personally. The last couple of days had been hectic. They'd been gearing up for war.

The old farts, on the VHC were in their third day of hearings over the vamp drug trade. A vote was expected in a few days. Not that it mattered. The fate of those old mutha fuckas was already decided. It was just a matter of time.

Arriving at his Charger, he reached for the car door. A chill hit him on the back of the neck.

"I'm disappointed, Padre, you haven't been back to see me."

Padre whirled about.

Anna.

"Was just bout to look you up, sweetness, how's it goin?"

Anna folded her arms across her chest. "I'm afraid I've suffered a minor setback."

"Yeah, I heard about that. The old dirty bastards sicced their big dawg on you."

"Argus' arrival wasn't anticipated, but in the overall picture, it changes nothing." Anna approached him.

He looked her up and down. Damn, she had the sexiest legs he ever laid his eyes on.

"So, you thought about our offer, querida?"

Anna ran her hands seductively up his chest. "I have, but I've thought of you more."

"Is that right?"

"Ummm hmmm, I've had so *many* sinful thoughts about you." Anna leaned in and placed a kiss on his neck.

He sighed, sure felt nice but... "Business before pleasure, sweetness, I need an answer." He held her at arm's length.

Anna smiled seductively. "Then I accept your offer. But, my alliance is to *you* not your employer."

"This ain't an either or."

"Oh, but I think it is. I'm not a fool, Padre, I have no doubt your employer is already taking steps to have me eliminated should I decline your gracious invitation. Let's be honest, he plans to do away with me the instant we conclude our business with the Council." She ran her hands over the back of his scalp. "I'm also aware that you're not the *least* bit satisfied with the pecking order."

"Got no idea what you talkin' bout, baby."

Anna stepped into his arms and kissed his lips. "Yes you do. I've read your mind. You want what he has. You're already at work making it happen. "Anna sucked on his earlobe and traced his ears with her tongue. "I can help you, Padre. I can help you take him down. I *know* it's what you want."

Padre sighed at what Anna and thoughts of being number one were doing to him. "Very temptin', but what you want in return?"

Anna ran her hand down his body to his pants and unzipped his fly. She slid her hand inside and caressed his growing hard on.

Padre groaned at the smooth stroke of her hand.

Anna's eyes sparkled, the bouquet of her arousal drifting up to his nostrils. "My last confrontation made me realize that to bring about the kind of change I have in mind, I need friends. And I think we could be *very, very* good friends."

He drew her against him, grinding his hips against her sex. "Umm hmm, and how do I know you won't take me out once we off the big dawg."

Anna leaned and kissed him, long and wet. She moaned. "You can trust me, Padre, we are alike, you and I. We are both trying to build an empire." Anna licked up his neck. "We can do it, Padre...together." She curled her leg behind the back of his knee and worked her hips, stroking his shaft with her body. "Besides, if I wanted you...mmmmm, dead, you'd already be."

No more convincing was needed. "Ok, baby, I'm down. But try and fuck me..."

"Oh I'm going to fuck you alright, just not outta what's yours. And I can be yours, Padre, all yours...if you play your cards right."

He squeezed her ass. "I like."

Anna smiled wickedly. "There's still one other matter. What about your female?"

"What makes you think I got a woman?"

Anna's expression darkened. "Don't insult my intelligence, Padre, her scent is all over you."

Padre grinned. "Busted. But she ain't here right *now*. I won't tell if you won't"

Anna returned his smile. "I *never* fuck and tell."

They embraced, coiling around each other like dueling pythons. Their lips locked, tongues wrestling as they locked in passionate embrace. He ripped open her blouse. She ripped away his shirt and yanked open his pants. He forced her against the car door. She gripped him and guided him in. Anna hissed as he pushed into her tight wet sheath.

They fell next to his car. He took her in long, slow thrusts. Their cries echoed down the alley and into the night, the sounds of birth of a new and deadly alliance.

# CHAPTER SEVENTY TWO

It was a posh, moderate sized cottage sequestered away from the city. When Anna bought it the year before, Trish was thrilled. The mistress splurged. The made additions included the usual furnishings, a walk in freezer in the basement filled with frozen blood and medical supplies.

Marie lay unmoving on the stainless steel table, hooked up to IV's that Anna, in her wisdom, had supplied. Trish couldn't be more grateful. Anna's foresight literally saved her mate. The instant they arrived, Trish carefully removed all of the silver buckshot from Marie's abdomen, hooked up the IV and began giving her pints of blood.

She'd already gone through six of the forty pints on hand. She hoped it would be enough. They needed to lay low for a while. With Argus, no doubt, haunting the shadows, it was far too dangerous to venture into the night.

Trish gazed at her mate. She sighed in relief. The color was returning to Marie's cheeks. With rest, she'd be fine. It'd been touch and go for a while. Her fangs extended, her hands curling into fists. That fat slayer, he did this to her. If it took her the rest of her unnatural life, she would hunt that prick down and kill him and his entire line.

She'd get him and didn't give a damn if Anna approved or not. Nobody hurt the ones she loved. *Nobody*! The slayer was a dead man, living on borrowed time. She'd see to it his bill came due.

*****

Neal lay on his back for how long he wasn't sure. He hadn't checked in with Maya in what must be days. By now, someone was on

401

the way to look for him. He tugged at his binding for the umpteenth time. There was no more give than when he gave the first yank. He had to figure a way out of this. Maya had to be warned about this new breed of vampire.

Vampire drug dealers, she'd think he was crazy. Hell, he wasn't sure he believed it. His captors had at least kept him fed and hadn't tried snackin' on him...yet. Best be gone soon, though before his luck ran out.

The door creaked open.

Jewel slipped inside, closing the door behind her. He swallowed. *Uh oh.*

The vamp sauntered toward him. "Mace stepped out, so I thought we could finish our conversation." Her fangs sank below her top lip.

Oh. Shit. "Your boss said no touching and no biting."

"Oh, I know, but I always was a hardhead. Actually, I kinda like him smackin' me around a little. Now hold still suga, this might hurt a bit." Jewel grasped his head.

"MACE. HEY, SOMEBODY, COME GET THIS BITCH!" Jewel opened her mouth wide. Great, just fuckin'great, the end to a lousy day and a fucked up life.

# EPILOGUE

Adalius and Kalleal stood atop a brownstone, waiting. Trey Thomas phoned to say he'd meet them in an hour. That was nearly fifty minutes ago. While they waited, he and Kalleal talked. Reminisced about the lives they each had led as vampires.

His phone rang. Adalius fished it out of his trench coat pocket. "I am here...Indeed, I should have suspected as much....very well, tell him to meet us at the Pennywise Bakery." Adalius ended the call. "Jericho has found something."

"Jericho?"

"My hooded associate from the factory, he has discovered where those weapons came from. They were delivered by an arms dealer I am quite familiar with. As soon as the slayer arrives..."

"Sorry, I got here as fast as I could."

They turned as the Trey climbed off the fire escape.

Kalleal nodded to the slayer. "How fare your brethren, slayer?"

Trey removed his riding gloves. "As well as can be expected, we lost a lot of friends. Have you any information on Anna's whereabouts?"

Adalius chimed in. "No. We do, however, have information about the weapons we discovered."

"Then what are we waitin' for, vamp?"

"We leave immediately. I've asked my contact to meet us at the bakery." As he turned, Trey held up a hand. "Hold on, there's something I need to ask before we go."

Adalius removed his shades. "Of course, what is it you wish to know?"

"As I understand it, Anna is both your makers and you're both Sandrians, living vampires."

Adalius nodded. "Correct."

"But Anna, she isn't Sandrian, is she?

Kalleal spoke up. "No, Anna is born of the clan Dracul, a child of the undead.

"Ok, then we're on the same page. Here's what I want to know, can an undead vamp, produce a Sandrian vampire?"

Adalius shook his head. "No, no undead vampire can give rise to the living."

"Then, Adalius, how can Anna be your maker?

He opened his mouth to speak, then paused. "She cannot. But how... has this escaped me?" He shut his eyes, focusing his concentration inward. "There has been...some sort of tampering with my mind, a blockage, subtle yet formidable." Adalius opened his eyes. "Kalleal, have you also such a block?"

Kalleal shut his eyes, his breathing deep and steady. "Yes, there is indeed some sort of...seal on my memories."

Adalius paced away. "Only one immensely skilled and powerful could have done this and concealed it from our consciousness."

"But who, my brother and why? And if Anna is not our maker, who is?"

"I do not know, but these questions we will address after we have dealt with this weapons issue. Let us be off, Kalleal. Safe journey to you, Trey Thomas, give our most heartfelt condolences to your companions."

Trey slipped on his riding gloves. "I'm staying. There's still a job to be finished here. Nessa would never forgive me if I left this undone. Best way to honor her, is to put Anna in the ground permanently. Beside, Gil said he'd bust my skull if I didn't."

He laid a hand on the slayer's shoulder. "Very well, our destination is the Pennywise Bakery."

"Shall I carry you, slayer?" Kalleal spread his arms wide, mischief in his eyes.

"You put yo arms around me, canines, and I'll bust a cap in yo ass."

Kalleal looked to his sibling. "I so like this mortal."

# Author's Biography

Keith is a happily married, frustrated Cleveland sports fan. He enjoys video gaming, reading, and writing. Keith is an original member of Critiques R Us, a writer's meet up group here in Cleveland Ohio. Hope you enjoyed Keith's first book in his action pack vampire series The Sandrian Chronicles: Written in Blood. Keith is hard at work on the second book in the series. You can find more updates and information about Keith and his work at:

www.facebook.com/AuthorKeithMont

www.optimusmaximuspublishing.com

CHECK OUT THE OMP WEBSITE FOR
A COMPLETE LIST OF OUR TITLES

WWW.OPTIMUSMAXIMUSPUBLISHING.COM

BOOKS ARE AVAILABLE IN BOTH PRINT
AND ELECTRONIC FORMATS

# RICKY FLEET
# HELLSPAWN
## SERIES

10.35 AM, September 14th 2015. Portsmouth, England.

A global particle physics experiment releases a pulse of unknown energy with catastrophic results. The sanctity of the grave has been sundered and a million graveyards expel their tenants from eternal slumber.

The world is unaware of the impending apocalypse, Governments crumble and armies are scattered to the wind under the onslaught of the dead.

Kurt Taylor, a self-employed plumber, witnesses the start of the horrifying outbreak. Desperate to reach his family before they fall victim to the ever growing horde of shambling corruption, he flees the scene.

In a society with few guns, how can people hope to survive the endless waves of zombies that seek to consume every living thing? With ingenuity, planning and everyday materials, the group forge their way and strike back at the Hellspawn legions.

Rescues are mounted, but not all survivors are benevolent, the evil that is in all men has been given free rein in this new, dead world. With both the living and dead to contend with, the Taylor family's battle for survival is just beginning.

Book 1 in the Hellspawn series.

Kurt Taylor and his family have battled the living and the dead and now find themselves on the run, their home reduced to ashes. With unimaginable horror lying in wait around every corner, the onset of winter and the plunging temperatures only add more danger to their precarious existence. They decide to forge ahead and try to reach the protection of others who have hopefully survived the zombie apocalypse. If this fails, their only choice would be to try and reach an impregnable fortress, a sanctuary that has stood for a thousand years.

Standing between them and salvation are the villages and cities of the damned, a path that will test their spirit and resilience unlike anything they have faced before. More companions are rescued from the jaws of death and join them in their perilous journey. Mysterious attacks befall the group and it becomes clear the dead aren't the only things that lurk in the darkness.

Tempers fray and personalities clash. The group starts to fracture and Kurt is forced to commit acts that cause him to question his own morality. Can they survive the horror of their new existence? Will they want to?

The Hellspawn saga continues.

## BALLYMOOR, IRELAND, 1891

Patrick Conroy, a young American student of medicine in Dublin, decides to take a break from the hustle and bustle of the big city and spend a month in the quietude of the wild and beautiful Glencree valley, County Wicklow. However, surrounded by local legends and myths, he is soon dragged into an ancient mystery that has haunted the village of Ballymoor for centuries. Set on the background of the tumultuous years preceding the War of Independence, and colored by Irish folklore, the Haunter of the Moor is a ghost story written in the style of Victorian Gothic novels.

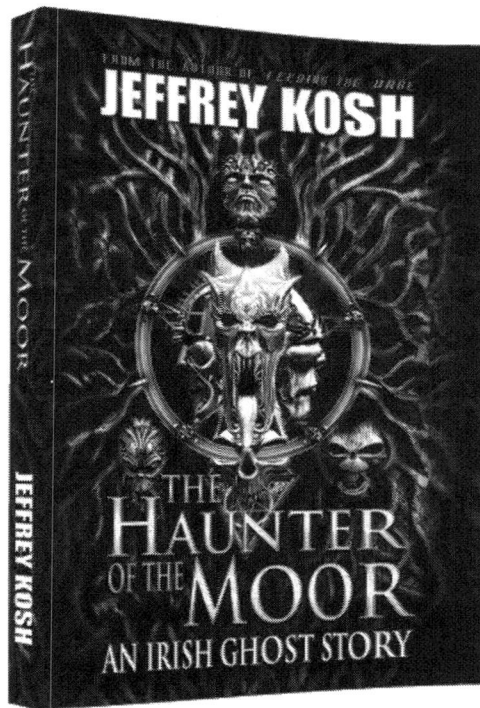

# To Fight Evil with Evil

England, 1392.

As the Black Death quickly spreads through the kingdom, the little hamlet of Blythe's Hollow suffers under the yoke of a sadistic Lord. Desperate, the villagers decide to seek out the magical help of a local witch, causing the wrath of the Church. Torture and murder befall on those accused of being in league with the Devil, adding more sorrow to the beset folk of Blythe's Hollow. Yet, one man will rise against the tyranny; a man willing to learn Black Magick to fight back.

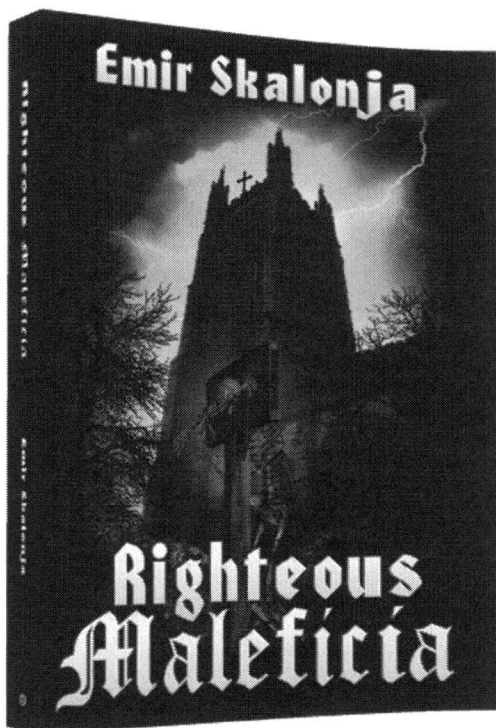